THE
FOX HUNT

THE UNIVERSITY

THE GUILDER WOOD

THE RIVER

THE MEADOWS

JERMYN COLLEGE

NORTH GATE

GABRIEL COLLEGE

ALBEMARLE COLLEGE

CARLISLE COLLEGE

THE HOUSE OF FOXES

ST. ETHELDREDA'S COLLEGE

GABRIEL PASSAGE

OLD HOB QUAD

GATE

SUSSEX COLLEGE

THE MATHEMATICAL BRIDGE

LADY MARGARET'S COLLEGE

HIGH STREET

MARKET SQUARE

PERCY COLLEGE

HIGH STREET

ST. DUNSTAN'S COLLEGE

THE ROSE GARDEN

BEAUFORT CRESCENT

GRANVILLE COLLEGE

WESSEX COLLEGE

DORSET COLLEGE

LIBRARIAN'S COTTAGE

DORSET COLLEGE

BEAUFORT COLLEGE

SCHOLAR'S ROAD

THE TURNBULL CLUBHOUSE

SENATE HOUSE

FINCHFIELD COLLEGE

COURT ENTRANCE

SCIENCE FACULTY

BEAUFORT COTTAGE

REGENT'S COLLEGE

THE SWAN PUB

RIVER PATH

RIVER PATH

THE RIVER

JASPER'S POOL

REGENT'S BRIDGE

HUT

THE LIBRARY

THE FOX HUNT

A Novel

CAITLIN BREEZE

LITTLE, BROWN AND COMPANY

New York   Boston   London

Copyright © 2026 by Caitlin Breeze

Hachette Book Group supports the right to free expression and the value of copyright. The purpose of copyright is to encourage writers and artists to produce the creative works that enrich our culture.

The scanning, uploading, and distribution of this book without permission is a theft of the author's intellectual property. If you would like permission to use material from the book (other than for review purposes), please contact permissions@hbgusa.com. Thank you for your support of the author's rights.

Little, Brown and Company
Hachette Book Group
1290 Avenue of the Americas, New York, NY 10104
littlebrown.com

First Edition: February 2026

Little, Brown and Company is a division of Hachette Book Group, Inc. The Little, Brown name and logo are trademarks of Hachette Book Group, Inc.

The publisher is not responsible for websites (or their content) that are not owned by the publisher.

The Hachette Speakers Bureau provides a wide range of authors for speaking events. To find out more, go to hachettespeakersbureau.com or email hachettespeakers@hbgusa.com.

Little, Brown and Company books may be purchased in bulk for business, educational, or promotional use. For information, please contact your local bookseller or the Hachette Book Group Special Markets Department at special.markets@hbgusa.com.

Print book interior design by Taylor Navis
Map illustration © HarperCollins*Publishers* and Shutterstock 2027

ISBN 978-0-316-59738-8 (hardcover); 978-0-316-60771-1 (large print); 978-0316-59740-1 (ebook)

LCCN is available at the Library of Congress.

10 9 8 7 6 5 4 3 2 1

CCR

Printed in the United States of America

For Dana and Jess,
Pip and Resham

Who make the world more magical

The City chooses who it keeps. It is old, it is vicious, and it remembers the time before. That was the time of blood promises. When even children knew that the price of knowledge was a fall from grace.

But knowledge is an intoxicating thing. It was the City's siren song. The first scholars came and found that their thoughts flew faster. Within the walls of the University, theories seemed to write themselves. Invisible hands pushed a flurry of quills onward, onward. Writers stumbled out of bed, catching at the words tumbling from their mouths. Where knowledge trod, fame followed, and riches. More scholars arrived, from the cold North and the ancient South, from the rough new nations across the Western Sea.

They spoke of the City in as many tongues as there were nations. The greatest seat of learning that had ever been. It filled the annals of history with discovery, peopled the world's halls of power. And generation by generation, those who came to its gates began to forget the ancient truth.

As each wave of scholars dressed the University in the finery of their age, it slipped on a cloak of civility. The buildings, now, are gracious. Soaring spires and honey-colored stone. Symmetry and order. Courts enclosing courts enclosing cloisters, like a rose blooming.

Or a fist closing.

CHAPTER I

THERE HAD NEVER BEEN SUCH A FLOOD. NOT IN LIVING MEMORY, at least. It came up silently. A dark tide clawed from the river, finger by finger, into the sleeping city. Under the cold gaze of the hunter's moon, it eased past the windows of students and academics, porters and librarians. It brushed their tangled dreams, lapping higher.

In the span of one nightfall, the waters claimed the University.

At sunset, the cobblestones had rattled with book-laden bicycles. The medieval mouths of the great college gates had gaped wide to welcome their gowned undergraduates and threadbare lecturers, to cradle the ancient dons tottering to their places at High Table. Bells rang out from myriad spires, and evensong silvered the air around Gabriel Tower.

By morning, all was drowned. Slick black ropes of water fingered the college foundations. Ankle-deep, knee-deep, waist-deep. Beneath its touch, gold stone weathered green. In the gray dawn, rows of bicycles bobbed at their moorings, as though lifted by ghostly hands. The straight march of the High Street turned wavering and sly.

And then the rain started.

It would become the tale of decades. The students passing precious paintings up to safety, bracing against waters that curled around hips and thighs. The lectures canceled, the tutorials postponed. In Persian-carpeted studies, professors settled in with their decanters. Underpaid lecturers huddled closer to their space heaters, submerging themselves deeper in Aramaic love poetry to stave off thoughts of the damp. The few cars that attempted to drive through the flood sputtered and died, bonnet-deep in swirling pondweed. Wading the streets was a task for only the bravest or the most desperate. For three days, the tourists had to stay out. The students had to stay in.

And in their absence, the other lives in the city rejoiced.

As the waters triumphed, dark fish swam up the steps of the Senate House. A shifting sheet of pewter covered the formal gardens, where eels wrestled in ecstatic knots among the drowning rosebushes. Spiders danced in the vaulted stone cathedral of St. Dunstan's College.

Then, on the third day, the flood receded. The river drew back its reaches from the modern outskirts first. Within a few hours, even the water at the ancient heart of the city stood less than knee-deep. The mortal world began its inevitable process of reclaiming and forgetting. Waterlogged college gates were pushed open again. An army of college servants swept river silt from the courtyards.

And high in Gabriel Tower, Emma Curran woke from a troubled nap with a start. Mist had laid moist fingers on her windowpane, clouding the city outside. She listened for the sound that had woken her and heard nothing. But something had changed. She was sure of it. It took her a moment to realize.

The rain had finally stopped.

She had listened to it through the three long days of her confinement. So long, the tapping water had begun to sound like whispers beyond the windowpane. They had seeped into her dreams. She rubbed at the window with her sleeve and peered out. At last, a few gleams of paving stone showed through the murk in the lane below. After three days of nothing but deep black currents, it felt like an omen of good luck, just for her. She laid aside the work on her lap and stretched limbs grown stiff from hours curled into the window seat.

A jolt pierced her heart. The rain was gone, and so was her last excuse. If she was going, it was nearly time. Everything she needed had been laid out on her bed in the morning, just in case. With hands she couldn't stop from shaking a little, she buttoned the crisp shirt, smoothed out one last imaginary crease in her good trousers. The chime of her phone distracted her for a moment only. Barely pausing to read the message, she dashed off a reply and went back to muttering under her breath. She'd memorized the facts. Only the opening still troubled her. Some people introduced themselves so easily. As though talking about themselves wasn't an insurmountable obstacle.

Her eyes strayed back to her phone. With a groan, she dropped the half-packed bag on her bed. Slipping from the room, she tapped on the door next to hers. They were the only two on the floor: Gabriel College had only recently converted the tower's crumbling cells into accommodations. It was not a popular option, thanks to the deafening cycle of bells from the belfry above. The monks who had first built Gabriel College had been dead six centuries, but still the bell tower rang out the joyful and thunderous pattern of their days, matins to compline. But for two second-year students who cared more about being close to the dining hall than the sanctity of sleep, the rooms were perfect.

"Come in."

Emma pushed open the door without ceremony.

Nat's bedroom was a collage of old film posters and flyers for upcoming plays. While the desk was buried under enough layers of books to qualify as an archaeological site, the area around the state-of-the-art sound system on the opposite wall was spotless. It was best not to consider how far the contents of that wall outstripped the value of her student loans, she'd found. Before the University, Emma had never imagined anyone her age with their own cinema-grade sound system. That had changed the day she'd arrived at Gabriel, a year earlier, when she'd seen fifteen unloaded with the new freshers from tasteful Range Rovers and Tesla SUVs.

The figure stretched on the bed grinned at her. Emma looked at the phone in his hand and sighed.

"Can it be?" Nat Oluwole threw his head back, gesturing to the heavens. "Can my own Emma Curran be abandoning me?"

He was the best boy alive, but he did like to declaim.

"I'm sorry," Emma said, but there was a smile in it. There always was when Nat decided to make her laugh. "I really don't want to let you down."

"Now that sounds likely," he said gravely. "You, the most faithful friend in history, a letdown? Well, of course. I mean, who would *not* have spent their last gods-given, lecture-free day pricking holes in their fingers to make me a costume — for no other reason than I mentioned it last week — and all for a party they now refuse to go to?"

"I tried to explain in my message. Nat, surely you can see? I won't know anyone, I don't know how to act at these things, and I'll go home feeling terrible about myself."

Nat shook his head. "I mention a party, and you start wailing like it's the last act of *Tosca*. But I make you hot-glue bottlecaps to a sleeping bag all night long — "

Emma's brow crinkled. "I really didn't mean to set off the fire alarm. I hope that lecturer above was all right. The burnt smell definitely reached his floor. And the alarm was so loud — "

"It was barely three a.m.," Nat went on with a dismissive flap of his hand. "And he chose to live in a bell tower. He'll be fine. But you, treasure among friends? You've glued and stitched away, and not complained or even questioned my sanity — "

"When you said this costume was for a party, I thought it was one of your theatre parties," Emma said. "I've done much madder things for those. Like when you had me sew you up in an actual shroud for the *Macbeth* cast party last year? You had to get the director to guide you around by the hand all night, to stop you tripping over chairs."

"I," said Nat with lofty dignity, "was the ghost of Banquo. You logical minds cannot understand the exigencies of art. Or parties."

"We logical minds are also covered in glue burns from last night's 'exigencies of art.' And we are not going to the party. There will be too many people, and I'm tired, and — " Emma flopped onto the bed. Nat shifted to make room. "That's what I wanted to talk to you about. I sent you that message, and then of course I started worrying that you'd hate me — "

"Which I don't," Nat interposed.

"And that you'd be angry with me — "

7

"Which I never have been."

" — because it was lovely of you to invite me. But I actually have something else this afternoon. And I don't know how late I'll be."

Nat propped himself up on one arm. "Do tell."

"It's — it's the Colefax-Lee Foundation program. The interviews are today."

Nat whistled. "Big stuff. Are you sure they'll be happening, though? Flood, and all that?"

"The waters are going down." Emma bounced, her body athrill with excitement again. "And it's not far. I have to try."

"Going down is not gone."

"Oh, I don't need to worry about that. Look — "

Emma dashed from the room. The sound of rubbery squeaking and a few choice profanities emerged from her bedroom. A few moments later, she pushed open Nat's door and stood framed in the doorway in all her glory.

"Good God," Nat said blankly.

A pair of voluminous, violently green rubber waders enclosed Emma from toe to chest. "I kept them from that time at the field station in Senegal." She beamed. "I thought they might come in handy if I ever wanted to do a survey of the caddis fly larvae in the river here. A colleague of my mother's in the US is writing a paper on how they might be linked to otter populations. Wouldn't it be amazing to actually find out if the same is true here?"

"Indeed," Nat agreed weakly. "Just what anyone would think. Now, take the hideous things off."

Emma wriggled obediently out of the offending articles. "Anyway, they're perfect for today. I'll be as dry as can be. Oh!" She dashed from the room a second time. "How could I forget? It's finished. Your costume." She dropped her armful of fabric into Nat's lap. Her friend let out a joyful squawk she was sure he would die rather than let his theatre friends hear. "I hope you make an excellent caterpillar," Emma laughed.

"I will," said Nat, with absolute confidence.

"And I hope you impress whoever all this is meant for."

"It's no one. Nothing. Just a friend." His neck had flushed bright red.

Emma fought a smile. She wasn't sure which boy had attracted Nat's attention this time. His many loves were legend. Unlike Emma, who dated seldom and with a scientist's detachment, Nat had a way of truly believing every time that at last, this one was true love.

"Lewis Carroll would be proud," her friend was muttering now, spinning in front of the mirror with the costume draped over his long form. The interminable hours she'd spent in the window seat — listening to the rain and sewing the hundreds of legs — had been worth it. He looked spectacular.

"But, Emma — "

Nat had stopped twirling.

"After the interviews. You could still come to the party, right? It won't matter if you're late. Just throw on that blue dress you have, and I'll say you're Alice in Wonderland. To go with me. It'll be fun. They'll love you."

Emma pulled a face.

"Em — " The caterpillar hugged her around the shoulders. "You're one of my favorite people. Truly. But you need more friends than just me. Let the world get to know you. You might be surprised."

Emma shook her head and busied herself with picking up her waders. "I don't know if I'll feel like it."

"I'm not going to press you if you don't want to go. You know that. And I love this newfound firmness." He raised one eyebrow at her, a trick she'd never been able to copy. "It suits you. I'm just tickled that, after all of the idiotic requests I've seen you give in to, this party is the one that broke the, er" — Nat eyed her long frame and grinned — "giraffe's back?"

Emma reached out and swatted him, without any real heat. "Giraffe yourself."

Then, as an afterthought: "It suits me?"

"Yes, Emma." Nat could go from theatrical to sincere in the time it took for Emma's voice to wobble. "And so does your height, for that matter."

Emma rolled her eyes at that.

"Go on." He grinned, herding her out of his room. "Go get the millionaire funding of your dreams. And see how you feel afterward."

Firm. Emma found herself repeating the word in her head. Firm. It did suit her.

CHAPTER 2

Among the tourists buying University sweatshirts, among the scramble of bicycles in its arteries and the punts gliding along its veins, the City sensed the life in one small square. Within the embrace of Gabriel College, a girl was hurrying across a flood-silvered lawn.

Women — as recently added to the intellectual life of the University as they were — were always thinking or reading or walking the City's paths now. The sight was no surprise to it. Nevertheless, it paused a moment before its attention rolled onward to the river.

For a girl whose posture did not betray an obvious longing for the spotlight, Emma Curran possessed features that demanded to take up space. She was built on taller lines than the average, with sharp shoulders and long, sturdy legs. Her nose and brows were striking rather than delicate. The strength of her features added a character to her little moon-circle face that time had not yet given. Everything else about her looked bare and fresh.

And, at the moment, a little damp. The last spatters of rain were blowing off the river, straight into her face. But at least her feet were dry. The waders were perfect. She splashed on across the marshland that had once been Gabriel's croquet lawn. A stray sunbeam lit the turrets above, striking gold from the weathered stone. And Emma's heart swelled, as it always did when she looked at her home. Gabriel College, crumbling and magnificent. Low of coffer but great of heart: its tapestries moldering, but its ducks the best fed in the city. It was where Emma's soul came to roost and had done since the day she arrived.

The college was the northmost of those lining the river. Beyond its august walls lay only the University Meadows and the Guilder Wood. Their paths were her favorite haunts. Curlews stalked the grasses; shadowy copses hid the elusive Guilder deer. Emma had even glimpsed a pair of otters at the bend in the river by the North Gate.

But she had no time to watch now. Emma checked the zip of her bag again, convinced it might have opened itself while she wasn't looking. It was tightly fastened. Not a drop could leak onto the papers inside. She tugged down her hood and slipped out of the North Gate. The floodwater in Gabriel Passage was only ankle-deep. Another good omen. The High Street was bound to be passable.

As Emma waded on, she saw signs that the colleges, so tightly shut during the flood, were coming back to life. Portly Granville College, lounging across two blocks of the city. Lady Margaret's, with its eerie twisted towers. Cheerful Sussex and austere Wessex. This place was like nowhere else. It called to her, an enchanting song of beauty and history and something beyond that, something she'd never been able to name. Everywhere, doors opening, college bedders sneaking cigarettes in the archways, the chatter of students piping among the chimneys.

Water was sluicing down the High Street, draining down cobbled lanes that sloped to the river. A procession of porters waded through the churn, bearing spadefuls of frogs. The floodwater rippled up around their calves and ankles like a preening cat, throwing out bewitching glints. It was almost mesmeric, watching it. Emma felt her breathing slow, her nerves drift.

Then the porters flipped their spades. Frogs splashed into the tide and were swept, croaking, back to the river. Startled from her daze, Emma jerked up. She'd been leaning toward the water, her hand almost brushing the surface. She didn't remember why. A porter tipped his bowler hat to Emma, and she waded on.

Her bag started ringing. Emma rummaged inside for her phone. She saw the caller and smiled. Madagascar was three hours ahead. Her mother would be having lunch in the research station canteen.

"Have I caught you before the interview?" Her mother sounded cheerful, as always.

Something in Emma's chest loosened. "On my way now."

"Oh, good. Sorry, we've had a mare's nest of a morning. First the water in the lab backed up, then we found a lemur nibbling the power cables outside."

Emma's mother was an academic. "A fertility expert," she liked to say at parties. "Only for plants, not people." And people laughed. They usually did, when she was around. Dr. Diana Curran was a square-set, petite woman with strong hands, often covered in soil. Thanks to her mother's trailblazing research career, Emma had grown up in six cities, four field stations, and eight different countries. She'd been told she didn't sound properly English, as a result. Her mother had always said that was a good thing.

For now, her mother was heading up a research station in Madagascar. Emma had been promised a rainforest trip for the Christmas holidays, so she was a fan of this latest posting.

"How's things at Gabriel? Still flooded in?"

"Just going down. People have gone mad, though, being shut inside. Everyone is talking about the fuss in the kitchen. One of the chefs is threatening to quit. Apparently, someone's been sneaking the desserts from the fridge overnight and leaving a crock of petals in their place. So Nat says, anyway."

Her mother chuckled. "Must be the students, surely. I've seen enough practical jokes in my time. And how is Nat doing? Did it go well, telling his parents? You never said."

"Turns out he didn't do it. Spent the whole summer working up to it, too. He says his family have just about come to terms with him dating boys, but him throwing over a decent career for a life on the stage would be, in his words, 'like hurling a grenade into a cage of poodles.' It's all a bit weird still with the traditional parts of his family, anyway."

"Oh, that's tough. But what does his father think he's doing all this time, outside of class?"

"Volunteering at the church, like he was supposed to."

"Well, tell him from me that it's best to be honest. Now, back to you, ladybug. Nervous?"

"A little."

"You don't need to be. You can do anything you set your mind to, and don't forget it."

Emma hung up, feeling a warmth in her chest. Not for the first time, she wished she had the assurance that came so naturally to her mother. Her fierce mother, whose only lapse in insight had been a brief, careless liaison with a man of more charm than principle. Who had brought forth her unplanned baby a week before her PhD viva, with no father in sight. The only thing that man had ever given Emma, she liked to say, was the surname on her birth certificate. Emma Pelham. And even that they never used. She had been Emma Curran to the world from the day her mother brought her home.

Diana Curran had marched in front of a panel of academics alone, baby Emma strapped to her chest, and delivered a blistering PhD defense. She had left destined for one of the brightest careers in her field. She would not have been afraid of a few questions at an interview.

Nerves thrummed in Emma's belly. By the time she turned into the forecourt of the Science Department, she felt her pulse in every part of her body. Emma followed the signs to a corridor lined with plastic chairs, and shed the waders. A single poster stuck to a glass door read "Colefax-Lee Foundation Interviews: Wait Here."

The lines of seats were empty. The other candidates were running late, she supposed. Emma chose the chair nearest the door, hid the waders underneath, and waited.

Purposeful steps echoed down the corridor. Emma's head jerked up.

The cool, oval face was one Emma knew well. At least by sight.

Julia Colefax-Lee's eighteenth birthday had been captured in lavish detail in *Tatler*. Her mother, it was rumored, was a paternal cousin to Princess Diana. Her godmother was a former lady-in-waiting to the queen. She had emerged from Swiss boarding school with the expected poise and accomplishments. She had also acquired a gracious smile that made those in its path feel included and special — however quickly its giver hurried away afterward. Like Emma, Julia belonged to Gabriel College. Emma had seen her returning to her room, surrounded always by a cloud of girls with hand-painted highlights and whippety torsos. They had never spoken.

The cool gaze took her in with a hint of surprise. "You're not here for the foundation, are you?"

"Th-the interview?" Emma stammered. "Yes."

"Mmm." Julia's gaze was dancing somewhere above Emma's shoulder. "Well. I'm sure the rest will be here soon. The other interviewers are running a little late too."

Emma couldn't coax her eyes away from Julia's dress, an exquisitely tailored confection of cream silk. It looked as though it had been designed for the boardroom of a California tech company. Emma darted a look down at her own plain white shirt and sole pair of smart trousers. They had seemed lovely in her room.

A redhead charged into the corridor, a sodden umbrella streaming in her wake.

"Jules! Bloody nightmare getting here. And Venetia nowhere to be seen, of course."

Julia sighed. "I'd wanted to wait for her, but — there! Beautiful girl!"

The object of her raptures stalked down the corridor, not visibly moved. She had a perfectly symmetrical face, delicately pointed chin, and long blond Alice in Wonderland hair. Not a drop of water clung to her skintight leather dress or the red bottoms of her boots.

"God, the taxi driver took forever. Well, if we're doing this, let's get it done."

Centuries of boredom oozed from that one small voice.

"Of course, darling. Let's set up. We'll leave some time for the candidates to arrive."

The door swung shut, leaving Emma alone in the corridor. She unclenched her fingers and muttered her way through her opening paragraph once more.

But before she reached the second sentence, she realized the glass door was not soundproof. She could hear every syllable of the girls' conversation. And — if she twisted in her chair at just the right angle — she could see them.

On the other side of the door, Julia sat in the central interviewer's chair, sipping a sparkling water. Venetia had propped her feet on the table. Imogen Baldock was pacing in front of them, red curls bouncing, breathless with news.

"You will not believe who's here."

"Who?"

"Three clues. St. Dunstan's College. Supposed to be racing his family's yacht around the world this year. Most beautiful boy in the University. Come *on,* darlings."

"Not Jasper Balfour?" Julia sat bolt upright. "Back?"

Imogen chuckled. "Oh, he'll be sure to scandalize half the University before term's out. But you have to admit, things would have been dull without the divine Jasper." She perched on the table and swung her legs. "Perhaps I'll have a crack at him myself this year."

She added, under Julia's wry glance, "Well, the demigod will have to fall in love one day. And why not with me?" She grinned. "Or the thousand others in the queue, yes."

"That's old news, surely." Venetia half closed her eyes. "Apparently, his father wasn't overjoyed about his only son taking a year off from the University to go yachting around the world — "

" — or maybe he wanted the yacht for himself," Imogen cut in, "to impress that film actress he's been seeing on the side. My dad's friends with him. He let that slip."

Venetia Kent rolled her eyes. Imogen's father owned a stable of the country's most slanderous scandal sheets. Gossip ran in the family.

"Don't try to be clever, Imogen dearest," she purred. "It doesn't suit you."

"So, Jasper's back at St. Dunstan's?"

"Yes, he seemed very disappointed when I spoke to him." Venetia shook back her moonlight hair.

"You've seen him already?"

"Did he say anything about *you-know-what*?"

"Oh, about" — Venetia looked up, the tiniest smile playing across her doll features — "being president of the Society?"

Julia spat a mouthful of water into her cream silk lap.

"What?" Venetia crossed one long, leather-clad leg over the other luxuriantly. Some people only feel truly at ease surrounded by discomfort. Particularly other people's. Venetia Kent was one such. "We're not five years old. This supersecret society nonsense is idiotic. But Jasper did tell me, actually. Now he's back — "

At this point, Emma's chair let out a loud scraping noise. She hastily rearranged herself. By the time Julia opened the door, she was facing innocently to the front, her hands clasped over the folder in her lap.

"Oh." The disappointment in Julia's voice was hard to miss.

She was looking over Emma's head to the row of empty chairs. "Well — why don't you come in."

Emma scurried past her to the seat facing the panel.

"But aren't we seeing Arabella Lennox and that girl from Jules' dressage club?"

"They were supposed to be here," Julia murmured fretfully. "I suppose the rain — "

"What, Tilly Harper-Graveney?" Imogen added. "Or that other one? Daughter of the Sotheby's chairman. Came to Eddie's birthday in Antibes — "

"Daisy Cadogan," muttered Julia, shuffling the papers in front of her.

"That's the one," said Imogen. "I thought it was all sorted that she'd get the Natural Sciences Fellowship and Arabella would — "

Julia had the grace to look embarrassed. "Nothing's decided. That's why we're interviewing candidates like, er — "

"Emma. Emma Curran."

Julia dove back through her pile of papers. "That's right, I saw my father's assistant had added an application. I hadn't read it yet. For the Science and Environment endowment? Let's see."

Emma knotted her fingers in her lap. Julia's delicate nose was buried deep in her binder.

"Application — conserving and renewing river habitats," she muttered. "Tracking population balances, find where to invest to make the most difference versus climate change — two-year trial here in the city. This is — " She looked up, a little wrinkle of surprise between her brows. "Well, it's exactly what we were looking for. Practical and academic. Local, but the end product is a model that could be applied anywhere."

She tapped her forefingers together, lost in thought. Then her gaze snapped back to Emma. "But it says here that you study law. Not natural sciences. An odd fit for a science endowment, surely?"

"Technically. But I've spent a lot of time around field research. I've had hands-on experience. There's a summary in my proposal — "

Emma slid it across the table. The shaking in her hands eased as she opened to the page on her methodology. The hours she had spent working on the tables and figures showed. What did it matter if her last three law essays had been handed in late?

"Emma, the Colefax-Lee Foundation Fellowships will support ten female students," Julia said. "With projects that will change the world, from the arts to the sciences. It is a significant investment in significant women." Her voice was beautiful, low and modulated. Emma couldn't imagine speaking with such poise. "So. Why do you think you deserve one of those ten fellowships?" Julia asked.

Firm, Emma reminded herself. *Firmness suits me.*

She began her rehearsed speech. "Rivers. They are key — "

"What year is she in?" Venetia rocked back in her chair. "You can't have another fresher, Jules. The first one was ghastly."

"Well, I'm a second-year," Emma answered. "Undergraduate, at Gabriel College."

"Second-year at Gabriel?" Julia leaned forward. "But that's the same as me. How have I never seen you before?"

"I'm not . . . out much." Emma hurried on. "But it is that dedication I would apply to this project, which could bring significant insight into the wildlife of — "

"Did you go to a state school?" Imogen broke in.

"Well — yes, when we were in England — "

20

"There." Imogen grinned at Julia. "She's diversity. You needed one of those."

Julia opened her mouth to speak, but nothing came out.

"It's not as though you have any other options." Venetia lunged to her feet. "For once, I agree with Imogen. Why waste our time? If Arabella or Daisy had really wanted it, they should have shown up."

She swept past Emma to the door, Imogen jostling behind her.

"Come on, Jules." Venetia tossed her hair over one shoulder. "Pick-me-up at Boddington's? I kept the taxi waiting."

"You go ahead."

The footsteps faded away. Julia stayed in her chair, cool gaze appraising Emma.

"This foundation is important to my family, and to me. Do you know why?"

Perplexed at this turn in the conversation, Emma shook her head.

"My father started it, back when the University wasn't so sure that someone who looked like him belonged here. The Lees are as old money as any family in England, don't get me wrong. But their currency was still a little too — *Chinese* — for the University." Her voice turned sharp. "For the college servants that refused to work for him. For certain lecturers and tutors. And now our name is on their buildings. The Colefax-Lee Foundation funds their key research. The University can no longer politely pretend that we don't exist, not when we're so important to its survival."

She wasn't meeting Emma's eyes. She was looking at something in her binder. Emma's heart sank. "This program for female students was my idea. My part of our legacy. Its success means more to me than you can know."

The silence stretched. Then Julia lifted her gaze. "And I think you take this as seriously as I do." She turned the binder to face Emma. She had placed Emma's proposal at the top of the applications.

"Nobody else did this. Among our accomplished candidates — and whatever Venetia says about us handing out fellowships to our friends, they are extraordinarily accomplished — not one built this kind of proposal. The detail. The numbers."

Warmth spread from Emma's cheeks to her neck.

"A Colefax-Lee science fellowship is open to you. If you want it."

"I — I do. Of course." Julia's outstretched hand was waiting. Emma stumbled up to shake it.

"There is one thing." Julia's eyes seemed to snag on Emma's shirt and trousers. "Being a fellow means being the face of the foundation. My father would expect you to represent us. In front of press, at parties. Could you do that?"

A single party with Nat's friends had felt impossible just hours ago. Julia's world would be something else entirely. Emma pictured the cameras, the crush of eyes on her. And amid the fear and doubt was something else, something she was surprised to find. Something like excitement.

"Yes," Emma said. "I can do that."

As she led Emma out to the corridor, Julia seemed to permit herself a real smile, very different from her gracious air. "Now that the official bit's over, I have to ask. How on earth did you get here so dry?"

"These." Emma pulled her waders from beneath the chair. "You put your legs into them, like so — it's a tight fit, so you have to wriggle a bit — there. Then you pull them up to — here."

Julia barked a laugh, quickly smothered in a cough. "I — I see. Well. There's a little launch party for the fellows to meet, a few days from now. At the new conference center in Beaufort College, if you know it? It's all architectural angles and glass, and achingly modern. The perfect backdrop for the program. Press will be arriving at seven thirty — at current count, we have *Tatler*, *The Telegraph*, good noises from *The Times* — oh, and a features writer from *Vanity Fair*, if we can sort her plane tickets in time. You won't have much to do, just answering reporters' questions."

"Right," said Emma. "An-answering reporters. Absolutely."

"And for the party. Do try to wear something a little" — Julia paused — "different, perhaps?"

As Emma strolled back down the High Street, she saw that the sun had burned all but a few silvery puddles from the cobbles. She tilted her face to the warmth. The flood was almost gone. And in its place, a world fresh and ready to begin again.

CHAPTER 3

THE PARTY WAS A STRESSFUL BLUR. A WALL OF LENSES POINTED at her, and people asking questions. Her own voice, talking from very far away. The Beaufort College conference center was dizzyingly bright, a kaleidoscope of chrome and glass and multimillion-pound design. But at least, in a black velvet dress that guarded her rib cage like armor, Emma finally felt the part. That was all due to Nat.

The day after her interview, she had met Nat for breakfast as usual. The wisteria-clad Great Hall at Gabriel College was famous for its beauty. Morning sun played over fluted stone. The smell of toast and butter rose to the rafters.

Nat had slurped at his fourth coffee. "So, you won your dream funding. And yet this is not a happy face?"

Emma groaned. "It's that launch party. Those people will take one look at me and know I'm not meant to be there, with their *Tatler* photographer and their dressage clubs. I'm nothing like them. I've never shot a pheasant. Or shopped at Harrods. I've never ridden a horse, Nat."

"I'm not sure that will be required, Emma," Nat murmured, with exquisite delicacy, "at a cocktail party."

Emma took the mature route and did not stick her tongue out at him.

"Em, it doesn't matter, that elite nonsense. I spent years with these people, at an *extremely* exclusive boarding school, no less. And it only gave them enough time to decide I wasn't 'quite their sort.' They met you once, and they've already given you a cartload of money and a golden invitation. Maybe they like you."

Emma pushed her food around her plate. "But you should have seen how they dressed at the interview, these girls. I have nothing to wear."

"We'll just get Helena to lend you something," said Nat, briskly scooping Emma's uneaten hash browns into his mouth. "She was all about society soirees and glossy 'it' girlfriends when she was here. And she has more clothes than she could ever wear."

"I love your sister, but — " Emma said.

"Everyone loves my sister." Nat heaved the long sigh of the martyr. "Alas, even me. Trust me, she'll be excited about this. I'll message her."

And Helena Oluwole had come through. She had not sent just one dress, but a whole box of gowns and jackets and jumpsuits with labels Emma barely recognized, almost all the right length. Helena was tall, too.

Emma could tell that in her own clothes, she would have felt small and ashamed in front of the girls at this party. They looked as though they had never questioned money; always had so much that it had sunk into their skin. They all had the same coin-like shine, the crisp edges of a banknote. There was china-doll Venetia Kent, leaning against a steel sculpture in an attitude of complete boredom. Julia, a bright jewel in a crimson jumpsuit, shaking the University chancellor's hand. Across the room, Imogen Baldock was vamping at one of the journalists. The other fellows flitted about, glowing in front of the cameras.

Batted around a gauntlet of photographers, Emma thought the night might never end. But as the last of the champagne dried up, so did the crowd. The journalists fled for the train back to London. Soon only Julia's little clique remained.

Emma looked down at herself. Just one in a row of girls perched on the tables in the empty conference center, legs swinging, passing a champagne bottle. She wondered why she couldn't remember ever feeling so happy.

"What next?" asked Elizabeth Lim, the fellow for history. Regal in a column of cloudburst silk, she was so beautiful that Emma could hardly look at her directly.

"The party at St. Dunstan's, surely," purred Antonia Viacelli, granddaughter of an Italian contessa, and the fellow for music. "Where else, darlings?"

An excited murmur shivered through the row of girls.

"Jasper Balfour's first party of the year," said Imogen, nudging Elizabeth in the ribs. "Let the scandal commence."

"*The* Jasper Balfour?" piped up little Tabitha Mountbatten, the youngest fellow.

"Yes, and he's *just* as wicked as you've heard." Antonia's smile curled like steam from hot chocolate.

"I haven't heard he's wicked." Tabitha was blessed with complete imperviousness to innuendo. "My brother Hamish said he's already on the Olympic sailing team. Or the reserves, anyway. And Hamish was at Eton with Jasper, and he says one of the geography masters was always giving them stupid homework, so Jasper took his car apart in the parking lot, then put it back together on the roof, the whole car! And he was on Hamish's ski trip in Courchevel, and Mummy said he was so charming, he was the kind of boy that just looking at him'd make you walk funny for a week, although I wasn't quite sure what she meant, and — "

"Gods spare us the views of the entire Mountbatten clan," Venetia muttered. "Someone muzzle the virgin."

Imogen shoved her. Venetia shoved right back.

As the group swirled into motion, grabbing bags and shoes, Emma stood uncertain.

"Are you coming?"

Julia had turned back at the door.

"Me?" Emma found her hand had fluttered up to her chest. She pushed it down. "I mean, of course I'm coming. Let's meet this Jasper you're all so impressed with."

She was worried for a moment that she'd overdone it. But the group laughed. And as they poured onto the sloping cobbles of River Lane, she felt Julia's elegant hand clasp her shoulder.

The girls hurried along the river path. A hint of fog hung over the water now. Autumn, only a breath away. The river lay quiet in its bed, with barely a sign it had been capable of flooding a whole city just a week before. The crenellations of St. Dunstan's College rose in the distance.

The group quieted as they shuffled through the college gatehouse. The silence they walked into had a weight to it. St. Dunstan's was the oldest and richest of all the University's colleges. Its students had the reputation of being the best-heeled in the University. Emma's father had gone here. She had seen the few photos her mother had kept. There was one of them picnicking in the St. Dunstan's gardens. Diana with her striking eyes and Greenpeace T-shirt, hair flowing past her waist. Hugh Pelham, blond and laughing, shoulders broad in a hand-tailored blazer. A strange match, even in a photograph. He had already been engaged then, of course, to his now wife. But Emma liked to look at the photographs and pretend. That there had been no other family for him. No one to leave her for. When she'd applied to the University, Emma had once had a vision of him showing her his old rooms at St. Dunstan's and parading her in front of the porters.

This is my daughter, he would have said, pride spilling from his voice. *Going here too. Chip off the old block.*

But visions and reality rarely aligned when it came to her father. And so the real Emma had found her home at Gabriel College and had never seen St. Dunstan's up close. It had the flavor of a medieval keep, she thought. Troops of gargoyles grimaced down, faceless from years of acid rain. Emma shivered, missing the jovial angels and chubby deer that framed the doorways at Gabriel.

Julia waved them on, and they passed through lushly planted cloisters and an endless parade of formal gardens. The yew hedges were clipped into the shape of dragons, the college's mascot. Twilight had pulled itself swiftly over the city in their wake, and now it overtook them. Emma could barely make out the shapes of the farther trees. Only a whisper to the left told her that the river was somewhere near.

All this time, Tabitha had been peppering the girls with questions about the party's host. Emma listened with one ear, half-sick of the sound of his name already. Whoever and whatever Jasper

Balfour was, he seemed likely to be as puffed up as a bullfrog. The way they talked about him. Such praises of his curling hair and broad shoulders; such tales of the private jet he packed with his friends. Most of all, the whispers about the hopefuls throwing themselves at him. Even models and celebrities. Even mothers.

Regal Elizabeth Lim stooped so far as to giggle, and Tabitha's cheeks were pink.

Emma found herself gritting her teeth. "Who else will be at this party?"

A cluster of surprised faces turned to her.

Julia recovered herself first. "Oh — well, there's his roommate. Richard. They share a set of rooms, so they're both throwing this party, really."

Venetia snorted.

"Richard is a little quieter than Jasper," Julia added. "That doesn't mean he's — "

"Boring." Venetia flashed white, wolfish teeth.

"No, no," protested Julia, in distress. "When you talk to him, you find he's really — "

"Boring." Venetia flicked her hair over one shoulder. "Honestly, Julia."

Emma felt a first stirring of interest. Quieter. Next to the oafish Jasper — she could already picture the rugby-field bellow and leering smile — she saw an unpretentious, friendly face. He would be perhaps a little slimmer across the shoulders, with less of the Eton swagger. Perhaps he also found it hard to talk about himself, at first. She found her step quickening.

"But apart from that?" squeaked Tabitha, breathless as much from excitement as from trying to keep up. "Who else will be there?"

"Most of the Society, I should think," Imogen said absently, checking her makeup in her phone's camera.

"What society?" asked Tabitha, eager-eyed.

Sharp looks telegraphed around the remaining girls. Elizabeth Lim hissed in a breath.

Imogen pulled up short, wearing a rather guilty look. "What? Oh . . ."

"And Imogen does it again," drawled Venetia, with a slow clap that lost nothing of its viciousness as it echoed off the fountains of St. Dunstan's. "You'll have to tell her something now, won't you?"

"Ah — hm. Tabitha, it's just Jasper and some friends. It's like a — a University-wide club. Mostly drinking and dinners and stuff, but it's properly old and historic. Anyway, there's not much you need to know, it's just a night out."

"But what is this club?" pursued Tabitha. "What's it called? Can I join?"

"No, you can't. Boys only, I'm afraid. And it doesn't have a name. At least, it does, but not one you can know. And you can't tell anyone about it. Not even that you know it exists."

"So it's a secret," Tabitha breathed, round-eyed. "Cool. My older brother Hamish will be so impressed I know a secret society now."

"You can tell *your older brother Hamish* —" Venetia began silkily. But before she could finish whatever crushing statement she had planned, most of the group had doubled over.

"What *is* that?" choked Elizabeth Lim. Beside her, Antonia Viacelli retched into a box hedge.

"It is the worst — "

" — I can't breathe — "

" — *disgusting* — "

A wall of rot curled up from the darkness to their left. It rose around them, foul and overripe. Emma felt it coat her tongue. Nausea shuddered through her throat.

It smelled of dead things.

"It's — I think — the sunken garden — " coughed Imogen.

Emma's eyes adjusted to the darkness. The garden below was a maze of rotting rosebushes, sagging with late blooms. Every rose blackened through; every thorn softened to mush.

"It must have been the flood. It drowned them."

"It's awful."

Even as she gagged, Emma found herself wondering if the flood had carried some contaminant, to leave the roses so damaged. A waterborne pest, perhaps? Her mother would have known.

But that was not what held her body rigid, a field mouse scenting an owl, scanning the garden. Something was *there*. It was a ridiculous thought. But for an instant, the fallen roses seemed like plucked eyeballs, pupils of rot rolled up to watch her. Then Julia tugged her arm, and Emma gladly stumbled away with her, toward the light at the end of the gardens.

They emerged in a vast, brightly lit quad, and Emma's macabre imaginings loosened their claws on her brain. She was rather inclined to laugh at herself.

"Old Hob Quad," said Julia, finally lowering her sleeve from her face. "The most beautiful student rooms in the University."

"But by God, they make you walk for them," growled Imogen, storming past in a blaze of red curls. She leapt up the first staircase and hammered on the door at the top. With one last look at the rot-scented darkness behind them, Emma followed.

CHAPTER 4

WHEN THE DOOR OPENED, EMMA HAD TO STEEL HERSELF NOT TO gasp. The University was lavish, but she had never known students could have such palatial rooms. Leading off the main space, Emma glimpsed a kitchen and at least two bedrooms. Dark paneling and velvet dominated. Portraits glowered from gaps between Gothic windows. Someone had set up a bar in one corner atop what looked to be a sixteenth-century sideboard.

Emma looked up to find she had lost the other fellows. Adrift in a sea of dinner jackets and blazers, she wandered until she spotted Julia Colefax-Lee perched on a sofa.

"Can I join you?"

Julia smiled. "Oh. The natural sciences fellow. Emma, was it? Sorry, come." She patted the cushion next to her, still scanning the crowd. "People watching is my favorite sport."

"I thought you captained the running team." Emma settled next to Julia, trying not to seem far too tall. "I see you sometimes in the Great Hall at Gabriel, with the other runners."

"Running is my second-favorite sport. You're observant. I'd

forgotten you said you were at Gabriel, if you'll forgive me. It can make you a little inward facing, this kind of thing."

She waved a hand at the party. Emma was surprised at how tired she looked.

" 'This kind of thing' is new to me," Emma admitted.

"Well, with your keen observation, we can make an expert people watcher of you yet. Now, where shall we start?"

Five minutes later, Emma's head was spinning. From their sofa, Julia had been classifying the rest of the party into the correct social taxonomies with Linnaean accuracy.

" — and don't even bother with the ones in the corner, dreadful social climbers."

"Julia! Brought you a drink. And your friend too." A large, solid boy had ambled up, his face shining with equal parts kindness and perspiration.

"In a second, Hugo. I'm just educating Emma here. Now, it's the University Union election coming up — picking the student body president, you know — so prepare for everyone's conversation to be the dullest. But nineteen of the last twenty prime ministers have come from the University, so perhaps it's fair this lot feel there are stakes."

"Over three-quarters of all the prime ministers in history," Hugo added helpfully. "They made us learn that one in school."

"That many? From one place?" Emma said.

"Well, the odd one came from the next rung down of universities. Oxford or Cambridge, Durham, Edinburgh. That sort."

"They're still excellent schools, surely."

Julia wrinkled her nose. "Fine, as later universities go. Oxford and Cambridge were actually born from offshoots of the University proper. But they've never really had any big names going for them, have they? Not like us. Imagine Newton going to Cambridge. Or Oxford being home to Shelley or Tolkien — you can't. The greatest works and discoveries are all from us."

"It does mean people expect rather big things from you, if you're here," said Hugo, in a doleful tone.

Julia laughed. "Some more than others. Emma, see that group by the fire?"

They wore tailcoats. Their cheeks were gammon pink with wine. They had the laughs of people who'd never worried about how loud they were.

The Society. The thought was instant.

It was the aura of power around them. They almost glowed with it, those boys by the fire. They stood apart, careless, while the eyes of the party absorbed their every move. Emma was almost certain she was right. But she said nothing to Julia, remembering that flash of fear in Imogen's eyes. Some secrets weren't meant to be spoken aloud.

Julia leaned in, her voice low. "There's your future prime minister right there. Perhaps more than one. Not Francis — the one who looks like Napoleon — or Hugo here. They're bound for family businesses and Labradors." Julia grinned at Hugo. "No. You'll want to keep an eye on that tall, dark one. Keeps his nose clean — in public, at least — and a shoo-in for the Union election. The one that looks like a Victorian schoolmaster, next to him? Philip, also a contender. Then Piers — well, I don't think he'll ever be top man. That weaselly sort never are. Minister, more likely.

"Richard was here a minute ago. I'm not sure where — " Julia's voice softened as she peered over the crowd. "Well, you might meet him later." She recovered her detachment and snorted. "Ed is still convinced he's going to be a grime artist. His family will stick him in a pretend job at a merchant bank until it wears off. Atticus Tremaine   the nervy, beautiful one? Very serious thesp. Film agents already swarming around those cheekbones. Then Guy's father is something big in property, so there he'll go too."

"And what about the famous Jasper?" asked Emma. "Which one is he?"

"He's not here," Julia said. "Nobody's seen him all night."

"At his own party?" Emma resisted the urge to roll her eyes.

"Jasper's funny that way. He likes to . . . surprise. It's part of what makes his parties so fun. You never know what will happen."

Hugo chuckled. "That one time, with the plane? Nobody knew, but he'd gone ahead and chartered a flight to Paris. Said nothing to anyone, let it sit on the tarmac all night. Then one of the girls happened to say she was hungry. And just like that, he flew us all to Paris for breakfast."

Julia sighed. "Because 'the only breakfast worth having is made by the pastry chef at Le Meurice, Julia.' I still dream about that breakfast. Oh, and there was the swimming pool in London for Piers' birthday — "

"Filled it with naked ladies," Hugo said solemnly. "Just filled it. Everywhere you looked, naked ladies. Well, they had little bits over their . . . ahem. Well. Point is, he's beyond me. I'm lucky if I remember what day I'm throwing a party."

Julia leaned forward. "Oh, what about that time he — "

They fell into a patter of unfamiliar names and places, and Emma felt more like an outsider than ever. So she slipped off, cross at the part of herself that wanted to stay and hear more. Her mind had no business wondering about the kind of person that might stay up plotting magical surprises for his friends. Or imagining the crunch of fresh pastry in a Paris sunrise, butter dissolving on her tongue.

A clock struck ten. She waited for the nagging ache to return to Gabriel Tower to strike with it. But there was a strange, empty space where the longing for her own room usually lay in wait. And how much more of a triumph would it be, she wondered, to return to Nat with something to show for the evening? *You need more friends than just me, Emma.*

Well, she would say casually, leaning against his door, *I've actually already made some.*

Unaware that her jaw was set and her face radiating determination, Emma forged her way into the crowd.

Behind her, a group had gathered by the window. Julia was holding court on a sofa. Next to her, Venetia Kent amused herself by freezing passing boys like rabbits with her cobra gaze, then releasing them with a slow smile. A sprawl of young notables lay at their feet, passing bottles of Bollinger.

There was only one topic of conversation.

"So now that Jasper's back, is he really going to be president of — *you-know-what?*"

"What, because he's changed his mind about 'finding himself' on a beach in Fiji?"

"Hugo, surely you've heard something."

Hugo shifted uncomfortably. "I can't say — "

The conversation cut over him. "But who else would it be?"

"Richard Wellesley-Jones was up for it."

"Bit of an odd choice. Quiet, isn't he?"

Julia's face softened. "Poor Richard. It was his year, really."

"I can't see him minding," Hugo volunteered, in his shy, slow voice. "It's not really his thing, all that being-in-charge business. Much happier with a book or a bottle, I'd say."

Julia threw him a warm smile, and Hugo blushed up to his ears.

Venetia tossed back her hair, straight into Imogen Baldock's face. "God, you're all dull. I already said: Jasper's back, and he's president. Move on."

Imogen fished several blond strands from her drink, glowering. Hostilities between Venetia and Imogen, always on the verge of breaking out, had been especially vicious of late. Imogen had already endured a full evening of unavenged barbs. Which is perhaps why she risked life and limb — and the likelihood of ever receiving another invite to the Kents' famous summer parties at their villa in Tuscany, which was far more important — by turning on Venetia Kent in public.

"You know, I don't think any of this is true."

"Really, Imogen darling, keep up. After I said so?"

"No," Imogen leaned back with a belligerent smile. "*Because* you said so. Maybe I think you're a liar, *Venetia darling*."

One of the boys actually laughed.

Venetia turned in his direction. He fell instantly silent. There was dead stillness as Venetia inspected her nails. "Well then," she said, in the softest of voices. "If we're calling names . . . No, perhaps not. We are at a party, after all." She stood in one flowing motion. "If you'll excuse me."

With that, she stalked off into the crowd, and the courtiers on the sofa dispersed.

Hugo lingered, offering a hand to help Julia up. "That was a relief. For a minute there, I expected Venetia'd — well, do the

37

usual. Blood and brimstone and all the rest. But she took it rather well, don't you think?"

"A little too well," Julia murmured.

Hugo tugged her arm. "Come on, Julia. They've set up a keg stand in the kitchen. Oh, I knew you'd look at me like that. The great Julia Colefax-Lee could *never* be seen drinking *beer* through a *funnel*," he teased.

"Oh, all right," she said. "But just for a bit."

So she didn't see Venetia stroll up to the bar and hand something to a girl there with a whispered laugh. Something that, when Imogen Baldock approached the bar a few minutes later, made its way into her drink without anyone noticing.

Emma, meanwhile, was not quite ready to admit defeat. She should, perhaps, have anticipated that the mating habits of the silkworm — as fascinating as they were — might not be a winning topic of conversation. But she suspected that the crowd in the room that night were just not in the mood to be befriended.

Worse, standing alone was attracting notice. She felt someone staring at the girl without friends, clutching her drink in an empty corridor. So Emma groped for the nearest door and slipped inside, away from the stranger's gaze.

She knew immediately that she was in Jasper's bedroom. It was just as she'd expected: Eton memorabilia on the walls, a gold-buttoned blazer slung over a trunk. A decorative saber hung above the bed. A persistent smell in the room nagged at the back of her throat: likely a mix of the unwashed rugby gear in one corner and the cologne that hung over everything.

She wrinkled her nose and sighed. There was no point being out for the night if she was hiding in a bedroom she didn't even like.

She put an eye to the crack in the door. The corridor was clear. She stepped out.

Someone had turned up the music in the main room. She could hear the cheers and feel the bass buzzing through the floor. But she hesitated, her eyes drawn to a second door. The one that would belong to Jasper's roommate. The quiet one. With a darting glance for any watching eyes, she twisted the second knob and slipped inside.

The room was a treasure trove. It was lined with framed photographs. Deserts. Rivers. Waves boiling on rock, waves crashing on sand, waves limpid in the flat calm of a bay. Some places she recognized. Like the cove in Tasman National Park, where eight-year-old Emma and her mother had run down to the tide pools. There, beside the famous organ pipe rock formation this boy's photograph had captured, she had watched the seal colony for hours. The eye behind the camera had caught the feel of the places. Had felt something for them, just as she had. She could see it.

There was nothing else in the room, she realized. No school memorabilia. No sports gear strewn in a corner. The whole was thoughtfully and peacefully tidy, as though to focus the eye only on the photography.

Quieter. Yes, she could imagine that the mind who had created these images knew about quiet. They had felt the peace that filled her mind in a silent crouch before a riverbank. They knew the wonders that nature would reveal only to the patient.

She had begun to feel conscious of her own intrusion in this boy's sanctuary. As silently as she could, she backed out of the room. And stepped neatly into the embrace of the person waiting behind her.

CHAPTER 5

EMMA SPUN TO FIND A YOUNG MAN WITH A SMILE SO GREASED, IT slipped from her face to her cleavage almost instantly. It was the one who'd been staring at her earlier.

"What's this pretty little piece, eh?"

He very nearly would have been handsome, if he hadn't looked so much like a weasel. Emma tried to edge past him, but the boy was blocking the corridor.

"Emma. I — I'm here with Julia," she said, unpleasantly conscious of the low back of her dress, the cold air pricking her exposed skin.

"Fresh meat? Oh, lovely stuff. Can't believe Julia's been keeping you hidden away. We're gasping for fresh talent around here. You don't fancy slipping off together and — No? Ha ha! Reckon the old GF wouldn't be such a fan of that either. She's lurking about somewhere. Not a word, eh? Got lost, did you? Don't blame you. We've nothing like this at Fenchurch College, it's all bloody Queen Anne architecture. Ups-a-daisy — the drinks are through here. Mind you don't let anyone lure you away to a shady corner — unless it's me, ha! Ha! Piers Popwell, by the way — one of Jasper's mates from school. Eton, that is. Everyone calls me Peeper — "

He ushered her along. She peeled her lower back away from his hand.

"Now, you park your bottom here a minute; I'll get us some — "

He turned back. "Where's she — ? Bloody females."

Pressed against the other side of a door, Emma chuckled to herself. Her escape from the corridor had brought her out somewhere at the back of the building, at the top of a flight of steps. They sank into a dark courtyard garden.

From the other side of the door, a particularly loud bump and a torrent of swearing indicated that Piers might have tried kicking the wall. Emma snorted, then clapped her hand to her face. It would be just her luck to give herself away. But the door didn't open. Emma waited, and Piers' steps faded into silence. The wind whispered through the olive trees in the garden below.

"Now, that was an intriguing entrance."

Emma whirled around.

From the darkness, a cigarette flared. In its momentary glow, Emma made out a bright eye. The sharp edge of a cheekbone.

"I wonder what brought you outside in such a hurry?"

The voice was cultured, hovering somewhere between boredom and amusement.

Emma stumbled down the steps toward it. "What — who — what are you doing out here, in the dark?"

"Couldn't I ask you the same thing?"

The speaker lounged against an olive trunk. The party spilled enough light to hint at the burnt-tan hand around his cigarette, the gold threading his messy curls. Emma moved closer. The boy was slim but powerfully built, like a big cat. After a night navigating rooms of waistcoats and blazers, his loose T-shirt was a shock to Emma's system. The cotton looked soft with age. Careless, comfortable. Emma wriggled inside her black velvet armor, feeling envious.

And as the boy turned his face into the light, Emma felt her throat catch. She had once seen a statue of Apollo at a museum, she remembered dazedly. And although usually she preferred the beauty of living things to the still, cold art humans kept in their galleries, something about this statue had gripped her. She had stared at the perfect lines of cheek and belly and thigh. The princely nose, the fierce eyes. That stone Apollo had looked as though he were about to leap from his plinth and sprint into the forest. The boy in front of her had the same sense of power, barely concealed in stillness.

Unused to being confronted by specimens of masculine perfection, Emma retreated into idiocy. She pointed at him — actually pointed — and asked the only thing that came to mind:

"What happened to your arm?"

The young man rubbed the welts that scored his forearm, rippling and purple. A rueful grin made him suddenly, and welcomely, more human.

"This? Being an idiot. I dove right onto a box jellyfish last year."

Emma couldn't repress a shudder. "A box jelly?" No wonder he still had the scars. Their venom was legendary.

"Yeah, just off the Tasmanian coast."

Emma had been inspecting the scars with awe. But at this, her head snapped up.

The stranger tossed the cigarette into the shrubbery and leaned against the wall. "It was after the Sydney-Hobart race, if you know it? The rest of the crew stayed with the yacht, but me'n one of the other guys, we rented a dinghy to explore the coast. The water was incredible, so — well, I jumped in, and found myself in a passionate embrace with a box jelly."

He looked at her, waiting for a laugh.

"You're the photographer," she said, a wordless joy creeping through her. She was certain. This slim young god, with the messy hair and careless clothes, was the one who had arranged those images on the walls.

"I've been in your bedroom," she added, before she could stop herself.

That startled him out of his languid lean. He cocked his head to one side, eyes sparkling. "Oh yes?"

"I saw a photograph there. In your room. Of the rocks outside Hobart."

"The organ pipe cliff," he said slowly. "Yes, with — "

" — the seal colony," Emma finished. "I loved it. I used to spend hours there, just watching them."

The knowing smile had slipped from his face. He looked years younger, and eager, as though he were running up on a beach to ask if she wanted to play skipping stones.

"You know it?"

"I lived near there. When I was younger." She grinned back at him. "We'd go to the national park on weekends. That photo caught how I remember it feeling, exactly. The sun, the waves. And that was you, wasn't it? Your photo. Your bedroom."

He shook his head in wonder. "Well — yeah. You got all that from me telling you about diving onto a jelly?"

43

"As soon as you said you'd been to Tasmania, really."

The boy let out a delighted laugh. "Just when you think there's nothing new in the world to surprise you — " He swung her around to a stone bench and sat them both down. "I think we should get introduced."

"I'm Emma. Emma Curran."

"Emma Curran, who lived in Tasmania. And loved the seals. And who still hasn't said why she's hiding at a party."

"I'm not hiding."

The photographer just grinned at her. Venetia had been mad to call him boring. The famous Jasper's roommate — Richard, Emma remembered, that was what Julia had said — was certainly not as loud as the boors in tailcoats inside. But fascination rolled from him, stronger than anyone she'd met.

"Fine. I am hiding. This party isn't for me. No offence to your roommate."

"My roommate?"

"The great Jasper Balfour. King of the so-called Society, or whatever that secret nonsense is," said Emma, made reckless by the warmth of several glasses of wine inside her. The photographer shifted on the bench beside her. "I'm sorry, I know he's your friend. But the way people talk about him. To make a big deal of inviting everyone here, and then not turn up to his own party? How pretentious is that?"

"Oh, very," said the photographer, picking a stray leaf from his jeans with a small and curious smile. "Seriously pretentious."

"Yes," said Emma, warming to her theme. "And the way people talk about him. Like his money makes him important. Like that's what matters, how extravagant his parties are. How many private jet rides he takes them on. It's just stupid. And sad. Don't you think?"

"Yeah," the photographer said quietly. He was shredding the leaf to pieces. "I actually do."

He shot a sideways glance at her. "And you don't care? About that stuff?"

A sudden vision rose in Emma's mind. She was in a ball gown, layers of tulle frothing around her seat belt. She watched the earth drop away from the window, felt Julia's hand in hers. *Next stop, Paris,* someone crowed.

Emma crushed the thought. "No," she said quickly. "I don't care. At all."

"Then you're cleverer than most people."

A bang made them both jump. The door at the top of the stairs had flown open. The noise of the party spilled out around a boy in a tailcoat.

"Come on, we're about to crack open the port old Cranner's brought. Spence said you were skulking outside."

The photographer's face crinkled in a grimace. He ducked his head.

The figure leaned out farther.

"Oy, Jasper. You still down there?"

The courtyard was silent for a moment.

"Er, yeah — be up in a minute, mate."

The photographer looked at Emma, who was sure her face couldn't have been more aghast if a tree root had burst up through the concrete and dragged the whole building down into the depths of the earth, like a kraken.

"Jasper," she said, in a voice of calm despair. "You're not Richard. You're Jasper."

A mischievous dimple hovered in his cheek. "I'm afraid so. The 'great Jasper Balfour,' as you put it."

She sprang from the bench.

"No — wait, don't go." He clasped her wrist, laughing, and pulled her back. "I'm sorry. You were right, anyway. About how stupid it is, all the people in there who only care about my parents' money."

"I'm sorry I said that."

"It's true, though." His voice was laced with bitterness. "None of those people see me. Not really. They want Jasper Balfour."

"And you don't want to be that?"

"Look, I wasn't even meant to be here this year. I wanted to be sailing the world, far away from — " He waved a hand at the building, where writhing shapes pressed against the windows. "My yacht was all ready."

"And they'd let you take the year off?" Emma asked.

"People do it all the time. And m'mother's good friends with the University chancellor, so they'd got it sorted between them. But my father put an end to that." Jasper's face had darkened. "He's got my life all planned out. Economics now, then straight into a job in finance, like him. I'll never get to live the way I want." He kicked at the bench. "So here I am, back in my box. My roommate wanted to throw this party. Richard. But when it all kicked off, I came out here. I couldn't face it."

"Why not?"

"The same fake stories and jokes and people *wanting* things. When I could be at sea right now, the spray on my face, where

I'm — my real self." He ducked his head and rubbed the back of his neck. "Or whatever. That sounded lame."

"Not lame," said Emma, reaching out. His forearm was warm, the scars rough under her fingers. "That's why the photos, right? When I was looking at them in your room, I thought they were like . . . windows. To somewhere different. An escape."

Strong tan fingers closed over her own. She felt a jolt in her chest.

"You do get it."

His gaze was piercing. Emma had the strange sensation that he was looking right through her, to everything that lay behind. His eyes were the most devastating blue.

"Of course." Emma feigned cool, though her heart was fluttering like a bat caught in a bell jar. "I know what it's like. To feel out of place, at parties like this. That's why I was in your bedroom in the first place."

"Oh yes." He smiled in a way that made Emma wonder where her insides had gone. "So you were."

"It was nice, seeing your photos of Tasmania," she said softly. "Like a piece of home. I miss it."

"Must've been amazing, growing up there."

"I grew up all over, really. But Tasmania was special. I got to stay there longer than anywhere else. Four years, nearly. Same school, same friends. And there was this beach right near our house — you could see penguins there. Can you imagine? Fairy penguins, they called them." Emma smiled and sighed. "I cried every day when we moved. The next place was the middle of Mexico somewhere. I remember refusing to learn Spanish, thinking it would force my mum to take me back to Australia. Eleven-year-old logic."

"Didn't work?"

"Not at all. In fact, after that we were on to the Philippines. Then Toronto," she continued, counting on her fingers. "The Côte d'Ivoire. Hertfordshire, strangest of all. My mum's work took us a lot of places."

"And your dad was okay with that?"

"They're not together. He — he was never really involved. With me. Phone calls now and then, that's it. So it was just her and me, and a few suitcases."

Jasper looked entranced. "What an incredible way to live. Country to country, taking only what you need. Living for the experience of it, not the material stuff. That's the life for me."

"As long as it comes with breakfast at Le Meurice," Emma teased, thinking of Julia's stories.

"Now, who told you that? No, I don't want to know." He laughed, eyes dancing. "I don't want to imagine what other stories you've heard. They're all probably true. Look, what penguin beaches are to you, fine pastries are to me."

The door above banged open once more.

"Jasper," bellowed the voice again. "Where the bloody hell are you? Come up for some port before I drag you up."

"Well." Jasper rose from the bench. "I don't think we can hide for much longer. Shall we?"

The moment they entered the main room, Jasper was mobbed. The press of people was overwhelming. Antonia Viacelli, luscious hair spilling from her bun, winked as they passed. Imogen danced barefoot at the center of a group of roaring boys, red hair flying. It was dizzying. Jasper caught Emma's hand and plunged them through an opening in the capering circle.

He steered her to a figure leaning against the fireplace.

"Emma," he said, "I'd like you to meet Richard, my roommate."

"And *best* mate," the figure corrected.

He was similar to Jasper, in that they both had blond hair and blue eyes. But if Jasper was an Aston Martin, Richard was a Land Rover. He was solidly built, shorter than she was. His hair was fine and light as a duckling's down, ruffled into an artfully tousled nest. A pale imitation, Emma thought, next to Jasper's naturally springy dark gold mane. Although he wore the same eveningwear as the others, Richard gave off a strong scent of corduroy, soon to become pinstripe.

The saber, the boarding school trunk, the blazer. It was a perfect fit.

"Welcome to our humble abode," said Richard. "Jasper, get the lady a drink. Where are your manners, boy?" He gave Jasper a fond cuff to the back of the head.

"Boy?" Jasper darted in with a sucker punch.

Richard doubled up but waved off Emma's horror. "Plenty of padding here." He chuckled, rubbing his stomach. "You clearly don't have brothers."

He saw Emma peer at the framed photo on the mantelpiece. "Yes, that's me and Jasper." Richard smiled over her shoulder. "And his father. The day he taught us to fish."

"You both look so young."

"Lived with them since I was ten. Best people in the world."

Emma's gaze drifted to Jasper, striding back to the fireplace with three brimming glasses. He was a lightning bolt streaking through the darkened room. Laughing with some groups, whipping a joke at others. Wherever he was, faces lit up. She'd been wrong to think it was just about the money. People followed Jasper like sunflowers leaned toward the sun.

He fetched up against the fireplace. "Sorry about that. It's like — there's a person I have to be at these things. I just slip back into it. Still, seems silly now to have been hiding in the garden, doesn't it?"

He offered her a glass. Richard and Jasper emptied theirs in one, so Emma tried to do the same. At some point, a pack of boys in tailcoats gathered around. The Society, she was sure now.

Even as the heat in the party rose and other shirt points wilted, theirs stayed sharp. Their tailcoats were cut from fabric so rich, the black of it seemed to drain the light around them. Firelight dripped from the brocade on their waistcoats, spinning from brass buttons and signet rings in dizzying rays. It was almost hypnotic.

Condensation dripped from the ceiling. Little Tabitha Mountbatten was pressed against a wall. Francis Carr's tongue explored her throat with the energy of a man rummaging through a coat stand to find his umbrella. Julia lay asleep on a sofa, her head in Hugo's lap. Emma was nearly knocked over by two boys ushering a staggering Imogen to one of the bedrooms. And over the heads of the writhing crowd, Emma met Jasper's gaze. Her heart was doing the strangest things in her chest.

Then Jasper smiled, and Emma knew she was lost.

Emma knew they must have said goodbye, but she couldn't remember it. As she slipped out of St. Dunstan's College, all she could

think of was the electric brush of his lips on her cheek. He had seen
her to the door.

"Would you like to — "

"Maybe we could — Oh, you first."

Jasper laughed and leaned against the doorframe. It brought
his face inches from hers. "So, you're interested in photography,
right?"

"I don't know much about it, but I wish I could take photos like
yours. Ones that tell a story."

Jasper rubbed a hand over his golden curls, looking pleased.
"I could show you a few things. Come out with me, next time I do
a session? Go on — put your number in my phone, I'll message
you."

Her heartbeat had not yet recovered. She hugged her arms to
her chest, reliving the match strike of his lips on her skin. Her steps
echoed from the empty city streets. From the cobbled lanes, where
fairy fogs muffled the lampposts. From the facades of the colleges,
turned to mother-of-pearl in the moonlight. And from the statues,
staring everywhere from plinths and rooftops. Stone eyes, blank
and pupilless, followed her path.

She passed Beaufort College, whose outer wall was shrouded
with the skeletal remains of a wisteria vine. It had been dead for
decades, withered fingers clawed too deep into the mortar to
remove.

Now, impossibly, it was blooming. Lush flowers glowed through
the dark like alien fruit, fleshy and corpse pale. Emma coughed,
dizzied. The scent of the flood leaked from them, an echo of the
rot in the rose garden. Emma backed away, repulsed and drawn at

once. The scent ran ghostly fingers through her hair, chased her all the way up Beaufort Crescent. Emma reminded herself that she was only interested, as a scientist would be. There was no reason to feel troubled. Or to walk faster.

If only she could shake the feeling of eyes on her back. Emma's heart made a determined effort to leap out of her chest. Those were drums, faint on the night air. The sinuous rhythm slid into her pulse. And wisps of human voices, like the chatter of a distant bazaar. She spun to face them. But the street was empty.

With a laugh that sounded like a gasp, Emma recovered herself. She was surrounded by student rooms. Students gave parties. Muffled beats from speakers, the sounds of laughter. What could be more expected?

Then, at the top of the High Street, something brushed her foot. Emma jerked back. But it was just a little frog. Another strange remnant of the flood, trying to find its way back to the river. The shape split. Not one, but two frogs. Squirming against each other.

Breeding. In September. It was impossible. It could only happen in spring. It —

It couldn't just be the flood. No single flood could change the patterns of millennia, surely. But what about climate change? There had been journal papers on climate-related behavior shifts before. She could do some research. None of this would feel so eerie once she found a reason. A peer-reviewed, data-backed reason, preferably. Her steps quickened toward Gabriel Tower. Purring croaks bounced from the shopfronts, following even as she hurried away.

Gabriel Passage was gloriously, gratefully in sight when Emma reeled back. There, stripped by the streetlight. A writhing mass of amphibious bodies, climbing and scratching at one another. One moist body slipped from the pile to the gutter, and another mounted in his place. They were croaking in a frenzy.

Emma stopped short. Her heart lurched. She seized a stick and pushed at the mass, sending the stubborn, rubbery bodies squirming away. Knowing what she would find beneath.

The lone female trapped at the heart of the pile. Legs broken at odd angles, ribs caved in. Her belly had split open. Emma could not dislodge the last frog from her back. He stared up with hopeful headlamp eyes, still clamped in position over his dead lover. Slowly, his head tracked down. Down, where the clotted crystal jelly of her insides peered through. His tongue flicked once. Twice. He gave a louder croak. Deeper. Without warning, he opened his mouth wide and plunged it into her side. The other frogs approached again, a hopping tide. They tore into the open seam of her belly, jellied innards dripping from their tongues. Guttural croaks ricocheted from the alley walls.

Emma dropped the stick.

Nature was itself. It was wondrous and it was wild and hungry. Even as a little girl, she had never needed it to be pretty to love it. Never needed to turn away at the sight of its appetite. And yet she found she was almost running now, straining for the North Gate ahead.

She huffed a laugh. If her mother could have seen her, running away from a few frogs. She deliberately walked the last steps to let herself into Gabriel College. By the time she reached her bedroom, her heart had stopped its nauseous dance. She wriggled out of Helena's dress, feeling as though she shed a skin. In her own soft nightclothes, hands cradling a moon-silvered cup of tea, the world felt right again.

She turned her back on the window, where the wind whispered at the pane. Where the dark called. Where, down below, the frogs still feasted on their love.

CHAPTER 6

THE NEXT DAY BEGAN FOR EMMA AS THOUGH HER WORLD HAD NOT just been rocked off its axis. The Great Hall echoed with the clink of cutlery. Nat was crunching his way through a bowl of sugar-coated cereal. Emma slid her phone from her pocket. No messages yet. She shouldn't have expected to hear from Jasper right away, of course. She stabbed at her porridge with her spoon.

Nat was agog to hear the details. When she told him about meeting Jasper, he looked closely at her face and just smiled. Much as she'd tried to make her voice sound offhand, she knew her cheeks were burning.

She pressed her hands to her face, hoping to cool it. "I never expected — It was all just so . . ." *Magical,* she managed to stop herself from saying.

"It is so much fun to see you like this." Nat slurped the last milk from his bowl. "Usually it's me who's stupid with love. I quite like being the superior, sensible one, for a change."

Emma snorted. "You will never be the sensible one."

"We'll see. Now." Nat clasped her shoulder. "Lectures, at last! Come on, we don't want to be late."

"Don't we?" Emma muttered. But she let Nat chivvy her from the Great Hall.

After the quiet of Gabriel College, city life outside hit them with an open-handed smack. Thirty colleges made up the University. And since colleges were only places to sleep and eat, that meant further buildings for lecture halls and classrooms, laboratories and museums. All filled with students and professors and staff, streaming from one to another until well after dark. The city was some distance from London, and not a tenth of its size, but its streets teemed with just as much chaos.

Streams of bicycles whirred past, incurring the wrath of cars and pedestrians alike. Groups of students wreathed the pavements, trailing chatter.

"Got a tute on Thursda — "

"Told you he had my gown, the — "

" — *puked* on the bursar — "

Seemingly intoxicated by the pearly September morning, Nat flung his arms wide. Passing cyclists swerved. "Is it mad that I missed — nay, *yearned* for lectures when the flood got them canceled?"

"Yes," said Emma flatly. "Mad as mad."

"Chaucer, *Beowulf,* anything," Nat continued dreamily, floating down the pavement. "But to come back to two hours on the sonnets with Professor Lindman? The gods do smile upon us mortals sometimes."

"And I have three back-to-back classes I know I'm going to fall asleep in."

"I thought it was better this year? Elective year and all."

"Law is never better. I thought land law might be more interesting, but . . ." Emma shrugged.

"You know, there's no shame in changing course, if something doesn't suit you."

But Emma shook her head and ducked away, leaving her friend at the corner between the law and English faculties.

Emma did not fall asleep during her classes. Instead, she let her mind drift. Imagined peaceful green hours in the river, fish flashing by her ankles. A Guilder deer stepping down the bank to drink, fooled by her stillness. The long glance they would share.

Class must have ended. She hadn't heard a thing. Emma gathered her books and dodged the exodus from the lecture theatre. Flood gossip was the spice on every tongue. A fresher who'd drunk floodwater on a dare — and started claiming that the University's statues were alive — had just been carted off to hospital. The Wessex chaplain, while supposedly logging water damage, had been discovered dreamily painting tree runes across the walls of their Christopher Wren chapel. And the Fenchurch rowing team had apparently bailed the last water from their boathouse that morning, and found their fiberglass boats sprouting branches of tender new holly. Emma smiled inwardly. People did love to embroider stories.

She drifted across the square to the church crypt café. Nat had saved their regular table. For Emma, the same thing every time. For Nat, whatever sounded newest and strangest on the menu.

He banged the table. "Em, you'll never guess what happened this morning. The *wildest* thing."

"Wilder than those people trying to walk through the wall next to the secondhand bookshop last week?" Emma helped herself to a forkful of Nat's broccoli. He never ate it. "Because that's the strangest thing I've ever seen. This term's barely begun, and it's already the weirdest one yet."

"I can't imagine how drunk they must have been. Their costumes were amazing, though, don't you think? They almost looked real, the wings and hooves and all. Must have been an incredible fancy dress party." He snorted. "I liked the one who asked if you wanted to bargain your hair for a month of good dreams."

Emma shuddered and patted her hair. "I did not."

Nat beamed. "Well, my thing today is *far* wilder. The theatre just called. They're recasting Tolstoy in *The Life of Tolstoy*. The lead, Em! The director just found out that Atticus gave her chlamydia, apparently, so he's out on his arse. Auditions tonight."

"No!" said Emma. "Well, you should have got the part the first time round, anyway."

Nat made her a bow over his broccoli. "This humble player dares to agree."

Emma caught amused glances at their table. She sometimes wondered if the other café regulars found them an odd pairing. Nat so vibrant and dramatic, she so muted and practical. She might have thought so herself, once. Meeting her best friend had been a matter of pure chance. Or, as Nat liked to put it, the universe shoving two unlikely souls together for their own good.

In her first year, on her very first day at the University, Emma had tripped over a pair of impossibly long legs. They were stretched out behind a tree in the Gabriel College gardens. And because they were exactly, inconveniently placed where nobody would expect legs to be, both Emma and her bicycle had gone flying.

"That was not," an unruffled voice had said, "what I expected you to do."

Sharp eyes glinted behind wire-framed glasses. The hands that put his paperback aside were gentle, even pausing to put in a bookmark. The side part in his Afro was carefully straight.

"Well, you're not the first and will not be the last to find me in the way of things. It is, alas" — a dramatic hand gesture — "my inescapable destiny."

He stood, an operation not unlike a daddy longlegs trying to free itself from a pat of butter. Emma took the hand he offered to scramble up.

"Nat Oluwole. Not Nate. And if you call me Nathaniel, we will have strong words. Other than that, it's generally a pleasure to make my acquaintance." He picked up her bike and handed it to her.

Emma had felt the first real smile since she'd returned to England curve across her face.

Nat never ate a main course where dessert was available. His room was plastered with posters for obscure art-house films from the seventies. His father had risen to the highest echelons of that august British institution, the Church of England. But in the hushed corridors of power, over the clerical sherry parties and biscuits with parishioners, Femi Oluwole had found that to be Nigerian was to be considered too loud, too vivid. Too different. He had hushed his voice, banished even the stray Yoruba word from his vocabulary, filled his conversation with Wodehouse and Elgar. And he was surprised at how entirely he was then welcomed into the fold of insiders. To the bishop's hat and the pulpit of Durham Cathedral. And so he had been anxious for his children to be as English as possible: boarding school, riding lessons, and a diet of toad-in-the-hole and roly-poly pudding. Nat's extensive Nigerian family might have looked askance at the gangly youth in a Dickensian suit at family weddings, among a sea of cousins in agbadas or bright blazers. But the bishop gazed upon his two clever, well-connected children, who spoke only English and had never tasted jollof, and was satisfied he had made them safe.

Safe, however, was not a state Nat lived in comfortably. He had steadfastly hated every minute at Eton, fallen off every horse he had ever been put on, and, piece by piece, was trying to build himself a Nigerian education. An auntie slipped him some recipes on the side. And so, when he wasn't rehearsing at the theatre, he was trying to teach himself to cook Yoruba food. The first time, he had looked at the recipe with a muttered "surely not," then shaken his head and dumped in the prescribed whole pot of hot pepper. He and Emma had gone through a gallon of milk each to quench the fire in their throats, laughing and crying alternately. But now his okra jollof was legendary, and Emma's spirits lifted when the scent of ewedu soup floated through the tower. Still, Emma would have eaten anything he put in front of her. It was so nice, finally, to have a real friend.

They had settled into a routine for their days that even their entry into second year had not shaken. And Tuesdays did not usually involve them turning right as they left the crypt café. Still less, heading over the Regent's Bridge.

"Nat, *where* are we going? We'll end up at the University Library this way."

"Wondered when you'd notice," Nat said cheerfully. "Yes, I

need to pick up some books, since it was cut off by the floods last week. I don't know what you have against the place — "

"Never been. Don't want to go."

Nat whirled around. "What do you mean, you've never been to the Library?"

"I don't see the point."

"But that's impossible. The set texts for your course — and extra reading — "

He looked quite ill.

"Why would I? I don't actually read the books for my essays. It's only law. I get some bits off Wikipedia and mash them up, and — " She sighed. "Well, if it's not good, then it doesn't matter. I am the dunce of the Law Department. They made a mistake when they let me in, one day they'll find me out, and — "

"Nobody thinks they belong here," Nat said, looping her arm through his. Leaves crunched beneath their feet, just beginning to turn. "It's the great secret of this place. You spend the entire time waiting to be found out and sent home. And then you realize that everyone else was thinking the same thing all along."

"You never," Emma said.

"I always." Nat groaned. "Could you live up to the bishop of Durham? When my father was here, he was a model young man. Beloved of the Theology Department. Head of a thousand serious societies. Forget telling him I've never set foot in the church youth group he recommended. The day he finds out I plan to abandon all serious professions to become an actor is the day his soul will crumple and die. I'll never be able to face him. He'd be too kind and too disappointed."

"You'll tell him when you're ready."

Nat heaved a dramatic sigh. "If only you could magic family into being happy with your decisions."

Emma only managed a small smile. "If only you could magic family into doing anything."

Her only family had been her mother. Since everyone else related to Emma had made themselves conspicuously absent — whatever she said or did — it was hard not to wonder if it was something about her that pushed people away. Like her father. And his wife, whom she'd glimpsed only once, through the window of her father's Porsche. Emma had just turned eleven, on one of those rare birthdays spent in England. They had been outside the Natural History Museum. Her father had stood on the pavement and tugged at the collar of his blazer, although it was custom-tailored and there wasn't a single wrinkle in it, as he explained why he couldn't spend the day with Emma, after all. He and Amal had had a call from their son's housemaster. Adam had fallen from his horse at school. He was only bruised, and the matron was with him in the dormitory, but you know how it is. They both wouldn't feel right until they'd driven up to Ludgrove and seen him. He knew Emma would understand. Emma, who had never met her half brother or been within touching distance of a boarding school, had nodded. Her father's hug was brief, and scratchy from his stubble. The woman in the car had not turned to look. She was very beautiful, even in profile. She had snapped the overhead mirror back into place as though she had wanted to break it. As the Porsche drove away, Emma's mother had held her hand tightly.

Emma never found out how Adam recovered. She wasn't sure if he or his sister, Poppy, had even heard of her. She had hoped, one day, her father might ask her to meet them. A family dinner at his house in Hampstead. Or a holiday together, crushed into the Porsche on the way to Devon, all three siblings in the back, laughing at their dad's music choices. But no invitation had come.

When her father had called to talk about choosing her degree, he'd sounded so pleased at the idea of her studying law, she'd thought he might come to the University to visit. But he'd never quite been able to make that work out either.

If there was a trick to winning over family, Emma had never learned it.

"Forget it." Nat shook off his gloom. "Now, normally I pride myself on being a supremely and exclusively decorative being." He struck a pose. Emma laughed, glad to see his mood lift. "But I have some real good to do in the world today, I see. Emma, we are going to get you to the Library. Has it not occurred to you it might be of some help in your fellowship project?"

"But — "

"No, don't try it. The Library has everything. Probably histories of the river, or archive photos and such. Wouldn't that be useful?"

Emma's feet slowed to a halt. The flood. The archives might tell her if there had ever been another like it. Or other freak events, like frogs mating out of season. And if she could prove the anomalies in the ecosystem were new, it could be the base for her case on climate change . . .

"You're going to see what happens when you actually crack a book. You may even discover how clever you are in the process."

At that, Emma snorted.

"Clever," Nat repeated, in a tone that brooked no argument.

"For one thing, you scraped through your exams last year without, apparently, having read a single book. Secondly, you are friends with me, which bespeaks a level of intelligence beyond most mortals."

So Emma stopped arguing. But she also elbowed Nat in the ribs for good measure.

CHAPTER 7

THE LIBRARY WAS ASTONISHING. EMMA HAD NEVER SEEN ANY-thing like it. Shelf upon shelf of books soared upward in dizzying towers. Walnut desks crouched below, with brass lamps hunched over them like gargoyles. The lamplight caught glints from gold-embossed spines, sank without a trace into leather bindings, slid over carvings in timeworn wood. Shadowy librarians flitted through the gaps between bookcases, silent as fish.

Yes, one librarian said, there were archive photographs of the river. But they had to be ordered a week in advance. Emma put in her request and headed for the exit. Three steps later, she groaned and tramped back. Her next land tort tutorial was in two days. Her tutor would fall over in shock if she actually came prepared. And the reading list he had pressed into her hand was still in her pocket.

It looked as though there was no avoiding it. Emma started for the law section.

She was still walking ten minutes later. The map in her hand had begun to seem like an elaborate joke. Emma wandered through painted galleries, shelves filled with scrolls, rooms whose occupants looked up as though she was the first person they'd seen in a hundred years. The quiet was oppressive. Emma was considering retreating the way she'd come, when she spotted someone her age in the reading room ahead. A student with spiked hair and leather trousers sat cross-legged at the base of a bookcase, bent over the volume in her lap.

"Is the law section near here?"

The girl's eyes widened, and she dropped her book. She leapt to her feet as Emma approached, and fled into the stacks.

"Wait — "

The shelves stretched into darkness, a catacomb of books. There was nowhere in those empty avenues the student could have hidden. Yet she had vanished. Emma stooped to pick up her fallen book.

A History of Magickal Bargains.

Prickles rose on the back of Emma's neck. Nat might have enjoyed the weird and inexplicable, but she did not. Quickly, before the part of her that wanted to investigate could lure her into the shadowed stacks, Emma shoved the book onto the nearest shelf and forged on.

The map finally came into its own. The rooms in this wing were modern, the books on the shelves no longer leather-bound. But if the rest of the Library had been quiet, this was silent. One floor from her goal, she found a creaky metal cage was her only way up. The lift screamed through the silence. Exiting, Emma found herself in total darkness.

The diabolical architect of the building had apparently decided that windows were an unnecessary luxury for the second floor, and dispensed with them. Emma's nerves did not appreciate this design choice. But she stepped bravely forward. The light above her switched on with a few sharp chinking sounds. *Like a teaspoon against bone,* Emma thought, and then wished she hadn't.

The room seemed to run the length of the building. Seemed, at least, because the lights only switched on for a few feet ahead of her. Melamine bookcases stretched to her left.

The receptionist had scribbled the shelf location code onto the map. The numbers on the bookcases almost matched it. She had only twelve more to go.

Behind her, the first light began to gently, silently wink off.

Emma had reached the right shelf. She knelt, puzzling over her tutor's scrawled list, and started pulling out books. Light by light, the motion sensors blinked off. Absorbed in her task, Emma didn't notice. Until the final light went.

Somewhere, in the darkness. A creaking.

It was coming from the opposite end of the room.

Emma froze. It was louder, closer. Now it was joined by a rhythmic, dragging rasp. Breathing. Someone was trying to breathe.

The sound came nearer and nearer, until Emma could no longer bear it. She jumped to her feet, coursing with adrenaline. The motion sensor light blinked on.

She was face-to-face with an old man.

"Hello, child," said a wandering voice. A chill flooded her chest. "I am the Librarian."

His hair reached away from his head like a cloud escaping a kettle. His eyes were the blue of sky reflected in water, fixed on a spot above and to the left of her head. They gave him a visionary air.

She found she was no longer afraid, once she looked at him. She was ashamed that she ever had been.

"Did you find what you sought, child?" he asked.

"Yes," said Emma gently, "thank you."

"Would I had your luck. You know, the Library has every book ever printed." He wheezed. "And yet, look though I might, I cannot find the one I seek. As you see." He fanned a hand behind him to a trolley piled high with books. Emma turned them over gingerly. More than one had the word "grimoire" on the cover. She saw another called *Compendium of the Beast*. The writing inside made her flinch. It was the color of old blood.

"What book is it?" said Emma, edging away from the trolley.

"I shall know it when I see it." His eyes were still fixed somewhere above her. "I hold it in my mind."

"Oh," said Emma, stepping back. "Good. I — I should be picking up my books. I left them — just here, you see. It has been lovely talking to — Thank you."

"Books of the law." He peered at the stack in her hands. "Not what I thought of for you. You are unlike the lawyers I once knew. They were men of tooth and claw."

"I — oh. Well." She wondered if he was really as vague as he seemed. "I actually meant to be a vet, at first. But my father said I should apply for law. That I could do more good for animals fighting for their rights in court, not patching them up one by one. And that's what I wanted. To make a difference."

An ethereal smile lit his face. "A kindred soul. I, too, love our brothers and sisters of fur and feathers. I had a dog, I remember. When I was young." His gaze wandered to times past. "Endymion. The very finest creature." A glint of humor crept into his eyes. "And when I wished to become an artist, my parents did not approve either. But we find our own ways in life. I wish you luck of the law, child. May you turn it to your own ends."

He bent over his trolley, still laboring for breath. He looked as though he might be scribbling something. But he was moving painfully slowly. When she peered over the trolley, she saw why. The hand around the pencil was a lump of meat, set sloppily around a tangle of bones. She bit back a gasp and stepped away. She did not want him to think she had been staring.

"I would not wish to alarm you." His blue eyes glowed. "But I ask that you have a care. The darkness is not always kind to a child like you."

He thrust something into her hand. She could not look at it without dropping her books, so she thanked him and stepped into the lift.

He was haloed under the light, white hair fuzzing around his head. As he pushed his trolley away, it creaked. The light blinked out, and he passed into shadow.

She did not examine what he had put into her hand until she was safely out of the Library. It was a scrap of manuscript with a drawing on it.

A monstrous eye, edged in teeth.

When she emerged from the Library, Nat was waiting for her at the café outside.

"Did you enjoy it? You look a little pale."

Her mouth tasted sour.

"Want my bacon butty?" He offered her the bag.

Emma, a vegetarian from the age of six, gave an elaborate shudder.

"Oh, of course not. Well, more for me." With a thoughtful air, he swallowed half the sandwich in one bite. She watched the lump slide down his throat.

A vision of the old man's hands rose before her, the flesh bulging over twisted bones. She forced her thoughts away.

"You are horrifying," she said to Nat. "Stop inhaling your food."

Her phone chirped in her bag. She pulled it out. An unknown number lit the screen.

hey emma. one photography teacher ready and waiting. go out tomorrow? J

Heat lanced through her chest. It was him. She felt a flash of something like triumph, and then the panic kicked in.

"Nat," she croaked. "Emergency. What do I write back?"

Nat seized the phone from her hand and whooped. Emma hovered over his shoulder as he typed her reply. She stuffed the paper slip into her bag. By the time she zipped it up, both it and the Librarian had fallen from her mind.

CHAPTER 8

A WEEK LATER, EMMA FOUND A SURPRISE BY THE RIVER. SHE'D come from the North Gate, hitching up her rucksack. The last person she'd expected to see was hunched on the bank, unspeakably chic in raw-hemmed jeans and a structured shirt. Watching the froth churn, one knee hugged to her chest.

"Oh, hello." Julia's glassy eyes focused on Emma. "It's you."

A cigarette wavered in Julia's fingers. There were smudges in her makeup and red rims around her eyes.

"I don't smoke. Usually." Julia ducked Emma's glance and crushed the cigarette into a patch of moss. "It's just — I had plans today with my friend. Imogen." She hugged her knee closer. "Without her here, I . . . I'm not quite sure what to do with myself, to be honest."

"I'm sure she'll be along soon."

Julia released a breath. "She just left the University."

"Oh. I'm sorry. I hope she's okay."

Julia looked at her as if for the first time. "She's not. But thank you. You're the first person to say that." Her eyes snagged on Emma's rucksack. "Where are you off to?"

"Meeting Jasper." Emma tried not to blush. "We — we're doing some photography together."

"Oh yes?" said Julia, with faint amusement. "Well, don't let me stop you."

Emma got four steps away before turning back.

"But later," she said. "If you're missing your friend. We could eat together in the dining hall? If you want."

"I'd like that." Julia looked down, blinking rather quickly. "Now, do get on." She lifted her chin, and Emma was treated to her real smile, crooked and glorious. "It won't do to keep Jasper waiting, you know. He's not used to it."

Emma hurried down the river path, her heart fluttering in time with the falling leaves. Around a bend, Jasper was waiting for her, bathed in sunlight. He'd chosen a pool in a curve of the river, a golden cup for the afternoon. A kingfisher flashed among the reeds.

"There you are — come see." He guided her to a tangle of greenery on the riverbank. Together, they pulled aside a summer's worth of knotted stems. Behind was a statue of a bearded man, his lower half a curve of fish scales.

"He's still here. I saw him last year, rowing past."

The statue's muscled torso reclined on a pitcher. Emma peered inside.

"It almost looks like a pipe here."

"Old storm drain, maybe? Running into the river?"

Emma ran her fingers over veins in the glass-smooth stone. "It's old, whatever it is."

"And perfect for your first shoot. Watch how I set up the framing — "

At first, she barely lifted the camera at all. She was content to sit in the sun, her arm looped around the stone merman, listening to Jasper explain.

But by their third visit to the river, Jasper insisted she try by herself. It was hard to concentrate on the viewfinder with his breath on her neck. Her subject ruffled its wings, preparing to fly. Jasper leaned over her shoulder.

"Adjust the focus — you've got the shot now. You see?"

And she did. The way the sunlight hit the lapwing's feathers. The beak questing up toward the sun. Hopeful, determined. Even as her finger brushed the shutter, she knew. It was going to be better than anything she'd ever taken.

"Just needed the right lens." Jasper grinned down at her.

"The right teacher, more like. Would you hold the camera? I want to see if there's a nest around here. If you don't mind."

"Go for it." Jasper stretched out on a sunny spot on the bank.

Sighting a likely patch of reeds, Emma splashed deeper.

"You know what I like about you?" came Jasper's voice. "You're peaceful. Not needing to talk all the time . . ."

So it hadn't occurred to him that she might be too nervous to think of anything to say.

". . . disappearing into your focus, like a proper photographer. You'd probably make a good sailor too. Same skill."

Emma resisted the pull of the vision. Jasper helping her onto his yacht. His arm around her waist as they reeled in a rope. A cabin below deck, just big enough for two . . .

"That's what travel does. People like you and me, travelers, we don't need to push a conversation. Because we're less possessive. Of places, of people. Of relationships . . ."

There was a mass bobbing under her patch of reeds. She crouched. Frogspawn. In September. Six months out of season, for this climate.

First the frogs mating on that city street, and now this. It was either a bizarre species mutation or environmental upheaval on a scale she'd never heard of. Her hand, stretching toward the cloud of spawn, stopped.

This had all happened after the flood. And she still had to check the University's archives to be sure, but her blood told her that both it and these anomalies were something new. Climate change in action. This could be genuinely groundbreaking research. Journal-worthy, even. Her fellowship project plan would have to change. She could survey the river in sections, checking for other anomalies. She'd need to assign more budget for equipment. Photograph it all. Run live-stream feeds, possibly.

There was a mystery here. And now that she almost had it between her teeth, she could not bear to let it rest.

Still musing, she turned to find Jasper's camera pointing at her.

"There," he breathed. "Just perfect."

Emma swiped a strand of hair from her face.

"No, hold still," he said softly. Their eyes met, and Emma could not look away. Under his gaze, her body was a river rippled by raindrops. Every inch of her, alive.

The shutter clicked. "Got it. Come on, you must be freezing in that water. Time for your rescue."

He pulled her onto the bank, and she stumbled against his

chest. Her head spun with his closeness. That clean cotton smell where his T-shirt clung to his neck. The animal scent of sun-warmed skin. And beneath, something she couldn't identify. Something smoky she had only smelled once, her nose buried in her father's blazer on some rare, long-ago visit. She breathed him in.

He smiled, his face inches from hers. "Now I have the best shot I'll get today. So . . ." He was going to kiss her. She knew it. Emma melted toward him. But then Jasper twisted, fitting the camera back into the padded bag. "So, what next?"

Emma swallowed her disappointment. Her eyes caught on a dome above the trees. "I actually kind of wanted to get to the Library today. For my project."

Jasper groaned. "You really want to spend your afternoon looking at old photos of a river?"

"The Library's archives are rare. I never thought I could find out so much about an ecosystem a hundred, even a hundred and fifty years in the past."

"I wish I cared about something here as much as you care about this project. Maybe then I wouldn't miss sailing so much."

"But you've got people. Your friends. The 'Society,' " she added, in strenuous air quotes, and Jasper laughed. "You have a gift. Leadership, or charisma, or whatever they call it. You're good at people."

"And you're not?"

Emma pulled a face. "Animals are easier than people. If you look long enough, stay still enough, you can see everything you need to know. About who they are."

"People are different?"

Emma smiled and nudged him onto the path that wound up to the Library. "I don't know. Maybe it's just that we can't stay still enough around other people to see clearly."

After an hour in the Library, Emma suspected that staying still might be a particular problem for Jasper. If he wasn't darting around to look over her shoulder, he was taking photos of her from behind a bookcase.

"Are you done yet?"

The river records had been fruitful. She'd not found one mention of another notable flood for the past eight hundred years. Whatever was happening, it was indeed new.

"Mmm. Sorry." Emma tore herself from a catalogue of photographs. There were strange annotations on this one: The Edwardian author had an obsessive belief that animals native to the area — the river's rats, foxes, ravens, and the like — were demonic forces, possessing "unholy and unnatural" traits. Emma forced herself to close the file and reach for the next. The historian's ramblings were entertaining, but not exactly scientific.

"Like I said, you really can go home if you like. I think I'll be a while here."

"Seriously?"

Jasper's face dropped. On anyone less beautiful, Emma might have described the lines between his brows as petulant.

"Do I need to remind you both that this is a no-talking area?"

They both jumped. The woman behind them had approached noiselessly. One eye was a hollow, an eyelid puckering over empty

76

space. Emma had seen her working at the reception desk, but always wearing an eye patch. Jasper's chair screeched.

"There's no one else here." He swept a hand at the empty reading room. "So what's the problem?"

She looked sharply at Jasper.

"You. Your voice is familiar."

"Happens to me all the time," Jasper said, stretching back in his chair.

"A Balfour," she pronounced, with the air of sentencing him for a crime.

"Yes." Jasper's smile faded. "How did you know? I don't remember — "

"You're just like your father." The receptionist had already turned her back. Her gray hair snarled past her waist. She was piled into a shapeless top and floor-length skirt. But her walk was surprisingly graceful, and her answer floated back to them with a hint of barely concealed merriment.

Jasper's face was white under its tan: with shock or anger, Emma couldn't tell. When he spoke, his voice was tight.

"God, what a harpy. Maybe my father banged her and she's been bitter about it ever since. Hard to believe, though — even my father has some standards."

For Jasper to sound so unlike himself, Emma knew, meant he had to be very upset. It did seem unfair for the woman to compare Jasper to his father. Without even knowing him, Emma thought indignantly. Children didn't have to be like their fathers. She wasn't anything like — and more to the point, Jasper wasn't anything like his father, from what she'd gathered. Jasper had spoken of him almost with fear, as well as resentment.

Jasper waved off her concern.

"Come on, let me buy you a drink. Let's leave the witch to her library."

As they were leaving, a familiar Humpty-Dumpty figure emerged from a side corridor.

"Rich!" roared Jasper.

"J-dog!" bellowed back Richard.

"We're going to Boddington's, Emma 'n' me, want to come with?"

"I just need to — ahem, lock up for the historical society," said Richard.

Emma saw the look of suppressed mirth pass between him and Jasper, as the latter said gravely, "Very good, mate, very responsible."

"You both go ahead," she said. Whatever secret they had, it could wait. "I have one more thing to do here."

Emma walked back through the stacks alone.

"Yes?" said the receptionist, without looking up from her computer.

"I — You gave me a map." Emma wasn't sure how to continue. "On my first visit here."

"And do you . . . need another one?" The receptionist swept a hand at a box on the counter, brimming with maps.

"Oh. Thank you, no, I — I wanted to ask about someone who works here. A librarian? I met him up on the second floor?"

The receptionist didn't say anything, but she did turn to face Emma for the first time.

"He was, um, an elderly gentleman, and he was breathing — That is . . . His hands were sort of . . ." Emma trailed off.

The receptionist had snapped back to face her computer.

"No, I don't think anyone like that works here. Could have been a stray professor. The dons are here all the time, and some of them are quite . . . elderly." She lingered on the last word, and Emma felt foolish. It occurred to her the receptionist might not be that far apart in years from the man she'd seen.

"But he said he was a librarian. No, he said he was . . . the Librarian," Emma realized.

The receptionist looked unimpressed. "Sorry. Is that everything? I have to get through this catalogue," she said, typing furiously. "It's full of errors."

Emma left the Library, but she couldn't let the problem go. It whirred round in her mind. She knew she had not imagined him, her strange librarian. Warning her of dangers in the shadows, pushing his trolley of blood-inked books. But the receptionist would have no reason to lie.

"What is it?" Jasper asked, as she slid into the booth at Boddington's.

"Nothing," said Emma, zipping up a pocket on her bag. It had been exactly where she'd left it on her first visit to the Library. A drawing of an eye and a monster's teeth. Proof. That her encounter had happened, just as she remembered it. That somewhere, deep in the entrails of the Library, there was an eerie old man hunting through books. And next time she came to use the photo archives, she would find him.

Then, two days later, Jasper and Richard's mystery revealed itself.

CHAPTER 9

THEY WERE IN THE SUNKEN ROSE GARDEN. THE SKY, MOONLESS. The smell of the river all around. Though the bushes were hunched and slimy as she remembered, this was not the black, rotting stench of the flood. Emma inhaled. It was the green, warm scent of the living river.

Jasper was facing her, still as a panther. His eyes bored into her. Sparks trailed her cheeks, her neck. Over the curve of her collarbone. Lower.

And then the first bud burst. Its insides startling pink. The rosebushes were blooming. The night air was thick with honey and musk, and still the buds split. Emma saw them straining against the black sludge of rotted stems. Heads swelling until the stems were bent and pleading. Then a snap. The first flower fallen, broken by its own weight. One by one, the roses burst and swelled and dropped, a carpet of pink and red.

Jasper knelt among the falling blooms and held one out to her. Red, deepening to purple at its heart. His eyes never leaving hers, he raised it to his mouth. A droplet of nectar clung to one thick, curving petal, there where his tongue just reached to brush it. Sweetness ran through Emma's core.

Slowly, Jasper parted his lips until the cavern of his throat showed, hot and dark. He bit into the blossom like a man starved. Emma cried out. She felt his touch as though the petals his teeth grazed were the smooth insides of her own thighs. He bit again, and again. Honey filled her mouth.

His hands pushed her, and she fell, soft, onto the thick bed of rose heads. Flowers rained around her as Jasper fitted his mouth to hers. His kiss, his kiss that scraped her skin against the hard gold bristles of his cheeks. Thorns forced themselves from his tongue, piercing hers. Emma tasted the salt heat of her blood, rising to meet him. Falling roses brushed her face. Somewhere, a whispering began. But she ignored anything that was not this moment, this movement. Her legs clamped around Jasper. The nectar sang in her blood, a music that soared. Petals flooded over her eyes, her mouth. Emma gasped. A tide of roses flowed into her throat. She choked on their flesh, clawed for a surface that would not come. The whispers hissed all around her, sinuous and insistent and louder than ever, and her lungs burned, and —

— and Emma woke, a fold of the duvet over her mouth. She tore it from her face, heaving in grateful breaths. The room was still and silver. Outside her tower, rain beat against the window. In the dark of the night, it almost sounded like whispers.

Slowly, her breathing quieted. Four in the morning, her phone told her. Then she saw the message. It had come while she slept.

midnight tomorrow night. meet at the library

the door will be open. trust me you'll want to be there. J

Emma fell back onto her pillow. Her last thought, before sleep claimed her, was of her tongue. She ran it around her mouth. She tasted blood.

The next night found Emma pushing through the bushes outside the Library. A ticking pulse pounded in her ears. Jasper had said to come at midnight, and so here she was. But it could so easily be a horrible joke, leaving her alone outside a locked door in the dead of night.

But the great doors opened easily under her palm. She padded through the deserted reception, as moonlight shifted over the marble floor. Jasper wasn't there. No one was.

And then she heard it. Whispers hummed, somewhere deep inside the Library. Her pulse beat harder. *Come,* they hissed, *come to us. Until blood cloaks each step, until bones crumble. Come, little mortal. Come.* Emma closed her eyes.

When she opened them again, she was deep among the dark alleys of bookcases. She looked around, confused. The prim little night-light of reception had disappeared. Corridors yawned around her like the mouths of caves.

She took a shuddering breath. She was not lost. There was no reason to panic. She had come this way because she had been following something. A sound. Emma wrestled with her memory. It was almost as though someone had been talking to her, although she couldn't think who, or what they might have been saying.

"Child." The voice behind her was so sudden, her knees threatened to buckle.

He was there again. The Librarian. Hair standing around his head like a dandelion clock, breathing labored. Emma took a step back.

"You should not be here." His voice was grave. "Those who wander after dark come to no good."

"I'm sorry, my friends said to find them — "

"You are with those others?"

So there were others. Relief spread cool fingers through Emma's chest. Jasper's text had not been a trick. There was something happening, and he wanted her here. With him.

A knotted hand hovered above her arm. Emma realized the Librarian was trying to guide her down the corridor to her left. "Come. Let us return you to the safe path."

An odd phrase. Surely all paths were safe. It was only an empty library. The most danger she was in, logically, was from a paper cut. Still, Emma glanced at the darkness over her shoulder. It seemed to have grown thicker, swallowing the nearest bookcases.

Abandoning logic for the moment, Emma broke into a run to catch up with the Librarian. With his steady wheezing beside her, Emma's pulse settled. She kept within arm's reach of him, all through the shadowed corridors and galleries.

At last, the Librarian stopped at the foot of a staircase. "You will be safe now. I leave you here. But do not stray again, child."

Emma felt a tug at her heart as he shuffled into the shadows. The darkness had not seemed so vast with him there. She listened as the creaking breaths faded into silence, wishing she did not feel so desperately alone. There was no sign of anyone else. Not Jasper, not those "others." She was not even sure she knew the way out.

Slim hands closed around her shoulders. "There you are."

Emma muffled a shriek. Julia spun her around. "Goodness, you're as jumpy as I was."

Jasper appeared behind Julia with a suddenness that made Emma flinch. He was holding the torch of his phone under his chin. The uplighting gave him a ghastly appearance.

"Stop it," hissed Julia. "Behave."

Jasper grinned. "The party's this way. Where've you been?"

"I got lost, I think." The last hour had begun to feel like a dream. It seemed strange now, how little she'd thought to ask the Librarian. What had he been doing here so late? Library staff might have to work at night, she supposed. Archiving, perhaps, or sorting new acquisitions. But he was surely too old, too frail for that? And why had that receptionist denied he worked there at all?

Then Jasper ran a hand down her arm, and the thrill of his touch banished her questions. Letting the Librarian fade from her mind, she twined her hand into his.

"How on earth did you get the front doors open?"

"That's down to Rich."

A sturdy figure met them at the staircase, twirling a key ring around his finger. "No problem in the end," Richard said in a plummy whisper. "Said I wanted to stay late to catalogue some new boxes of Cromwell correspondence."

"The Library's Military History Society was founded by Rich's great-uncle." Jasper trained the phone light in his friend's eyes. Richard squinted and batted him away. "So Rich gets prime position as student curator. They're very . . . trusting with the keys."

"That's because I'm responsible," Richard said, offering his arm to Emma. Jasper passed him the light instead.

"Lead on, then, prick."

The room Richard led them to was awash with candles and brimming cups on every surface. Light flickered off embossed spines. Emma recognized most of the people from the last party, lounging against the bookcases, swapping gossip and sips of wine.

Her heart sped. She leaned to whisper in Julia's ear. "Is this 'the Society'? The one Imogen — "

Julia's voice was barely above a breath. "Don't let anyone hear you say that. Jasper bringing you here is a test. The boys are watching you tonight. No, don't look around."

Watching her? A slow chill crept down Emma's back.

"They'll want to see you're not a gossip. Try you out."

"And then?"

"Then? It's Jasper's decision; he's the one that wants you along. But he clearly likes you. And once you're in on the secret, you're in."

"But not in the Society."

Julia gave a tiny shake of the head. "Men only, I'm afraid. But as guests, we're invited to the events. The secret ones. They're the most fun. Come." She swept Emma across the room with the air of a mother duck. "Guy, I think you remember Emma? My fantastic fellow for natural sciences. I'm sure you'll love getting to know her." And with a wink, she slipped into the crowd.

Guy Cavendish, of the Windsor Cavendish clan, took a slow sip of his wine. "Friend of Julia's, eh? Let me place you. Bedales?

Cheltenham Ladies'? Milly Fotherington was a Roedean girl, mentioned an Emma Talbot-Weston there — that you?"

Dizzied under the assault of names, Emma pieced together that Guy was asking about schools. More precisely, the most exclusive and expensive boarding schools in England.

Guy rattled on. "Not a boarder? One of the London day school lot, then. Bloody St. Paul's, of course. The Univ's swarming with you Paulinas . . ."

Trying to convince Guy that she had not gone to boarding school, or any fee-paying school at all, would clearly be like trying to turn around a steamroller with a breadstick. Instead, Emma drew herself up in her best imitation of Julia's poise and redirected the conversation.

"This wine. Such an interesting choice. I wonder what it is."

That was one thing she remembered about the academic donor dinners she'd been dragged to with her mother. The richer the donor, the more they yearned to tell you about wine. As a plant scientist's daughter, Emma had often been presumed to have more interest than she did in cultivars or chalk soils. It served her well now.

Guy's face lit up. "Yah, yah. Really has the perfume of a Château Margaux, doesn't it? That gorgeous balance. But it's actually from a little vineyard at the arse end of the Médoc. Thinking of buying it up, taking this lot out there. You should come. Spend much time in France?"

He wasn't talking about buying the wine, Emma realized. He was talking about buying the *whole vineyard*. With as much nonchalance as though they'd been discussing gravy, or Irish dancing.

"Oh, do let her be, Guy." Venetia Kent stood at Emma's shoulder. "The new girl's bored with you already."

Before Emma could protest, Venetia was pushing her across the room.

"Delivered her for you, gentlemen. Now, where's my fee?"

One of the two boys waiting by the window tossed Venetia a bag of powder. Atticus Tremaine and Rory Clarke made languid introductions while Venetia tapped a line of white onto the nearest reading desk and made it disappear up her tiny, perfect nose.

"Always with the good stuff, Tremaine." Venetia stood and traced a finger along one of Atticus' famous cheekbones. Emma did not miss the way he flinched. Nor the way that Rory, the supposed future prime minister, hopped out of Venetia's path as she left. Venetia might look like a china shepherdess, but she wielded fear like a scalpel. Even among this perfect constellation of pedigree, privilege, and private banking.

And before Emma turned back to Atticus and Rory, she wondered what that might be like. If she were the one with the power to make people jump out of her way.

But instead, she followed Julia's lead: smiling, gracious. She let Atticus and Rory put her through her paces. Then Philip Cranbottom, and Eddie Spencer with his girlfriend Arabella Lennox. After that, she lost track of the names. Always, as she moved around the room, she felt Jasper's eyes: two points of heat, tracing her back. But he kept his distance, chatting with Richard. Part of the test, perhaps.

The candles were burning low when Jasper finally slid an arm around her waist. He was looking at something over her shoulder.

Emma twisted. Nine boys were dotted around the room. One by one, they nodded.

Jasper raised his glass to Emma's, his eyes glinting in the candlelight. He never dropped her gaze, not as the crystal touched, not as she took the first sip.

The wine spread across Emma's tongue, rich as a blackbird's wing. Perfumed, just as Guy had said. The taste of people who did not buy by the bottle but by the vineyard.

Emma tilted her glass and drained it to the last drop.

CHAPTER 10

AFTER THAT, EMMA FELT LIKE SHE WAS LIVING ON FAST-FORWARD. Her nights were sprinkled with glitter. Each one brought a new party. Lounging in someone's rooms, candlelight sparking from crystal glasses and luxury watches. Or out to a club, where every bottle came with a sparkler on top, and every dance with Jasper made her heart shine brighter. Nobody spoke of the Society. Not to her, at least. But she felt the secret hovering just beyond her reach. Every event felt like a step closer to being trusted. She saw it in the way the boys had begun to roar her name when she arrived, just like they did with Julia. Or how they all treated it as a given that wherever Jasper was, she would be invited too. It felt like acceptance. Maybe even liking. Without realizing, she had stopped thinking of the party crowd as Jasper's friends. They finally felt like her own.

Night after night, she plundered the magic chest of Helena's clothes. In a vintage Halston jumpsuit, she sat behind the velvet ropes at a nightclub for Antonia Viacelli's birthday, thigh to thigh with her circle of trust fund socialists and Turner Prize darlings. A leather blazer and shorts saw Emma through a harrowing

Tatler shoot for "Inspiring Women of the Future." Helena's silver chain-mail dress shimmered down the carpet at the private screening of Atticus Tremaine's new short film.

"You're getting quite a reputation as a looker," said Julia, as they sprawled on Emma's bed with the University newspaper. "Look at those long legs of yours, all over the society pages."

But Emma always felt best in her own clothes. In bed, hunched into a disgusting old sweater, she pored over her research. The initial data she'd gathered at the river stacked up. She almost had a complete case for how to use the Colefax-Lee funding over the coming two years.

"I'm impressed, Emma," her mum said one night. Emma was holding the phone to her ear with one hand and typing up her latest dataset with the other. "I showed what you sent me to the others at the station, and they agree. Professional work."

Her laptop screen had gone blurry. Emma blinked back the tears. "Thanks. Coming from you, that means a lot. With time to recruit volunteers, the full trial could even start in spring."

"You sound so happy," Emma's mother said. "Confident. This project has been good for you."

"It has. I just know there's something behind this flood. And with this project, it feels like I'm a breath away from finding out what it is."

"That's the beauty of science, ladybug."

Soon after, a shy email on Emma's part had led her to Dr. Asima Banerjee. A round, unabashedly loud woman, she was just as fascinated by the anomalies in animal behavior after the flood as Emma. They spent many a morning in her office in the Department of Natural Sciences, debating theories over coffee.

"Climate change, you think? Faugh! It's definitely happening. But does it explain everything here? Flooding and frogs mating in the fall, and more besides? The caddis flies have been doing things you wouldn't believe. Otters practically tap-dancing along the banks. Strange times."

She nodded at the jar of frogspawn sitting on her office desk. "Thanks for bringing your samples. We'll keep them in the lab. See if anything exciting happens."

"No problem," said Emma. "I wondered, would you take a look at my first species survey? I want your opinion before I send it to the foundation."

When Dr. Banerjee finished studying the document, she let out one of the laughs that seemed to roll up from her belly. "Stellar. Good as anything my third-year zoology students turn in, the lazy sods. It's a shame you're not on my course."

"Do you — do you ever get people switching?" Emma murmured.

"We do," she said. "They have to start from the beginning, from first year. But the people who join us often find they love it."

She handed back Emma's data with a smile.

Emma wandered from the faculty with an unfamiliar lightness in her bones. She was so distracted, she had to rush to make it to the Great Hall on time.

Formal dinner at Gabriel was a special occasion. Candlelight flickered from oil paintings and crystal glasses. Courses came on silver platters, and guests in dinner jackets and academic robes. Emma usually avoided it: The grandeur and Latin made her nervous. But tonight she was there for Nat. As one of the college's highest-achieving scholars, he had been chosen to read the ancient opening ceremony for the dinner. It was an honor granted to only ten students a year, and Emma had been determined to be there to cheer him on. She hadn't seen enough of Nat, of late. Rehearsals had him at the theatre at all hours.

He fidgeted behind the lectern, academic gown ironed to a crisp, looking like a large and very nervous bat. Emma waved, then ducked into the last empty space at the long tables. The only people nearby were a trio of academics. Emma recognized tweed-jacketed Dr. Peasewhisker, the Gabriel College bursar. With him were Professor Aguilar, chic and chignonned, and a cheerful, curly-haired older woman Emma vaguely placed among Gabriel's history dons. Emma hadn't meant to listen, but the dining benches pressed them all so close, she couldn't avoid it.

"Decent wine tonight." Dr. Peasewhisker smacked his lips.

"Better without the extra legs, I imagine." The curly-haired woman's eyes twinkled.

"*Alison.*" Dr. Peasewhisker groaned. "Sorry, Beatriz, you'll not be up on the latest gossip."

"Do tell." Dr. Aguilar curled manicured nails around her wineglass.

"High Table at Granville College last night. Cellar master uncorks what should've been the finest claret. A '45 Bordeaux, no less. But what pours out — directly over the Sumatran president's shoulder, mind? Spiders. A flood of spiders. Imagine the chaos. They think the flood must've got to the wine cellar."

Emma's interest sharpened.

"Hearing a lot of that these days."

The bursar sighed. "Our own head gardener practically banged down my office door once the flood went down, raving about hawthorns popping up everywhere. 'Just chop them down, man,' says

I. And what does that do, but send him wibbling on about demon trees that regrow as fast as he cuts them?" Dr. Peasewhisker took a long, consoling swallow of his spider-free claret. "I ask you."

"Hawthorns? Perhaps the fae folk're taking back their land." The bright-eyed history don winked directly at Emma, as if to include her in the joke.

"You and your folklore studies, Alison." Dr. Peasewhisker blew a breath from his jowls, ignoring Emma. "No, I don't know what things're coming to."

"And the porters were complaining of trespassers in the Old Music Room." Professor Aguilar took a dainty sip of her wine. "Animal masks, drums in the night. Petals scattered all over in the morning."

The history don chuckled. "Probably just early Samhain celebrants. We're harmless enough, we pagans. And it hardly takes a criminal mastermind to creep into University buildings after dark."

At the lectern, Nat lifted the ceremonial book. The dining hall quieted. Emma's heart swelled with pride as Nat read the Latin, his voice soaring and sure.

It was a quirk of the University that formal dinners started with this weird remnant of centuries past: not a grace, but a bizarre sort of bargain between diners and their food. Nat was reading the nonsense text with charm and humor, promising their dinner the best of their attention and delight in return for the privilege of eating it. Nobody remembered the origin of the bargaining tradition, but everyone enjoyed it.

When the last Latin phrase had rolled from his tongue, Nat flopped onto the bench next to Emma. Close up, his eyes were red-rimmed and glassy, and the shadows under them stretched to his cheekbones. Emma felt a twinge of unease.

"What are those rehearsals *doing* to you? Tolstoy himself wasn't this tortured."

Nat rubbed his hands over his face. "This performance is pulling something out of me I didn't know I had. The whole play's special, Em. Inspired. But we're all drained dry by it. Hannah, our director? Came to the last three rehearsals with her shirt inside out. She's also convinced foxes are following her home at night. Swears they actually wait for her to leave the theatre. Apparently, they're different from normal foxes. Shinier."

"Shinier?" Emma coughed. "Oh, wow. So you're all cracking up, is that it?"

"Pretty much," Nat said cheerfully. "How're things with you? Tell me tales of the real world, please."

"I'm going on another photo outing."

"With Jasper? That's going well, then?"

"I don't know, exactly. When we're talking, I'm sure how he feels about me. His eyes — and sometimes he's almost said — but then it's the end of another trip. And he's gone and still nothing has happened."

"Ah, that energy like he's absolutely, desperately in love with you, but he's not sure whether he left the oven on at home, so he just has to run off and leave you — under duress, darling, of course."

"That's it, exactly. How did you know?"

"Em, I hang around with theatre people. What you're talking about is charm. Tell me, how much do you talk about him, on these trips of yours? And how much do you talk about you?"

"What do you have against him?"

"Nothing. We just met at school." Nat pushed his dinner around his plate. "Which was not a good time for me."

"You don't like him."

"It's not that. It's more the — halo he has. The world rearranges itself around him. He's never had to step outside that golden circle of being handsome, and lucky, and universally adored. And he doesn't even realize that's not what everyone else starts with. He's happy to assume it's all because he deserves it. Never a doubt or a challenging thought."

"You'd be surprised. Jasper is very conflicted. And complicated." She caught Nat's sardonic eye, and a giggle she didn't intend escaped her. "He *is*. He just doesn't spend his entire life questioning himself from his head to his shoelaces."

"*I* have never questioned my shoelaces," said Nat, the picture of injured innocence.

"Only because you haven't thought of it yet," Emma shot back.

They traded jokes until the dessert plates were empty and the three academics long gone. The dons had been interesting, Emma reflected. She'd have to sort through all they'd said about the flood. The bit about hawthorn trees could be promising. Any imbalance might be worth tracking in her data.

At Nat's first yawn over the port, she hauled him to his feet. They wove through Gabriel's shadowed cloister together, and Nat managed a smile. "I miss you. Isn't that silly, when you're right here? You're just so busy these days. All your new friends. I mean, it's great, but — "

Emma pulled him into a sideways hug. "Old friends come first.

You were right, I did need more people than just you. New friends are fun. But you're always my favorite. So, how about film night this week? My turn to choose."

He fixed her with a hawkish stare.

"Emma. Try and pick a *film* this time."

"*Planet Earth is* a film. It's very film-esque, anyway."

"I don't have the energy to argue with you. That's how dire things are." Nat groaned as they climbed the last step to the bell tower. "Right. My Golden Age playwrights essay is upon me. Though I may skip this one in the name of sleep, and risk Professor Lindman's wrath tomorrow."

Emma watched him go unhappily. Nat had never even joked about missing an assignment before. She would have to check in more often, until that glassy look left his eyes.

But by the time she'd rolled into bed, her mind had already slipped back to Jasper. Their photography trips brought him so tantalizingly close. His hands around hers on the viewfinder. His breath on her neck. It was all building to something, she was sure of it.

As if the heat of her thoughts had summoned him, demon-like, from the void, her phone beeped. And the message made her breath catch in her chest.

something special tomorrow.

can't wait for you to see it. you'll die.

Underneath the message, a row of skull emojis winked up at her.

CHAPTER 11

OLD HOB QUAD GLEAMED GOLD IN THE SUNLIGHT. AN AUTUMN breeze tumbled leaves across the flagstones and batted Emma's hair around her face.

It felt good to get out of her room. Her fellowship dataset was misbehaving. No matter what analysis she applied, it threw up glitches. Like insisting the river animals were larger than they could possibly be, compared to previous years. It had to be data error, unless they'd all somehow found an extra energy source to feed on. Nothing of the kind showed in her surveys: no new species, no change in prey populations. It was infuriating.

Emma jogged up the stairs to Jasper and Richard's rooms. Nobody answered the door. But it was unlocked, so she slipped inside.

There were voices from the living room. Jasper was squared up to a man whose eyes were as bright blue as his own, and whose face was dark with anger.

" — for God's sake, Jasper, try to get it right. Don't let yourself down."

Emma had meant to declare herself, but the rage in that voice stopped her where she stood.

"Dad, it's just a dinner. I don't know what you're so bothered about."

"You need to be more bothered. This is important for you. The impression you make here will be — "

"I know, it'll determine the course of my life forever and ever."

His father slammed a hand onto the window frame, inches from Jasper's face. "You will take the Society seriously. I won't have you throwing your chances away with your arrogant, lazy — "

"I'm the president now, not you. This is my dinner. And I'm doing it my way."

Jasper's father loomed over him until their faces were inches apart. "It may be your dinner. But it's my Society. Mine and all of the other old boys. And you're not going to humiliate me."

Jasper and his father locked gazes in silence like dogs sizing each other up, the air thick between them.

"Fine," Jasper muttered.

As Jasper's mouth tightened, his father's smile broadened.

"Now, Jasper, what do you reckon to this suit? My tailor is ready to disown me. Says the peak lapel makes me look like an American, but I'm quite partial to it."

Emma thought the time was right to show herself. She sidled into the room.

"Oh — Emma. I was meant to — Never mind. Dad, this is Emma Curran."

"Pelham-Curran," said Emma, and immediately wondered what had possessed her. She'd never double-barreled her surname, though she'd long suspected that the Pelham family's place in the annals of the peerage would have unlocked doors for her. She'd always been proud to be her brilliant mother's daughter, first and foremost. But something about the tailored man in front of her reminded Emma of her father at his most unreachable. She found herself wanting to impress him.

Jasper's father looked at her closely. "Not as in Hugh Pelham?"

Emma nodded.

"*Pelham*. Good man. Jasper, why didn't you tell me about your little friend?" Jasper's father smiled at Emma, all charm. "I see your father in town sometimes. I didn't realize his daughter went here. I thought you were up at Manchester."

Emma felt something hard and hot in her throat.

"That's his other daughter," she said woodenly. "Poppy. We're about the same age."

"Mea culpa," Jasper's father pressed his hands together in apology. The laurel wreath on his signet ring glinted. "I'd thought, for some reason, that Hugh and Amal only had the one daughter. Isn't she a lucky woman to have two girls? And your brother — is he finishing up at Harrow soon?"

"I don't know," Emma gritted. "I've never met him."

Jasper's father raised one brow.

Emma had to force the words out. "They're his other family. His proper one. My mum and I happened to him before that."

"Before? And so close in age?"

"There was some overlap." She couldn't — wouldn't — look at Jasper.

"Ah, of course. Understood." Jasper's father smiled, suave as a film star, and Emma scolded herself for her suspicions. He couldn't have been needling her deliberately.

A throat cleared. Emma hardly recognized Richard in the shy schoolboy hovering in the doorway. He had combed his haystack hair into a semblance of neatness. His tie and blazer were precise to a pin.

"My boy!" Jasper's father beamed. "What's this?"

Richard was offering him a box. "Snuff, sir — I took your advice and tried it. I hope you'll do me the honor?"

"Of course." Jasper's father snorted a pinch. "Exactly what I like. You have taste, my boy."

"I should hope so, sir." Richard's face was shining. "I sent down to Yardley and Walters and asked them to make me a mix of your sort."

"Good lad," Jasper's father roared. Emma looked from them to Jasper, alone by the window. He was clenching the sill so hard, his knuckles were white. She saw his father glance over, smile at Jasper's reaction, and turn back to Richard. "Now, what have you been up to, my boy? I want a full update."

"Certainly, sir. Military History Society keeping me busy. If you want to step into my room, there are a few things I saved. I thought they might interest you?" Richard was practically frisking at his heels.

"So thoughtful. But I still have business to attend with Jasper here. If you'll excuse me?"

It was a dismissal. He turned his back on them and steered Jasper into a bedroom. Emma saw the look on Richard's face as the Balfours left. The chagrin and hurt, raw in his eyes. She stood with him by the ancient window, and the silence stretched.

It galled her, seeing Jasper's father play them off against each other. Constantly shifting the balance of favorites, turning a word of praise for one into a barb for the other. She looked sidelong at Richard, his hair slipping from that neat schoolboy comb-over, and felt desperately sorry for him.

"You could show me those military history things," she said. "I'd like to see them."

Richard rubbed a hand over his face. "No, you wouldn't. But thanks. You're a good sort."

Dust motes danced in the sun. Their shadows stretched long on the floor. The voices of Jasper and his father were a dim buzz from the other room.

"My father can be like that," Emma said. "Like there's something much more important over your shoulder, and you're keeping him from it."

Richard laughed, then stiffened as though stuck with a cattle prod. "I shouldn't — They're the best family in the world, and they've been so good — "

"No, of course," said Emma, feeling like an idiot. "I don't know what I'm talking about. I don't even see my father much. At all, really."

"My father's not here either. Dead, though."

Emma was taken aback. "Oh. I'm sorry."

"Long time ago. But it's like there's a shape, everywhere I go. A shadow cutout, where he's not."

"I get that," Emma said. "Sometimes I wonder what my life would be like if he was here. How things would be different."

"Me too."

They leaned against the windowsill, framed in the arch of medieval stone. The sun warmed their backs. Her other friends loved to talk. But Richard seemed as comfortable in silence as she was. For a moment, she wished Jasper were more like him.

A door slammed. Jasper burst into the room like a hurricane.

"God, he's such a *dick*. He said he wants you in there now, Rich. Probably to lecture you too." He grabbed Emma's wrist. "Come on."

"Where?"

"Away from here." Shouldering his camera bag, he pulled her from the room and out onto the quad.

Jasper kept up a stormy pace through the courtyards and cloisters of St. Dunstan's. The famous spires of St. Dunstan's Cathedral rose above them.

He finally slowed. "Up there has the best view of the University."

Emma looked at the roof, impossibly high against the sky. "We're not climbing it, are we?"

"There's a secret staircase. I bribed the warden. Come on, it's perfect for a shoot."

He led her up narrow spiral stairs inside the vestry. They emerged into the open air on the cathedral roof and waded up the tiled slope together. The ridge at the top was just wide enough to sit on. So high up, the city lay before them like a gift, washed gold in the dying light. Emma breathed it in.

"I didn't come back to the University because he told me to," Jasper burst out. His vehemence was startling.

"What, your father? I wasn't think — "

"I only came for my mother. She asked. I didn't care what he said. It's not like I'm scared of his threats or anything. I actually couldn't care less."

"I — I get it."

"I know you do." A smile spread across his face. Like sunlight, like butter. "No one understands me like you."

For a moment, Emma wasn't sure if he really had said it. He lounged back on his elbows, grimacing at the skyline. "I hate this place. It's all been laid out for me. Who I have to be, what I have to do."

"Like heading up your mysterious 'Society'?" Emma teased.

"Oh, the Turnbulls?" Jasper yawned. He shot upright. "Oh God," he groaned, clapping his hands to his face. "Not supposed to say that yet. I am not cut out for this. Put me on a boat, point me at a horizon, I'm your man. But all these rules, these traditions — "

He dropped his head onto her shoulder. Emma forgot how to breathe. "I know you're cool. I can trust you. Just don't tell anyone else, yeah? I'd be in so much trouble."

She could feel the warmth of his cheek, even through her jacket. She wondered if he could hear her heart beating. "I won't tell."

"The Turnbulls've been a secret society since the founding of the University. It'd be embarrassing if all our mysteries got splashed around on my watch."

"But that would be — what? Founded a thousand years ago? That can't be true."

"Can, actually. The founding chancellor of the University, John de Turnbull? He had this group of scholars that were his mates. Or his followers? Same thing. Anyway, they started the club and named it after him. All in the records."

"Really? So is the University chancellor still involved?"

Jasper snorted. "I think he's heard of it, but he'd never have been in it when he was a student. His father was a postman or something. I'd have to ask m'mother."

He groaned and collapsed back onto the tiles, worrying at a rip in his jeans. "But there's this big dinner coming up. There's this really important tradition that goes way back to the founding of the University, and I'm the president, so I have to organize it."

"Don't worry." Emma smiled. "You'll be brilliant."

He kicked his heel against the roof. "My father was president, too, while he was at the University. He doesn't think I can do it."

"Your father was in the Turnbulls too?"

"Yes, and my grandfather." Jasper's mouth curved up for a moment. "Apparently, when he was president, he shot a sweet hole right through the St. Dunstan's weathervane in Great Court to settle a bet. It's still there."

Somewhere below, the injured weathervane creaked.

"Oh," Emma said softly. "I can't imagine what it's like to have so much of your family history right here, around you. It's like you're part of a story. That sounds stupid, I know — "

"No, you sound like Rich. After his dad died, he got really into history. It took him a few years, but he found records of Wellesleys stretching back to the founding of the University. Piers had some Tudor ancestors who built a college or two. Hugo beats us all. He's got a direct line back to William the Conqueror — "

"Richard told me about his dad."

"What? Oh, yeah. Awful. Died when we were ten. The housemaster had to tell him. After that, he lived with us."

"What about his mother?"

"That old tart? Too busy hunting for her second husband. She packed up his things, sent him over to us, and that was that."

He was silent for a moment. "I think my dad likes him best."

There was a note in Jasper's voice that made him sound very lost, and very young.

"You know Rich, he — he dresses right. He and my dad like so much of the same stuff. I feel like, I have to try so much harder for him not to get at me, you know?" Jasper's mouth had set. "I'm going to show him, though. Be the perfect president, and for once he'll have to admit I didn't mess up."

"Well, if you're in charge now, you could just throw all of the old boys out of the club," Emma pointed out, with a mischievous glint. "Declare a new dress code. T-shirts only."

Jasper let out a roar of laughter and flung back his curls. "Oh, I feel so much better when I talk to you. Wish I could take you along in my pocket to this dinner."

Emma held her breath. It was happening. He was going to ask her. She pictured herself sweeping into dinner on Jasper's arm, the hot joy of his mouth on hers. The way their friends' eyes would linger. *They make a beautiful couple,* someone would whisper. And later, in his rooms, he would make her his, tongue tracing unhurried spirals on her skin. It all began with his next words.

But as Jasper leaned in, his foot knocked the camera bag. It slid down the roof, gathering pace. Emma flung out an arm. Too late, she realized she was leaning too far. The world tilted. She heard Jasper shout. Then the slates bit into her cheek. She was rolling, faster and faster. The crenellated wall loomed, the last thin strip of matter between her and flight into the sky. The cathedral was ten stories high. She clawed at the tiles. Rattling filling her ears.

Then her back hit something solid, and the sky stopped moving. She drew in a shaky breath. She was lying in the shadow of the wall around the roof, the camera bag wedged into the small of her back. It hadn't been clear from above, but the roof evened out into a flat space here. She lay still a moment in silent gratitude.

Thunderous rattling announced Jasper's arrival. His face appeared above her, glowing with enthusiasm. "That was amazing. The way you threw yourself after the bag. So reckless. You're properly adventurous, aren't you?"

"Mmmph," croaked Emma, feeling rather battered. "Yes. So adventurous. Could you — ?"

A strong hand scooped Emma's head and helped her sit up.

"There. Any better?"

His arm was around her back, his legs tangled with hers. Her skin thrilled. There, where his breath brushed her cheek. Where his hand rested at the secret curve of her hip.

As though someone else moved her, Emma saw her fingers curl around Jasper's neck. Heard a sound burst from her lungs when their lips touched. Felt the wondrous sharp heat on her scalp as Jasper buried his hand in her hair, and pulled. Her body melted where they touched, until she was supine and almost keening in his grip. Jasper drew back. A slow smile wreathed his face.

With delicious deliberation, he lifted the camera bag and placed it behind them. There, in the narrow strip of stone between roof and sky, he began undoing her buttons. Behind his head, glory-tinged clouds soared in an endless sky. His fingers, roughened by ropes and salt air, traced her smile. She was warm and liquid, atoms of sunlight held together by longing alone.

She pulled him to her.

She was going to implode if she couldn't tell someone, right away. And there was one person she knew would want to hear. Who would know exactly what she was feeling, and gasp in all of the right places.

Julia's room was in East Court, a little jewel box of a courtyard covered in drifting vines. Julia answered the door in a pink bathrobe, her hair twisted in twin buns.

"I slept with Jasper."

Julia pulled Emma inside the room with something perilously close to a screech. "Tell. Me. Everything."

Within minutes, Emma had been tied into a spare robe, and a parade of Korean face masks and snacks laid out on the coffee table.

"Right." Julia cozied herself next to Emma. "Full story, please."

It took an hour to go through the details to Julia's satisfaction. By the time they were done, the muscles in Emma's stomach hurt from laughing so much.

"What about you?" asked Emma, smoothing a sheet mask over her face.

"Me what?" said Julia, from the depths of her own mask. Only the slits at her eyes and mouth moved. It gave her a wonderfully ghoulish look.

"I've nothing as exciting as you. On a roof, no less? Although. Richard Wellesley-Jones. I've always — and I never thought he — but lately, I wondered . . ."

Emma had never imagined the poised Julia Colefax-Lee speaking anything less than a full sentence. Let alone twisting her fingers in her lap like a schoolgirl. It was impossible to see a blush through the mask, but Emma would have bet her month's student allowance that one was there.

"Julia."

"Right. Well. He hasn't exactly said anything. But Rich isn't obvious like that. He just looks, you know? I've not told anyone else. Just you."

Only months before, Julia had looked at her without recognizing her. Now, Emma had worn almost everything in Julia's wardrobe. The star maps that plastered Julia's walls were as familiar as her own room. She had never thought she would have a best friend besides Nat. And yet, somehow, it had happened.

Julia sat up straight. "Maybe I should ask him out."

Emma squeaked. "Yes, do it. Absolutely."

"Really?"

"Imagine a double date. You and Richard, me and Jasper."

"Date?"

"You know, Jasper and I — after what happened today — "

"Emma — Wait, let me take this thing off. Look." She took one of Emma's hands in her own. Her face, freed from the mask, was troubled. "Jasper is all very well for a fling. For fun, you know? But he's not really in the market to settle down. He doesn't date, shall we say? I don't want you to get your hopes up."

"I like fun," protested Emma, peeling off her own mask. "That's a good thing, surely, that we have fun together?"

"I've heard he's already 'having fun' with a few people. He's always had so much choice. He doesn't like to be tied down. And that's fine and lovely as long as nobody gets hurt, but you seem — "

"Jules, I think — I know — I'm different. For him," said Emma. She let the quiet confidence in her words sink in. "With other people here, he feels out of place. But we get each other. On a deeper level. It's like we were meant to be. You don't need to worry."

"Well, if you're sure," said Julia, not sounding very convinced.

"I am." Emma smiled and tossed a marshmallow into her mouth. "He wants more with me, I know it. Just wait. You'll see."

CHAPTER 12

THE TURNBULL SOCIETY

REQUESTS THE COMPANY OF

Emma Curran

AT THE ANNUAL DINNER
7PM SUNDAY NOVEMBER 16TH
AS THE GUEST OF JASPER BALFOUR,
PRESIDENT OF THE SOCIETY

EMMA DRIFTED OUT OF THE MAIL ROOM, CLUTCHING THE INVITAtion. So she hadn't been wrong about what it meant, the way he looked at her. When he'd kissed her.

No one understands me like you.

Beneath that thrill lay another. The Turnbull Society, whose secrets stretched a thousand years, had invited her into their inner circle. Soon their secrets would become hers. Hers and Jasper's, to share. Emma almost skipped to her room. She had a week to figure out how to look perfect.

On the night, Emma arrived alone. Jasper had to be at the Turnbull Clubhouse early to set up, he'd said. But it was easy enough to find the building: They owned a whole town house off Beaufort Crescent. The first thing she saw was the hall, dominated by a grand staircase and lit by a chandelier the size of a horse. She tilted her face to stare at the piped-icing plasterwork and the oil paintings, sure she looked like the worst kind of tourist. The marble around her echoed with the voices of the Turnbulls and their dates.

A uniformed server glided forward, holding out his hands. Just beyond she saw Venetia Kent, insolently beautiful in green satin, dropping her coat into the hands of another server. Emma shrugged her own jacket from her shoulders.

"Wouldn't leave anything in the pockets," someone said in a stage whisper. Piers Popwell leered into view. "Jasper's hired a criminal-looking lot, hasn't he?"

The server's face remained so rigidly expressionless, she knew he had to have heard. Emma's cheeks flamed as she handed over the jacket. "I'm sorry," she said.

But the server only bowed silently and moved away.

"Oh, they're not allowed to talk to us. Or at all. De Turnbulliis silentium est."

Piers chuckled and ran a finger up her arm. "My, we are looking luscious, aren't we?"

The gown was Helena's finest: a firebird-red silk that draped softly around her chest and left her shoulders bare. Lying close around her waist, the heavy skirt flared out to blaze around her ankles. She felt like a living flame in it. Her skin sparked with awareness. On her walk to the clubhouse, she'd noticed heads turning as she passed. Eyes lingering. She had imagined over and over how Jasper would look when he saw her in it.

She had not imagined Piers pawing at it. A few couples were already starting up the staircase, so she extracted herself from his grasp and hurried to join them. She caught up with Julia and Hugo on the steps. He in tails, she like a white lace mermaid. Julia seized Emma's hand and squeezed, her eyes sparkling. An air of excitement had begun to catch. The girls around them were giggling, clutching the arms of their escorts.

And there was Jasper at the head of the stairs, a lion prince. Each couple came forward to be greeted. When it was Emma's turn, Jasper swung her by the waist and kissed her.

"Jasper." Emma had to laugh, breathless. "Stop, you're crushing me."

"No." His eyes were too bright. He vibrated with nervous energy, his grip hot through the thin silk of her dress. "Shan't."

"Jasper, they're waiting. Behind me."

"Oh, all right." He released her as abruptly as he had grabbed her. Unsettled, Emma turned and trailed Julia and Hugo through an open door. Within, a dining room glowed by the light of candelabras. It was set for twenty, with the finest crystal and linen seen outside a palace. Silver domes covered each plate.

Nine Turnbulls, dressed in tailcoats and bow ties, lined the table. Jasper made a tenth at the head. Emma went to slip into the chair on his right, but he stopped her. "Oh, damn. I should have said. You're not here."

Lady Alice Blount, read the place card. "But all the other girls are sat next to their dates — "

"I'm sorry," said a musical voice. "Have I made things difficult?"

A second Grace Kelly stood beside her, gleaming in a satin sheath. Her hair a fall of blond silk over one shoulder; her figure all willowy elegance; her smile clear and sweet, like a painted Madonna. Emma had seen that face, and that name, in the magazines in Julia's room. Lady Alice Blount hailed from a family of acclaimed beauties. One of her sisters had even married a duke. That was, apparently, still a career path in this particular crowd.

Jasper pulled Emma aside. "My father asked me to look after her tonight. Family friend. She transferred from the Courtauld this term, so she doesn't know anyone. You're farther down the table, but it's only for dinner. Don't be angry."

She gathered what dignity she could to smile at Lady Alice and walked stiffly down the table to find her seat. It was a long table. She passed Elizabeth Lim and Antonia Viacelli, leaning over their dates to gossip. And Venetia Kent, holding a fascinated Eddie Spencer in her gaze like a blond, bored cobra. Even little Tabitha Mountbatten was seated before Emma. She was almost at the end before she spotted her place card.

Emma had never spoken to Francis Carr. He was a third-year from Granville College and the proud possessor of an overbite, a limited vocabulary, and enough acres of farmland to rival the Prince of Wales' estate. Now he pulled out her chair. "Care for some punch?"

"Gladly." Emma flopped into her seat. At the head of the table, Jasper was smiling at something Lady Alice had said. Emma took the glass from Francis and drained half of it. The punch tasted like cough syrup. She knocked back the rest.

Julia settled into the seat opposite Emma. Hugo followed, as glum as Emma had ever seen him.

Julia's cheeks were pink. "I was just saying hello to Richard. He explained the history of the clubhouse. Then he was telling me about the heraldic designs on the walls . . ."

"Richard does like to explain things," Hugo muttered into his wineglass.

"I didn't know you and Hugo were together, Jules," said Francis.

"Oh, we're not," Julia laughed. "Just here as friends."

Hugo wilted. Emma knew just how he felt.

"I think it's starting. Get ready," Francis whispered.

A row of silent servers had lined up, one behind every chair. A gong crashed, so loud Emma flinched, and the servers leaned as one to whip the silver dome from each plate.

It was bleeding. That was all Emma could think at first, seeing the mass on the stark white plate. Cubes of raw meat had been carefully molded into the shape of a heart. Anatomically accurate, some part of her mind noted, while she tried not to be sick. Someone had even taken the trouble to shape arteries from strips of dried meat.

At the head of the table, Jasper stood.

"With our flesh, we sustain the Society."

"We sustain the Society," the Turnbulls echoed. A cacophony of knives and forks scraped. Teeth ripped into ragged strips of flesh. Down the endless table, silver candelabras threw back distorted reflections of jaws working, throats swallowing. There were spatters of red on the damask tablecloth. Emma's skin crawled.

"Why're you not eating?" Francis scarfed down a mouthful. "Venison tartare. S'gorgeous."

"I'm vegetarian," Emma managed to force out, between lips shut as tightly as possible to hold in the nausea.

Julia looked up, appalled. "They've given you the same as us? Didn't you tell Jasper?"

"He must have forgotten."

"Bad luck for you," said Francis. "It's a running joke for the annual dinner that the president designs the menu with every kind of meat he can think of."

Jasper hadn't mentioned that. Emma ladled more punch into her glass.

"Except pork. Not allowed to serve that here. Tradition," Hugo mumbled.

Julia's tone was arch. "Though I heard there was something *rather* unsavory with a pig in your Society initiations."

"Ah, but we don't make the new boys *eat* it," chuckled Francis.

The silent servers reappeared to remove the plates. Emma saw Richard signal to Piers. They both slipped out. They returned and placed something with great pomp on the sideboard behind Jasper. A bowl made of a strange veined stone — or was it glass?

"What's that?" Emma asked.

"The Turnbull bowl. For the ritual, after dinner," said Francis. "That's why we're all here, really. The annual dinner is just to get us together for the ceremony. Turnbulls've done the same rigmarole every year since the University started. Same words, same stagy bits, same bowl."

"Same *bowl*? That's a thousand years old? Shouldn't it be in a museum?" Emma asked.

Francis chuckled. "That's sweet. Half the National Gallery is on loan from Eddie Spencer's family. Rory Clarke's fourth-nicest bathroom is papered with Picassos. Museums are for people who don't have their own collections."

The gong crashed. A new plate thumped down in front of Emma. A rib cage clawed for the sky. It had been forced into a ring shape, like a crown. Some kind of meat held the thing together, but Emma refused to lean closer to investigate.

Jasper raised a glass. "With our bones, we defend the Society."

"We defend the Society."

A loud cracking from her left sent a shiver of nausea up Emma's throat. Francis was slurping at one of the spokes of the crown. "By God, a different flavor marrow in each one! Jasper's outdone himself."

Emma felt stomach acid slosh around her insides. She hadn't eaten a thing since breakfast. She'd been too nervous. Her vision of dinner had been so different. Jasper in the candlelight, laughing just for her. His golden head bent close.

Emma twisted to look at him. Jasper, at least, was just as she had imagined him. Smiling, leaning in to whisper. But Lady Alice was sitting in Emma's place.

She was getting to know the bottom of her punch glass. It was proving to be a beautiful friendship, although she'd somehow knocked over Hugo's wine and lost her napkin. The room had also decided to sway just a little, which was off-putting.

She had to talk to Jasper. As she made for the head of the table, she seemed to be drawing some odd looks. More fool them, because she was Jasper's guest. Jasper wasn't even talking to Lady Alice anymore. He was staring into his wineglass. Of course, because it was Emma he really wanted there. She would make him happy. But when she reached his chair, his face was all wrong, like a stranger's. She'd never seen his forehead so rigid, or that twitching muscle in his jaw.

"What's wrong?" Emma reached to stroke the line from his brow.

116

"Nothing." He flinched away. "Just the ceremony after dinner. It's complicated."

"The one you have the bowl for?"

Emma drifted to the sideboard, ran her finger over the glass-smooth bowl. There were dark veins inside the stone. A candle guttered. Now the veins were crawling across the bottom. Horrible. Alive. Emma jumped back.

"What are you doing? Don't touch that." Jasper had her wrist, like a naughty child's. "Go sit down until dinner's over."

Emma slid into her seat, chastened. He was being so different. As though something terrible hung over his head. His precious ceremony, perhaps. She only wanted to help, but he'd flinched from her. As though seeing her somehow made things worse.

Francis patted her hand. "We're not supposed to stand until the president releases us. But here's dessert, so it won't be long."

Emma's stomach welcomed the news. Dessert was, at least, a reliably vegetarian course.

The gong crashed. A hand put down a plate. And Emma stared into the skull of a small animal. Otter, if she had to guess, by the extra-sharp molars. They'd turned the head upward, so the jaws yawned open. Its little eye holes had been stoppered with resin, so it made a cup for the brandy inside.

Emma tried to banish the memory of her otters dancing in the foam, at the bend in the river near Gabriel College. It wasn't Jasper's fault. He couldn't have imagined the caterers would use real animal skulls. He would never have asked for that. Across from her, she saw Julia gingerly prodding the skull. Disgust wrinkled her delicate nose. Farther down the table, Venetia was already holding hers up with a grin, testing the sharpness of the teeth against her thumb.

The table cheered as Jasper stood for the last time. "With our spirits" — he grinned — "we honor the Society."

"Spirits," said Hugo, sloshing the brandy. "Clever."

"With flesh and bone and spirit," Jasper continued, "we serve the Society of Turnbulls."

"We serve the Society of Turnbulls."

Jasper raised his skull cup. "The president says you may rise. The ceremony begins at midnight."

He tossed back the brandy and grinned, wet-lipped. "Open house rules till then."

The gong crashed a final time.

On her plate, the otter skull looked up at her in mute appeal. But Emma threw a napkin over it. She was at a party. It was time to enjoy herself.

CHAPTER 13

S OON NO ONE WAS IN THEIR PROPER SEAT. C HEEKS FLUSHED AND
laughter reached a wild pitch. They passed a mint around the table,
mouth to mouth. Two of the girls lost a forfeit and had to swap
underwear. Emma was pitted against Julia to race down the table.
Their high heels dodged the crystal and silver, evading the grasp of
the Turnbulls who tried to catch their ankles as they ran.

But she'd made a mistake, somehow. The world warped as she
ran. Faces shouted up at her, red and leering, like a nightmarish
carnival. That punch. Had it been stronger than it tasted? Ahead,
Julia wobbled, about to tread on the head of one of the Turnbulls.
He had passed out in grand style, forehead down on the table.
Emma knew with awful certainty that if she stopped running, she
would fall. So she leapt past Julia and on to victory, dropping into
Richard's arms at the end of the table.

The room roared with applause. Emma stood, turned, raised
her arms in triumph. She was a marvel. How had she never realized that? She was going to curtsy. But the floor got away from
her. It shifted under her feet and she staggered, arms windmilling.

Something solid hit her back. A table. It was tilting, a heavy object sliding past her —

The Turnbulls' bowl fell through the air, smooth and whole. Then it hit the floor. A crash in her ears, a grenade explosion of shards. Chips of stone skittered across polished wood.

Then silence. She knelt. The pieces, could they go back together? They were sharp. Dots of pain on her fingers.

She looked up. They were staring at her, the people. Deadly still. What was in their faces? She lifted her hands to block out the room, but they had blood on them. A long, angry slice on her palm, dripping red.

"My God."

The voice was a snarl. Emma flinched from the frightening man stalking toward her. But then he was close, and how silly she was, because it was only Jasper. She swayed to her feet, reaching for him.

Richard was herding people from the room. "No problem here, just go on out to the drawing room." He closed the door on the last of them.

Jasper pushed Emma away, his face hard. "No — stop, get off me. How could you? God, Emma, this was important and you — "

He was shouting. The room was spinning. Why was she so dizzy? The drink. What had been in the drink?

Richard stepped between them. "Jasper! Stop."

"What am I going to do? Rich, couldn't we use another bowl? I mean, does it matter for the ritual if — "

Richard was silent.

"It does, doesn't it? It has to be this one. Oh, God. My father's going to — "

"Calm down. Jasper, we don't have to do the ceremony tonight. We get the bowl fixed and do it next time. God's sake, man, what do you think they did in World War I? Or the Civil War, for that matter? Do you think they worried about getting together on the right date with a war on? That bit's not the tradition. You won't be letting anyone down."

Jasper was hugging Richard. "I'm sorry. I just wanted to get it right — "

But it wasn't right. Something was wrong. She was. She was wrong all over. Her stomach pushed itself up through her throat. Sick spattered her shoes.

"Oh, for God's sake."

"Patch her up, Jasper. Some plasters or something, for the hands. I'll sort it all for next time."

Emma stood, shivering with shame. The retches kept coming.

"Come on, mate. I'll clean up over here. Don't be too hard on her."

Someone was helping her over to a chair. It was Jasper, wonderful Jasper, come to rescue her. His warm hands on her back.

She was so sleepy. Emma wriggled her head against the back of the chair and let her eyes drop shut. She was just going to have a little rest. She heard Jasper moving. Sparks of pain flared and died on each fingertip. She jolted up. Jasper jumped and darted a look at her.

"It's just the bandage. Sorry if it hurt. Lie still. You'll feel better soon."

His expression seemed important, somehow, but the reason why drifted beyond her reach. Somewhere far away, a door closed. Emma sank into black nothingness.

"Oh, Emma."

Jasper was gone. It was Julia kneeling in front of her.

"I didn't know you drank the punch. I should have warned you, I never touch it. I don't know what they put in it. I should have been looking out for you. After what happened to Imogen — oh God, your hands. Do they hurt?"

With Julia's support, Emma lurched out of the dining room. The world was still unsteady.

"I was so wrapped up in my own night, and me and Richard — "

"You and Richard?" Emma repeated, sliding into a wall that seemed to have moved since she last looked at it.

"Oh, well." Julia negotiated Emma around a tricky corner. "It turns out he's not quite as indifferent to me as I thought."

Julia was smiling, so Emma smiled too. Then she had a thought.

"Wait — stop. We need to get Jasper. I can be with him, and you can be with Richard."

She wondered why the smile was slipping from Julia's face.

"I don't think that's a good idea right now."

"Not a good — why?"

"Just let him cool off. Give him a few days. He'll see it's not your fault."

Julia didn't understand. Jasper wanted to be with her. He'd asked her to be here. He'd looked after her hand. But Julia was guiding them through the front door, and they were already outside, and it was too hard to argue.

"Come on. Hop in the cab."

Emma moved obediently. The top of the car wobbled and caught her head as she sat down, but she didn't complain. Julia was talking to the driver. Emma twisted in her seat. The Turnbull Clubhouse was right behind them. The curtains in the dining room were open. And he was there by the window.

Waiting. He was waiting for her.

"Julia, look. He wants me — "

But when she turned back, Jasper was not alone. Framed in the light of the window were two silhouettes. Emma watched as Jasper pulled Lady Alice Blount to him, slender and yielding. As she swayed in his hold. As he captured her lips with his.

It didn't make sense.

"But — "

There was a hole in her chest. It was roaring.

The engine was starting.

"Wait — "

The clubhouse shrank to a dollhouse in the rear window. Julia's hand was tight around hers. It hurt. Her hand hurt. All of her hurt, all the way back to Gabriel College and up the steps to the tower. She sat on the bed watching Julia hunt pajamas out from drawers. It felt like ice, the pain. It sat in her chest, in her lungs, in the hollow place where her stomach used to be.

The pain thawed, just for a moment, when Julia leaned over and tucked the coverlet around Emma's neck. "Sleep tight," she said.

But then Julia was gone.

And it dawned on Emma that something was wrong. The darkness beyond her bed was shifting, bending over her. She vaguely remembered being too cold. A moment before, an hour before, what did it matter? Now she was blazing hot, a furnace beneath her skin. The walls were warping. Pressure building against her eardrums. Hissing.

It was the whispers.

They cascaded from the corners of the room. And at last they took off their masks of raindrops and tapping branches. They separated out into voices. As they always had been, underneath.

They muttered and pleaded and cried, these whispers. Frantic scraps of poetry, lists of numbers. A high, cracked laugh ran fingernails over Emma's neck. She hugged her face into her knees and rocked.

...and did he not the hero's way on trembling step incline?...

...fourfivesixseven, in the thousands, the thousands...

...please, i'll do anything. take it, just leave me, please leave me...

...from what is owed on said bargain's contract. the terms were indicated...

...and with his heart's blood dripping from his mouth, he sings still...

...so ripe for the draining, poor little mortal all lost and alone...

She jerked. The room was still and dark. She had been dreaming.

Somewhere, far off, her hand throbbed. But her head was thick and sweat chilled her chest. She lay with her gaze trained on the inky square of her window, careful not to close her eyes. Sleep had declared itself her enemy, and she would not visit its camp. She counted each cloud blowing across the moonless sky.

Something laughed. Her heart gave a terrible wrench.

A figure loomed at the end of her bed. Darkness hooded Jasper's features, but the chill in his fine blue eyes was clear. His mouth twisted.

"Oh, Emma. Why do you ruin everything?"

His smile was horrible, a knife-edge.

"It's like you want to make me hate you."

She struggled backward, but her limbs wouldn't move. They pinned her to the bed. Fear bloomed in her stomach, and —

Jasper wasn't there. Now her father loomed above her, wearing Jasper's tailcoat. Cold loathing radiated from him. She squeezed her eyes shut to block him out. Opened them, and the figure at the end of her bed was a shadow, pulling any light from the air. The tinny orange streetlamp outside the window faltered. Her breath was being driven from her chest.

"No," she whispered. "No, please, no . . ."

The walls were squeezing in. Emma sobbed with the pain, the pain —

And woke again. Gray light filtered in, scraping over the college spires. Four in the morning, her phone said. Outside, something screamed. A fox, probably. But in the dim confusion of the dawn hours, it almost sounded like a woman.

She pushed herself up. Pain pounded through her hand. Someone had tied a square of white fabric around it. Wincing, she pulled open the knot and stared at the cut on her palm. It glared back, livid and accusing.

She remembered a bowl. A smash. Jasper's face, turned from hers. And against a window's glow, the dark outline of his body, entwined with a shadow girl.

She flexed her fingers. Bright new drops of blood beaded the line on her palm. The pain felt cleansing. So she did it again.

The next day, she decided to send Jasper a message. Just a little one, to say hello.

She waited.

It took a week for her to admit that, in fact, the silence between them might just be permanent.

November was cold.

The end of November was even colder.

Emma stopped checking her phone for messages.

CHAPTER 14

HOPE IS A DANGEROUS THING. IT CAME FOR EMMA ON A MONDAY, in the mail room of Gabriel College. Porters in waistcoats and bowler hats streamed about her, ferrying parcels. Students dug through their post like industrious moles, wrapped to the ears in college scarves. Emma stood in the middle of the rush, staring at an envelope.

She would have known the handwriting anywhere. Fine and firm, a product of the most exclusive education money could buy. Jasper.

She could not open it there, in front of a crowd. She fled to the tower. She had to shove piles of fellowship notes from her window seat to clear a space. It didn't matter: They were mostly stills from a river camera near Regent's Bridge that had corrupted, leaving strange flares on the night footage, as though the river itself had been glowing. A problem, but not one that needed her immediate attention. She slid the card from Jasper's envelope.

THE TURNBULL SOCIETY

INVITES

Emma Curran

TO AN OPENING MEET

7PM TUESDAY 2ND DECEMBER

GENTLEMEN IN SCARLET, LADIES IN TAILS

A few taps into Google unraveled the mystery of the "opening meet."

Emma pressed her knuckles to her mouth.

It was a fox hunt. An opening meet was what they called the first fox hunt of the year, in those corners of England where horsemen still gathered with their coats and family trees in perfect order, ready to chase down their prey. She hadn't been able to understand it when she was younger, and her mother had tried to explain the picture in the newspaper. Why would a group of grown humans bestride their horses, gather a pack of dogs, all to chase down one fox? To gallop laughing through fields and over hedges, while a shivering little creature fled in blind, uncomprehending fear?

"It's how it's always been," her mother had said. "Some people find that comforting. It's not cruel to them, when it's tradition. That's Britain for you." Diana had turned her face up to the Australian sun, as if grateful to be there and nowhere else. "Old ways run deep."

Emma let the envelope fall. Blood sports were the opposite of everything she held to be right. And the invitation was for the next night. Only a day's notice. But Emma knew what her answer would be. She had known from the moment she opened the envelope.

Because Jasper would be there. She had ruined the most important moment of his dinner. Of course he'd been disgusted with her. But now she had a chance to see him again. She could make it right. She squeezed the card to her and winced. Blood shone from her palm. That cut was still refusing to heal, but she could bandage it later. Right now, she had to find her phone.

"Hello?"

The golden voice, so close to her ear.

"Jasper, it's Emma. I've just, I — " She cursed herself and started again. "I've just got your invitation."

"I hope you're calling to say you can make it. Don't let me down."

She felt her breath come in a rush of relief. "Oh, no — I mean, yes, I can make it."

"Meet me before. We can go in together. It feels like ages since I've seen you."

Emma felt a rush, as though a hand pinching her heart had released its grip.

"Me too. Though, Jasper? The invitation says to wear tails. You know I don't have a tailcoat."

"Not actual tails." He laughed. "It just means the ladies dress as the foxes."

"Oh. So 'scarlet' means the men are the hunters?"

"Exactly." A teasing note entered his voice. "All clear?"

She managed a laugh. But the line was already dead.

Emma assumed she would wear Helena's chainmail dress, or the firebird gown. But the next night, she found herself walking past Helena's box entirely and reaching into her own wardrobe. It was there, at the back. The dress she'd stolen from her mother when she turned fifteen. Black jersey, soft from wear. Her mother had said nothing when she saw Emma in it. Just brushed Emma's hair behind her ear with a look so sad, Emma had known she must finally have looked grown-up.

She slipped it on now and was instantly at ease. Her skin felt her own in a way she hadn't realized she'd been missing. It had probably cost a fraction of any of Helena's outfits. It was, to be honest, rather shabby by now. But she was herself in it.

The bells of Gabriel Tower were striking six. Jasper had said to meet him at the clubhouse early. That he had a fox costume for her, the same the other girls would be wearing.

It sounded like an excuse. Emma hoped it was an excuse. To see her alone, because he wanted things to be as they were before. Because he missed her.

The door of the clubhouse opened and there he stood, looking her up and down.

"You look nice. Not great to run in, though."

Emma stared at her feet as though that could make trainers appear. She would have remembered if he'd told her to dress for running, surely? If only she remembered their phone call more clearly. She'd been too caught up in her vision of winning him back. What else might she have missed?

"Later? When — Oh, never mind." Jasper turned away from the door. Emma darted in to catch it before it swung shut.

He took her through to the dining room.

"There."

He was holding out cloth ears and a tail. It hadn't been an excuse.

Jasper turned to the dining table, where a hunter's gear was already laid out. He tugged his T-shirt over his head. The unexpected fire of a December sunset poured over him, bare-chested before the window. Emma became very aware of her breath.

He was outlined in light. It stroked over the rippled honey of his back, the shadowed paths of muscle tapering to his waist. Even indoors, in the dead of winter, he gleamed like a bronze statue. As though a private sun shone on him alone. Always golden.

He tossed the T-shirt aside, and she watched the muscles of his stomach, hard under his skin. Her fingers itched to reach for him.

"How have you been?" she ventured.

"Fine."

"I just — I haven't heard from you for a while."

"God, Emma, it's just been a busy time. I didn't think you were the kind to get possessive with people, not after all of your traveling. I thought you understood." He flashed her a smile. "What are you going to do when I sail around the world, then, if you get upset at a few weeks apart?"

Jasper swatted at her with the waistcoat he'd been about to put on. Emma gave a laugh of pure relief. She saw how unreasonable she'd been. She had misjudged him.

"And you're sure it's okay to bring me tonight? After last time?"

She thought she saw his face darken, just a fraction, and regretted bringing it up.

"Why wouldn't it be? I'm the president. I'm inviting you. Who else has got anything to do with it?"

"It's just — I can't remember — I thought the others might be angry at me. After I broke — that thing."

"No, the opposite, really. I was the one who got worked up

about the bowl. Rich calmed me down and got it fixed, and the others never shut up about how great you are."

Seeing Emma's face, he put down the waistcoat and crossed the room to her. "Honestly, Piers practically begged me to get you back to one of our clubhouse parties, and Richard told me I looked miserable and should invite you. Even Hugo asked if you were coming tonight, and I didn't think he had enough brain cells to notice anyone but Julia."

Why would they have to be so insistent? a small, miserable voice thought. *Did Jasper need that much persuading?*

"So you're making a big worry out of nothing." And with a funny face for Emma: "Don't get paranoid on me."

She felt strange when Jasper was fully dressed. The costume was exactly as she'd seen in cartoons: red coat with tails at the back, breeches, shining top boots. She watched him, absorbed in adjusting the white stock around his neck. She'd known that Jasper's parents lived mainly on their country estate. Why had she never thought to ask him about hunting?

"Is that yours?" she asked. "The hunting outfit."

"What? No. This is fancy dress."

"Oh." Emma smiled, relieved. For a moment, she'd felt a dizzying shift. As though her vision of Jasper had always been a smoke screen, and she'd just seen the complete stranger beneath. A person whose edges were made up of questions she hadn't thought to ask. But she shouldn't have doubted. Of course this was only fancy dress for him. She knew who Jasper was.

He did up the last button. "My hunting gear's black, not red."

Her mind was a chaos of shattered thought fragments, and she had no time to straighten it. Jasper was already leading her down a corridor.

The room they entered was dark. Clusters of candles cast flickering shadows over the audience that waited for them. Hushed, expectant. Emma hesitated in the doorway, but Jasper led her on by the wrist. A table had been set in the middle of the room, like an altar. Emma saw crumbling parchment, the gleam of a knife, a jug of red liquid. And at the center, the Turnbull bowl. Spiderweb cracks marked where they'd had to glue it back together. Emma's cheeks burned, but no one was looking at her.

They all watched Jasper. Squaring his shoulders, stepping forward to the table. The Turnbulls crowded round him, all in red coats and hunting hats. Among them, Emma recognized nasty Piers, Richard, and Hugo.

The girls stood apart, huddled by the fireplace in fox ears and tails. Emma was relieved to see they were wearing gowns and heels, just as she was. Julia was a cloud of crimson in a satin halter dress; her only possible concession to practicality a tightly pinned crown of braids. She beckoned Emma to join them. Venetia, beside her, was almost vibrating with fury, her hands clenched against the black mesh of her jumpsuit. The girls had been pushed to the sidelines, Emma realized. They had a terrible view: the Turnbulls' backs blocked the table. For once, Emma was grateful to be tall. If she stood on tiptoe, she could see Jasper and the bowl.

"What is this?" Emma whispered.

"They're doing some sort of ceremony first," Elizabeth Lim whispered back. "The one they didn't do at the annual dinner."

"I've not seen it before," Antonia Viacelli added. "We were too soused at the end of last year's annual dinner to take it in. I was asleep with my head in a soup tureen."

"The punch," said Elizabeth. They all pulled a face.

"So we're supposed to stand in a corner, like good little girls, until they're done?" Venetia Kent's eyes gleamed dangerously. "We're supposed to be the most powerful generation of women the University has ever seen. And look at us, waiting all nice and proper until we're wanted. We can't even see."

"Don't," said Julia, pulling Venetia back. "It'll only make a scene."

"Is that a bad thing?" Emma said, surprising herself.

Venetia flashed her something that was almost a smile.

"It's starting," Julia said, with a quelling stare for both of them.

The hush was unnerving. Jasper held the parchment before him, ran a finger over the spidery writing. His voice shook as he intoned the first lines. Then it grew in power, until someone else might have been speaking through him, it sounded so unlike Jasper. Snatches of words winged around the room. Brotherhood. Sacrifice. The Turnbulls watched every movement of his lips, eyes glazed in the candlelight. Then the speech dropped into Latin.

Emma knew only as much Latin as she'd been able to pick up from species names over the years. The words rolled over her. The air in the room was heavier, somehow. She licked sweat from her upper lip.

There. *Sanguis.* She knew that one. It meant *blood.* And *mortis,* like *rigor mortis. Death.*

Piers glanced back at the group by the fire with a horrible smile. Emma bit back her revulsion and looked past him, to where Richard stood at Jasper's elbow. He lifted the jug and let the red liquid splash into the bowl. The veins in the glass-stone glowed scarlet. The spicy, sullen scent of wine rose in the air.

The Turnbulls roared a chant, harsh and rhythmic. There was something ancient about the sound, something raw. As though centuries of civilization had fallen away, leaving only the hunger of a pack.

Jasper slid the knife under the seal of an envelope. The paper inside was covered on both sides with typed text. Illuminated for a brief moment in the candle's glow, it looked like a list.

Jasper let it fall into the wine. Patches of scarlet bloomed across the paper. It struggled to stay afloat, then plunged down into the depths of the bowl.

Richard handed Jasper a stone jar, edges softened with the wear of centuries. Jasper tilted it until a single red drop fell into the bowl at each compass point. The Turnbulls had been repeating the same phrase, over and over. Now their chant rose to a higher pitch.

The knife flashed. Jasper had plunged it into the bowl. He stirred the wine. Fragments of paper spun and dissolved. The liquid had taken on a dark, viscous look.

Jasper lifted a battered silver cup and dipped it to the bowl. He drank deeply. Wine ran over his fingers, dark as blood. He pulled his lips from the cup, dripping red, panting. The room thrilled to his voice.

"Gentlemen. By our flesh, by the bones of our fathers, and the spirit of the chosen: The Society of Turnbulls lives on."

"The Society of Turnbulls lives on," the room thundered back. Each Turnbull dipped the cup and drank.

When the last one had drunk, Venetia broke from Julia's hold and charged forward. But there was nothing left in the bowl. Nothing but a few specks of wine sediment, like dried blood. Emma knew she was imagining it, but the veins in the glass-stone walls of the bowl seemed fatter now. Almost as though it had been fed.

Afterward, they brought out the champagne. Someone had hurried the bowl away. It was a good thought, because in the mess that followed, of wine and large male forms being flung around the room, Emma doubted it would have survived intact.

"No, but really, the thing about fox hunting," Emma heard someone say behind her, "is the adrenaline high. More than paragliding or other extreme sports, which I do a lot of."

"Really." Venetia sounded excruciatingly bored. "Fox hunting."

"Yeah," the boy added impressively. "Because you could actually die."

"Right, right, that's it," another voice boomed. "Hunting's all about skill."

"And the fox mostly gets away anyway," added little Tabitha Mountbatten. "But they never put that in the stories."

Emma turned away. Perhaps it was because she'd been avoiding drinking, the memory of the Turnbull punch too horrible to shake. But the rest of the party felt as though it was happening on the other side of a glass wall.

"Come on, mate."

A few steps away, at the center of a pink-flushed group, Eddie Spencer was trying to shove Richard toward Antonia Viacelli, lolling by the fire. But Richard shook him off and fled for the far window, where Julia waited.

Eddie downed his glass. "Only trying to help. That man needs a girlfriend."

Piers stumbled against Eddie, giggling. "Not him. He's been sticking it into something secret."

"Sly dog, who?"

Piers let his eyes snag on Julia. Queenly, radiant in crimson satin by the window.

Guy Cavendish whooped. "Oh, good lad. Best call the ambulance, lads. Seems our Rich has a spot of the *yellow fever*."

The group screeched like macaques.

Yellow fever. Emma could have ripped out their eyeballs for daring to even look at Julia. Or their stupid, shrieking tongues. And all at once she realized: She was done here.

She looked around: at the boys with red coats and redder faces; the girls shrieking and slapping away errant hands. The bottles knocked over and forgotten, slopping champagne onto the floor. And she couldn't remember what it had felt like to want all of this so badly. It was empty. The money, the sheen. The jealous eyes following them from party to party. None of it made the people here worth spending time with.

Jasper stumbled across the room.

"You are so gorgeous," he whispered. Speckles of saliva sprayed her ear. He kissed the rim, a wet wash of tongue on her skin. "And you're mine. Pretty, pretty Emma."

Five minutes before, that kiss would have set Emma's skin tingling. Now it was a blank.

Jasper leaned in again, but before Emma had decided whether

she wanted to duck — and why would she do that, Emma scolded herself, what was wrong with her? — Piers clapped his hands.

"Right, you lot! These are the rules of the Opening Meet," he announced.

Venetia rolled her eyes. "It's a pub crawl."

"Men-hunters!" Piers bellowed over her. "You are one team. Lady-foxes! The second. Between each pub, foxes, you must run. Hunters, you must chase them. That is the hunt. If a fox gets to the next location without being caught, she is safe. But if a hunter spots a fox, he may call all the other hunters to chase her. And then, watch out, foxes! Because the hunters only have to catch one fox to win the round. And" — he waggled his eyebrows — "the winning team gets bought drinks at the next pub."

"What happens to the fox that gets caught?" ventured one of the girls.

His eyes glittered. "Why don't you find out?"

A low laugh went around the room.

Emma's hand itched in Jasper's hold. She twitched it away. "Jasper, actually I — "

"Oh no." He pinned her to him. "You can't leave. Not now."

Sweat-damp fingers ran down her spine. Wriggling away from him, Emma overbalanced.

"All right there?" Richard asked, with a steadying hand. She wasn't sure what he saw in her face, but he sighed.

"Emma, I know Jasper's very excited. But it's really just a pub crawl. Don't stay if you don't want to. People usually lose track after the first stop. I mean, Hugo's already passed out in the coatroom, so not everyone even makes it out. And you look tired already."

"Thanks," she said. "You know what? I really am."

Impulsively, she leaned into Richard for a one-armed hug. He stiffened, and then a hammy hand closed around her shoulders.

But the group was gathering. The grip on her wrist was Jasper's, towing her to the street outside.

"Hunters," Piers bellowed. "It is time."

In the hours they had been drinking, the streets had emptied. The tourists back to the train station, the market sellers driving home. The city was left quiet and cold.

"Next stop, the Swan," cried Piers.

Piers had named a pub near the river. It was a clear run from the Turnbull Clubhouse if you took Scholar's Road. But on an open path, the Turnbulls would outrun her. No, this required cunning. Emma sifted through side streets in her mind.

Piers raised his hand. "Foxes, on my signal."

Emma tensed. Piers blew a long blast on a hunting horn.

The girls raced into the cold dark. The scattered drumbeat of high heels on stone echoed from buildings and statues. Julia was the first of the pack, outpacing them all with a runner's easy stride. She swerved into a side street, her gown a blood-hued flicker in the dark. Venetia tore off her fox ears with a savage smile and sprinted straight down Scholar's Road. The other girls scattered like a shoal of nervous fish. Emma watched them flit into one side street and another.

She was already tired. Her lungs stung in the icy air. Perhaps she could leave the Turnbulls to their games. Then the tinny cry of the horn came again.

The boys were coming.

Her pulse thrummed. She was the only one left hesitating. She would be the first to be caught.

An idea came to her with the suddenness of divine inspiration. She doubled back. The Senate House was locked at night, but the gates were low enough that a child could climb over. She might even get to the pub first.

Just one drink, she promised herself, *and then home.*

Nat would be watching a film in his room. He'd already been muttering about his costume for *The Life of Tolstoy*'s cast party. She suspected he was in front of a Werner Herzog classic, attempting to cut out a Russian military cape in the style of Prince Andrei Bolkonsky. Perhaps she could even be back in time to stop him from slicing off a finger or two. She set a steady pace, and the pillars of the Senate House soon loomed before her.

It was dark and echoing inside the colonnade. Generations of scholars had added carved plaques and marble statues until the whole complex looked like a strange stone menagerie. Emma shuddered as she skirted a man with a boar's head, a screaming deer. A towering merman reminded her of the bearded statue on the riverbank, from the first time she'd been out with Jasper.

And then Jasper was there. Not in the rolled-up jeans and bare feet of her memory. In the red coat and white breeches of a hunter.

He leaned against the statue with a satisfied grin.

"How did you know?" asked Emma. Her words echoed off stone eyes, stone horns, stone tails.

"I guessed. I was lucky."

"Aren't you going to call the other hunters?"

"No, silly. I haven't had you alone all night. Come here."

"What about the game?"

He gathered her to him. Gone was the scent of cotton and clean boy. There was wine on his breath. There was cologne on his skin, a cloud so thick she finally recognized what it was. It was money, that smell. The dark wood of paneled studies in stately homes. The leather of a luxury car, gleaming new. The smoke at the end of a cigar. It made a stranger of him. Someone older, more assured.

"Caught you," he slurred.

He surged forward and mashed his mouth against hers. The column was ice against her back. Emma closed her eyes, tried to summon the golden magic of the cathedral roof, the way his fingers had felt like small flames flickering across her skin. It was no use.

"Stop," she said. "Sorry, I'm sorry, could you stop a moment — "

"Em-ma," he moaned into her neck.

Now she felt the way her neck was twisted, with his hands holding her head in place and pressing her into the column. She couldn't breathe.

"Jasper. Jasper, wait."

"Fine, fine." He lifted his hands in exaggerated obedience, releasing her. "You're confusing me, Emma. I thought this was what you wanted."

She looked down, uncomfortably aware of the blank where she should be feeling desire. Or embarrassment. Or anything except a tired longing for bed. Her own. Alone.

"I'm sorry. I thought I wanted — I do, it's just . . ."

He took it as an invitation and pulled her against him with renewed fervor.

It was worse than before. He was crushing her. She couldn't breathe and she couldn't think. *Move*, she screamed at her stupid legs, her lazy arms. *Just move.* Her traitorous body remained still, a doll, a shell. It was as though she watched floating from somewhere above. The beautiful boy sheathed one hand in the tangled hair of the girl in his arms, pulled her face to his. She was limp, insignificant. She was nothing in his grasp. He stopped, breathing hard, and switched his attention to the front of her dress, twitching and ripping in his haste to undo the buttons.

She woke. Her blood *screamed;* that was the only way she could describe it. A song of bared teeth and fury echoed through her, curling her fingers to claws. She wrenched at Jasper's wrist.

He jerked in shock. They stared together at the welling crescent marks on his arm, the blood on her nails.

"I'm sorry. I didn't mean — I'm sorry — "

"You keep saying that," he slurred.

"But I am."

He advanced on her.

"Fox."

It was soft, like an insult. He was staring at her with unnerving intensity.

"Fox."

He raised his voice, still not looking away.

"Fox."

The sound echoed through the colonnade, bouncing off the pocked stone tiles.

Foxfoxfoxfoxfoxfox.

The first halloos filtered through the night air.

Jasper smiled, and it held no kindness.

His coat was red. His boots were tall. And his eyes were hard.

He stepped toward her.

She ran.

CHAPTER 15

THEY WERE BEHIND HER.

"Fox! Catch the fox!"

The horn blew jaunty blasts through the night air.

She could hear them. Their boots, their hunger.

She ran faster than she ever had. Streets and squares and cobbles blurred into one. The city was hard stone. Gargoyles leered. She whipped around a corner.

Her breath was coming in gasps. She could taste blood.

A statue screamed for her with outstretched arms.

"Fox! It's the fox!"

She hazarded a look behind her and choked. They were coming for her. Red coats dark in the night like wine, like blood. Jasper there in front. Their faces alight, nostrils flaring. The scent of the kill.

She was the kill.

She stumbled and could not risk another look back

She had thought they were boys but no, now they were hunters, no trace of boy

Where were the ones that were drinking and laughing with her
catching her ankles as she ran down a table
    oh god could they catch her ankles and send her sprawling on
stone
    the boys they were hunting
    hunting her they were hunting her
    "help," she cried out
    but her breath was gone her voice would not come
    please oh please help
    help me run help me hide
    they are hunting the fox i am the fox
    heart thump blood in her ears breath sharp blood in her mouth
blood in a bowl drinking the blood they were drinking the blood
they would drink the blood her blood
    run run run run run run run
    run

"SECRET SOCIETY" EMBROILED IN MISSING STUDENT CASE

By Olivia Farquhar and Mus Khan

Why were nine of our University's wealthiest students running through town, dressed for a fox hunt, on the night Emma Curran disappeared? And why do all of them claim to have had no idea she'd been in a room with them that very night?

There has been rising anger in the student body at the lack of progress in Emma Curran's case. We reported on Jasper Balfour's questioning – and subsequent release – by police, in the days after she disappeared. New information has since come to light that Balfour was part of a wider group: a clandestine society for the wealthiest and most powerful male students, whose existence has been concealed by the University. They, it seems, coaxed Ms. Curran to a private party that night. This was revealed in a brave statement to the press last month by party witness Julia Colefax-Lee.

But the University administration has chosen not to answer these claims. Instead, they heaped praise on "The Turnbull Society," as we now know them to be called, in a press conference at the Senate House.

(Image above, L–R: Piers Popwell, Richard Wellesley-Jones, Francis Carr, Eddie Spencer, Philip Cranbottom, Guy Cavendish, Atticus Tremaine, Rory Clarke, Jasper Balfour)

Standing by their side, the University chancellor came out with strong support for the boys: "I deplore the cruel disruption to their studies, the harm to their reputations from these baseless, discriminatory rumors. What happened to Emma Curran was a tragedy, as the young men next to me have expressed. Evidence suggests she must have met an unknown assailant while walking home alone. Sadly, inebriation was a factor. It is unfortunate but true that criminals target those that make themselves vulnerable. We urge all female students to take sensible precautions: perhaps stay home rather than travel after dark; limit your alcohol consumption; and refrain from wearing headphones, which offer such an invitation to predators."

The press conference encountered a bombshell: Student Venetia Kent interrupted proceedings to harangue the young men, revealing photographs of Emma Curran from the night of her disappearance (pictured, inset). Many show Emma in conversation with Jasper Balfour, Piers Popwell, and others – despite the young men claiming they had not seen her that night.

"We were training for a charity race," said Popwell, explaining the evening's activities, in which the group ran from pub to pub in hunting gear. "The girls were there to support. If Emma was around, nobody told us. I don't recognize those photos. They've clearly been doctored."

Jasper Balfour declined to answer questions. His family later released a statement, repeating that Balfour had "little to no relationship with Emma Curran," and was "entirely uninvolved with her disappearance."

And in the absence of new leads – or perhaps, of police and University energy to pursue them – the case appears to be slowing to a halt. It is months since Emma Curran's disappearance. And we are no closer to knowing what really happened to her that night.

The horn blew jaunty blasts through the night air.

"Fox! It's the fox!"

She hazarded a look behind her, and choked.

She had run straight into their path.

They were coming for her.

run run run run run

run

the city changes its skin
green spring for summer gold
autumn blows from the trees
in a flutter of russet and brown
leaving one copper patch
glowing against snow

a fox

fox wanders the stone forest
the days have claws of frost
the nights freeze fox's heart

too long alone
she has no song of her own
though rich hot prey-blood
steams on her tongue
fox stays cold

till it happens
a shaking comes
from within it tears her
fire lancing paw and pelt and tail
she shrieks
falls
stone ground hard beneath her

and with a scream that is fear
fox is lost

CHAPTER 16

EMMA OPENED HER EYES. ABOVE HER, CLOUDS CHASED ACROSS A pale blue sky. She was just wondering, lazily, where she was, when a barrage of panic scrabbled at her mind. The safe, familiar smell of fox was gone. She scented a predator.

She jerked up to meet the threat, teeth bared, and froze. Her legs were long and smooth. Her claws were round, flat little moons.

Human. They were human legs. And the smell, the not-fox smell — it was her. Emma. Human. Not fox.

"Can you hear me, girl?"

Two faces loomed above her. Tired faces with silvery pelts. *Hair,* she reminded herself. The speaker, a woman, had one eye covered with a patch. The man beside her had a dandelion's head of white hair and a faraway smile.

Emma pushed herself up to face the strangers. Cool air brushed her gums. Her lips had curled back, baring her teeth. A growl tunneled up from her throat.

"Very nice. But as I've no use for flummery, I'd rather you stopped making a fuss in the street."

Emma's growl faltered and died in her throat.

The cold, hard surface beneath her was indeed a cobbled street. She looked up from it to a row of crooked cottages. The door of one stood open, and the glow from inside spilled onto the street. Warmth. Emma unconsciously stretched for it. Her skin was almost numb, she realized. The air around them was sharp with cold.

"You're half-frozen, girl, and no wonder," the woman said gruffly. "Dressed like that. Come in, we'll get you properly clothed."

Emma ran her hands down her arms. Her sleeves were a tapestry of rips and mildew. *This must have once been a pretty dress,* she thought. Soft and black and clinging. Now it was a mess of threads, as though someone had been crawling through dirty streets in it for a long time. It seemed familiar, but she had no memory of putting it on. Icy air lanced through the rips in the fabric, and shivers shook her. Warm. She needed to get warm. Perhaps then she might remember.

Emma lurched to her strange, unclawed feet. The moment she rested her weight on them, she pitched forward. Her face collided with a domed stomach in a waistcoat. Knotted hands set her on her feet and held her until she could stand. Those hands. She knew them. Her mind flooded with memories.

"You're — " Her voice emerged from her chest in a creaky whisper, like a rake through leaves. She tried again.

"You," she said carefully. "You work at the Library."

The old man nodded.

Emma continued, more confident with every word. "You were the librarian who helped me that day. You gave me — a drawing. Of an eye. You warned me about . . ."

But her memory became hazy at that point — what was it he

had warned her about? — so Emma switched hurriedly to the old woman. Her eye patch was familiar.

"And you . . . work at reception in the Library. You came over once to tell me to be quiet."

"You were right, Henry." The woman's voice was grim. "Come, we must get her inside. There may still be time."

The old man gestured to the house with the open door. Emma followed him, stumbling on the cobbles. Her feet were bare and blanched with cold.

Inside, a fire crackled merrily in the grate. Everywhere else, from the whitewashed walls to the battered rug, was given over to books. A thread of open floor wound through the maze of footstools and hardbacks.

The woman shut the door behind them. She inspected Emma. "You're pale, girl. Henry, some brandy, if you please. We've much to tell her and no time for fainting fits."

Emma sank onto a footstool, fingers tangling around a glass of brandy she didn't want.

"Drink up. My brother's brandy collection is well worth the while, you know."

The old man chuckled assent.

"Your brother?" Emma coughed, brandy burning a trail down her throat.

"Yes. He is the Librarian. I am his sister. Have you a name?"

"It's Emma." There had been a second part, surely. She almost had it, it was — "Curran. I am Emma Curran."

Of course she was. She was Emma Curran. That wasn't the kind of thing a person forgot.

Except she had.

A storm broke in her head. What was she doing there? Why couldn't she remember? Tangling her mind, the strange dream that she had been — not human. Emma began to tremble. She still felt, at every nerve ending, strange impulses she was sure hadn't been there before. A second self, a beast, a —

" — fox."

For a moment, Emma thought she must have said the word aloud. But the Librarian's sister was looking at her expectantly.

"Can you remember, girl? How you came to be a fox?"

"Came to be a . . ." Emma repeated dazedly. "You're saying — I was really a fox? Not dreaming, or — "

"Or mad?" The Sister snorted. "No. Where do you think you got those charming teeth-baring habits from, hmm? We saw you ourselves. I was in my workroom — the spell I was trying to nail down was the finicky sort, you know — when the aftershock of some magic rolled in from outside. Blasted my working to pieces, it was so strong. Henry felt it just the same. It quite upset his books. So we ran out to the street, and there you were. Flickering in and out of fox form on those cobblestones."

Spells. Emma couldn't remember if she had been the kind of person who believed in magic. Perhaps she was. And for a moment, it all made sense. She *had* been a fox. She knew it. Her mind shivered with sense memories: paws on frozen ground; head lifted in a song to the moon; the warmth of sun on her pelt. But then a tide of disbelief surged. It was nonsense.

She was Emma Curran. She lived at Gabriel College. She could see it, with her window seat and her leaf-patterned bedding. She'd picked that pattern with someone. A warm voice over her shoulder, calloused fingertips that brushed hers as they stroked the fabric. A scent like sun-warmed earth, and rosemary crushed in her palm.

Her mother. Forgotten, until now.

Horror stiffened Emma's joints. With the memory of that scent, her mother's face swam into focus. And Emma saw that face crumple, frantic with fear. How long had she been away? A day? A whole week?

Emma clenched her hands to still their shaking. What would her mother do, if she hadn't heard from Emma in a week? She had never gone more than a few days without a message. And Nat, and — more faces came back with a rush — Julia and Venetia, Hugo and Richard. Her friends. What would they have thought? She winced against the onslaught of memory now. Her lecturers, the University officials, they would all have been notified. They probably would even have called her father. Little as he might care.

She had no explanation for where she had been. Her chest was searing. Emma realized that she'd been holding her breath.

"I have to go." Brandy spilled over her skirt, the glass rolling to the floor. "My friends, they'll be — "

"You cannot, child." There was an unbearable sadness in the Librarian's voice. She thought it might be pity.

"You're going to keep me here? Are you — Is this some sort of kidnapping?"

"No. We would not keep you against your will."

"Speak for yourself," muttered the Sister. "She doesn't believe any of it yet, that's plain to see, and she'll be a danger to herself wandering out there with no more sense than a mortal on a moonless night."

With an air of decision, she dragged a footstool opposite Emma and sat upon it.

"I am going to explain a few things to you. I am sorry if this comes in too direct a form, girl. It's important you understand quickly, as there's no saying how much time we have before — But no, we won't begin there."

Behind her, the Librarian smiled encouragingly at Emma. But as he then proceeded to smile at the fire, the doorway, and his own shoe with equal amiability, Emma was not as reassured by his support as she could have been.

"There are some things you must believe, girl, and believe fast if you wish to survive," the Sister said. "The first: You were a fox. Not ten minutes ago, you were lying on the street with ears and a tail. But when you regained your human shape, my brother and I knew we had seen you before. So we also knew that you were not always a fox. It is a thing that can happen, girl. A magic. A transformation. Those who call upon a power in the dark may be answered."

"What power in the — "

"Nothing picked you off while you were a fox, so I can only assume the shape hid you. A small mercy. But now I've loosed you from the shape, it's only a matter of time before something sniffs you out. And then they're bound to come and take you — "

"Who?"

The Sister could be quite selectively deaf, it seemed.

"That's the thing about magics like yours," she went on. "They come at a cost. A wish made, a bargain struck: There's always a price."

"A bargain? But I didn't, I don't remember — "

"I am afraid there is no other possibility. You made a bargain, as many others have before you. And with this kind of bargain, you cannot pay what you owe with gold." The Sister shifted on the footstool. "You pay with yourself. With the mortal part of you, the part that anchored you in the human world. That is gone now."

Gone. Strange how certain the word sounded in the Sister's gruff voice.

Emma looked down at her forearms. Right there, the scar from when she was five, stealing her mother's rose shears to cut her own hair. The familiar sprinkle of moles on her left elbow. Her body might feel strange right now. But it looked extremely normal to her.

"You may look like a mortal, but that is just a skin over what you are. Those of us who have been touched by magic, we belong to the power that claimed us. That saved us, or granted our wish, and changed us in so doing. You belong to the Night City now."

She looked into Emma's face, as if hoping to see her words sink in. For a moment, Emma was caught by her urgency. By the mystery in her words. *The Night City.* There were worlds of meaning in the way the Sister had said it. Fear, but awe too.

But nothing could pull Emma from the call of home and her mother, and a real life that made sense. The longer she stayed here, the more tangled she was getting. The more she believed things that could not be true. Emma pasted on a smile. "Well. This has been so — interesting. All those things you wanted me to know, I understand now. I'll think them over, I really will. I'll just head home now." She backed toward the door, panic clawing her throat, counting the paces to freedom.

"Nonsense," snapped the Sister. "You cannot go home. There is too much danger for you to try something so idiotic." Her good eye flicked toward the door, glittering with unease. "Not here. Not now. Things have been . . . unstable, of late. A dangerous time for any of us. Folk are on edge enough already, looking for something to blame — "

The Librarian gave a wheeze, and the Sister broke off. Emma looked between them, curious. She had thought before that the Librarian was not as vague as he seemed, and now she was sure. He had cut his sister off before she said too much. About some danger.

The Sister turned back to Emma. "For now, you'll stay with us. Nobody visits, so you'll be safe enough. Perhaps we can find a way to unpick whatever bargain you made, before they — "

Her face contracted. It was dead white under her eye patch. Someone was pounding on the front door.

"Open, by the Night City's command."

The blows redoubled. Loud as hunters' boots slamming the ground. Loud as her heart crashing in her ears. Reflex took over. Emma found herself in a crouch, lips bared in a snarl.

The wood around the latch was splintering. Mouth set, the Sister marched to the door. It opened on a figure in a green tunic embroidered with a great tree, chafing his hands to shake off the cold.

The Sister lifted her chin. "Strange times, when messengers of the City force entry to a private home."

The messenger rubbed a hand over his hair in some embarrassment. "I know, mistress. It's not as we would wish. But these are indeed strange times. Least said on that, the better. Let's have the business done with. The City has summoned the mortal debtor. I'm to take her to the Court to pledge her service. The Oath is due."

Emma backed away, fighting a whine in her throat. Predators. She had the scent in her nostrils. It sang of hurt and tearing teeth waiting just out of sight.

The Sister frowned. "Allow me at least to lend her some boots. A cloak too. She cannot walk the streets barefoot."

The boots the Sister brought out were hobnailed and laced above her ankle. They made her feel like a Victorian schoolchild. They were too big, but Emma still found her toes curling inside them, as though anxious not to touch the edges. She had to fight the strangest conviction that it was all wrong for limbs to be trapped in prisons of cloth and leather. That she ought to feel the ground under her, to dig bare toes into earth as she ran. She wrestled her thoughts into obedience. Human feet were meant to be in shoes. She wouldn't make it far barefoot, if she had to run.

Then the messenger grabbed her arm, muscling her through the open door. She felt herself go limp, prey in a predator's jaws. An instinct, far deeper than thought, told her to be still. It was not yet time to run.

They emerged onto the cobblestones. Opposite the cottages was a row of shopfronts, their signs turned to "Closed." The old-timey Fenchurch Fudge shop, beloved of tourists. A newsagent's. A chime of hope rippled through Emma. She remembered this street now. The spire of Sussex College towered over a nearby roof. Gabriel College had to be in running distance, even if she couldn't yet remember exactly where.

"You'll have to bind her," the messenger said. "If she escapes, there'll be the Night's own breath to pay."

The Sister pulled a silver chain from the belt-purse at her waist. She held it up for his inspection.

"That'll do," the messenger said.

The sight of the chain sent an electric charge through Emma. Her muscles coiled. And just as the wind veered to the perfect place, she felt a prick at her limbs. A fox-shaped shriek at the recesses of her mind.

Run.

She sprang, cobbles pounding beneath her feet, hearing the shouts at her back.

"Catch her," the messenger howled. "Night's sake, I'll have to tell the City — "

Emma swung around a corner, and the rest was lost. Her heartbeat was pounding in her mouth. She was sure, any moment, a hand would land on her shoulder. The chain would circle her wrists. She would be dragged back to whatever her kidnappers had planned for her.

She ran.

CHAPTER 17

EMMA'S FEET FOUND THEIR WAY BEFORE HER MEMORY DID. SHE would double back down a side passage as if at random and only afterward realize that she had once known that bookshop, or sat in that churchyard with a coffee. At last, when her lungs were at bursting point, she stumbled into an open space filled with the hum of ordinary life. Sunlight bounced from colored awnings. She was in Market Square, and the chill in the air told her it was a crisp winter's day.

The market was bustling with the last trade of the day. A student whirred past Emma on a bike, close enough to clip her as he went by. She debated shouting after him but found herself grinning instead. She was back where she belonged. Lightness flooded through her at the beautiful normality of it all.

As she wandered the stalls, the events since she awoke began to seem like a dream. In her last clear memory, she had been lost after — was it a dinner of some kind? But there had been something else. She had been running. A picture surfaced. Red coats in the dark, faces twisted with hunger. One face more beautiful than the others, but she wasn't going to think about that, about him —

The name sprang from her memory, fully formed.

Turnbulls.

And the memory was all around her now. She tasted the blood in her mouth, heard the boots pounding behind her. Her breaths were ragged plumes of mist as she ran, and ran and ran . . .

She stumbled, and she was not on a dark street but in a sun-warmed square. Her borrowed, too-large boots had tripped her. She came back to herself, breath by breath. And it all made sense now.

That night, wandering the streets in the cold, she must have become ill. Her feverish state could have called up all sorts of wild visions. Like being a fox, of all things. Perhaps the Librarian and his sister really had found her, shivering and delirious, on the street. And if she had memories of them saying strange things about foxes? Well, that would be part of the hallucinations too. But now her fever must have broken. And here she was, back at the heart of normal life. She scurried along the pavement, barely pausing when a lecturer walked straight into her and bounced off, muttering apologies.

Gabriel College glowed in the afternoon sun. Its entrance was always manned by bowler-hatted porters, poised to defend the college from marauding tourists. Emma sprinted past them and tumbled into Front Court, but none of the porters even turned to look.

She was home. The world, which had been making so little sense, righted itself. She let her hand trace the walls as she hurried through the college, the touch of the golden stone an anchor. She only had to reach her staircase in Gabriel Tower, and the nightmare would be over.

She could already imagine the way Nat would squawk with laughter at the visions of her fever dreams and the strange clothes her rescuers had given her. She knew how his brows would snap together when she told him about the Turnbulls, and the horrible hunt through the streets. About Jasper, and how wrong she'd been.

She bounded up the last step. "Nat!" she said, banging on his door.

The silence stretched out eerily. "Nat?"

Her breath came fast and shallow. Someone else's name was above Nat's door. There were, she told herself, reasonable explanations. That none came to mind just now did not, in fact, invalidate their existence. She turned and almost cried out.

Her name was gone. The sign above her room had been painted over in thick black strokes. Emma pushed back her hair with shaking hands.

"I don't understand," she whispered. "I don't, I don't, I — "

She needed her mother's voice. That practical, warm voice that made everything all right. She had to call her.

Wandering from the bell tower, she heard the buzz of voices and cutlery. The Great Hall. This close to dinnertime, it was bound to be heaving with people.

The first person she tapped on the shoulder seemed reluctant to be disturbed. He was a square-shouldered rower type, quietly shoveling protein from plate to mouth with only a book for company. It was only after she'd tapped him three times that he turned around.

He seemed friendly enough when Emma asked to borrow his phone. But then he turned back to his dinner, his phone untouched by his elbow. When Emma tapped his shoulder again, he turned around with the exact same expression of polite inquiry. As though — Emma's stomach dropped — as though he'd never seen her before.

The same thing happened with the next person she tried. And the next. Emma felt panic rising. She returned to the first student. Half hoping that somebody would catch her, that somebody would see her, she snatched the phone from his tray. No one in the dining hall reacted.

The calls wouldn't go through. She dialed the number and then — nothing. She took more phones, from pockets and bags. None of the phones would make a call. Dinner was over by the time she admitted defeat.

She pushed her way out of the college, buffeted by bodies who tried to walk straight through her. Sunset bloodied the face of Granville College. Shadows stretched across the cobbles. It was time for a new plan. She only needed time to think, somewhere quiet and alone. In Market Square, the crowd had thinned. The traders were packing up, stripping the awnings from the stalls. Leaving. They all got to leave and to go home. Where would she go?

Someone collided with Emma with enough force to set her staggering. Her wavering control snapped. The tears lying behind it flooded up. It was only a small hurt, physically. She'd been shoved against a shop window. Her shoulder ached. But that was not what made the sobs rack her chest until she could not breathe. She was crying like a small child: helplessly, hopelessly. Lost on a street corner. Invisible. As though erased from life itself, devoured whole by this Night City, the thing the old woman had spoken about with such fear.

She ducked into one of the alleys that branched, capillary-like, from the bustle of Market Square. It was dark and dank, but it was quiet. Emma put one foot in front of the other and tried to breathe in time with her steps. Her sobs started to slow. She almost felt in control of herself. If she hadn't been so absorbed, she might have noticed sooner.

The snorting came from the shadows behind her.

run run run run

Something moved. Emma ran.

The animal part of her knew in an instant: The thing was behind her and closing the gap. It was fast. Faster than a human. She felt a breath of air rake her back. As if a set of claws hadn't reached quite far enough. Grimly, she set a swifter pace down the alley. The snorting was as loud as a train. If she concentrated, she could place it. Muscles around her ears twitched, as if by habit.

two leaps
four foxlengths
behind
closening
three foxlengths

She could see the end of the alley. A sunny patch. A bench and an old water pump, leaning together like confederates. She sped into the tiny courtyard. Sunlight spilled across her back, sudden and warm. Emma risked a glance behind and fell hard, scraping her palms against stone. Face down, she fought to free her ankle from the water trough she hadn't seen under the pump. It was too late. The thing would be upon her any second.

When no attack came, she looked up. It was there, at the end of the alley, glaring at her. It had stopped a millimeter before the courtyard, where sun and shadow made a sharp dividing line.

It had the head of a boar and the muscled torso of a man. Wickedly sharp tusks sprang from its snout. Two weapons belts crossed its bare chest. Trousers hid its lower half, but Emma couldn't miss the powerful muscles of its thighs.

Its eyes fixed on her, vicious and glinting. It slammed one meaty hand against the alley wall — no hooves, she noted with numb interest, just human nails filed to a point — but still didn't take the single step that would have carried it over the threshold of shadow.

Maybe it couldn't.

Then a cloud crossed the sun, plunging the courtyard into gloom. The boar-man swung one booted leg into the half-light. Triumph gleamed in its eyes. It moved slowly through the lighter shadow in the courtyard, as though wading through water. But still it came, inexorably, toward her. The razor tips of its nails reached for her with yearning. Emma wriggled back on her elbows, her breath coming in gasps.

From somewhere behind, hands wrapped around her arms and lifted her upright.

"Come," murmured a voice in her ear, velvet as summer moss. "This way, and we shall outrun it."

CHAPTER 18

SHE STUMBLED IN THE WAKE OF A BLUR DRESSED IN GREEN, OVER sun-streaked cobbles and around tourist groups. Shops and colleges flashed by, a jostle of bicycles and shopping bags bruising her thighs as they pushed across Scholar's Road. She could see nothing of her rescuer but the outline of a curly beard and a whorl of dark hair. Then the ground sloped, and Emma had to watch her footing. The Sister's boots seemed determined to trip her at every step. Finally, the stranger's pace slowed.

When she next looked up, it was to a familiar view. The river, its banks stirring with winter-browned bracken. The water shone in the dying light, flinging back reflections of bridges and colleges. Emma dropped the stranger's hand and stepped forward into a wash of warmth. At the river's edge, there were no more buildings to stand between them and the last of the westerly sun. She tipped up her face and breathed slowly, until the sear in her chest and tremble in her legs faded.

"And the lady is saved. The beast cannot follow us into the sunlight. We have enough of that here."

Emma turned to find the owner of the velvet voice standing behind her, along with a forest-green tunic and a face made for mischief.

He scraped a bow that managed to be elegant and impertinent at once.

"My lady. The Court is all agog to see you, and here am I " — he caught Emma's hand and lifted it to his lips — "stealing that first honor." He twitched expressive black brows.

Emma suspected he was making fun of her, but it was hard to be cross with anyone so merry-looking. Under walnut skin, his cheeks glowed robin red. A little black beard sprouted from his chin, curling upward. When he smiled, his eyes turned up at the edges too.

"Who are you?"

"Just a well-wisher and a stranger. A mysterious, *handsome* stranger," he corrected himself, all hopeful innocence.

Emma eyed his clothing. No human had worn anything of the kind for several centuries. But Emma's mind had begun to admit — under mounting pressure from the evidence of the last few hours — that the man-shaped being before her might well not be human. She peered closer at his green velvet tunic, noting the tree embroidered across the chest.

"You're . . . a messenger of the Night City," she guessed. "Like the other. You wear the same tunic."

The stranger feigned shock. *What? Me?* Then he tipped her a wink.

"Quite right. You've rumbled me. I am but a humble messenger, not a dashing young courtier fit to win the heart of a lady like yourself. Although I might be a lord in disguise?" he tried.

Emma pressed a shaking hand to her temple. Nothing made sense anymore. Least of all this conversation.

"Why *did* you run from your Court summons, by the way?" the stranger went on. "It was a most original reaction."

"How do you know what I was running from?"

He laughed. "Come. When you fled a City messenger, the alarm spread to all of us at the City's disposal. It is why that beast was sent after you. Not many would resist an invitation to Court."

"I wanted to go home."

"Home? You weren't likely to find that among a pack of mortals — " He looked at her face. "Ah. You come from mortal stock, do you? I was born in the Night City. I sometimes forget that there are other ways into our realm. What a jewel of resourcefulness you are."

He put his head on one side to study her. "How did you manage it? Are you a spellworker? A scholar?"

The sense of unreality washed over Emma again. This stranger spoke as though she belonged to some other world, just as the Sister had. As though the familiar town around her, the colleges and libraries, the bicycles clattering over the cobbles, was some mortal realm she no longer had any part in. It had not escaped her, the name they had both used, with such a similar mixture of pride and fear. The Night City.

"I'm not either of those things. I am — "

What was she? A name, whirling through space. A collection of memories: a mother's hands scented with rosemary, a friend declaiming poetry over coffee, a tower room littered with tables of figures . . .

"I'm — a scientist," she finished with wonder. In a sea of

wavering memories, it was reassuring to find something about herself that felt certain.

"How unusual," the stranger said, sounding delighted.

The sun was lower in the sky than she liked, the shadows like deep bruises. It was too easy to imagine a dark shape looming, and the outline of cruel tusks.

"Could we move? A little? The sunlight's going."

"Even my charm cannot halt nightfall, my lady. Much as I weep at my shortcomings."

"But that monster — "

"Will walk easier as the shadows grow stronger, yes. But I think we may be cunning enough to evade him." Eyes crinkling with mischief, he offered Emma his arm. "Come, O beauteous fugitive. It would be my honor to escort you to safety."

They waded through undergrowth until the riverside wall of Beaufort College loomed above them. It was overgrown with swathes of wisteria, pulsing and pale in the gathering dusk. The stranger heaved aside a swag of vines to uncover a door. The fleshy scent of the wisteria rolled thick into Emma's throat, and her head swam with it. As she passed through the door, she seemed to see strange lights play across the flowers. For a crazed moment, she thought of nothing but drawing closer to those lights, of stretching her tongue to the sweet heady secrets at the base of those flowers.

"Come now, lady."

The stranger's hand on her arm was firm. He towed her away through the Beaufort College gardens. Emma shook her head, clearing the scent. What was her tongue doing outside her mouth? She tucked it away.

"Should they be — doing that? The flowers?"

The lights were still pulsing over the wisteria. She could hear the hum of desire in her mind. Her tongue crept toward her lips.

The stranger spared a glance over his shoulder. "Far be it from me to deny any pleasure of yours, O star among ladies. But there are other enchantments more worth your time."

"Enchantments?"

"That one being more suited to insects and bats."

"But — enchantments?"

"Oh yes." He opened a panel carved into the college wall and bowed her through. "At the fading of the sun, it is not just the monsters that have free rein of the streets. With the dark, the beauties of the Night City also come into their own."

The messenger led her through an earthen passageway and opened an answering panel at the end. Emma stepped out. They had cut through to the corner between Granville College and the Senate House.

Dusk had fallen on the cobbled streets. But above, a strange light shifted across the walls of the colleges and faculty buildings, climbing and swaying like something alive. It was as though the northern lights had fallen from the sky and come to rest in the stones.

Emma watched the play of pinks and greens in awe. "I've never seen anything so — beautiful. It's strange, I always felt something was here. In the streets, the buildings. Calling me, almost. The University's famous for it, that feeling. But I couldn't have imagined this. This light . . ."

"The Night City sits upon the mortal city like a veil of shadow. They share the same streets but not the same qualities.

This light is but one of our beauties. You did not see it when you were mortal?"

Emma shook her head. Then unease flashed through her mind. He had spoken of her mortal self in the past tense. As something gone. And for the first time, she had not argued with the idea. Not even in her head. When had she crossed that invisible threshold?

As they passed Granville College, the statue that guarded its gate — a griffin rampant, with furled wings — moved one stony claw to its nose and gave it a good scratch. Beside it, a group of students strolled on with no sign of having seen.

"*That* never happened before," Emma said emphatically.

"The statues are all such fidgets. I had no idea mortal senses were so dulled."

"How does it work, that glow? I wish I could study it." She swiped her fingers across the college wall. The glow did not rub off. Instead, it fled her touch. "Fascinating. Is it bioluminescent? Like an algae of some kind, or — "

"I hate to disturb, lady. But the beast on your trail is still loose."

"Oh." Emma wiped her fingers on her skirt and hurried after him. "So the Night City is like . . . a layer? On top of the normal city?"

"Beneath it, more like. The mortals who built these streets did so under instruction from the Night City, little though they knew it. And we have pockets all our own, where no mortals can walk."

Somebody collided with Emma. "Sorry, clumsy of me. Cool outfit — you going to the vampire party at Wessex?"

A freckled girl grinned up at her. She was wearing a hockey hoodie, with a laptop bag slung over one shoulder. She was also, unmistakably, from the mortal world. Unlike the students in the

Gabriel dining hall, this one clearly realized Emma existed. The messenger smiled at the girl and nudged Emma on.

Emma tugged him back. "But — she saw me."

"What did you expect?"

"Nobody else did, earlier."

"Ah, but observe. That was in daylight. Now it is dark. Humans can see the folk of our world in the night hours, if we take the trouble to make them. We mostly choose to slip past unnoticed. We do not appear in their gaze as strongly as those of their own world, even in the shadow hours."

Emma filed that away. Another group passed, this time with cloaks and gowns that trailed the pavement. Stubby horns peered from the curls of one figure. Another wore an amethyst gown and a carnival mask. Emma's first thought was that they must be students in fancy dress, going to the party the freckled girl mentioned. Then the gowned figure laughed, and Emma realized that she wore no carnival mask. A gull's beak truly sat across the lower half of her face, where a human mouth and nose would be.

"Now, *those* folk are of our own realm," the messenger whispered.

"You don't say," Emma replied with deadly irony.

They passed an arch where a statue screamed with outstretched arms. Emma watched the statue yawn, shake out her wrists, and return to her pose. She turned to the messenger to remark on it, but he was no longer there. Strangely, he was lounging in a doorway far across the street.

"Well, lady mine, I leave you here," he called.

"You leave me . . . but this is the middle of nowhere."

"Ah. So it is."

The darkness pressed around her. "But — what about the monster?"

"Ah, the monster." The messenger's teeth gleamed in the dark. "I'd suggest you run. That way."

He pointed to a column of light beneath the screaming statue.

"But what — "

Emma turned back. The shadows were empty. He was gone.

Alone in the dark, Emma tried to steel her shaking legs. A sound from the far end of the street made her decision. Not waiting to see if it was the grunt of a boar-man or simply a passing car, she sprinted for the strip of light. Just as she was close enough to see that the light came from an open doorway, her borrowed boots tripped her. She clutched for the doorframe and missed, sprawling into the space beyond.

And the door swung shut behind her.

CHAPTER 19

EMMA PEELED HERSELF FROM THE FLOOR. SPECKS OF GRIT WERE embedded in her cheek. She spat a mouthful of dust and flexed her wrists. Nothing broken, it seemed.

She was in a tiny cell, lit only by slits of light around the door that had slammed behind her. Emma threw herself at it, but it would not budge under her fists. As her eyes adjusted to the dim light, she saw a deeper square of shadow in one corner. It was a flight of stairs, leading underground. With a sinking feeling, Emma recognized the silver shape etched into the first step. The same tree she had seen on the Night City messenger's tunic.

This was a place of the Night City, then. Emma thought of the messenger's smiling assurances and ground her teeth. He had, technically, led her away from the boar-man. Exactly as he promised. *I just never asked where to,* Emma thought. *So he brought me exactly where the Night City wanted me in the first place.*

But there were no uniformed messengers here, no chains, no one forcing her through dark passages to a dungeon. Just the staircase leading into the earth. There was nowhere else to go.

The staircase ran so deep, roots grew down the walls. Down and down went the spiral, until Emma's breath was a hypnotic wave in her ears, the thud of her feet on the steps her only mark of time. At last, the stairs ended. Emma came out into an earthen passage, its walls streaked with glowing minerals. She stretched out a hand and felt dirt crumble beneath her fingertips. Her mind began to slide back into focus. The wall was real. The boar-man had been real. Perhaps everything the Sister and the messenger had told her was real too. That she was not a mortal; she was — something else. That the Night City wanted her for something. That the consequences would not be a dream she could wake up from.

Emma felt panic lock her lungs. She steadied herself against the wall. This was not a death sentence. She was alive, and free to wander. She would think of it as an opportunity for information. If she could find out how and why this had happened to her, then she could find out how to undo it. She pushed herself upright, balling her hands into fists.

To one side, the passage was cobwebbed and dank, with a single door. But the other end of the passage glowed gold. Emma blinked, blinded by pearlescent light, and saw in the distance a great gilded hall, held up by living trees of gold and silver. Fruits carved from gemstones dripped from the branches. Beneath, music floated over a crowd dressed as brightly as a bower of spring flowers, their laughter tinkling like bells.

"Oh," Emma breathed. Was this what she had been summoned to? The Court of the Night City. She could not think why she had been so afraid. It was beautiful. And she would be beautiful within it. The music would run through her like rivulets of sunlight, and she would dance. Her feet were already servants to the melody. They sped faster, faster, toward the golden hall.

But the harder she ran, the farther the shimmering court retreated. The golden hall became a pinpoint of light beyond a corridor that stretched into infinity. Winded, Emma braced her hands on her knees. The passageway did not want her to get to the golden hall, that much was clear. What, then, did it want? When Emma raised her head, the answer seemed to be looking straight at her. The single door she had seen in the cobwebbed corridor was right before her, as though daring her to open it. Squat, carved with fanciful figures of beasts and people, knobbed with a handle of raw crystal.

Emma turned the handle cautiously. The chamber beyond was octagonal, lit by a strange cold light. Five plinths stood at its center, holding five glinting objects. But there was nothing else. The room did not lead deeper into the Court, where she might overhear useful information. She shut the door. Luckily, there were suddenly more to try; they now stretched down the cobwebbed passage.

Emma tried one on the opposite side. Impossibly, it, too, opened on the octagonal room. Emma huffed out a breath, half grump, half laugh. Stubbornly, she reached for the next door, and the next. The octagonal room looked back at her every time. The corridor clearly had an opinion. In some ways, she was glad of the game. Grateful for the bite of her frustration. It kept the cold, oily well of fear tamped down far enough to ignore it.

"You're going to keep me here forever, is that it?" Emma tilted her face up to the ceiling. "Really? Until I go mad?"

As if in response, the crystal-knobbed door appeared again on the opposite wall. Suggestively. Emma kept walking. The door kept pace with her, always a step behind.

"It's not a choice if you're not given any other options," she complained to the air.

The door slowed, almost hopefully, as her steps did.

"Fine," she muttered. "If you insist."

The crystal knob gleamed under her hand. As Emma stepped into the clear, strange light of the octagonal room, her skin puckered with shivers. She edged toward the pedestals and their tiny glittering objects. Perhaps there was a key there, one that would let her leave the endless loop of corridor and doors, and she was meant to find it.

Something crunched underfoot. Emma felt her muscles clench. *Just a chip of stone*, she told herself. *See how old this room is? Crumbling at the edges, ancient mortar. A chip of stone, or an old twig, or—*

It was a bone, cracked under the Sister's borrowed boot. Emma's eyes followed it. A slant-jawed skeleton yawned from the wall behind. The bones were bleached with age; whoever it was had been slumped against the wall for some centuries. Emma backed away blindly, groping for the door. It had disappeared. There was no way out. It was too cruel. She had been lured here, just to be buried alive.

"Mind yourself," said a voice. It was a scratchy sort of croak, and when Emma whirled to face it, she found a figure with an appearance to match.

It was a wizened creature as tall as her waist, with skin in tones of mushroom and moss. Its fingers were long and seemed to have a few too many joints. Her eyes lingered on the needle-sharp nails, the same length again as those fingers. The creature fanned these as it spoke, running them like little flaying knives across the skin of the air.

"So, there you are." Slightly-too-large black eyes gleamed up at Emma. "Took you long enough."

Emma squared up to it. "I'm not going to just let you kill me." Despite her best efforts, her voice was shaking. "So, it's in your best interest to make a deal with me."

"Kill you?" The creature tilted its head. A membrane snapped across its eyes and away again. It seemed to be blinking. Like a snake, or a bird of prey, Emma thought. "That is not my purpose."

"Your purpose?"

"This little once-a-mortal made a bargain with the Night City. And for bargain made must price be paid," the creature said in a singsong croak.

"I didn't make one," Emma protested. "It was an accident, I didn't mean to — "

"All who enter have made a bargain. Their own words, of their own free will. The Room of Choosing would not have admitted you otherwise. Let us see what this little one has asked for."

Emma went still. Razor-sharp nails roved over her skin, close enough to slash.

"You were running," the creature said. "Hunters in the night. Help, you cried out."

The memory formed around her. The air was ice. There was blood in her mouth.

"*help,*" *she cried out, but her breath was gone and her voice*
    would not come
they are hunting
please oh please help
help me run help me hide
they are hunting the fox i am the fox

"There, little once-a-mortal. You see? Your bargain. An unusual one, indeed."

"That? *That* was my bargain? But I never asked — I didn't know — "

But she had. She had felt it there, in the memory. The listening dark pressing from all sides, like blades wrapped in velvet, as she ran and begged.

help me hide
i am the fox

She was shaking. Oh, it was a cruel way to interpret what she had said. What she had thought.

"The Night City made me a fox. It helped me hide." Her voice trembled. "But why did it listen to me? I didn't mean it."

The creature grinned. "You were in need. You opened the way with blood. There are rules about these things. The Night City had to listen."

Blood. The cut on her hand, spilling spatters of red to the cobbles. Jasper's blood, shining wet on her nails. She had opened the way.

"So I did this. I made the bargain."

"And when a little mortal makes such a bargain with the Night City, they must pay for what they receive." The creature fanned its nails luxuriantly. "But so generous is the Night City, it blesses these fortunate ones with immortality, so they may work off their debt. One mere hundred years of service, and they are freed."

One hundred years. Emma's throat constricted.

"With still greater kindness, the Night City grants every debtor the freedom to choose: how they may serve, and which of the Lower Houses they shall enter. And so they are sent here, to the Room of Choosing."

"To you. And your wisdom," said Emma, trying a smile. It seemed worthwhile to charm the creature. There might yet be some way to turn its friendliness to her advantage, if she could but spot it.

The creature's eyes crinkled in return. "Indeed."

"And there is no other way?" Emma wheedled.

"If you had some great talent that pleased the City, it might have taken you into the Court itself instead. Do you?"

Emma had to admit she did not. She even managed a rueful laugh.

This seemed to please the creature. "Fear not, little once-a-mortal. I shall steer you aright."

It drew itself up to its full height and puffed out its chest, clearly ready to perform:

"Debtor, for the City's payment
You must choose which way is yours.
One joyous gift of beastly raiment,
One servant's task, one house of four."

The creature folded its hands modestly. Applause was obviously expected, and Emma did not stint. The creature glowed.

"I wonder, wise one," Emma ventured. "A 'gift of beastly raiment,' you said. So when I choose, I transform? Into a beast. A certain beast for each 'house,' " she said, watching the creature's face. It seemed to be willing her along. "Do I stay that way? As an animal?"

"Raiment" — the creature eyed her significantly — "is something that may be put on and taken off at will. But I cannot say more."

"I already was a beast," said Emma. "But I didn't get to take it off."

"Yes." It tilted its head to study her. "You have already worn another skin. Which makes you strange, you know. None of the other once-a-mortals here have been like you. Their bargains asked for wealth or freedom or beauty. They came to this room weeping, the bodies they were born with all they had ever known. They could not imagine the joys of a new form." Emma thought she heard warmth enter the scraping voice. "But you—you alone asked for transformation as your gift. A year and a day in another form. A true nightdweller's choice. As though within, you already belonged among us. Never before has it happened this way."

"Belonged?" Was that true? Had there always been some part of her that beat with the pulse of the Night City?

"Night is the time of change, little once-a-mortal. Daylight fixes the world in place. To be seen is to be trapped in another's eye, is it not? Known only as the shape they perceive. But unseen in darkness, things are free to shift. And so darkness reveals the true nature of things."

"What does that make my true nature, then? A fox?"

Curiously, the creature chuckled. "As though she were meant to be among us," it muttered, turning to the pillars at the center of the room. "I've never seen the like."

"What is that supposed to mean?"

The creature cleared its throat, a sound like a rusty garden chair unfolding. "It does not matter. For the City's rules are firm. All who come to this room must have free choice of their Lower House and their beastly form. No matter what their bargain may have been. So you must choose your way."

The needle nails waved Emma toward the pedestals. Five objects hovered above them.

Emma looked along the row. "And what are these? The choices?"

"A test. The little once-a-mortal must enter the Lower House most suited to her. The shape that calls to her inner nature."

There was a black feather, carved from iridescent obsidian. On the next pillar, a perfect crystalline droplet. Trapped within, Emma saw a fin like a delicate fan. The central pedestal held a ball of pure light, pulsing like a small and furious sun. After that was a strange, twisted golden square of four points. Emma leaned closer. Teeth. Four of them, two short, two long, molded from dull gold. *Rodent,* a voice in her brain insisted, although she could not ferret out the memory to back it up. She stopped at the last in the row. A curved amber claw, its ridges picked out in copper. It glowed with a warmth that did not belong to the cold chamber, as if a fire blazed at its heart.

Emma's fingers crept toward it. "This is a fox claw. I remember this. How it felt." Slashing the air. Sharp under moonlight. Emma looked down at the creature. "I was a fox. Does that mean I have to choose this?"

"You have indeed lived as a fox, by your own bargain. But that need not be your choice forever. If another of the Lower Houses might suit you better, then you have now the chance to choose: to change your path. This is your test."

"And if I don't choose at all? Am I free to do that?"

"Oh, yes. You remain here." The creature jerked a needle-nailed finger at the skeleton in the corner. "As this one did. A monk." The creature shook its head in disgust. "Always praying and moaning. I think it enjoyed dying, although it took a long time about it. No others refused, or not for long."

Emma refused to give in to the stab of fear in her chest. A choice had to be made, then. Her future depended on it. But one of these Lower Houses might offer a better chance of escape than the rest. She just had to find out which one.

"Someone as clever as you must know all about these Lower Houses."

The creature tilted its head to one side, flattered. "All who enter the Room of Choosing may hear the riddle. Should you care to?"

Emma nodded, and the creature puffed out its chest once more:

"Which beastly skin shall wrap your own?
Which Lower House, which service owed?
First, with coat of amber burning
Might ye skim of mortal fires;
Or nightwinged, eyes on shadows turning,
Unveil secrets from on high;
Perhaps by magic's pathways minding
Could ye snake the river's bends;
Or long of tooth, with steady grinding
May ye serve the City's ends.
One hundred years shall lap time's shore
Till unbound shall ye be once more."

"And this is telling me about my choices? The things on these pillars, and what they mean?"

"I can perform it again," the creature said hopefully. "If you didn't get it all the first time."

"Please." Emma smiled winningly. "You declaimed it so well. The greatest mortal actor could not have half so much skill."

The creature swelled, whisking its needle nails together in a pleased-sounding susurration.

"If you insist," it said with pride.

In the end, Emma coaxed it to repeat the puzzle three times.

"So: *coat of amber burning*. The fox claw. I take it and become a fox again."

The creature crowed.

"The obsidian feather. That's the *nightwinged eyes*. Crow?"

"Not allowed to give clues," it said. "The other once-a-mortals didn't get them. Not allowed to have favorites." But it winked at Emma and shook its head broadly.

"Not crow? Similar, then . . . raven?"

The creature grinned.

The fin in the crystalline drop stumped her, and led to many pantomimed headshakings from the creature as her guesses missed the mark.

"*Snaking through the river's bends* — but I've gone through the fish I can remember." Her memories were still a blur, that was the problem. "Unless — it's not a regular fish at all? *Snaking*. Eel — is it an eel?"

The creature was almost hopping up and down with excitement.

The teeth were much easier to guess. "Rat," she said, and that was that.

"House of Foxes, House of Ravens,
House of Rats and House of Eels:
Each Lower House owes loyal labor.
And one of them your choice shall be!"

chanted the creature, clearly in high spirits.

What would it be like to fly? To breach the clouds with her wings? To breathe under water and tumble through the silken currents of the river? It shouldn't have meant much, not beneath the shadow of a hundred years' servitude. Besides, she had just regained her own shape. The itch of an unasked-for fox pelt still rippled across her skin. She ought not to have felt anything like a thrill in her fingertips, in the veins of her chest. But from the few memories of mortal life that had returned, she knew herself. Knew that to see the world in an animal's form, to live among them and know their secrets, was a dream closer to the essence of who she was than anything else. But something obvious was nagging at her.

"Four houses," she said. "Five pedestals. What of the glowing ball? You missed it. What choice is that?"

The translucent film flickered over the creature's eyes: once, twice more.

"Ah, that," it said carefully. "That is a different choice. By this choice, you will be made mortal."

"Mortal?" Emma's head swung to the pedestal.

But the little creature hopped in front of her, nails shivering like striplings in a gale.

"Those who walk the path of power
Wear the gift of mortal skin:

They shall owe no gift of service,
But only that which lies within."

Emma gazed at the ball, lost in the swirl of its fires. Mortal again. No hundred years of service. She saw her hand closing around it, saw the fire leaking through her veins, scouring them of whatever strange magic the Night City had touched her with. She saw home.

The sound of the creature's nails reached a clashing crescendo. It was almost vibrating with the effort to keep its mouth shut.

"It's too good to be true, isn't it?" Emma said.

The creature let out a great breath, and its nails stilled. It nodded.

"What's within a mortal, then? Ah." And she saw it. It was so simple, it was tragic. "Mortality. You give what you contain. Everything that you are. And you're gone. A far higher price than a hundred years of service. A trick."

The creature nodded. She paced before the pedestals. "So my choices are here."

She'd never had a wish to be a rat; still less, to serve with *steady grinding*. But Ravens *unveiled secrets* with *eyes on shadows*. Sentries, perhaps. Was she not cunning and quiet? She had lain in wait watching animals often enough in her mortal life. She might make a good sentry.

And Eels *minded magic's pathways*. She liked thinking of herself as a guardian. Swirling around the same bends in the river as the otters she had loved. She might see the walls of Gabriel College there. Or watch her friend sitting on the bank, refracted through the water's surface. Julia. Emma stretched her hand for the droplet.

She could not take it. A call in her mind stilled her fingers. Emma turned to the amber claw. It glowed with the warmth of a secret spilled, with the light of a winter's fire. She pictured jaws strong with teeth. A pelt, rough and cozy. A song from her throat, piercing the sky. And it felt like something known. A part of her that had always been there, waiting for the fire spark of fox fur to unfurl.

And a phrase from the riddle came back: *skimming mortal fires.* Whatever service the foxes performed, they were close to mortals. If she did not escape, if she had to serve a hundred years — Emma pushed down the screaming in her mind at the thought of it — she could not bear it without sight of her friends. Nat, a strong memory: bright with music and laughter and the sting of chili on her tongue. Julia, a quieter note, winding through her clouded memories like a ribbon of pale silk. If she could only be near them, she would survive.

"I've chosen," she said. "The House of Foxes."

She reached for the claw. Once more a fox. But this would not be like her cold, panicked run through the streets, fear sweat clouding her eyes. This time, it was a choice. She knew what would come.

How her smooth skin, plucked and shaved to the hairlessness so pleasing to humans, would change. Coarse hairs would sprout through her pores, a thicket against invaders. No hint of camouflage. She would be red, only red. A blazing warning to predators: *Touch me, and you will burn.*

Her softness would go. The curves of her breasts, the small belly like a cushioned pear, the spread of her thighs. Lost. Winnowed into the lean tension of a fox frame, a coiled spring made flesh. Her long, sturdy legs would shrink, shedding the strength she had built from years of hiking with her mother or climbing the steps of Gabriel Tower. So much of herself lost with that woman's shape.

But she would be fierce. Her jaws would rend; her claws would tear. She would dance, copper armored under the moon, a huntress in the night. Was that not something she had always longed for, deep down? The Emma that would be, if only she could shed her skin of fear and niceness. Running free through the streets. Elemental. Beastly. Alive.

Emma's hand closed around the claw. Heat streaked up her arm and settled like a heavy cloak, falling over shoulders, waist, head. Her ears were full of noise. Joyful barks bounced around her skull until Emma could not think, until she felt her lips pull back and her throat echo the cry. She fell, and the stone chamber became vast around her. Her nose twitched, now a bright, damp blackberry at the end of a long snout. Every particle of scent sang to her of its source. And through it all, a russet voice frisked through her mind.

we are fox
so quick so clever
blood on claw and jaw

Emma balked. She had been trapped with just such a voice, in a fox form that had been a prison. It had eaten her whole. She could not lose herself again. Emma gasped in a breath, and her senses flooded back. She was bent over, girl hands braced on girl thighs. No longer fox-shaped.

She had not been trapped. This fox form was a choice, not a prison. Emma forced her breathing to slow. The amber claw pulsed firefly bright in her palm, then crumbled into glowing particles that sank beneath her skin. She felt the change, beneath the workings of her mind. The barest whisper of the fox voice. A brush of autumn leaves, skittering in the wind of her thoughts.

"Fox maiden." The creature looked her up and down with approval. "The test has spoken true."

It waved. The stone wall fizzed, and a door pushed its way through.

"The Night's luck go with you, little once-a-mortal." There was warmth in the rasping voice. It had been kind to her, she thought.

Emma turned with thanks on her lips, and stumbled back in horror. Reality was stretching, creature and pedestals and walls sliding together like strands of dough. The room was collapsing on itself. In another moment, the walls would fold entirely and take her with them. Already, the force of it was pulling her inward. Emma clawed through the rippling world for the door. She pulled it open and threw herself through.

CHAPTER 20

EMMA STUMBLED FORWARD, DIZZY AND SICK. FOX SONG COURSED through her blood, chiming against her bones like a knife drawn across marble. Emma reached her hands behind, thinking to steady herself against the door. There was nothing at her back but a wall of earth. She wiped her fingers on her borrowed cloak, and her vision at last steadied itself.

She was in a sparse room. A jug and basin stood next to a dressing screen. Cracks spiderwebbed the mirror, and the rows of cloaks and boots along the wall were old and worn. There were two chipped chairs before a fire. And there, on one of them, sat a figure with wild gray hair and a tapping foot.

"So there you are." The Librarian's sister hauled herself up. She clasped Emma's shoulder with a warm, calloused hand. "You've scuffed up my boots, girl."

For a moment, Emma wondered if her tumble through the door had scrambled her mind. She could not imagine how the Sister had come to be in front of her. Or why the old woman looked entirely unsurprised, when the shock was coursing through Emma's body like an ice-cold shower. "How are you here? What is this?"

"It's where I was told to wait for you. You've an ordeal in front of you, girl, I won't lie."

"An ordeal? What's — "

"Answers soon. We're to rest here first, so you'll be ready." She waved Emma to the chairs.

Emma sank into one with relief. "You're not afraid I'll run away again?"

The Sister barked a laugh. "Did it do you any good to run, hmm? What did you learn out there?"

"I can't be seen by mortals. They don't hear me; they can't remember me. After dark it seems easier, but — I'm still not like them. Not anymore."

She told the Sister of the boar-headed monster that had hunted her. Of the emptiness she had felt, wandering the streets unseen.

"And with what you saw, do you want to run away again?"

"There's nowhere for me to go, is there? My old life is gone." As the words hung, trembling, in the air, Emma realized she could not take them back. Grief hit her with a force that made tears impossible. Crying would have been a relief. Instead, her eyes burned, dry as cracks in the savannah.

To her surprise, the Sister pulled her into a hug.

"I know what it is to be lost to the world, girl," she whispered fiercely. "I'll not tell you to forget your mortal life all at once. I've not managed it. But you must start again. You cannot spend your life yearning for what is gone."

Emma gave way to sobs at last: ugly, body-wracking ones. The

Sister stroked her hair and made gruff soothing noises. "So you met one of the Boars, did you? Seems extreme to send one after you for a simple summons. But nothing is simple these days, I suppose."

"What are they?"

"When the City's laws are broken, the Boars are sent after the offenders. May you never spend time in their cells, girl."

It had not been civic duty that made the thing's cruel eyes light up. It had wanted to hurt her. The fact it had an official role made the bile rise in her throat. What kind of place was this City, having predators as lawkeepers?

A squat figure in an apron bumped the door open. Her cheeks had the moist green-brown spotting of a frog. "So that one's for the Oath? You be sure she's ready. They'll be sending for her soon."

The frog-servant spun on her heel. She let the door bang behind her.

"Calling you now?" the Sister growled. "Oh, that's the Court for you. *They* can spend two hundred years of their immortal lives composing an ode to the moss beneath a toadstool, but *this* they want done immediately. We need more time . . ."

"Calling me for what?"

"The Oath. A swearing-in ritual of sorts, now that you've chosen a house." The Sister's mouth twisted, as though she would have said more but had stopped herself.

"My house." Emma uncurled her palm. The fox claw was gone, though a trace of its warmth lingered on her skin. "The House of Foxes. I chose it."

"A house I know well." There was affection in the Sister's voice. "My brother and I have plenty of dealings with the fox maidens. I should think you'll like them." She pulled writing materials from

192

her belt-purse and dashed off a note. "I shall send my brother to bring them, since you'll need sponsors for your Oath."

She winced as she rose to hand the note to a servant outside the door.

"This Oath." Emma pictured a knife slicing her palm. A brand pressed to her flesh. Fear curled in her belly. "Do I have to?"

"Your house cannot take you in, not until you are sworn to the City. Once you take the Oath, you are a citizen and protected by the City. Those who do not, live the dregs of a life at the outskirts. Preyed upon by whatever monsters are off their leash that night. It's no life, girl."

A small foot nudged open the door. A diminutive creature blinked at them, one whose eyes were too large for her face and strangely far apart. The twitching velvety ears of a wild hare rose from her cap. "If you please, miss? I'm to see to you."

Within moments she hauled in a steaming jug that dwarfed her. She steered Emma to the basin, peeled off her cloak, and tugged at Emma's waistband with tiny paw-hands traced with puffs of fur. Emma squeaked.

"Don't raise a fuss, miss, and let me take your clothes off proper. I have to get you scrubbed. You've half the muck of the streets on you, by the look of it."

Emma submitted, and soon stood shivering behind the dressing screen. The servant dipped cloth after cloth into the basin and scrubbed Emma's skin until it glowed. Emma looked down at her body.

It was her own, down to the last scar and freckle. But it was also new. The outlines of it were sharper, somehow. Her skin had a sheen to it. And her limbs felt loose in a way she didn't recognize, as though she were made from a different material.

"So what is she?" the servant said.

"Fox maiden," the Sister answered.

The servant wrapped a sheet around Emma, taking a good look at her as she did.

"The House of Foxes? But she's got no collar. I thought she might be one of the Upper Houses — she's so tall, you could take her for a noble. Will-o'-the-wisp blood or the like. Not that there's anythink wrong with the Lower Houses, mind. My own cousin's girl went into the House of Ravens, seeing as her father got into a spot of debt, and it's only stiff-rumped folk that're funny about it, these days."

She held up a hank of Emma's hair with an expert squint. "Nice wave you have. I can do it proper for you, if you like. The Dawn Rose style, maybe? It's the most popular with the nobles. But — it's maybe not fitting for you. We barely see the Lower Houses at Court, so I don't know. Don't want them officials thinking you're reaching above your station."

Before Emma could wonder how low, exactly, her station was that a mere hairstyle could overreach it, the maidservant bent her over the basin and began rinsing the dust from her hair. Through the sodden strands, Emma heard her peppering the Sister with questions. "Is it true you work in the Library? Do you really get to see mortals? Up close, in the daytime? Did you ever . . . touch one?"

"I do. That one you're washing *was* a mortal, not too long ago."

"No, truly? Born mortal and everything? Not a curse or the like? I heard the City made the lordling of one Upper House a mortal for a week and a day, and he came back pale and thin as a spider's thread. You lived as one for . . ."

"Nineteen years," said Emma, into the basin, fighting to keep her face expressionless even as her heart sped. Someone had been turned mortal. As a punishment, no less. So there was a way to reverse what had happened to her. To go home.

"Well, you must be glad as anythink to be here now. Mortal for nineteen years, imagine . . ." She ran a scented paste over Emma's hair, and the strands fell to Emma's neck in waves, shiny and dry.

Emma did not answer. She was staring at the looking glass. If nothing else convinced her she was no longer mortal, her reflection would have. Her face had changed, honed into cold perfection. It was an inhuman beauty. Dark hair tumbled from her brow like the sea under moonlight. Her lips were red as dark fruit; her lashes and brows, crow's-wing black. Her eyes were pools of liquid night. Tiny glints lit their depths, like cold stars winking in the deep.

"No fussing with the hair, now." The maid interrupted her thoughts. "I hope it goes well for you, miss, with the Oath. It'll all be over quick, either way."

With that reassuring utterance, she tripped from the room. The door clicked shut behind her. And Emma sat down to marinate in her own uncomfortable thoughts. She barely registered the door opening again and the Librarian shuffling in. Not even as two foxes padded past him.

Then the foxes disappeared in a swirl of copper fur. And that absolutely did hold Emma's attention. She fought the impulse to rub her eyes like a yokel, staring at the two upright figures where the foxes had been. At first glance, Emma would have called them girls. Then she wasn't sure. *Girl* was such a human word. The sheen to their skin was too perfect; the harmony of their fine bones and bitten-red lips too uncanny. They wore broad silver chokers, each engraved with a curved claw. She recognized in them the same strange beauty that had stolen her breath in her own reflection.

One of the pair stepped forward. She was an unnervingly pretty girl — *girl?* Emma wondered again — with bouncy auburn hair around a narrow face. Her little nose was dusted with freckles.

"I'm Nancy. I hear you've a story and a half."

Emma couldn't help smiling back.

"We've not had a new fox maiden for decades. We're a tight little clan, the House of Foxes. Just eight of us, if you'll believe, but we make it work. You'll fit right in. Saskia," Nancy called back. "Come meet the new girl." And, in an undertone Emma suspected was not meant for her: "*Be nice.*"

The other fox maiden straightened from helping the Librarian into a seat and stalked over. Her trousers bristled with buckles and ended in well-worn combat boots. She leaned back on one hip, arms crossed. The look she gave Emma was ambivalent in the extreme.

"Hi," she said eventually.

Saskia's hair was an explosion of spikes, standing straight out in jet-black glory. She'd shaved the sides, leaving a layer of soft stubble. Within a ring of eyeliner, her eyes were fiercely, deeply blue. Emma took in the high cheekbones and diamond jawline, the layers of leather and studs.

She looked Emma over. "You were trapped as a fox? Brutal."

"That didn't happen to you?"

Nancy squeezed her arm. "Night above, no."

Emma's breath came faster. "So what happens next?"

Saskia winced and pulled at her silver choker. It was cutting into her skin. The closer Emma looked, the less it looked like a necklace. There was no clasp, no way to unfasten it. It was more like a collar.

The Sister sighed. "Where to begin? Easier to start with the basics, perhaps. The Night City is a power, girl. Intelligent, ingrained in the earth around us. It has always existed in this stretch of land, if the records do not lie. Our hidden world grew around it. Ancient mortals worshipped it. Later ones built their town and their University on top of it. Mortals have been calling on the power of the City for centuries, most without even knowing. The inspirations and discoveries that make the University famous? All drawn from the City's power — for a price. And the mortals do pay, little though they know it. You follow, girl? Over centuries, more mortals came, and the City's power grew. It surrounded itself with its Court, laid down its laws. As citizens, we live under its protection. In return, we must pledge our loyalty. The Oath is the rite that binds you to the City, so its power can live in you."

"Will it hurt? Is it — dangerous?"

The Librarian's hand was on her arm, gentle as a landing dove. "We will be with you, child."

The little servant was at the door. "Mistress? The tailors've sent word. Her things're ready. Should we have the Boars come to guard her?"

"No, please. I can do all that is necessary." The Sister drew out the silver chain Emma had seen earlier. "Your wrist, Emma?" She lowered her voice. "You trust I will not harm you, girl?"

The silver chain snaked around Emma's wrists like a living thing, sealing itself in a shining circle. The Sister held the other end and tugged her forward.

Emma tried not to imagine her progress through the corridors as a walk to the scaffold. She looked around, determined on distraction. This part of the servants' halls was busier. She saw a flurry of white-aproned maids, whose feet peeped from under their hems in an unexpected variety of hoofs, talons, and paws. Sweating footmen hefted platters, four men to a dish, that held strange confections: a spun-sugar swan with a golden beak; an improbably tall tower of tomatoes that hummed with a chorus of small voices; and a meat roast they had dressed to look like a winged dragon. The roast bent its head to spit a shower of sparks onto the nearest footman. He patted frantically at the singed patches on his moss-colored wig and livery.

Emma slowed to stare, but the Librarian nudged her onward.

"It would be well not to show your surprise, child. The Court has a liking for tender meat. Let them not find it in you."

Emma shivered and schooled her face to stillness.

The tailor's chambers were vast: at least nine dressing platforms, and rack upon rack of dresses and doublets. All in plain, sturdy cloth and sensible colors. Servant's colors.

Emma stood with arms stretched on her dressing platform, as a seamstress tugged a dull brown gown into place. She peered to the side. The Sister, the Librarian, and the fox maidens were huddled in conference at the door, out of earshot.

Emma kept her voice low. "Make the bodice loose and the hem shorter. No, even shorter than that. Above the boot."

The seamstress grunted and knelt. She made quick work of the seam, even with one hand shaped like an eagle's talon. Emma twisted and found she could move freely. Now this was a dress she could run in.

"Turn," the seamstress croaked, and Emma obeyed.

A voice rang across the room.

"I am sent for the fox maiden. All is prepared for the Oath."

At the sight of a green tunic, her heart leapt. But it was not her messenger. It was another, who looked her over with a bored expression. Emma clenched her hands and found them slick with sweat. It was time.

The seamstress twitched a last seam into place. "All done. Just needs the final touch. This." She held out a charming little shell on a chain. Her eyes gleamed.

"With your dark hair — oh, it would be the Night's own beauty on you. If you had this, you'd look so pretty, no one'd hear a word you say."

Emma looked at the shell dangling from her claw. She had never seen a necklace so delicate. She could almost feel how it would warm against her skin.

"I think only my gown is paid for."

The seamstress's laugh was a caw. "No need for coin. Something from me to you. Go on, take it."

Emma stretched out her hand. Steps sounded behind her, and her wrist was knocked aside.

The Sister stood there, gray hair in snarls around her shoulders. "Be off," she growled at the seamstress.

The creature scuttled away, with a nasty smile for Emma. "Can't blame me for trying."

Emma's arm dropped to her side. "What was that?"

"That, girl, was you being a mortal-addled fool. Everything has a price in the Night City. Remember that."

The Sister's good eye was steady and clear. "City dwellers do not give, as a rule. Almost always, a gift they offer will be a bargain in disguise. And the worse for it. You're lucky I overheard, before that harpy tricked you into giving your voice away for a bauble."

"My voice?" Emma's hands flew to her throat.

"Oh, it was cleverly worded. All the better to hide the trap. Words are weapons here, girl. Be on your guard."

Emma rewound the seamstress's words as she was marched from the tailor's, her wrists bound by the Sister's silver chain. *If you had this, you'd look so pretty, no one'd hear a word you say.* Cleverly worded indeed.

The messenger had been the same. There was a trick to this world, she realized. The precise words chosen. The ones left unsaid. Every sentence a web to catch the unwary. And she would not survive if she stayed the person she had been. So trusting, so happy to follow. Whatever the ordeal to come, she would have to match cunning with cunning. To lay out words like hunters' snares. And if the thought of it clawed at her like grief, what then? She would not be their prey. So she would have to be their equal.

The Sister flicked the silver chain. It uncoiled from Emma's wrists and slithered back to the Sister's purse. They had halted before a wood-paneled chamber. Inside, figures in robes and fluffy green wigs flurried around. Wax seals and gavels lay strewn across desks.

The messenger led them to a corner. The sheep-faced clerk there glanced up with such boredom, Emma's racing heart slowed. This was hardly the look of someone expecting to lead a dark ceremony. There were no burning brands on the desk, no goblets of blood. Just a pile of papers. The clerk pushed a stack over to Emma.

"Say this."

Emma bent over the parchment. The top sheet had a few lines written in large script. But underneath were many more pages, packed with tiny text.

"What about the rest?"

"That is merely the details of the contract. The only piece you need to say is here."

"No, I want to read it. The whole thing."

The clerk spluttered. "You have the right, but — "

Emma ignored them and stooped over the contract. The language was almost impenetrable, but flashes of meaning gleamed out between clauses. She blessed her diligent, determined law lecturers. Despite her best efforts, they seemed to have taught her something. She managed to decipher some terms of her service.

She was swearing loyalty to the Night City and obedience to its laws. She must abide within the City and never leave. In return she was to receive her rights as a citizen, and a new life as a fox maiden. She read that fox maidens earned their wages as huntresses for the Night City. She would have a wage, then. That was a relief, knowing she might have something of her own to trade with, or perhaps to bribe her way out. It was difficult to tell what form those earnings would take, and what the hunting duties entailed. The language became obscure, laced with complex references to payment and debt.

Emma let the last sheet fall. The terms bound her to the Night City and to the House of Foxes, on pain of death. The word "eternity" had appeared several times.

Emma bit the inside of her cheek. She had to choose a path. She'd never done it when she was mortal, when it should have been easy. She had lived where her mother had taken her and moved when she was told. She had changed her degree at the University at her father's insistence and stayed on a course she hated, too afraid to choose for herself. Now she had a decision. Under her hand, the words that would seal an eternity of service. Outside, a life of running from monsters in the shadows, never safe enough to rest.

She could crumble, or she could decide. That whatever she chose, she would have the strength to find her way back to her mortal life. The contract in front of her was only words, after all. And words were malleable things. She could spin them to her advantage, just as the creatures here did. It was a strange feeling, the certainty that coursed through her. She had never thought anyone would believe in her — least of all, herself.

Emma picked up the parchment. She got the first line out with only a slight waver.

"I pledge myself to the service of the Night City."

The clerk rose, a tab of silver in their hands. They pressed it to Emma's neck, and the metal slid around it, a molten snake. The pain was instant. Light flared from her throat.

"I—I pledge myself to the House of Foxes," she continued. She had to force the words. The collar was a vise. Agony seared her skin, until she could no longer tell which part of her screamed at its touch. Colors danced before her eyes. She would die of it, she was sure. She struggled upright, fighting her spine's cries to curl in on itself. She spat the final phrase.

"I am Emma Curran.

"By my will

"This contract is sealed."

As quick as it had arrived, it was gone. The pain, the screaming in her blood. The collar lay around her neck, quiet and cool to the touch.

The doors to the chamber crashed open, hard enough to splinter.

Four boar-men shoved through the entryway. With them was the tailor. Pointing at Emma.

"That's her."

Emma's lips had peeled from her teeth. A hissing came from her throat. The Boars were knocking clerks aside, gavels and quills flying, clearing a path to her. She leapt for the nearest desk, papers scattering beneath her scrabbling limbs. But unseen hands dragged her back, legs flailing, arms scratching at anything she could find.

bite them claw them kill they will kill

"Unhand her." The Sister's voice cut through the hubbub. "What is the meaning of this?"

A growl burst from Emma's throat, rising to a screech. Two Boars had her, one on either side.

trapped
hurt them bite
blood on claws and jaws

"She is being taken to trial," said the tailor.

"Trial?" the Sister growled. "For what? By whose order?"

"The Judge decides her fate." The tailor cackled.

The Librarian stood stricken. Behind him, Saskia and Nancy scrabbled through their pockets.

"We don't have enough." Saskia sprang into motion. "I'll run back to the House of Foxes. Enough coin there for a bribe — to keep her from the cells, at least."

The Boars almost had Emma to the door. Close up, a stink rolled off them: sweat-grimed leather, the undertone of old blood. The fox's voice was a shriek in her mind.

hunters
they will kill
they will kill

"Emma!" The Sister was jogging alongside. "Say nothing. We will follow to the courtroom. But you must not — "

Emma could not hear the rest. The Boars shoved the Sister against the chamber door and dragged Emma backward. She bucked against their hold. No matter how she kicked, her feet only slithered across the smooth stone floor. On they went, through corridors hushed as a mausoleum.

Above her, the ceiling became dark, jagged rock. Twisted shapes cavorted among the cracks, carvings of trees and beasts warped by time. She recognized none of it, and knew she had no idea where they had brought her. If they released her, she would not even know which way to run. The growl in her throat died to a whine. The Boars pulled her on, deep into the underbelly of the Court.

CHAPTER 21

THE AUDIENCE CHAMBER WAS MORE CAVERN THAN ROOM. WHISpers bounced and fractured on its uneven walls. The audience of clerks and courtiers was seated behind her. The Librarian, the Sister, and the fox maiden Nancy had been permitted to stand before the dais.

Emma looked up at the robed figure on the throne. The Judge's hair was white, but his spine was straight and his face strangely unlined. He could have been twenty or two hundred. His eyes were uncompromising, intelligent, and a deep ruby red.

"Bring the fugitive for judgment." His voice was the whisper of fingers over parchment.

The Boars seized Emma's shoulders and muscled her up to the dais.

"My lord, she is no fugitive." The Librarian's voice wavered across the chamber.

The Judge lifted a finger, and the cavern fell silent. The Boars released Emma's arms.

"It has been some time since we saw you in these halls, Librarian.

You may speak in defense of this fox maiden, if you wish. The City has assigned no other."

The Librarian seemed to shrink. "She fled her call to the Court only because she did not understand."

A jeer came from the back of the cavern, where the audience sat.

"It was — She — There was no need to send a Boar for her, for such a small misstep — "

Emma watched with a failing heart as the Librarian stammered. Before the crowd, his wits were sand escaping an hourglass. One courtier pretended to fall asleep, snoring loudly for the amusement of her friends. Another took the peel of the fruit his servant had sliced for him and flung it at the Librarian's back. Emma heard titters from the audience.

The Judge did not hurry the old man. Impassive, he heard the last of the Librarian's plea.

". . . and so, for the child, a pardon. Yes, yes. Pardon. So then, when she is safe, I can continue with my search. It is so lost, it is so . . ."

The Judge lifted a long, pale hand. "Your statement is heard. But her Oath is of no account. Delay or no, it would have come to pass. The Boars pursue her for a far greater offence. That of dishonoring a bargain."

There was a ghastly silence. Then a seething hiss of whispers boiled from the audience behind her. Emma twisted. They looked alternately sickened or alight with malicious fascination. The Librarian's face was horror itself.

Emma sketched the lines of morality in her new world as quickly as her brain would work. The Boar's vicious pursuit of her in the mortal world was apparently allowable. The tailor's attempt to steal her voice? An inconvenience to be brushed aside. But this crime was so serious it could hardly be spoken. Emma's stomach clenched. They would expect a punishment for such a crime, that audience. She felt their hunger for it.

"This 'Emma Curran' is a fugitive: The full essence of her soul has already been promised in a contract. Yet here she stands, intact."

"The full essence of her soul . . . My lord, you cannot mean — a full draining? The City could not allow . . ." The Librarian staggered where he stood.

The Sister strode forward to steady him. Her eyes flashed with righteous fury. "It would be barbarous. Drain the entirety of her soul? There would be nothing left of her. A shell. It is worse than death — what contract could call for this?"

The Judge's voice sliced through the din. "Those are the terms of the bargain between the Night City and the Turnbulls."

Emma jerked as though a knife had traced down her spine.

Turnbulls.

Her face felt entirely numb; her lips, two chips of ice. She might have been deep under water, the sounds of the chamber a distant storm above the waves. Here she was. Mortal no more. A ghost in the world she had been born to, a stranger to every soul she had loved. There was a collar around her neck. There were bruises on her arms. And she felt them as little as she felt the pulses of her own heart, which should have been tearing at her chest. She could look at it all, turn the whole knotted horror over in her mind, quite without any feelings.

So she had been promised to this dark. They had known, the Turnbulls. Known of this power, known enough to bargain away a girl who had turned up at their parties and drank what they gave her, but would never be one of their own. Had she not thought that it made no sense for her to be with them? Hadn't she felt it every moment, in the exchange of names she did not know and schools she could never have attended? She had never been able to copy their glow. That invincible ease, gained from knowing what it was to belong all their lives. There she had been, so full of desperation and longing. With them, but never one of them. She had been so convenient.

Someone had been clever enough to see that.

The Judge continued, somewhere far away.

"It is a bargain of long standing, and always paid before now at the appointed time. The Turnbulls selected her for sacrifice, a full winter ago. And yet the payment has not been made."

Yes, someone had been very clever, to choose her.

The pain bloomed through her. It was frostbite put before a flame. It was waking too early on the surgeon's table. She saw his laughing eyes, his careless smile. He had steadied her hand on a camera viewfinder. He had kissed her bare skin on the rooftop of a cathedral.

He had dressed her in ears and a tail and set her running through the dark.

He had called the hunters to her path.

"She has prevented this payment from being extracted, firstly by transforming into an animal whose form obscured her, and then by fleeing the City's officials."

The Judge turned to Emma. As though her fate depended on memorizing the tiniest of details, Emma noticed for the first time that there were no whites around his eyes. They were pure ruby, split only by a snake-slit pupil. Hunger glowed from their depths. She could not look away.

"So, Emma Curran. Your soul was promised to the City by the Turnbulls. And yet it was not given. You made your own bargain with the City to become a fox, and hid in animal form so that your pursuers might not find you. And now you have sealed that bargain further by swearing to the City within these very walls. A clever scheme."

It was clearly pointless to protest her innocence. Emma only wished that she was as clever as he believed her. Someone that clever might yet find a way out of this.

"None may betray a bargain with the City. Your very existence is a conundrum. To honor the Turnbulls' contract, you owe the entire essence of your mortal being. But you are no longer mortal, are you? Your current state prevents the payment of the Turnbulls' debt."

Emma straightened her back, as her mother would have. Distant afternoons in lecture halls filtered back to her. It seemed unlikely that any of the mortal law she had studied would apply here. Who at the University had ever written an essay on the finer points of a contract to drain the soul of another person? *But what if this were just another tutorial,* she thought. *An exercise to be solved? Think. Just think.*

"Current state. You can turn me back? Make me mortal again?"

The Judge's eyes flared, hard and glittering as rubies. He watched Emma shrink back, then continued. "You owe a debt of your own to the City, from your later contract as a fox maiden. One hundred years of service. A fox maiden must hunt. An employment you cannot undertake if we take the essence of your soul, as is owed. You see? You cannot fulfill the contract with the prior claim without reneging on the second. But you cannot fulfill the second contract before the first has been honored. This is a thing which has never happened before in the annals of records."

"I see. By honoring the Turnbulls' bargain, I would default on my own debt to the Night City. If that draining is so complete, so final, I would have nothing of value for the City to take. Nor even the faculties to earn payment elsewhere."

"Indeed. By either path, you default on one of those bargains. For which death is the only sentence."

Death. With that word, Emma found that every particle of cold had seeped away. In its place, she finally felt the pain. It was rage and fear and grief. It was a tangled throbbing mess of wanting, and it screamed its need to live. In that instant, Emma knew she would tear through the world with her teeth for a chance to survive.

Emma raised her voice for the whole Court to hear. "Then I wish to make a bargain with the Night City."

The chamber erupted with murmurs.

"The debt that the Turnbulls offered must be paid. And I will do it. But not with my soul. With payment that I earn in service of the Night City. I am a fox maiden, so I have a trade to earn with. This is my bargain: Add the Turnbulls' debt to my own, let me repay it in my own way, and I shall see that the City receives what it is owed in full."

The Judge's pale brows rose.

Emma continued. "My death would not only be entirely unnecessary; it would prevent the Night City from receiving the payment that is owed."

The chamber behind her roared. But Emma's gaze was locked with the Judge's. *I dare you*, she telegraphed with her eyes. *Go on.*

The Judge leaned forward in his throne. He was alight with the same animation Emma had seen in her own law tutors, when a student finally made a point worth hearing. "A bold demand, indeed. And yet the City cannot find fault with your terms: Your bargain is acceptable."

At her back, she dimly heard the chatter bouncing from the cavern's walls. A grunt close behind reminded her of the boar-men's presence. "And I will no longer be hunted? You'll call off the Boars?"

The Judge gave a silent "ah" and waved spidery fingers.

"I cannot. You are marked by the bargain with the Turnbulls, and that will call to the Boars as long as the debt is not paid. I do sympathize." He inspected the Boars guarding the dais delicately. "Yes, I would not wish for such . . . crude companions, myself."

The Boars stiffened at the insult. Emma saw fists clench, shoulders tighten.

The Judge dismissed them with a glance. "But the mark is affixed to your soul: I cannot remove it as long as the contract exists."

His eyes were glinting. *He's enjoying this,* Emma thought. *He's testing me. Fine.*

"Then make a second mark," she fired back. "If you cannot remove the first, or stop the Night City's officials from hunting me while I bear it. Give me something that will tell the hunters not to harm me when they find me."

"Such as what?"

"A token of protection, perhaps, my lord?" the Librarian's voice quavered from the side of the chamber.

"Hmm. They are usually for visiting dignitaries, but that might do. Yes." His eyes snapped back to her face, and if she hadn't known better, she might have thought the quirk to the straight, dry lips was a smile.

"The Night City hereby grants you a token of protection. Any Boar who comes across you will spare you. But the payment owed by the Turnbulls' bargain will be added to your debt. One mortal soul is equal to one thousand years of service. You may pay it off in any way you choose, but pay you must."

The buzzing in her ears was applause. It caught like fire across the chamber. Emma was too relieved to notice. She stumbled from the plinth. The Sister's arm caught her, and Nancy pulled her from the cavern.

CHAPTER 22

EMMA SAT ON THE BENCH OF THE ANTEROOM IN A DAZE, AS green-wigged clerks and mincing courtiers eddied from the judgment chamber. One thousand years.

If it took that long, if she paid off the debt on the final day of the thousandth year, and found a way back to the mortal world, what would it look like? It would not be her world. It would be empty of any who had known her. Her mother would have been buried generations before. And what would she recognize of herself, after centuries of living in the Night City? Emma pictured her kinder feelings worn away, her face wearing the same mask of glittering malice as the audience at the trial. That would be its own kind of death.

The chatter of the anteroom faded back around her, and Emma realized that the red-haired fox maiden — Nancy, she reminded herself — was talking in a soft murmur.

" — so brave as you were. But how're you ever going to pay off that debt?"

"I'm not going to think about it," said Emma, more cheerfully than she felt. "So how long do you have left? Before you get out, I mean."

"Out?" Nancy looked blank.

"Your years of service? How long until you're free?"

"Oh, that? I don't know," Nancy said, with a listlessness that surprised Emma. She spoke as though it were something she barely thought of, recalled after long effort. "A fair while to go yet, I suppose."

"You suppose?" Emma couldn't imagine not keeping track, down to the week. Down to the day.

"The City'll let me know once I'm through. I don't like to question." She ducked her head. "I'm not the same as you. Or the rest of our sisters."

"What do you mean?"

But the fox maiden leapt to her feet. "There's the Librarian with your token. Come, let's go meet him."

The token was a slip of waxed parchment the length of her thumb. When she saw it, Emma fell silent. She didn't say a word, not all the way back through the earthen corridors of the Court, not as they climbed up to the tiny chamber with the door to the outer world. There on the parchment, in gleaming black ink, was an eye ringed with monstrous teeth. A shape she had seen once before. When she was mortal.

It should not have made her want to cry. But she remembered that girl, so confident of failing her law tutorials, zipping a piece of paper into her bag and forgetting about it, and wished she had known. Known what it had meant. That someone was watching out for her. That someone cared for her. That she was worth caring for.

"You gave me this symbol," she said. "The day we met in the Library."

The Librarian covered her hand with his own crooked, lumpy one. "Mine did not have such power, child. It was but a poor copy. I knew the rune, that is all. I thought it might protect you, with my hope and will worked into it. Would that it had been enough."

"But how could you know I would need protection?" Emma whispered. "I'd only just met the Turnbulls. Met — Jasper."

She had spoken his name. A howl echoed in her chest.

"There was something in the air around you." He stroked her cheek with one gnarled finger. "I had seen something like it in my youth. When I first painted the University. Even as a mortal, I sensed there was a wonder about it. A power beyond what should have been. I saw the truth of it, and I saw the truth of you. You are precious, child. And the precious often becomes the hunted."

Carefully, as though his bones were made of glass, Emma reached around to hug him. She buried her face in his brocaded front. She hadn't realized it before, but safety had a smell. And it was an exact blend of old toast and dusty paper.

There was a harrumph behind them.

"Well then," the Sister said. "Now that's settled. Nancy, it's high time you take her to the House of Foxes. Dawn's on the horizon. We will see you soon, my brother and I."

Emma's spirits dropped as their steps faded down the street. With the Sister and the Librarian went the last connection to her mortal life. Her new world felt cold. Gray light seeped over the turrets of Fenchurch College. The dawn chill seeped through her borrowed cloak.

Nancy curled an arm through hers and squeezed. "Don't look

so sunk, love." She steered Emma along the High Street, then past Percy College into the maze of cobbled alleys beyond. "They'll all be waiting up, you know. Your sisters."

Despite herself, Emma found her pulse picking up. "Who? Where?"

"The House of Foxes, of course. Your new home."

Nancy led them into an alley so narrow, the moon only found its way there in slivers. It was choked with industrial bins from the restaurants that backed onto it. Even as she wrinkled her nose, Emma was aware of some remnant of fox at the back of her mind, sorting the stench into its component scents with delight.

grease and bird and sugardrink and old meat and foxsmell and

"Wait. I can smell them. Foxes." Emma lifted her nose to sniff the air.

foxsmell greenstuff foxsmell meat foxsmell foxsmell foxsmell

"Here. Right here."

There, in a thicker patch of shadow, the molten gleam of a foxy brass nose caught her eye. It was a doorknocker. The door nestled between the bins was ornate enough, but Emma suspected that if she had not been looking very hard, or directed by a fox's unerring nose, it might have slid from view unnoticed.

"Right you are." Nancy grinned. The claw on her collar glinted silver in the streetlight. "Welcome to the House of Foxes, love."

Nancy raised the knocker and beat the fox's head against the shadowy door. It gave them a long, slow wink, and the door swung open.

Emma saw a russet-paneled corridor —

burrow home burrow

— *corridor,* Emma thought firmly. There was an underground feel to the House of Foxes, with its low ceilings and bowed walls, which ought to have been oppressive. Instead, it felt comforting. As though a warm hand were smoothing the prickles from her fur.

"You're back." The beautiful eyes and dark skin of an older maiden peered from a doorway, framed by a lace cap. "And with our new sister? Saskia will be glad. She tore the house apart looking for enough coin for a bribe, before we got the message."

Nancy's face was torn between amusement and regret. "Oh, Frances, no. Not the pantry, at least?"

"Especially the pantry," Frances said, and Nancy groaned.

"Night above. We came back as soon as we could, but the Court had to sort a token of protection for Emma."

The older maiden made a noise in the back of her throat.

"I know, I was flummoxed when I heard. An actual token of protection." Nancy shook out Emma's cloak and hung it up with her own. "Getting it took an age and a half. You know how it is at Court. The Upper Houses keep the scribes running about on solstice invitations and poetry and the like, so they hardly have a breath for Lower House business, even when it's official."

"I do know." The maiden looked grave. "Our sisters are still awake. They were shaken, hearing about the Boars."

"Thinking a troop would burst in any moment, to take us all away to join Emma?" Nancy sighed. "I'd have spared them that. Come, Emma. They'll be glad to meet you."

They passed through double doors into a large space. A baronial fireplace dominated one wall, holding court over a trio of squashy russet sofas. Across the room, lead-veined windows looked out into dark earth laced with roots. Beneath them stood a claw-footed dining table. Mildew webbed the tapestries, and the brocade wallpaper behind had been ripped in several places, as though by claws. The strips that hung down fluttered in the draft of their entrance.

Emma's eyes were drawn to the figures by the fireplace. Flickering firelight shone from hair that gleamed like silk in the dark, and faces whose lines were eerily perfect. The fox maidens, she supposed. Most of them were curled together on the sofas. The two youngest, who didn't look more than fourteen, wrestled on the hearth. Saskia sat apart in one of the window seats, a barricade of books on her lap. At their entry, she buried her face in her reading with studied unconcern. But Emma felt a fierce gaze tracking her over the rim of the book.

Like Emma, the others in the House of Foxes wore the silver collar with the claw. But their dress was a jumble of decades. The two young ones — the twins, Nancy said — were dressed identically, in school uniforms no teen had worn in more than a century. Gertie was the one buried under swathes of spangled black veil, like a Victorian mourner. She spoke only in eerie hums and, apparently, was fond of snacking on beetles.

Lounging on the sofa opposite was one of the more glorious specimens of femininity Emma had ever seen. Selina was a peroxide-blond confection of cone bra and curves, lipsticked to

perfection beneath the wave set of a fifties starlet. Half-eaten choc-
olates littered the cushions around her. Beside Selina sat the beautiful older maiden, Frances, who refused to go out unless properly
attired in a bonnet and pelisse, and whose voice still held the song
of her birthplace in Jamaica.

They were curious and welcoming, and Emma felt herself
shrink under their kindness. She did not want it. She could not let
them draw her into feeling she belonged. The House of Foxes was
not her home. Her real home was in the mortal world, and she had
to focus on getting back to it. So she ducked her head and answered
in monosyllables. She heard the fox maidens murmur in sympa-
thetic tones about how tired she must be, after her ordeal.

"We all ought to be abed, late as it is. Has Sara gone already?"
Nancy said, scanning the room. "Well, you go join her. It's past
dawn already."

"I'll stay a while." Saskia unfolded herself from the window
seat. "The new girl's not eaten yet. She might be hungry."

"I'm really not — " Emma was cut off by a gurgle from her
stomach. "Oh."

She was ravenous.

"Good idea, love," Nancy said. "We can see Emma right."

The other fox maidens filtered out in a cozy, yawning group.
Saskia gestured Emma toward the dining table. It groaned under
the weight of empty dishes. From the feathers left on the largest
platter, it seemed a roast peacock had been the centerpiece.

Nancy pulled a face. "Sorry, love, there's not much left for you.
We're not a house of delicate appetites."

A clunk shook the table. Saskia had dropped a platter onto it,
whisked from beneath the chairs. She pushed it across the table

without meeting Emma's eye, and flopped into a claw-tipped dining chair. "Saved what I could," she said.

Nancy slid into a seat opposite. Emma sat next to her and inspected the tray. A luscious little rectangular tin was calling to her. It was all she could do not to tear into the metal with her teeth. She couldn't place the smell, but the animal voice pulsing beneath her thoughts was enraptured.

eat

tear with teeth

tongue bright and sure

Peering at the gold tin, she recoiled. FINEST PÂTÉ.

Many things she had forgotten. But not that she, Emma, was a vegetarian. *Oh,* she thought, with a sickening twist in her belly, *but when I was a fox, I . . .* she forced her gaze from the tin and clenched her hands.

"Is something wrong?" Saskia offered a serving spoon of peacock with icy courtesy. When Emma shook her head, Saskia wolfed down the lot and licked the spoon.

Emma fought not to shudder. She pulled a dish of spiced rice toward her. It tasted like ashes.

Nancy tore into her own haunch of peacock as she recounted the twists of Emma's trial. When they reached the point of Emma's debt, Saskia sucked in a breath.

"A whole mortal life? Night above, that's steep. And you told the Court it was better for them to let you live, because you'd be able to pay back the debt as a fox maiden?" Her face cracked in a silent laugh. "That's too good."

"I will be earning," Emma said, a little defensively. "The contract said so, when I swore to the house."

Saskia crunched on a peacock bone with vim. "It didn't say how much, though, did it? I don't think anyone from the Lower Houses has ever earned as much as half a mortal life. Not hunting, at least."

"Hunting on behalf of the Night City." That was the phrase the contract had used, describing her duties as a fox maiden. But hunting what? *Skimming mortal fires,* the riddle had said. That was the service of the House of Foxes.

Hunting. Mortal fires. Emma bit down hard, nipping the edge of her tongue.

The shivers started between her shoulder blades. "The mortals. We aren't — we don't *hunt* them?"

It would be too cruel. She'd only wanted to be close to her mortal friends. What kind of sickening trick would force her into a life of hunting them, instead? She thought again of a fox's gleaming teeth, of the blood-hungry gullet of its throat. Her throat.

Saskia snickered. "Your *face*, new girl. It's not like that. No blood and body parts. We hunt what's inside them. There's a vitality to mortal life. Their lives are so short, and all that intensity is bottled up, and — "

"And it has a power of its own," finished Nancy.

"And we can hunt that?" asked Emma, fascinated. "Doesn't it hurt them?"

"No, love. We only take a little at a time. To mortals, what they lose might feel like a night's sleep. The color blue from their dreams. The memory of their first hiccup."

"That sounds useless to me," Emma said frankly. "I can't see what the Night City would want with it."

Saskia waved a bone at her. The peacock's talon was still attached, gnarled and crispy. Emma was not going to wonder what it would taste like. She shoveled another spoonful of rice into her mouth.

"Mortals, especially the ones at the University, they feed on the power of the Night City without even knowing. They get knowledge, power, all of the good stuff. And in exchange, the City feeds on the mortals. On their vitality — the thing it's our job to gather. That gives the City more power, and the next mortals feed upon that power — and so on."

"Symbiosis," said Emma, and Saskia and Nancy looked rather blank. "Host and parasite live in mutually beneficial balance. You see it a lot in nature."

"A scientist among us," said Saskia with an ironic bow over her plate. "We're honored."

Nancy scraped her bowl clean. "And one with a token of protection, no less."

Saskia whistled. "That's rare enough. You've got diplomatic immunity, new girl. You can get up to all sorts of trouble now."

"Then how about starting with a proper drink?" Nancy grinned. "I stowed a bottle of firefly brandy in the fire scuttle last solstice."

There was no harm in it.

Sprawling with the other two on the sofas by the fire, Emma meant to feel strong. She took a swig for it being a day she had not died, and another for the thousand years she did not want to think of. But then she had to swallow away the Boar lurking in an alley, and the red coats that came swarming from the dark corners of her mind, every one wearing Jasper's face. Sip by sip, she drowned them all.

Someone had carved a row of foxes above the fireplace, Emma noticed. Each with a swooping tail wrapped around the next, so they were linked together. Linked, or chained? In a thousand years, that might be her. Sitting in just such a line, too changed by centuries trapped in the House of Foxes to break free.

She could not bear it. She would not.

She rounded on Saskia and Nancy. "But how can you *stand* it? The Court is all golden halls and parties and feasts, but we have to work hundreds of years for something that wasn't even our fault? Do you not see how unfair it is, the whole Night City?"

Saskia gave her a strange look. "Yes, we're workers. And yes, that means the deal we get is unfair. Did you really find the mortal world so different? I'm not sure England can have changed much since I was mortal, but I'm happy to be proved wrong. I never found out what happened to Thatcher once I was gone."

"Dead," said Emma. A light glinted in Saskia's eyes.

"Of natural causes," Emma hastened to add. "I think."

"Oh. Well." Saskia was downcast only for a moment. "I would have preferred deposed over dead, anyhow. Still, you're not wrong about the Court. Bunch of gilded bladders bumping into each other. The Upper Houses swan around, intriguing and subjecting each other to their poetry. They're not stuck with any work, or tied to just one beast form, like us. They get to play with the higher magics too. No collars, of course." She flicked the silver band at her neck.

"They're nobles, love." Nancy laid a hand on Emma's arm. "The lords and ladies, and their households and servants. The City granted them their power a long time ago, and they've a lot of it. They swear oaths to the City, but not like ours."

"Their oaths'll promise loyalty, but never labor." Saskia snorted viciously. "Still, as long as we pay our dues and don't dirty their hems, they're happy not to think much about us. The Lower Houses work for a living."

"But not at Court," Emma guessed.

"Exactly. And there's a reason for that. Think of the Night City as like — a layer, almost, over the mortal world. We share the same space as them — the same streets, the same river, the same college buildings — right on top of them, but they can't see us."

"But at night? Some mortals saw me."

"They get glimpses. But it's like they're on the other side of a thick veil."

"Only we get to see the full glory of the Night City." Nancy clasped her brandy glass reverently.

"Or the horror." Saskia ducked Nancy's swat with a grin. "But the Court is different. It's underground, beneath the mortal streets. And it wouldn't show on any mortal map, or turn up under the spades of mortal diggers. In the mortal world, that space does not exist. It's pure Night City. It's the source. Imagine it as a generator, powering the whole layer of the Night City above ground. Which means?" She raised her brows at Emma in challenge.

Memories unglued themselves from the blur in Emma's mind. In most environments, the organisms that secured closest access to a power source — like the sun, or water — tended to be the strongest.

"The closer you are to the heart of the City's power . . . the more important you are?"

Saskia clinked her glass, grinning. "Yes, new girl. That's what the Court is about. Upper Houses only, a few City favorites and hangers-on. Most other citizens, and all of the Lower Houses, have to find places outside the Court. Above ground, mixed in among the mortal spaces."

Emma remembered the alley at the entrance to the House of Foxes, choked with the bins and smells of restaurants that mortal Emma had known well: the late-night chip shop she'd dragged Julia to after nights out; the discount pizza takeaway; the vegan bakery her mother had loved when she visited.

"There are places above ground that are just for City folk, though." Nancy picked out a plump date. "Pockets, like secret rooms. Mortals can't see 'em or wander in. There's bits of the Library — and Saskia, we have to take her to the night market — "

Emma's head was whirling. She could not be drawn in, though the scientist in her longed to investigate it all. A veil separating mortal and magical worlds, held in place by a power below ground. Mortals and immortals sharing the same space, feeding from one another. Thought of as an ecosystem, it was beyond fascinating. It would be groundbreaking to study.

"And there's still so much we *don't* know about the Night City, that's the thing." Saskia propped herself on her elbows for a long, gleeful slurp of brandy. "I bet they don't tell us half of what's really going on. I've heard stories . . ."

"Get out of it." Nancy chuckled. "Our Saskia is a bit of a conspiracy theorist."

Saskia bolted upright, grinning. "Am not. And just because we haven't seen the filament spiders in the sewers, that doesn't mean . . ."

225

Emma nestled close to Nancy, watching the debate spark. A cozy sort of feeling was settling over her. She realized, to her horror, that it was contentment. Something about this room, and these companions, felt like home. Perhaps it was not so bad to find a little comfort, for the time being. She would be no more likely to escape by staying tense and lonely. Perhaps the fox maidens and their knowledge might even be the key to helping her escape. She held out her glass for another round of brandy.

In the end, Nancy forbade them to sleep on the sofas, even as the firefly brandy was making Emma a persuasive case to the contrary. Nancy swatted Saskia to her feet. "It's our own beds we need. You'll thank me for it later."

Saskia peeled off at a doorway covered with a moth-eaten velvet curtain. Nancy led Emma down a third flight of stairs, to a door decorated with deep-scored claw marks, and left her there. Staring uneasily at the violent pattern, Emma braced herself to be brave. She opened the scarred door.

A face glared through the darkness. The threat it emanated was quite undimmed by a long ruffled nightgown and the bow that topped its nightcap.

"Who are you?"

"I — This is my bedroom, I thought?" Emma trailed off.

The fox maiden in the bed looked at her scornfully.

"I am not," she said, enunciating each word as if for somebody particularly slow, "sharing my room. Go tell Nancy to put you somewhere else."

"I don't know where Nancy is — she said to go here, so — ?" Emma stammered.

"For Night's sake," snapped the girl. Then she seemed to make an effort to speak softly. "Fine, you can stay. Whoever you are. But first, could you step outside so I can get changed?"

"Oh, of course," Emma moved toward the door. "Sorry, I understand, I'm — "

The door shut in her face with a slam. Surprise turned to rage as she heard the unmistakable sound of a lock snapping into place. She pounded on the door, to resounding silence.

Planning ten kinds of revenge, Emma stalked the darkened corridors of the house. She tried door after door. None would open. And with a tearing inside that felt like relief, her fury poured out. She'd had no room to feel it, not as the Boars dragged her off, or as the Judge stared at her with those clever eyes. It had not been safe then to feel something so fierce and all-devouring. Another door, slammed in her face. Another hour of wandering, footsore, heartsick, with no place to call safe. Because of them. *The Turnbulls.* The hiss seared her throat. They would pay. And she would be the one to make them.

There had to be a way back to the mortal world, with or without the City's permission. In thousands of years, someone must have managed it. Every city had an unwatched exit; an illicit trade route; an underbelly. There would be stories. She just had to find them. And then the Turnbulls would be the ones made heartsick and afraid.

Then a door slid open beneath her hand. The room was carpeted with a layer of dead leaves. Its only contents were a four-poster bed festooned with drapes of spiderweb, and a corner given over to a mound of bones, laced with shattered twigs and the skulls of small rodents.

Emma looked at the bed, uneasily aware she ought to have been more drawn to it. Her eyes were heavy. She was ready to sleep. But something about that mound of bones and twigs called to her. It smelled of earth, of juicy worms and warm burrows.

safe smell
burrow smell

She knew that voice in her mind as well as she knew the shape of tail and pelt and paws. But she was not a fox now. She was a girl-shaped being and she ought to have wanted a bed. The other fox maidens read books and wore fine fabrics and ate from shining platters. They did not sleep on bones, she was sure of it.

safe

the voice insisted, a sinuous brush of fur in her mind.

Well. There was no one around to see. Wrapping herself in her cloak, Emma curled up on the bones and fell deeply asleep.

CHAPTER 23

WHEN SHE WOKE, EMMA STEPPED BACK INTO THE CORRIDOR. SHE might have slept for minutes or untold hours, for all the difference she saw in the House of Foxes. The rosy lamps, dotted along the walls, cast the same soft light as before. The wood-paneled passages were just as deserted. There was no way to tell if it was night or day. The only windows faced onto earth packed with roots and stones.

If I were a plant, I would die here, thought Emma. But then again, a plant was a living thing. And she was — not. Was it possible to exist and not be alive? Pausing on the staircase, Emma fumbled for her pulse. It was still beating. Her breath still slid into her belly. It was possible, then, to not be mortal and yet not be dead. In a world that had changed, a life with no roots, a home with no night or day: Still her body followed the same physical commands. It was an anchor. She had not changed, even if her world had.

As Emma reached the door to the common room, the twins pushed past, small faces horror painted.

"She won't stop," said one.

"Run while you can," said the other.

Grabbing each other's hands, they fled.

Emma stepped into the room, feeling for the place in her mind where she heard the fox's voice. It was silent. Nothing smelled like a threat. Saskia was curled up under a mountain of books by the fire. The dining table looked freshly polished. And at the far end of the room, Nancy was flitting from grimy armoire to gramophone, feather duster in hand. A dreamy smile lit her face.

"Clean, clean, clean."

The tuneless croon floated back across the room.

Saskia's eyes glinted over her book. "No one can stop her when she gets like this. Put something down for a second, and you'll never see it again. Gertie's already barricaded herself into the broom closet with her tarot cards. The others ran for it."

Emma plumped down on the other sofa. "Terrifying."

A soapy hand landed on her shoulder. "What's terrifying?" came Nancy's chirpy burr. She settled herself at Emma's feet, tossing the feather duster onto the pile of books. Saskia sneezed and scowled.

"Did you sleep, Emma?" Nancy asked. "It'll be odd for you at first, sleeping through the day and waking for the night. It's the way of the City."

"Is it night, then?" Emma said. "I couldn't tell."

The sameness of the House of Foxes was unnerving. The enormity of a thousand years in this house, with these people, settled on her. Her sisters, Nancy had called them. And yet they were strangers. Emma had been ready to trust the tailor at the Court. And she might have lost her voice for it. The Night City was dangerous. What might these new sisters truly want of her? She would need to know more about them to be sure. Saskia, all spikes and clever eyes, would be tricky to crack. The nightcapped maiden had refused to share a bedroom, and the twins had run as soon as they'd seen her. The others — Selina and Frances and Gertie — had also made themselves scarce. But Nancy could be open to a friendly approach.

"Would you like help cleaning? I'm not bad at it," Emma lied.

Nancy gently took the duster from Emma's hand and turned it right side up.

"That's kind of you, love. But I'm all right on my own. This lot would rather live in decades of dust and crumbs — "

Saskia made an approving noise from behind her book.

" — but they put up with the cleaning, since I enjoy it. I find it calming, like. I couldn't always have things as clean as I wanted, before."

"Before what?"

A shutter seemed to fall on Nancy's face.

"Before she was a fox maiden," said Saskia.

"Now, here's me with a right good idea. Saskia, you'll have run out of books in an hour or two, knowing you. Why don't you take Emma to the Library?"

The Library. Emma darted a glance at the spines on Saskia's lap. *Choromancy. The Allusions of Illusions. A History of Magickal Bargains, Part III.* Those did not sound like mortal titles. The Night City must have its own books in the Library. Books of magic. A place to start looking for her escape. They might contain stories of crossings to the mortal realm. Or explain how the *Turnbulls* — her mind spat the word as though it were poisonous — had known about the Night City and made a bargain with it. Fury flamed into purpose. She was going to bring them down and she would find something in the Library to help her do it, even if she had to search every book.

"It might be nice for Emma to see the Librarian," Nancy pushed on. "He seems right fond of her."

Saskia glanced at the avalanche of books on her legs and opened her mouth. Whatever she saw in Emma's face seemed to change her mind, and she snapped it shut again.

"Oh, all right. New girl, you'd need to be ready to go soon."

"I'm ready now." Emma jumped to her feet and promptly tripped over the boots the Sister had given her. They were far too big. As she hauled herself upright, she heard Nancy speak in an urgent undertone.

"You'll take her the back way?"

Saskia nodded. "Down the mortal high street, to be on the safe side. The patrols've been seen as far as the river tunnels."

"Patrols?" said Emma.

Two pairs of startled eyes turned to her.

"Boars," Saskia said shortly. "They're all over at the moment. *Just keeping order,* supposedly. Making sure we're *safe from lawbreakers.* But the only real way to be safe? Stay out of their way. Of late, people say they're a law unto themselves. And there have been . . . accidents."

The bruises along Emma's arms prickled, as though the Boars' fingers were still pressed into the flesh.

"But I thought they were the City's guard?"

"You could call them mercenaries, I suppose. The City uses the Boars like a security force, but they're not part of any house. They just turned up centuries ago, apparently. Millennia after the City and the houses first came into being. And no one seems to know where they came from. The Boars answer only to the City itself. Or" — Saskia leaned forward — "to whoever has enough coin, apparently. Although that's a thing it's best not to whisper on a moonless night."

Emma had not been afraid enough, on that street with the sun sinking below the horizon. That was clear. Now, thinking of the way the Boar had clawed through the air to get to her, Emma's body felt like a violin string tautened to snapping point. It had been so close. If it had not been for the messenger pulling her out of the way —

"There, love." Nancy was patting her arm. "You've got that token of protection, don't forget. Everyone's just a little jumpy right now."

"That's what the Sister said." Emma thought back. "That things here were . . . unstable."

"Unstable's right. It's all whispers and disappearances, recently." Saskia lowered her voice. "People're saying things in the market. That the barrier between the mortal world and ours is strangely thin all of a sudden. That the City's power is — slipping."

"Fools of people," Nancy said. "That's dangerous talk. You just focus on staying out of the way of those patrols. Get our Emma to the Library without running nose-first into trouble, hmm?"

Saskia waved her away. "I will if she can keep up. Come on, new girl."

She strode from the house. Emma scurried in her wake, eyes flicking round for patrols of cold-eyed Boars at every corner. But the streets were almost deserted. The statues of Wessex College turned miter-hatted heads to watch them pass. The Night City's strange light chased over the cobbles of the High Street. It was familiar and strange at the same time. Emma felt in her pocket for the slip of parchment the Judge had given her. The token of protection kept her safe from the Boars as long as she had it, he had said. Perhaps she could let go of feeling afraid. Just for now.

After all, there was so much else to take in. The wondrous lights of the Night City, dancing across the buildings. The moon high over college spires. The few passersby, huddled into heavy parkas against the cold. At that last sight, Emma had a new thought.

"Hey." Emma trotted to keep up with Saskia. "How come you're dressed like that? Not like the others?"

Saskia scowled, tugging the cuffs of her leather jacket over her hands. "Well, I can't please everyone. You think I care if you don't like how I look, new girl?"

She stalked ahead, and Emma felt a pang in her stomach. Five minutes into a conversation, and she was already a failure. She scurried after Saskia.

"No — I just meant, why are you dressed like modern people?"

Saskia's shoulders unwound. Her back began to look slightly more friendly.

"At the Court, it was all cloaks and tunics." Emma smoothed her hands over her own borrowed cloak. Underneath, the tailor's gown felt none the fresher after a night sleeping on bones and leaves. "But you, you're — "

"Modern?" Saskia said, with a wry smile. "Nice of you to say. I've been in the City forty years, nearly. I mostly have to steal these from mortal secondhand shops now. Eighties punk was a long time ago. The City is stuck in some nightmare Renaissance perma-loop. The hose and the doublets. The curtsying."

Emma tried to think it out. "Is it because they've always had magic? They never had to keep up with technology, so their world . . . didn't change?"

"Dead on. And immortals don't like change much, I've found. Even in fashion. Time moves slower for them."

As if by agreement, their feet drifted to a halt at the top of a bridge. Emma looked across the once-familiar river, the bridges, the colleges lining the banks. Now the lights of the Night City played over them all.

"My theory is, there used to be more flow between the mortal world and ours. Back when people really believed in magic. And as that belief drained away, the Night City shut up on itself . . ."

"And stayed as it was?"

"That's immortals for you. A mishmash of olde worlde nonsense, and no sign they want to update. You won't find such a thing as a union anywhere about. Forget constitutional monarchy, or having a vote. Feudal fairyland here has the political sophistication of a bucket."

She nudged Emma's leg with a combat-booted foot and grinned. "Come on, new girl, don't look so grim. There aren't many things that make up for the bad here. But the Library is one of them."

She raised reverent eyes to the far end of the bridge, where the Library's dome glowed in the moonlight. Their feet crunched down the shadowed path toward it.

"I've been there before. As a mortal."

"Then you haven't really been." A smile like a wisp of smoke curled across Saskia's face.

She tapped one of the Library doors. It swung open under her touch. Emma was about to protest about locks and security cameras, then stopped herself. Human rules no longer applied.

"The Library is the only place the mortal world and the Night City exist together. As equals."

The reception was buzzing with life. A figure in a monk's cowl trailed by, taloned feet scritching over the marble floor. Groups stood debating and waving books at one another. Emma saw several silver collars like her own. Saskia ushered her through the crowd and into the dim glory of the reading room beyond.

"We can walk around the mortal streets and buildings out there. But we don't own them. We pass through, leaving marks mortals can't see. And most of our own spaces are like pockets, hidden from mortal eyes and feet."

"Like the Court."

"Right. But here" — Saskia turned soft eyes upon the shadowy shelves — "it's both. Magic and mortal, at the same time. Like two floor plans laid over the same space. Technically, we have our own rooms with our own books, but really there's nothing to stop a mortal wandering in. They can stroll into a room that shouldn't exist in their world, and which won't be there again when they come back the next day. *Centuries* of scholars have found this place baffling."

Her voice was full of glee.

Emma remembered her first visit to the Library with Nat. Walking into reading rooms she'd never been able to find again. The way the readers had glanced up at her, all sporting the timeless academic uniform of tweed patches and beetle brows, as though she were the first person they'd seen in a century.

Perhaps she had been.

And in a place where the two worlds overlapped, Emma realized, there might be more odd edges like that. Frayed seams, tiny gaps where a patient, determined person might wriggle through to the mortal world, leaving their debt behind.

"We're mostly meant to come at night, after the mortals are gone. Since they can actually see us here, and we stick in their memories."

"They can see me here?" said Emma, her heart lifting. "Remember me properly, in the daylight?"

Nat came to the Library all the time. He could bring her mother. And together, surely, they'd find some way around her debt to the Night City —

"Don't get your hopes up." Saskia led them up a warped staircase. "The punishment for courting mortal attention here is something fierce. I've had to make a run for it before, when a mortal's got too close. Only the Sister and the Librarian are allowed to talk to them, and that's because of their jobs."

"Shelving books?"

"They're more like guardians. The Library's precious to the City. One of the few things I like about our ruling power."

"Why?"

"Because a proper appreciation of books is a mark of decency. Oh, why's it precious to the City, you mean? Best ask the Librarian. He explains better than I can. I was going to drop you at his study up ahead. I've a few more books I wouldn't mind borrowing, and I don't want to have to drag you round with me." She pointed to a door in the shadow of a tapestry.

Emma felt a flash of warmth in her chest. She realized that she did not want Saskia to go. Instinct urged her to trust this spiky-haired, spiky-tongued stranger. In fact, it told her that she already trusted Saskia. That she could ask the question burning in her throat. Emma lowered her voice. "Saskia — the Turnbulls. Do you know anything about them?"

"Only to stay away from them."

"The Judge said that they made a bargain with the Night City, and made me part of it. But they're only mortals. *Boys.* How would the Turnbulls even know the Night City exists? What would they bargain for? I thought — you had all of those books — maybe you'd know where to look . . ."

"Yeah, I could take a look for you. Maybe." Saskia inspected her chipped nail polish with an air of unconcern. "It's not like I'm going out of my way. Whatever."

Behind her, the little door flew open. The scent of toast floated out.

"Child. It is you."

The Librarian's delight cleared the gritty feeling from Emma's throat. The Turnbulls had owned enough of her thoughts.

"And young Saskia. Well met, both. Will you take some tea with me?"

Saskia begged off, but Emma stepped into his study. Tea sounded excellent. And she would not feel guilty for having a second purpose. The Librarian knew so much of the Night City and the contents of the Library. If there was a secret weak spot in the City's barriers she might creep through, or a book that told of illicit crossings to the mortal world, he would know it. But she could not let him know what she intended. With his scattered wits, he might let it slip. And he would suffer punishment along with her, if was found she had escaped and that he had given her the tools to do it. She saw him dragged away by Boars, bruises flaring under his brocade waistcoat, childlike eyes puzzled at the hurt. She could not bear to think of it. It was safest for them both to keep her hunt hidden.

The Librarian bowed her into the best armchair in his study: the one that still had both arms. He shuffled about with an air of joy, fetching teacups and fussing at butter dishes. Books were piled in a waist-high labyrinth. A little old-fashioned Primus stove sat atop a desk, a smoking toaster beside it.

"You carry your token, child?" A dish of hot buttered toast was put down in front of Emma. She fell on it, tearing with her fingers.

"Yes," she said, through a dripping mouth. Butter was so *good*. She wiped her hands on her cloak, thinking an apology to the Sister, and pulled out the slip of parchment with the fanged eye.

The Librarian settled in the armchair opposite. "That is well, child. Keep it with you always."

He filled Emma's teacup. The stream of tea wavered as he poured, but Emma would have bitten out her tongue rather than say anything.

"Though you would have nothing to fear from the Boars here, in any case."

Emma raised an inquiring eyebrow, her mouth too full of her third slice of toast to attempt speech.

"The Boars do not come to the Library," the Librarian said. "It is not permitted."

"That sounds very final," she said.

"It is." A frost hardened the Librarian's eyes. "They are creatures of violence. They have shown they do not respect this place, or the knowledge it contains. The City may find them useful elsewhere, but it will not stand for that here."

"Yes, Saskia said the Library was important to the Night City. But not why."

"Why, child? This is its very heart."

"Not the Court?"

"The Court is its golden bauble. But this is its holy place. Where knowledge lives, and where mortals come to seek it. One the Night City's greatest gift, the other its greatest fascination."

Emma wondered why she had once thought him vague. When his wits focused, as now, she almost shivered in their beam.

"At Court, the Night City rules. Here, it loves." He waved at the stacks around him. "Think of the books, child. Books are dear to the City, for they contain knowledge, and knowledge is its power."

The Night City loved books for the knowledge they contained. So even if a book contained secrets the City might not want shared — like how to flee its boundaries — what were the chances it might let that book survive anyway, from a pure love of knowledge? She knew that someone, at some time, must have found a path from the Night City back to the mortal world. And people wrote things down. All she had to do was find the right book.

"There are so many books here," she said, pouring milk into the Librarian's cup. "I remember you told me, once. Every work ever printed."

"And many before the printed word. The collection here is like no other."

Emma tried not to sound eager. She stirred his tea, then turned to her own. "So how might you find one? If you were looking for something in particular, I mean?"

The Librarian let out a louder wheeze than usual. Emma realized after a moment that it was a laugh.

"Might I but solve that."

"What do you mean? Librarian?"

He seemed to pull himself back into the room with great effort. "Forgive me, child. It falls to the Librarian to find what is lost. The one book I cannot find. It fills my thoughts, my dreams . . ."

He trailed into silence. After a while, Emma leaned forward. "Librarian? One book lost isn't so bad. I'm sure everyone has forgotten about it by now."

"I cannot. All I am is bent toward it. Such were the terms of my return."

"Return?"

He clasped her wrist, sending her teacup toppling to the floor. She felt the strange set of the bones in his lumpy hand, the splayed spokes grinding against her wrist.

"Librarian?"

He had been about to say something. About his book hunt, perhaps, and the "terms" that required it? That had sounded like a bargain, to Emma's ears. And what had he meant, talking about his "return"? A return to where, or from where? Could he have meant the mortal world? Emma felt an electricity in her chest. An escape story, not hidden in an unknown book, but right before her.

"I am tired." The Librarian looked smaller, suddenly. Tiny as a coin lost down the back of a sofa. He released her wrist. "So tired . . ."

He had sunk into vagueness, and Emma knew she would get no answer from him. But she still had the Library. She could approach it like her research project. Scientifically, methodically. Catalogue the areas to look, then survey in squares until the species she wanted to observe appeared. She folded another slice of toast in four and put it whole into her mouth.

It was a good enough plan.

She stood. "Shall I leave you to rest?"

He nodded, apparently too exhausted to speak.

Emma closed the study door. She could not think of the pain in the Librarian's voice or she would start to cry. No, she would focus on her plan. The Library held every book ever printed. As much knowledge as a building could contain. It would have the secret to returning to the mortal world.

Emma straightened. The book-lined archway at the end of the corridor was calling her. With or without the Librarian's help, the knowledge she sought was somewhere in these rooms.

She had work to do.

CHAPTER 24

EMMA HAD WALKED THROUGH THE READING ROOMS QUICKLY AT first, trying to get a feel for what they held. The problem was, as soon as she turned back, the rooms behind her had switched themselves round. She recognized none of them. It had been worse once she'd thrown stairs into the mix. Tired as she was, she had to smile. The Library had a sense of humor, it seemed.

And then this room had turned up. Tall windows, a tapestry of a river winding around a fruit tree. And shelf after shelf of books titled things like *Mortal Theory: Man and Manifest;* or *Perish the Thought: A Brief Philosophy of Mortality.* Magical texts devoted to mortals, written by residents of the Night City. She hadn't dared leave for fear the room would disappear on her.

But after hours of backbreaking work, she had covered exactly a tenth of the upper gallery. Nothing had held the secret to crossing into the mortal realm. She slumped on the top step of a spiral staircase. Perhaps if she hadn't spent so long dodging Nat's attempts to take her to the Library, she might have had a more realistic idea of the task she was undertaking.

But then, if it were easy, then anyone might have done it. And if there was one thing Emma knew about herself, in the flood of her returning memories, it was that she was patient. As a mortal, she had sat unmoving for hours, until her stillness set the creatures around her at ease. She had watched a seal colony until her fingers wrinkled from salt spray. She had seen a Guilder deer and its fawn pick their way to the river's edge, even as the current numbed her feet. She stayed when others admitted defeat and went home to hot drinks. It was why the otters had danced for her alone, in the bend of the river outside Gabriel College. Seeing what was hidden from others had been a wonder, equal to any of the Night City's. And she had only ever needed her own mind and eyes to do it.

"Loved your speech." The velvet moss voice came from behind her, in the gallery.

Emma jerked round, spilling books from her lap. The messenger — her messenger — lounged against a stepladder.

"*Quite* a showing, your trial."

"You were at my trial?"

He widened his eyes, which did nothing to hide the dancing mischief in their depths. "I? Would this humble vassal miss the trial of my own dear lady fugitive?"

At her hearty scowl, his grin widened.

"Oh yes," he continued, fingering his curly beard. "I was there. To face down the Judge with a bargain of your own, and win? La! My dear."

He produced an apple from nowhere and tossed it high into the air. Catching it in one hand and biting down, he said, "Sh'been a long time sh'ince I've seen old Misery enjoy himself that much. But you've got that nasty extra debt now — a whole mortal life, no?"

"I'm not going to think about it yet," Emma said firmly.

"A thousand extra years of service? You should."

"*You* should try not abandoning people on the street."

"I prefer to think of it as delivering people back to the bosoms of their friends. Are you not a fox maiden now, and among sisters?"

Emma was on her feet before she knew it. The remaining books in her lap cascaded down the spiral staircase. She ignored the protests from the reading room below. Her eyes were narrowed on the messenger.

"You dropped me outside the Court on purpose."

"Perhaps I did leave you where it might be — ah, easier for you to find your way in. But no good would have come of your avoiding your summons."

Emma turned to pick up her fallen books, hoping her silence conveyed the full chill of her disdain.

"But it *would* be a mistake, you know," the messenger said quietly.

"What would?"

"Not to think about how you can pay off that debt."

Emma's eyes snapped to his. "Why would you care?"

"There are ways, you know." Tossing the apple up and down, he looked at the ceiling, at the walls, anywhere but at Emma. "For someone who's clever. There are things they could do."

Caught despite herself, Emma moved closer. She tasted secrets. "Like what?"

"I am sent by one far more powerful than I. Perform for them the smallest favor, and the rewards will be great. What do you say?"

It was what she had been looking for. What Saskia and Nancy

245

had not been able to tell her, and what none of these books had contained. A way to earn more than a fox maiden could. To be free of her debt. To go home. She was about to open her mouth, when she heard the Sister's voice, and her warning: *City dwellers do not give, as a rule. Almost always, a gift they offer will be a bargain in disguise.*

Emma's lips drew back from her teeth in a fox snarl. "No, thank you. Unless you care to name your terms. I won't be taken in by your gift."

The messenger gave a delighted laugh. "Oh, I'm half in love with you already. Right you are, my lady. Business it is. I tell you what my sender wants of you — "

"And who is this sender, messenger?"

"Robin."

"What?"

"Messenger Robin." He swept a deep bow, eyes twinkling. "My lady."

"That's not an answer to my question."

"No fact escapes your cunning eye, lady fox. My sender does not wish to be known." Robin sighed, tapping the tree on his tunic. "And as a lowly City messenger, I obey. But I assure you, they are more than generous."

Emma made a noncommittal sound. She had always liked to know all the facts before making a decision. To lay out her data and analyze before giving her conclusions. She mistrusted simple tasks with anonymous instigators.

"So what do they want from me?"

"Share all you know of the Turnbulls, and there will be a nice little reward for you. Enough to pay off — oh, perhaps two hundred years of your service?"

That was double what any of her sisters owed to the House of Foxes, for information she would have given gladly. It would be a relief to talk about the Turnbulls, to release the gall choking her insides. She wanted to know why so much would be offered for so little. But she had learned enough of the Night City not to show her hand. "Of course. No one else could tell you, because — because there's never been anyone like me in the Night City before." She tried not to sound as though she were guessing. If the mystery patron thought she had value, she would act like it. "Someone connected to the Turnbulls."

"Certainly nobody close enough to have useful information. Your coming stirred the hornet's nest of the Court. How many newcomers to the City do you think are called to a full trial in the great chamber, with the Judge himself?"

"Not many, I hope," said Emma, rubbing the tender spots on her arms where the Boars had bruised her.

"Which gives your knowledge great worth. You were even with them during a sacrifice."

"I *was* the sacrifice," she reminded him drily. "So tell me more about this generous bargain. What are your terms?"

"Our terms, O Gorgon of suspicion, are these: You tell me all you remember of the Turnbulls. Even details you might think unimportant — on this matter, no corner of your knowledge should remain unshared."

"And if any part of the bargain is not met?"

"A little transformation. Frog's legs for twenty years. Webbing and all," Robin said promptly.

Emma nodded as though thinking it through. In reality, she was remembering the tailor at the Court. The trick in her words.

Emma had sworn to match cunning with cunning. To turn the Night City's game to her own ends. And she had just seen her first opportunity.

She tried to sound casual. But she held every word in her mouth before saying it aloud. She had to get it right. "So this is our bargain. Your sender wishes to know all about the Turnbulls: We will share complete confidence on this matter. Everything there is to know. You and I swear this bargain now, and I will receive a reward at the end. If the terms of the bargain aren't met, that means twenty years with frog's legs. We agree?"

"It's a bargain." Robin shook her offered hand.

Emma kept her face smooth to hide the unholy glee within. She kept her end of the bargain. She told Robin every last vicious, rage-filled detail about the Turnbulls. It felt like soaring, letting her vitriol flow free. She particularly enjoyed describing Piers Popwell as a bloated weasel intestine. Robin blinked, but wrote it down. At last, with a sheaf of scribbled notes, he stood to leave.

"Oh no, Messenger Robin," Emma told him. "Not yet. Time for your part of the bargain."

Robin turned, eyes wary. "Lady?"

"I believe we just agreed to share full confidence, on the matter of your sender wishing to know about the Turnbulls? Such full sharing between us, I believe, would include the identity of your sender." She paused, enjoying herself immensely. "Would it not?"

His face went comically blank. Then he broke into a roar of laughter. "Oh, you are magnificent. You have tricked me. Me!"

"I have. You must tell me who sent you, or suffer the punishment we agreed. What was it again?" she mused, gazing up at the reading room ceiling. "Something about frogs?"

"But I am fond of my legs," he complained. "Truly, the beauties at Court have said that they are my finest feature."

"How sad for you." Emma grinned. "But just think how much faster you may deliver messages. Bouncing down the corridors of the Court. All who look on you will be stunned."

"Enough, enough." Robin buried his face in his hands. "Lady fox, you have me."

"So who sent you?"

He raised his head slowly. "The Night City itself."

She had expected some courtier, hungry for gossip. It took her a moment to recover her breath. "It can't be. The Night City's power is knowledge. It must have all it needs on the Turnbulls."

"It does not," Robin said quietly. This time, his voice was deadly serious. "And that is something no one can know. A single sign of weakness can unsettle the Court. The Night City cannot have that. There can be no official records of this inquiry. So it sent me."

"Why does the City need to know more about the Turnbulls so badly?"

Robin lowered his voice to the barest whisper. Emma had to lean in to hear him. "Here it is: The City wants to be free of the Turnbull bargain. And yet the contract has never been undone. Never worked around."

"And the City would usually do that."

Robin chuckled. "With the ease you might crush a beetle beneath your dainty foot. Let us say a mortal wishes for endless riches all his life, and the City is not in a mood to comply. How easy, instead, to fill the mortal's belly with gold coins, without stop or cease, until the very force of the hoard splits his flesh open from the inside. Riches without cease, until death."

Emma pressed a hand to her own stomach.

"The City delights in finding ways to turn a wish on its head. Especially for those who think to trap it for their own advantage." Robin pulled at his beard in abstraction. "But not this contract. It seems forced to fulfill their demands. And the City does not like being crossed."

Emma had seen the Night City as all-powerful. It was unnerving to think of it trapped under the Turnbulls' command.

"But how can that be? Why would this bargain be so different?"

"To undo a contract, we must know how it was first done. And for this bargain, my beauteous fox maiden, that very pertinent information? It is gone. The original contract, alone among all others in the City, is missing. Without it, the usual means of dissolving a bargain are lost to us."

"Which makes my knowledge valuable," Emma said. "I see."

She did see. In fact, an idea was forming.

"Indeed. In the absence of the contract, the City values every stray piece of information on the Turnbulls. In time, who knows what crumb might bring an opportunity to weaken the Turnbulls."

Emma had been nodding. At that, she turned with a snap.

"Weaken?" she spat. She had expected the Night City to turn the Turnbulls' entrails to snakes or force them into eternities of service. Not to hope for a minor reduction in comfort. "I don't want to *weaken* the Turnbulls. I want to destroy them."

Fury crystallized her idea to a single thought. "My value is far more than what happened to me."

"I can see that," Robin murmured. "In fact, O radiant one, I wager I'd want you on my side in a fight."

"So forget just compiling my mortal memories. Let's change

our bargain. What if I find a way to help destroy that contract? To stop the Turnbulls ever making a sacrifice again?"

Robin's face was alight. "Could you do that?"

"To undo a bargain, you must know how it was done, you said." She leaned in, her voice intense. "So what if I discover how my particular sacrifice was done? Could we not also work backward, and outward, and discover the key to the bargain as a whole? To undo it, completely?"

"Centuries of Night City scholars tried to find the secret. None have done it."

"How could they? They've never been mortal. They don't know how to think like one. But I know these boys. If they have hidden their magical workings, I'll be able to figure out how."

"If that is indeed the bargain you offer, I will accept it on behalf of the Night City gladly." He swept a bow. "Lady fox, you are a marvel among marvels."

She waved aside the hands attempting to clasp her own.

"Can you please be sensible?"

"I am not sure," he admitted candidly. "I never have before. But for you, I will try."

From the twinkle in his eye, she was not sure if either of those things was true.

"You know," he went on. "It might not need to be anything as great as the key to the whole contract. Any new information on what magics the Turnbulls have been using, or how their ritual is worked, could be weapon enough for the City."

"And if I found that, what kind of reward would there be?"

"I would have to ask. But if you delivered something that helped the City break the Turnbull contract, the reward would be . . . breathtaking. Enough to cancel your debt entirely, I am sure. Perhaps even enough to get you what you want, O dawn-flower of the river marches."

"What I want?"

"To leave the Night City, of course." Robin watched Emma stiffen. "Come, lady fox, what else would you want? We all long to return to where we belong, when we are far from it." He seemed sincere, for once.

"And the Night City would let me go?"

"The Night City would hand over your freedom on a jeweled platter, if you can deliver what you've said. Especially now. It needs a good show of power. With things as they are — You've heard the whispers?"

"That something's — not right, with the Night City. That it's losing its grip. And people here are on edge."

"They are. Things have been off, since just before the flood. Something was thinning the veil between mortal and magic. I don't know what, but I do know something's shaken the City. Enough that it would gladly take a victory wherever it can, especially over an old grudge. And reward richly for it."

"I will find you the Turnbulls' secrets. And you will get me home."

He held out a hand. "Our new bargain. You would need to keep this secret, though. No blabbing to your sisters."

"Understood." Emma did not move yet. "And no frog legs this time?"

"No, indeed."

Emma fought a grin. It was almost fun, dueling wits. She took his hand. "Then I accept this bargain."

"Very well, O pearl among raindrops. See what you can find. Tell no one. And know that I await your discoveries most breathlessly." He smiled, bright and sudden, like sunlight through leaves.

"Emma!"

The spiral staircase shook with the pounding of heavy boots. Saskia hauled into view, panting. "You have to come."

"But my books — I haven't tidied — "

Saskia's hand closed around her arm. "We have to leave. Now."

Emma flung a glance back to the stepladder. The messenger was gone, as she'd expected he would be. But her books had been stacked neatly on its rungs. So Emma let Saskia drag her away, trying as hard as she could not to stumble over the borrowed boots. Reading rooms flashed by, and still Saskia did not slow.

"Nancy sent a message. We have to get back," she said, as though through frozen lips. "It's the House of Foxes."

"What about it?"

Saskia set her jaw. "There's been an attack."

CHAPTER 25

THERE WAS AN AWFUL STILLNESS IN THE HOUSE OF FOXES, LIKE the moment before a scream. The fox maidens huddled in the hall. They barely glanced up as Emma and Saskia slipped in. After several minutes of tense waiting, the front door swung open again. Nancy went rigid, and one of the fox maidens let out a choked cry. Two male shapes in green uniforms carried in something on a litter. Something twitching and bloody. They deposited it on the floor, none too gently. A snarl rumbled around the room.

"You've done enough. Leave now." The Librarian's sister stood outlined in the doorway. The look on her face would have frozen mercury. The two carriers ducked past her. She slammed the front door after them.

"I came as soon as I heard." The Sister knelt over the bundle on the litter, resting a battered leather bag beside her. "Nancy, take the others and ready the sickroom. And you, come here. I need you with me."

Emma realized that this was directed to her. The Sister's voice

254

had sounded gruff, but the hand that beckoned her trembled. Emma knelt with her.

The bloodstained bundle on the floor was a person. Someone had covered it — her — with a blanket. Red blooms had already soaked through the fabric.

The hair was matted, not smoothly tucked under a nightcap. Instead of glaring, the eyes were unseeing. But the face was familiar. The Sister looked at Emma closely. "You know her."

"We met last night. We had a disagreement. About me sharing her room." Emma looked down, saw her hands clutching her elbows tight to her body. Realized she was shaking. "What happened to her? Did those men — "

"Do this to her?" The Sister smoothed the hair from the girl's forehead. "No, this is what happens when you cross the Night City."

The Night City had done this. The sick feeling clawed up from Emma's stomach to her throat.

"Sara must have fled the house while the others were sleeping."

"Is that why she didn't want me in the room? So she could leave — "

"Unnoticed. Indeed. The girl believed she could escape. Start a new life, outside the City."

Emma looked down at the figure on the litter. Sara's lips were moving soundlessly.

"She did what is forbidden. She tried to flee the City."

Emma's voice shook. "What happened?"

"There are beasts that guard the outer reaches of the Night City. Monstrous, ravening things. Answering only to the City. There was no hope of making it past. It was madness to try."

Saskia's pale face appeared in the stairway. "Sister? The sick-room's ready now."

"Right." The Sister got to her feet with a grunt of effort. "All of you. Lift her gently. We can only move her once. She's close to the end of her strength."

The fox maidens gathered around their sister, each taking hold of an edge of the litter. Emma joined them. Her panic was threatening to spill over. Fugitives were not treated kindly. There were consequences for those who crossed the Night City. She saw them now, etched in blood on another girl's face.

What would happen if she were caught searching old books for the secret to crossing between worlds? If she were discovered planning to escape?

When they lifted the litter, Sara screamed.

The sickroom had the cold look of a barely used space. The Sister set her bag on a countertop and began whisking labeled jars from its insides. Emma watched her sort linens into baskets by the bedside, lay out instruments in precise rows on the worktop. There was an ease to her movements Emma had never seen. In the sickroom, the Sister finally looked at home in herself. She lit the candles and beckoned Emma to her side. The other fox maidens filed out. When the Sister finally lifted the blanket from Sara's body, Emma flinched. But after one rebellious roll, she forced her stomach to stay put.

"You have no medical training, I suppose?"

Emma shook her head. "I studied law." She clamped her lips shut again quickly. The salt-metal scent of blood was in her mouth.

"Pity."

"Did you? Have medical training?" Emma asked, watching the deft way the Sister's gnarled fingers unrolled bandages.

"I might have done. Had I been born in a different age." Before Emma could ask what age she had been born into, the Sister had turned to rifle through a drawer. "You might give her some water."

Emma tried, but the water mostly dribbled from the sides of Sara's mouth. Emma forced her eyes downward, to what she had been trying not to see. Beneath the blooms of blood, the sticky gleam of raw flesh. Emma realized that her hands were knuckling into her stomach.

"Will she — " She could not say it.

The Sister joined her at the bedside, a jar in hand. "No, she may not die of this. But with these wounds . . ."

"What can I do?"

"Good girl. Fetch me that jar — no, don't open it yourself. I have everything here secured with alarm spells. Let me . . . there."

The Sister drew out a pinch of purple powder. "This is deathsleep, girl. It's best swallowed, but inhaled will do." She held the powder to Sara's nose. "This will keep her asleep while she heals. Now, come close. We'll start by cleaning these wounds."

The figure on the bed became the center of Emma's world. They sponged and sewed, set and splinted, until her eyes were as heavy as her hands. But hour by hour, Sara slipped away from them.

"Enough," the Sister said eventually. Her face looked gray, the eye patch digging into her wrinkles. "We've done all we can, for now."

It took a moment for the sensation to travel from Emma's tired brain to her fingers. They were starting to cramp around the mortar and pestle. Freeing them, she joined the Sister in her vigil by the bed.

The sound of the door opening made them both start. Emma

257

recognized the labored breathing even before she saw the Librarian. The Sister tugged a dusty book from his grasp.

"How does the child?" He approached the bedside. A misshapen hand, like a gnarled tortoise, crept toward Sara's face but never touched her.

"You found it?" The Sister's wrinkled face was alight. She leafed through the book with swift fingers. "The regular cantrips only did so much, and I remembered something in this volume that . . . Ah! Here it is. The vervain preparation. We'll try this next."

The Librarian shut his eyes, as though to ward off a memory. "So cruel. Such cruel punishment."

Emma saw the moment when something changed in his face. It was like a ripple crossing a pond. His eyes popped open, as vague as Emma had ever seen them.

"I must leave," he said to the air, with some surprise. "How did I come to be here? The book is lost, I cannot spare this time . . ."

"Oh, Henry." The Sister reached for him, but he shuffled past, eyes fixed on a point invisible to all but himself. The sound of his mutterings trailed away down the corridor.

It was not the first time Emma had seen the vagueness take him. It had been the same in his study, when he'd been about to talk of his "return." An escape story, she had hoped. To the mortal world or back again. But she hadn't followed the thought to its logical end. Whatever journey the Librarian had made, the Sister might well have been with him. She would not let her brother go into danger alone. And the Sister had no fits of vagueness. She might answer a question, if it were put to her.

Emma considered how to start. Lightly, she thought. On a safe topic. "Were you very fond of Sara?"

"Barely knew her." The Sister emptied a jar of roots onto the worktable and started chopping. "But I have seen what the City does to those who displease it. I have learned how to help. Not always enough."

A tear trickled from under the eye patch. The Sister caught her looking.

"I am an old woman, Emma," she said, creasing her face into a wicked smile, with some effort. "They tell you incontinence starts and ends with the bladder, but the eyes are just as bad. Just you wait."

"You were like Sara, weren't you?" Emma said slowly. "The Night City hurt you. It did that to you. Your eye."

The Sister made a half-hearted movement, as though to cover her eye patch.

Emma thought again of the Librarian's mangled fingers. "And your brother's hands."

The Sister shook her head. "It is a bad story, girl."

Emma pulled the book toward her. "I can work as you talk. Please."

The Sister looked deep into one of the candles.

"The England of our youth was one of carriages and ball-rooms," she said. "My only destiny, or so I thought, was to marry. A gentleman of rank and fortune, an estate. My brother was an artist, and my favorite person in all the world. He painted things of great beauty from his studio near the University, rising in renown and riches.

"Until he disappeared. He told me once of a strange magic that summoned him.

" 'There is a power in this place,' he had said, looking not at me

259

but through me. 'It fills these streets with beauty. I try, but paint cannot capture it.'

"Then he stooped to pick up one of his smaller canvases. It showed a rear aspect of the Library. A door peeped from behind swathes of creepers. 'If I am gone, little sister, it will be here. They have told me the way. Just through this door, a place more wondrous than any we could imagine. A land like the tales of old.' He smiled. 'Perhaps Queen Mab may take me as one of her own.'

"But I did not believe him. Not until he was gone. Then, I believed. When my parents told me, I slipped to the stables and took my dear old horse, Bess. I did not stop until we reached the Library. There I found the door, just as in Henry's painting. To open it, I made my own bargain. Fool as I was, in my innocence, I swore I would give anything for my brother's safe return. Thinking I might lose my pretty fan, or my favorite horse. Instead, the City took my youth, and Henry's, as price for the crossing, and sent us ragged into the streets of the mortal world. Wrinkled as we were, none recognized us. We were barred from our home. Worse, things were not right with Henry. He could not bring himself to paint. He said it was as though the mortal world were washed of color. His body had left the Night City, but his mind did not. I watched it drift away from me, day by day.

"And so I made another bargain, to bring him back. But the City was angry with us. For it had loved him. Unlike so many others, Henry had not been forced into a collar or a Lower House. No, the Night City had taken him straight into the heart of its Court. The City prizes great minds and talents, you see. It likes to take them for its own, those special mortals. And Henry was special. With his genius and skill, he painted the Night City with its true face. He showed its beauty. And for such a favorite to leave all the City's wonders to return to the mortal world — it was a betrayal. To be taken back, we had to submit to a cruel price. I lost this eye. Henry, the grace of his hands. Now, he cannot even hold a brush. But we became members of the Night City, even if only at the outer fringes. We are exiled to walk between the mortal world and the magical one. And so we have been given charge of the Library, to watch over it and every generation of mortals that comes to its doors.

"Mine is a lowly enough role. I have no title. But my brother is the Librarian. Even in disgrace, I believe the City cannot forget the love it once bore him. Above all others, it chose him to guard its most precious place, and the knowledge within. My brother is happy, if not entirely whole. He sees the beauty of the City, and I know it comforts him. He cannot paint, but he smiles again. Some things are worth the sacrifice."

"You make it sound like it happened long ago."

"It did. I walked through that door two hundred years ago, and more."

Two hundred years. Emma shuddered at the thought. But if the story had told her anything, it was that desperation put people at the mercy of truly flesh-rending bargains. And like the Sister, she had just made another bargain. How much did she know about the messenger? He had not told her much of himself. Or mentioned the consequences of failing to find the information he wanted. Cold trickled through her, as she entertained exactly how stupid she might have been.

The Sister cleared her throat. "You've done well, girl. Have you readied everything the cantrip requires?"

"I have." Emma banished the messenger from her thoughts.

"Then come, we'll have to be quick."

They tipped the vervain mixture down Sara's throat. Her eyelids flickered, and her breathing seemed to ease.

The Sister collapsed into a chair. "To bed with you. I will watch over her."

Emma lingered at the door. "I never asked, Sister. Why do they call you that?"

"Because I have no name here. Henry is the Librarian, and I am his sister. That is all anyone needs to know."

"But what was your name, before?"

The Sister glared at the wrinkled hands in her lap. She forced her words through stiff lips, twin spots of shame burning in her cheeks. "I cannot use it now. It was the name of a beautiful woman. I am a ruin."

Emma looked at her, from her tangled gray hair to the tree-ring lines of her face.

"No," Emma said stoutly. "You are not a ruin. You are better than beautiful. You are whole."

She did not stay to watch the effect of her words. She slipped out of the room.

The Sister stayed a week, until Sara was stable. When she went home to the Librarian, Emma missed her. But the fox maidens took over watching Sara in shifts. In the cool of the sickroom, Emma helped Gertie lay out a tarot spread for Sara; she read from *Fordyce's Sermons* with Frances; let the twins braid her hair into mad spirals;

sat in companionable silence with Saskia or noisy merriment with Nancy. Every hour made it harder to armor her heart against the fox maidens. She was going to escape and leave them behind. It made no sense to get attached. She had to remind herself that they were of the Night City. And she could not trust the Night City.

But one morning, as Emma returned yawning from changing bandages and sponging wounds with Nancy, a voice stopped her at her bedroom door.

"Hey! New girl."

Emma turned. Saskia stalked into the light of the corridor's lamps, holding a pair of boots. She was scowling ferociously.

"You keep tripping." This, in an accusatory tone. But she was scanning Emma's face, as though what she saw there mattered.

Emma still wore the boots the Sister had lent her. They did trip her at least twice a night. It warmed her to think that somebody had noticed, and cared.

"Got these in the market," Saskia growled. A blush was staining her cheeks.

She shoved the new boots into Emma's hands. Tiny leaves danced around the ankles, embossed by some delicate hand. Emma stroked the silvery leather. They were narrower than the average, just like Emma's feet. They might have been made for her.

"Are we friends?" she teased, earning herself a truly feral glare from Saskia, who crossed her arms and muttered something about idiot newcomers. Emma grinned at her. "I thought gifts weren't to be trusted round here."

"We'll make it a bargain, then. I give you these . . . you have to wear them to the Beasts' Ball at Midwinter. And dance."

"A ball?"

"We all go. The City puts it on every year for the Lower Houses. Sounds lame, I know, but . . ."

"No. It sounds perfect, actually." Emma swallowed back a sudden wave of emotion. She'd never got to sweep into the student ball at Gabriel in a twinkling gown, to run wild in ancient halls with her best friends. She would have danced all night with Julia and Nat. Taken endless photographs on the grand staircase. She would have remembered it always. Perhaps, before she escaped, the Night City could give her this one thing. One night to feel what she'd missed.

"You'll dance? It's a bargain, then." Saskia looked pleased as she turned away.

"Thank you. I mean it. If I can ever — "

Saskia mumbled, "Don't bother," and fled.

Emma grinned. The leather and spikes looked a lot less intimidating when they were scurrying away. Next time, she'd try giving Saskia a hug. It might send her into an all-out run. Emma cradled the boots to her chest, still smiling, and shut her bedroom door.

CHAPTER 26

EMMA SETTLED INTO THE RHYTHM OF LIFE AT THE HOUSE OF Foxes. She still scoured the Library stacks for any mention of a way through the veil between the Night City and the mortal realm. But she was coming to think that a small delay in the Night City might not be so bad. She had the messenger's task, for one. If she discovered something to help the City break the Turnbulls' bargain, that would damage them much more deeply than anything she'd manage as a mere mortal girl. Whatever the Turnbulls had bargained her for, it had to be important. And she was far better able to hunt out their secrets as a fox maiden, with the protection of invisibility around mortals, and the promise of fox form to help her.

But it would not do to wait too long to escape, however useful her new powers might be. She was afraid of what might happen if she stayed too long in the Night City. There was something deeply disturbing about her new home. She had seen it in the fox maidens. There was an apathy that chilled her, and seemed worse the longer they had been in the City. They seemed not to care about escape. If she asked about their plans for wheñ they were mortal again, or whether they ever thought about crossing between the worlds, they mostly shrugged. Said vaguely that they wanted to be free, but somehow they had stopped thinking about it. Emma sickened at the idea that the same might happen to her, with enough time.

The other fox maidens tried to explain it to her. Memories faded, they said. At first, it was like looking at a picture through a glass pane. Then the years passed, and the glass became dirtier and dirtier, until it was hard to see the shapes beneath.

"Unless you go to the water hag," Saskia muttered. Despite the chatter around the rest of the dining table, she was nose-deep in a volume on theories of shadow.

Frances drew in a sharp breath. There was a flutter among the other fox maidens. Emma leaned in. There was a secret here.

Saskia let her book fall, looking absurdly guilty. "Sorry. Best not to mention in polite company, I forgot."

"Oh, it's only an old legend." Nancy grinned across the table and tipped a platter of crisp, salty bacon onto her plate. "The water hag's a whispered monster in these parts, Emma. Supposed to do dark spells for the Lower Houses, to help them remember their old lives."

"To really feel the memories again, with the same fire you had when you were mortal." Selina leaned her chin on her hand. "It would be nice."

"Not for the water hag's victims, it wasn't," Nancy teased. "How did it go? She'd do her wicked ceremony using something of yours. A personal item, that was it. One that held the memory. But after she was done, that memory became hers, not yours.

Forever. As if it never happened to you. Poor trade, I'd say. If she ever existed, she's gone now. 'Seeing the water hag' is for drunks and fools."

Emma scented something. "Then people still see her?"

Nancy snorted. "Oh, I've no doubt someone's dressed up in a parcel of reeds and riverweed, to take honest folks' good coin for a magic ceremony that don't exist. I've not come across them, but then I've no leisure to be gulled." Nancy nibbled a rasher thoughtfully. "Pr'aps it's a con we could run ourselves. Invent a nice scary mother vixen, with the power to make you taste your dreams, or summat just as useless. Doll up Saskia with a shaggy coat and a mop handle for a scepter, and charge a tidy sum."

The others shouted with laughter.

Quiet Frances shook her head. "You miss the point of the tale. The water hag speaks of the fear we all carry, we who have come to the Night City. That in enjoying its wonders, we lose ourselves. The feelings and memories that made us. And that once lost, they cannot be regained."

The table was silent. Her sisters' faces had become bleak. And it cut Emma to the heart.

"Then you should remember," Emma said. She had tried so hard not to get involved. To keep herself separate, ready to leave them all behind. But she could not bear their sadness. She looked round at each of them in turn, willing her strength into them. "You could fight the fading of your memories. Do it together. We can tell each other of who we were, and what mattered to us. Remind ourselves how we felt. How we can feel."

"Share our memories." Frances nodded. "And keep them thus alive."

Nancy brought out her firefly brandy. And as the night wore into dawn, her sisters told stories. The ones Emma had wondered about. She learned that the fox maidens came from as many decades as they did backgrounds. Even Saskia unbent enough to tell an anecdote, which made Emma laugh until she snorted brandy from her nose, about her dive into the 1980s punk wave, and how horrified the students had been when she arrived in halls for her first year, Mohawked and leathered to the wrists. She had been a scholarship student, Emma was able to gather. The only one from a state school in her entire college.

Wordless Gertie turned out to be a fortune-teller: once a mayor's daughter, until she ran away to join the circus. Selina had been a nightclub dancer, whose furs and teddy-boy beaus barely concealed the traces of Mattie, the scared evacuee who had arrived on a train with a label around her neck.

Every story ended in the Room of Choosing: facing the imp, picking the amber claw. But her sisters' paths had differed from Emma's in one key way. Many had made bargains in desperation, as Emma had. For safety, for freedom. But their shape had not changed with those bargains. Only when they became fox maidens did they transform. Emma alone had been pulled from human into fox form before then.

The reasons for their bargains varied. Loss. Betrayal. Senseless violence. But the sadness of them did not. Emma found a fullness in her heart. Her sisters could understand pain. Even hers. The loneliness that had wrapped around her from the moment she arrived in the Night City began to recede.

Emma noticed that not all of them shared their stories. Frances spoke only of a particular flower she had loved as a child, then folded her hands. Nancy seemed conveniently called to tidy plates whenever the conversation turned her way. In turn, none of them pressed Emma to talk about Jasper or the Turnbulls. They were content to accept her as she was, with whatever she had to share.

The candles wore down. They finished the last of the brandy. Only Gertie, seeming to float upright in her chair among her veils, looked even halfway sober. Selina propped her feet on Emma's lap.

"So, what are we all wearing to the Beasts' Ball?"

"Something appropriate," said Frances firmly.

Selina giggled. "I suppose you don't think my pink number with the feathers is *appropriate*."

"Appropriate has never been in the same *room* as that pink dress." Saskia snorted.

"You would look so elegant with a pair of gloves." Frances sighed. "A young lady should always wear gloves to a ball. Gertie agrees with me, is that not right?"

Gertie looked up from her tarot cards and pushed back her veil to grin, waving hands encased in black satin.

"Oh, I know, darling, they look divine on you," said Selina. "But Midwinter's so close. We've not enough time for me to order a whole new outfit, which I'd need to go with the gloves, of course . . ."

"What'll you be wearing, Emma?" Nancy said absently, trying to tease a snarl from one of the twins' hair.

"This, I suppose." Emma looked down at her brown dress from the Court tailor. It had been ugly enough when it was new. Now it was smeared with Sara's ointment and Library dust. Though she knew it shouldn't matter, not against her escape and her business with the Turnbulls, Emma's cheeks heated at the thought of wearing it into a ballroom.

Her sisters exchanged looks.

"Your face will shine the lovelier in a plain setting." Frances patted her hand with sympathy, which made Emma feel worse.

"You are *going* to look smashing, darling." Emma was pulled into a cloud of platinum curls and Shalimar. Selina's enthusiasm was so overwhelming, it sometimes sounded downright threatening. "*Trust me.*"

"Is it time to go?" Saskia set down her book, seemingly bored by the talk of ball adornments. The other fox maidens fluttered to their feet.

Soon only Emma was left helping Nancy clear the table. She heard her sisters call farewells from the hall. The front door slammed.

"Where are they going?"

"To hunt," Nancy replied.

Emma's gaze dropped to her feet. She had not been on a single hunt. The thought of it made her stomach clench. Despite the fox maidens assuring her that they drained only the smallest sip of energy from a mortal. That it barely hurt the mortals, or not so badly they couldn't get over it in a few days. Their defenses only made Emma feel worse. Because they wouldn't call it a hunt if someone wasn't about to become prey.

"What if — if I don't want to hunt mortals?" Emma stammered.

"Emma, it's not just ball gowns and frippery we buy. The meals we eat, the warmth of this house? It's all paid for by our hunts," Nancy said gently. "The City doesn't give them for free. All those costs add to our debt, which means more years of service. Why do you think Frances has been here so long, or Gertie? More'n a hundred years, both of them. We've all been covering your costs till now, love — and happy to do it — but it's time for you to try."

Shame flooded Emma's cheeks. "I didn't know."

"I didn't think you did." Nancy patted her hand. "Hunting's also part of your contract with the Night City, so you'd be getting a mighty unpleasant visit from the Boars if your dues aren't paid. When you're ready, just ask one of us take you to hunt. Best have fox form ready for that." She took in Emma's face. "You have transformed back into a fox, haven't you?"

Emma grimaced. "I tried reaching down into my mind, where I feel the fox, and — nothing. Managed to switch my fingernails for claws, but that's it."

"Hmm. And what did you feel, when the change started?"

"It was like drowning. I — I couldn't breathe." Even remembering it, Emma felt that same awful vise around her chest. "I heard the fox inside me." The taunting whisper, so close to the surface.

we are the hunt
prey hung limp in dripping jaws
teeth so sharp to rip the meat

"And I was afraid — am afraid," Emma corrected. "If I shift, she could devour me, all there is of me. I'll be stuck, just like before."

"Ah, the fear. That would do it. Magic is a force of will, like Saskia says. All in the mind. Fear can throw it off in funny ways. You can choose to believe it." Nancy held Emma's gaze. "Or you could sit with the fear, breathe through it. See what's on the other side. And if you don't want to be lost to the fox, then don't be. Up there, maybe you were what other people decided. But here, you can be what you believe yourself to be. You decide."

"I decide," Emma repeated. She had not been good at that as a mortal, she realized. At saying who she was, or what she wanted.

She had hated moving around with her mother. Losing her friends, her home, over and over. But however much she had wanted to stay, it had never seemed like it mattered. Not when her mother needed to move for her next big academic chance. As a child, she had never stopped to consider whether her pain at leaving her home might ever outweigh the damage to her mother's career. Whether what she wanted was important, even if it hurt someone else. Perhaps here, she could be different.

Nancy heaved another stack of plates with a sigh. "Now, let's get this lot into the kitchen. It's my turn to watch over Sara later, but I've enough time to hear more about your mother's tree-home."

"Research station," Emma corrected, with a laugh.

"Right enough, love. And tell me again of the snake-tailed striped beast — lemur, did you call it?"

Emma's mind had split in two. She agonized over it in the Library; in long night watches over Sara; curled in her claw-marked bed at the House of Foxes.

The longer she refused to hunt, the more she betrayed the other fox maidens. She could not let them keep paying for her from their own earnings. But if she went hunting, she would become someone she didn't recognize. The real Emma, the mortal one, never hurt anything. She freed the spiders in the bathroom rather than killing them. When it rained, she walked with her eyes trained on the ground to avoid stepping on snails. Going hunting would feel like giving up on that Emma. It admitted the possibility that she might never return: that there would be no escape from the Night City. It was too hard let her old self go.

Then, days before Midwinter, Emma trailed in from the Library. She was weary and sore, smudged with sweat and dust from another fruitless book search. But her bedroom was not as she had left it. There was something on the bed. A ball gown, silver-white and glimmering, like a dress of morning mist. And beside it, a note:

Should be your size, darling. We all chose it. Call it a Midwinter gift.

I said you'd look smashing at the ball, didn't I?

Love from us all
(and especially Selina)

Another gift. Another kindness. The dress shimmered up at her, lovely as moonlight. And something shifted within Emma. Since the tailor's trick at the Court, the Sister's warning had blared in her mind: *City dwellers do not give. A gift they offer will be a bargain in disguise. And the worse for it.*

But Emma had become so focused on looking for hidden spite, she had missed what was in front of her. Not everything in the Night City was a trick. The fox maidens were offering true friendship. Emma ran gentle fingers over the dress, feeling tears prick her eyes. She was among people who cared for her. She was part of the House of Foxes. The old Emma might not have known what to do with that. But the new Emma did.

She could afford to change. It was time to stop being so afraid of the Night City, and what she might become within it. After all, she had her sisters at her back now, and the Turnbulls to bring down. She could try being fierce. And the Beasts' Ball would be the perfect place to start.

CHAPTER 27

There were many ways into the Court. This one was hidden in the crypt beneath Regent's College. Among the sleeping stone crusaders and long-dead college proctors, the lid of one tomb had been pushed aside, revealing a shadowed staircase. Emma clambered over the lip of the tomb and down into the dark. Before and behind her, a line of cloaked nightdwellers murmured and jostled. There was no light. Only by reshaping her eyes into a fox's could she make out Saskia, striding immediately in front.

They emerged in a part of the Court deep below ground, hewn from dark rock. Emma followed the crowd through a labyrinth of caverns. A glow the size of a stamp beckoned. It grew gradually to a majestic doorway, the breadth of two elephants, thrown open at the head of a grand staircase. Sconces flamed every few steps. A low buzz of sound became a thunderstorm. Laughter. Music.

Emma looked over the staircase and caught her breath. The ball below was a whirl of shadow and firelight. The hall was vast, supported by endless columns that faded into the dark. It looked to have been hacked from the earth millennia ago. Great stalactites dangled overhead, like savage chandeliers.

At the center, a polished obsidian dance floor writhed with masked dancers. At first glance, they seemed human-shaped. But here and there, like carefully planned accessories to the doublets and gowns, Emma spied the outlines of wings, tails, and fins alongside hands and feet. Some of the Lower Houses evidently preferred to enhance their two-legged forms.

Their dancing was a strange mix of formal and fierce: a curtsy followed by a swipe of the claws; a baring of the teeth as partners traded turns. The dance of the hunt. The musicians were sawing away with bows of sharpened bone, on strings that sprouted thorns. The music they made cut straight to Emma's marrow, setting her feet twitching. *Dance*, it whispered. *You shall dance your feet to the bone. You shall dance until blood marks your steps, until your skin falls like rotting leaves. You shall dance.*

Emma felt her blood sing in response. She tightened her mask — fox-shaped, with velvet ribbons that tied under her hair — and smoothed the silver skirts of her ball gown. Her sisters had chosen well. From the classical drapery at the shoulders to the long, twinkling folds that fell to her feet, the gown was designed for someone with height. In it, Emma forgot to hunch. She strode forward, the gown wrapping her body like a cloud of mist, cool against her skin. Layers of shimmering gauze swirled with every breath of air. She felt like a dancing wind herself in it: mercurial, free. Seen from the corner of her eye, the fabric seemed to drift like a real morning mist, spilling tendrils of vapor into the air.

Saskia leaned on the balustrade, pulling her own mask into place. "So, what do you think?"

Emma raised her voice over the shrieking strings. "Isn't this a Midwinter ball? I thought it might be more, er . . . quaint? Holly. Pine cones. Silver bells?"

"Midwinter has never been a tame festival. But neither are we, now. Would you rather have the holly and bells?"

Emma looked at the ball again. The music ran teeth of honey and velvet over her skin. The fire of the dance licked at her, driving her pulse to a throb, drenching the bare skin at her neck in delicious shivers. She was not back in the mortal realm just yet. The Night City beckoned. And for one night, she was ready to answer the call. To revel in having claws of her own, and a pack of fierce sisters to dance among.

"I don't want the bells," she said.

Saskia offered her arm. "Then welcome to the Beasts' Ball."

As they descended the grand staircase, the heat rose to meet them. Silver collars winked from the sliding shadows of the dance floor. The ballgoers wore masks to show their affiliations. And Emma was astonished at their number. The House of Foxes must have been an outlier, to boast so few as nine. The fox maidens were drowned in a sea of beak-masked Ravens, sharp-nosed Rats, and silvery Eels. The other Lower Houses of the Night City, who served the City in its most menial roles.

But to Emma's mind, it seemed that waste removal and cleaning, repair work and guard duty — and, yes, tax collection, which was what the foxes' drainings came down to — were hardly of menial importance. What place could run without them? That, Saskia had said, was the point of the Beasts' Ball. On Midwinter's Eve, the workers of the lower orders were given a lavish feast to reward them for the year's labor.

The fox maidens clustered around Emma, arguing good-naturedly about what they should do first. Some were for joining the dancers, others for exploring the feasting tables. Selina yearned for the shadowed tables where gamblers challenged one another to duels of bargains; Frances to rest on the fur-draped benches around the dance floor, where the gossips chatted. Emma's chest pulsed with a dark, joyous greed. Everything was enchanting and vicious and impossible to resist. She wanted it all.

A figure climbed the dais at the end of the ballroom and dropped into the central throne. A murmur raced through the ballroom, quickly hushed. Nightdwellers bowed as one to the piglike head, the muscled human chest.

Something caught in Emma's throat. "What is one of *them* doing here?"

The Boar beckoned a trembling server and speared a grape on one sharpened nail. He ground it to a sticky pulp between stained teeth. Behind him, a troop of Boars filed into position on the dais. At a nod from the throne, they snapped to attention. The soldiers had plain leather bandoliers, Emma noticed, while the commander wore gold.

The commanding Boar ran cold eyes over the crowd. "Bring that one. The sweetmeat in purple."

The voice was guttural, as though forced with difficulty between the razor-sharp tusks. Emma shuddered. She had not known they could speak, these boar-men. A tiny Raven in a blackberry gown was pulled to the dais, the shiver in her body visible even through her bodice. The Boar's eyes glinted.

"The Boars've been put here to keep order tonight," Nancy

whispered, her face tight. "And they may pull any maiden or male from the crowd to suit their pleasure. Their station allows it."

But the commander ran his eyes up and down the tiny Raven, and seemingly did not find his pleasure there. With a snort of disgust, he shoved her back into the crowd. She fled gratefully, small shoulders shaking.

The Boar threw himself back into the throne, beckoning roughly for wine.

"Ordered to watch over a Night-poxed ball like a pack of wet-nurses?" Emma heard him mutter to a soldier. Resentment snarled through his voice, a forest of brambles. "Us? The City's forgotten where respect is due."

He paused, tilting his goblet. He had seen Emma staring. She ducked her head, wishing her dress truly were a cloud of mist she might hide in. She felt the graze of Boar eyes on her bare skin. It made her feel small and exposed, a field mouse trembling in an open patch of ground.

"Enough." Saskia's eyes glinted defiance. "We don't stand here shaking. That's what they want."

"Too right." Selina hugged Gertie around the shoulders.

Nancy bared sharp little teeth. "And what do we want, loves?"

The others growled in response, grins widening.

Emma heard the growl in her own throat, felt the cool air on her sharp, exposed teeth. She raised her head. "We want to dance."

The fox maidens exploded into yips and barks. Then a hand grabbed Emma's and they were all running through the crowd. The room was a howl of color and noise. Ratfolk crowded the gambling tables, while giggling Ravens swapped kisses on the benches.

Shadowed figures flitted among revelers to slip a bracelet off a wrist here, an amulet there. Eels lay under the open spigots of wine, gulping without the need to breathe: Frilly gills had appeared beneath their ears.

Someone thrust a goblet of star wine into Emma's hands: black as night, its depths glowing with tiny white lights, like constellations. Then it was empty, and she was knocking back another, and a third. When she hiccuped, tiny motes of light floated from her tongue. She swayed as the music bound itself to her pulse, sharp and sweet and agonizing.

"Boots look nice." Emma whipped round. Saskia stood behind her in a spiked black tunic and silver hose. Dabs of glitter on her cheekbones made her eyes look bluer than ever.

"The ones you gave me?" Emma tried to straighten up. She pointed one silver-booted foot at Saskia. "Yes, they're perfect."

"Didn't give them, new girl. It was a bargain, remember?" Saskia leaned back on one hip, silver hose gleaming. "One pair of boots for a dance."

"With you?"

"Who else?" Saskia bared her teeth in a fox grin.

Despite herself, Emma found herself grinning back. She let Saskia pull her to the floor. At the touch of hands around her waist, her pulse warmed.

Then the other fox maidens descended.

Selina seized them. "Darlings, we've been searching everywhere for you. Dancing time. Come on."

Saskia shrugged and let her hands slip from Emma. At the sudden kiss of cold air around her waist, Emma felt strangely bereft.

The fox maidens plunged into the center of the dance floor and threw themselves into the music, arms twined, hair flying. Emma spun with them, a star in orbit. All around her, bodies pressed close, rippling into one another. It brought back flashes of sweaty nightclubs with Julia: hair falling into her face, someone's hands on her hips.

But everything in the Night City was richer, fiercer. And now it burst on Emma: She was too. Now she was a fox maiden, and immortal. The lines of her limbs sharp, her movements cold and swift as night air. Finally, she recognized the unfamiliar feeling in her body, the clawing energy trying to burst from beneath her skin. Power.

The strings shrieked to a crescendo. Her sisters circled her, a blur of hips moving and teeth flashing with laughter. Emma let her head fall back. She spun, seeing claws trace through the air at the ends of her fingers. She turned on one foot: once, twice, three times. She was newly light, like spider silk slung, or fox song leaping to the night sky. It was beautiful, this body. This power.

And the knowledge struck her that she would be bereft for the rest of her days, if she returned to the mortal world. The normalcy there, the mildness, would chafe her soul almost to bleeding. The air would not taste of incense and adventure. She would not snarl through the streets, or feel the pulse of magic beneath her skin.

As the dancers whirled around Emma, a seductive little whisper wondered why she would want to escape. She could give up her fruitless search for a way out. Forget the Turnbulls and sink into the Night City completely. Live one endless, dizzying adventure with her sisters, century after century.

The idea was exhilarating. Emma could not think why she had held herself back from it. She was sure she'd had a reason. But it slipped from her. The music had command of her body, and her mind was wiped clean. At the opening chords of a new song, the fox maidens looked at one another with comical joy. They flung back their heads and let out a piercing chorus of fox screams. Emma joined them, loudest of all.

As a gong rang out, they piled into the feasting hall. Beads of juice ran like dew from fresh-roasted meats; domed loaves of bread steamed in trenchers with golden roundels of butter and thick amber honey to drizzle on top. There were towers of quince and wild currants; greengages and plums scattered like jewels in a dragon's hoard. Pitchers of chilled mead and lacy elderflower dripped icy tears from their rims.

The fox maidens tore into the feast. But Emma sat still, her plate bare. A song blazed through her mind. A different kind of hunger. For her true self: powerful, fierce. As a mortal, she had spent so long pretending to be smaller than she was, she had even fooled herself. But no more. She was ready.

"Saskia."

"What?" Saskia paused, tooth-deep in a roast fowl. Grease painted her cheeks.

"I want to ask." She would have to say it fast, while the power of the dance still flooded through her.

"You fill me with foreboding — Emma? What's wrong?"

"I want you to take me hunting."

"Hunting?" Saskia looked her over, as though for weak spots. "All right. When?"

"Now," Emma said. "It has to be now."

A slow smile spread over Saskia's face. She licked the grease from her fingers and dropped the half-eaten fowl.

"By all means, new girl. Let's see what you've got."

They fled the ball for the icy air of the streets above. Saskia taught Emma to pull the shadows around herself like a cloak, until she barely registered as a presence to the mortal eye. They went to an alley outside a nightclub. Though it was close to Christmas, and most students fled home for the holidays, the queue was packed. The wild-eyed revelers, eking out the last celebration before being forced back to sober families; the graduate students, set free at last from labs and frowning supervisors; the young college gardeners and cooks and admissions staff. They were loud and flushed. Ties loose, eyeliner smudged. So unwary. Emma almost couldn't remember what that felt like.

And there was something else, too, something all the mortals had and she did not. She felt a huge, beating warmth inside them. And she finally understood what the fox maidens meant, when they talked about mortal vitality. It was a fire, inside those bodies. And she hadn't known, until that moment, that she was so cold. Being near them hurt. It was like frostbite in front of a fire. Like looking in on a bright, cozy house on a winter's night, when you're all alone and cold outside.

So that was what it felt like. That thing she didn't have anymore. Mortality.

That was what a fox maiden hunted. And after all her worries, the hunting proved easy. Saskia showed her. Emma just had to pass her hand over the nearest body. And as her fingers brushed a boy's arm — a shadow's brush, too light for him to notice — she felt a spark of that bright blazing mortal energy peel away, up into her arm. And oh, the beauty of it. Her blood sang. She was warm, finally warm. The silver collar was humming around her neck.

Then she tried to pull more of the mortal's warmth to her. It wouldn't come. She could still feel the energy in him, the boy she'd chosen. She wanted more. But the collar squeezed her neck, like a warning. She'd taken all she was allowed from him.

Saskia guided her hand to the next mortal, and the next. They moved through the crowd, taking a drop of mortality from all they touched. Emma felt the blood pool in her cheeks and pound through her chest. Thought given way to pure instinct. So this was the hunt.

It was a daze that stayed with her all the way back to the House of Foxes. And when Saskia called back to Emma to turn, and her body twisted into a flurry of red fur and white teeth, Emma followed her into fox form without question. The world shifted.

and oh her senses are alive now
for there is a new music in her
the song of claw
to pierce the air
of jaw
to grind and crush
for this is the hunt
and she is fox

It lasted only a few breaths. Then Emma's thoughts caught up and spat her back into girl shape. She fumbled on hands and knees, pavement cold beneath her skirts, and retched into the nearest storm drain. But she had done it. For those few moments, she had been a fox.

Saskia ran back, swirling out of fox form with obnoxious ease.

"All right there, new girl?"

Of course she was snickering at Emma. But she also looped an arm under Emma's shoulders and eased her upright. Saskia had a bigger heart than she wanted to admit, Emma suspected.

"Fox form and star wine do not a match make, in your case. Let's get you home."

Emma let Saskia tow her back to the House of Foxes and slide her gently into bed. The room that had once belonged to Sara was now all her own. She had softened the brutality of the claw-marked walls with a few bunches of flowers, stolen from college gardens. Her meager possessions were piled on the desk. And Nancy had given her a cozy patchwork quilt, which she cuddled to her in the dark as Saskia left. The feel of tail and paws filled her mind. She had been a fox. Truly, nose to tail. A whole other being. She was dazed with the wonder of it. But as Emma's stomach spent the next few hours ejecting every last drop of star wine into a basin Saskia had left by the bed, she had time for the haze of the evening to drift away.

Beneath lay horror at herself. She had known that the Night City was tempting. But she had been so swept away in one night, she had forgotten her mission. Forgotten her mother, and Nat, and the thousand reasons calling her back to the mortal world. Blind to the evil of the Turnbulls, numb to her true rage and the call of her vengeance. Emma spat grimly into the basin and waited. There seemed to be no more wine to bring up. She pulled herself onto the bed and flopped over the covers, fully dressed. It did not seem worth taking off her ball gown. She was too sleepy.

But as her eyes drifted shut, a smile wreathed her face. She would not trade the magic in her limbs or the warmth of her sisters for anything. And it had not been such a loss for her mission either. Because, by succumbing to the Night City, she had learned her own power. And that power made her fast enough and cunning enough to face down any Turnbull. It was a weapon. She had learned that she did not need to block out the Night City entirely. To forgo star wine, perhaps. But there was so much else she could let herself explore. So much awe and darkness. In the mortal world, she could not have brought down the Turnbulls. But now she was changed. The Night City was helping her grow.

Tonight, she had become a fox. In the nights to come, what else might she do? Emma rolled onto her side and pulled a fold of the quilt over her. First, it was time to sleep.

CHAPTER 28

JANUARY SAW ITSELF OUT WITH RAIN; FEBRUARY, WITH SLEET AND hail. On the first day the sun tremulously returned, Emma went straight to the Library. As she had hoped, it was deserted. Most mortals were out basking in the lukewarm weather. So Emma tucked herself into her favorite reading nook and folded Saskia's note into her pocket. An important discovery, or so the scribbled message said. Saskia would tell Emma all when they met, in the Librarian's office.

But Emma had come to the Library hours early, while daylight still glowed through the warped windows. It was useful to have time alone to hunt through the stacks. But for all her work, she'd found no clues to crossing between worlds, and nothing of worth to the messenger either. Logically, she knew that the key to the Turnbulls' downfall would not be out where anyone could find it. She would have to get closer to them. To go where they were. But it was easy to find excuses. It would have been pointless to look in December: The University had emptied for the holidays. And she ought to master fox form first, so if they spotted her, she'd be able to hide.

The truth was, she was afraid. That if she went looking, they would find her, and they would hurt her. So for now, Emma busied herself with her notebook. She had outlined three clear paths of inquiry. Firstly, what had the Turnbulls bargained for? If she knew what they wanted, their vulnerable spots might become clear. Next, how had she been brought into their bargain? On the night of the ritual, had it been something she drank, or touched — or none of those things? The Judge had said she had been "marked" with something "affixed" to her soul, but not how or when. And thirdly, had there been other victims? The Judge had said that the Turnbull contract was of long standing, after all. In finding the other sacrifices, she might be able to piece together more of what had happened to her.

Emma's pen froze at the hiss of approaching whispers. One word caught her: *Boars*. She ducked beneath the desk and crouched, quieting her breath. In the gap beneath the bookcase, she saw two pairs of feet: one booted in leather, the other with talons like an eagle.

The taloned feet edged closer to the boots. Like someone with a secret. "There, s'quieter in here. It's all over the market. Raids on four traders, all innocent folk, like."

The other made a noise of disgust. "You never saw so many Boar patrols, before the flood."

Emma frowned. She hadn't thought about the flood happening in the Night City. Silly of her, really. The nightfolk did share the same patch of land with the mortals. If the mortals had been under water, it stood to reason the City would have been, too.

Emma watched the talons scrape into the floorboards. "That *flood*. It's all been amiss since then, and none as is brave enough to talk about it. And you know the City started it in the first place?"

The boots backed up a step. "Hush yourself. That's bad talk."

"Go on, try'n tell me you didn't recognize the magic behind that water. City, through and through. We all know it."

Magic in the water. Hunched beneath the desk, Emma sorted through flashes of memory. The river swallowing the colleges in a single night. Unnaturally fast, surely. And when it receded, that odd, intoxicating scent it had left behind. Rot and sweetness. The sense that something was strange, somehow. Animals breeding out of season. The knot of frogs on the pavement, writhing and devouring.

Magic. The flood had been swirling with magic. And now it seemed obvious. A flood that rose a whole day before any rain started? Hardly natural. How had she not noticed, not suspected? No wonder nightfolk said mortals were blind.

The boot voice scoffed, though with an edge of unease. "Night's sake, it was enough water to drown the Guilder Wood. Come, why would the City raise all that magic?"

"Maybe something happened. Something the Court's scared to talk about. Like an attack."

"You want us both dead? Night's breath, you can't *say* things like that."

"I wouldn't, near our kind. I'm no keener to see the inside of a cell than you. But it's only cloth-eared mortals here." The voice veered between belligerence and fear. Emma blessed the instinct that had sent her scurrying beneath the desk.

The pair's argument drifted to guild matters. Emma's legs had time to grow stiff in their cramped curl against her chest by the time they moved on. Finally, their voices faded.

Emma crawled from under the desk, muscles complaining. So much time lost working on her notes. The flood was interesting

289

enough, to be sure, but she'd learned nothing she actually needed to know. With a sigh, Emma flipped her notebook shut. She would catch up another time. The afternoon was getting on, and she had a far more important reason for being at the Library during mortal hours: The English Department's last lecture ended at three p.m.

Emma knew this because at three fifteen sharp, a familiar lanky figure would push open the entrance doors and emerge from the stacks. Nat wore his hair short these days. He had a favorite seat near the window.

The punishment for drawing mortal attention inside the Library was fierce, Saskia had said. And Nat would have recognized her the moment he looked up. So Emma watched from behind her bookcase. If she unshelved a few books, she had a gap large enough to see him clearly.

She was never bored, watching him. The way he mouthed parts of the essay as he wrote it, as if performing for an invisible audience. How he crammed a book against his nose when he read a point that excited him, or tossed it onto the desk in disgust when he thought the author was an idiot.

She had been gone more than a year, so it was Nat's final stretch at the University. And Julia's, and Venetia's. Her mother had probably moved to a new posting by now. She always got itchy feet around the eighteen-month mark. Emma was surprised to find herself smiling, as though it were something she loved about her mother, rather than their biggest difference. But if Emma had been mortal, she would have been preparing for a move too. Her head full of final exams, but spinning with the world opening up beyond. This time, she would have been able to choose those places for herself, to stay as long as she wanted.

Emma let her fingers curl, imagined the hunt song of a fox flowing through them, and watched with satisfaction as her nails lengthened and curved themselves into claws. Dark as night; sharp as flints. She dug them into the bookcase, glorying at the yielding scrape of the wood. She was practicing fox form, in her off moments. Shaping her nails into claws came most easily. Knowing she could rend and slash quieted something inside her, a voice that murmured of hunters and danger and boots slamming after her in the night. She didn't have to make a conscious effort. Sometimes, she would just look down and the claws were there.

But if she concentrated harder, she could switch her ears for a fox's keen hearing, or her eyes for a predator's night vision. A full transformation was still an effort. She found fox shape uneasy and hard to hold. It was too animal, too savage: too far from the idea of herself she clung to. The slightest distraction sent her rocketing back up into human form. The claws seemed to be the only thing she could hang on to.

Emma forced her nails back into human shape — although it always felt like a loss — and brushed the sawdust from the ruined shelf. It was the moment she waited for every day. Nat was gathering his belongings. Then he would take his usual path to the readers' café and eat a bacon sandwich at a table outside.

Outside the Library, that is, where the laws of the regular world applied. Where, at four thirty on a bright March afternoon, a creature of the Night City was all but invisible to mortals. Where there was no punishment for being close.

And so, as she had every afternoon she watched him, Emma slid into the café seat next to Nat. He was hunched against the chill, his hands cozied in gloves. He looked up vaguely at the scrape of the chair, but returned to his sandwich and his book. He still hadn't mastered the art of chewing his food before swallowing.

"Hello, stranger," she said.

He looked straight into her face with the beginnings of a smile she had seen a thousand times. When he had spotted her in a crowd, or waved her to the lunch table he'd saved. But it faded, and she knew he had not seen her.

"Well," Emma said, bringing out her own packet. It was only a little crumpled from her crouch under the desk. "I'll have to eat fast to catch up with you. I brought dawn cakes today. I think you'd like them."

He was so intent on his book, Emma could almost imagine he was listening. Two best friends, sitting in the sunlight together, just like always.

"They're best fresh fried, but I saved them to show you. They're from Saskia's favorite vendor at the night market — Saskia, the one with the dark hair and the nuclear tongue, you remember? I've got another story to tell you about her . . ." She had time. Nat always lingered over his book. Telling him about her new life made it all feel almost normal. Even if he couldn't hear her.

"I went hunting again. By myself, this time. It wasn't as bad as I'd thought. Nat, it scares me, but I even *liked* it. I passed Granville College and heard music. It was a party, in someone's rooms. The window was open, and I slipped in, a shadow among all those bright blazing mortal fires. But Nat, this time it felt like power. To be unseen. Unstoppable.

"So I brushed up against a girl here, a boy there. Peeling away that one spark from the fire of their mortality. I don't know what I took from each of them. Maybe the music they heard in a dream.

292

Or the last good night of sleep before their exams. I wonder whether they'd have thought it a worthwhile trade, if they knew what they'd taken from the Night City's power in exchange. A textbook memorized the night before finals. An electric performance onstage. The kinds of things mortals care about. That I used to care about.

"You know, I'd not stopped to think what I might have taken from the Night City, when I was mortal. But now I remember my river project: how methods leapt to mind, and my reports seemed to arrange themselves to point to the right conclusions. I would have been proud of that work, if I'd been allowed to finish it. Even if I'd known I was bargaining away pieces of myself to do it, I would have called it a fair trade. Some things are worth the sacrifice.

"I know *you'd* agree with me." Emma smiled at Nat, picking at the last few crumbs of dawn cake. "I'm not sure anyone will forget the time you decided to learn eleventh-century Gaelic in time for your first *Macbeth* rehearsal. For 'proper character grounding,' I think you said."

A ghost of a smile flitted across Nat's face. Emma knew that he must have read a sentence that tickled him. He could not have heard her. It still twisted her heart.

"But don't worry." She propped her chin on one hand. "I'm not going to drain you anytime soon. It'd be too strange, between friends. I wonder if anyone has, though. If it was Saskia — well, I think you'd like her. She's grumpy, but she's got a big heart, under all the scowling. She loves books as much as you do. And Nancy's looked after me, every moment. She's much sharper than she lets people think. At first, I didn't see past the cleaning and the housekeeping, but Nancy has secrets she doesn't tell any of us, I'm sure."

Nat was still reading. Emma leaned as close as she dared.

"I just wish I could let you know. That I'm all right, and I have friends. I don't want you to be sad."

There were tiny lines around his eyes now. He was too young, surely, to have those. What had the last year been like for him, to draw such lines on his face?

"I mean, yes, the Night City is a pit of monsters and impossible tasks. But if I could only show you some of the wonders. There's a shimmer that dances through the streets. Every ancient wall, every cobblestone. It's all alive. Remember that strange archway — the one by the secondhand bookshop? It looked bricked up to us, but to a nightdweller, it's a passage. To the night market. Oh, Nat, if you could see it."

So she told him, as if it would smooth the lines from his face. About trailing Saskia through the maze of billowing cloth and incense. The music of the night market beating into her pulse, the winged lanterns floating above the stalls like stars. About the vendors, a flurry of hands and paws and talons thrusting goods beneath her nose. Melons with the sheen of jewels. A fairy horse smaller than her palm. A heart in a crystal jar, still beating.

She described for Nat the stall of the jeweler with dragonfly eyes, and the dainty bracelets she had bought there. One for each of her sisters. Not pure silver — her purse could not stretch that far. But the chains were as fine as rivulets of water, and the jeweler had shaped her a tiny winking fox charm for each. The first purchase made with earnings from her own hunts. Her sisters had used their savings to buy Emma's ball gown. They had cared that much that Emma felt part of things. Emma only hoped her gift showed what their bond meant to her. That it was worth as much as any promise made to the City. And unlike the City's silver collars, these brace-lets were something they could choose to wear. A mark of friend-ship, not servitude.

She told Nat how Nancy had cried when she put hers on. Selina and Gertie had held her in a hug so tight, Emma had to claw her way out, laughing, before the breath was crushed from her. Saskia had looped the bracelet twice around her belt, quick and casual, and fastened it there. But sometimes, when Saskia thought herself unseen, Emma had caught her reaching to stroke the fox charm.

A shadow crossed the sun. With a glance at the oncoming clouds, Nat sighed and scraped back his chair.

"Wait — " Emma said.

He was tucking his book into his bag.

"No — "

He was gone.

Emma sucked the inside of her cheek. Less time than usual, today. Desolation ran sharp fingernails down the inside of her throat. It was not as though she had not known it would end this way. It always did. But she still had to breathe through the hurt.

She scuffed her way into the Library to wait for Saskia, taking the back stairs. Nat was not the only mortal who might know her, after all. She had seen Julia here once. How she had longed for that moment, before it happened. Often, when her new life had seemed too strange to bear, Emma had called on the memory of Julia to hold her together. The Julia behind the elegant facade: crooked smile and snorting laugh, kind and silly. Making up nonsense lyrics to their favorite songs, toes shining with wet polish. But Emma had barely recognized the gaunt figure in the Library's astronomy room. It had hurt to see Julia so thin and hunched, worrying at a strand of greasy hair like a rosary. When someone asked to borrow a pen, Julia startled from her seat as though she had been shot. Emma had not seen her since.

But she had seen Jasper's friend Richard, zooming like a happy bumblebee between the stacks and his military history room. So earnest. So dimpled. She still found it in her to pity him, and it frustrated her. She was determined to hate all Turnbulls: They deserved no less. But a memory kept presenting itself: Richard picking at the mortar of a windowsill, speaking thoughts that could have been her own. What it was to be without a father, and to long for one. Looking at him now, she saw a lost rag doll dragged in the wake of the Balfours. Straining for the attention of a man who would never see him as a son. It made her angry for him, which made her angry at herself. None of them deserved her thoughts. Especially not the one whose face flooded her dreams. Night after night, she would close her eyes and find herself in a rose garden. Rot dripped. Flowers fell. And there he would be. Jasper, golden and cruel. Burying her in a shroud of petals. His weight on top of her, dangling a barbed stem above her eye. Pushing it through the socket. Smiling. She woke snarling from those nightmares.

It was too much, all of it. She longed for just one sleep without any dreams at all. Emma tapped on the door to the Librarian's office. It was mercifully empty. And there were hours before Saskia and her mystery were due to arrive. Emma coiled herself into an armchair, trying to keep one ear open for danger. But she could fight sleep no longer. She closed her eyes.

CHAPTER 29

EMMA WOKE TO THE SOUND OF AN AVALANCHE NEXT TO HER EAR.
A stack of books wobbled an inch from her nose.

"Good. You got my note. I've finally made progress with the
Turnbull question." Saskia, resplendent in tartan and leather, and
offensively awake, plunked herself on the arm of the chair. "Do
you want to take the first book, or shall I?"

"I swear I locked the door," Emma croaked.

"Me? Well, if I must." Looking pleased, Saskia reached for the
top of the stack.

" 'The Society of Turnbulls has existed as long as this University has, and they have performed their ritual every year since its
founding.' A ritual. Any clue?"

Emma rubbed her eyes. "The night I turned. I saw it. There was
a chant in Latin. And a strange bowl . . ."

"Latin chants." Saskia cast her eyes to the heavens. "I swear,
they beat all the imagination out of them at boarding school."

"So Jas — " The name stuck on her tongue like a barb. She
cleared her throat. "So the head of the Society, he filled the bowl

with wine, and he put in a paper covered in writing, like a long list — "

"Fine. List sounds promising. Written terms of a bargain? Let's try another of these." Saskia patted the first book fondly and put it aside.

"The club is something to do with the founder of the University," Emma said. "They told me. Were there any bits on him? John de Turnbull."

"Yes. It looks like he founded the Turnbull Society itself, at the same time as the University. It was a group of his closest circle."

"I knew that. Anything else?"

"Not much. Just a history of how John de Turnbull founded the University. He picks a small town with not much going for it except a river and some Roman bits and pieces. Drawn by divine calling, he said."

"The pull of the Night City?"

"Safe to assume. So he builds on top of the City's power. And the scholars here made advances beyond other mortals: in alchemy, medicine, philosophy. The University gathered fame. And as more scholars came, the City granted them knowledge. In exchange — "

"The Night City fed upon them."

"Exactly. The more scholars it had to feed from, the more the Night City's power grew, and the stronger its call became to mortals." Saskia flipped open another book. "Human scholars described a power that 'hung like a fog in the air' around the University. Mortals back then claimed to see strange sights. Supernatural hazes over buildings. Creatures in the shadows. The townspeople thought the University must be the devil's work, and a mob attacked to drive the scholars out. John de Turnbull and his circle were besieged. They were weeks, then days from surrender. He disappears for a few nights. And then — triumph. Out of nowhere."

"How?" Emma asked.

"There is a story. Some of the historians mention it, but — it seems so unbelievable. They say that John de Turnbull made a bargain so clever, he got the better of the Night City itself. He could force its power to his will, to win his battle.

"There are no details of what that bargain was. None. The historians I read seemed scared to admit it even existed. They said that all traces of that knowledge were destroyed. That the City's rage at being tricked was boundless. But no punishment fell on de Turnbull and his followers, as though they were immune."

Saskia turned another volume open at a bookmark. "After that, the scholars build more colleges, more libraries: They flourish. Every man in the Societas Turnbullia rose to unusual power: archbishops and generals, dukedoms and even kingdoms. John de Turnbull became the richest man in the realm. Although he stayed at the University all his life, and refused all titles, he was the whispered power behind every throne. For — " Saskia whistled out a breath. "*How* many kings and queens? No mortal lives that long." She lowered the book, eyes wide. "Emma, if there's no mistake here, he would have been over two hundred years old when he finally died."

"He can't have been." Emma felt a twinge of unease in her stomach. For some reason, her mind pictured John de Turnbull as Piers Popwell. The same nasty sneer. Watching her, eyes cruel and still. His face crumpling and aging like sped-up footage of a rotting apple.

"A scholar notes that, when asked for the secret of his success, John de Turnbull dated it all back to the pivotal moment at the battle for the University. When, he said, 'he came into his power.' This historian goes on to say: 'Those who inhabit the mortal world, who find it easier to believe in a power in the sky rather than one that lives, as they do, rooted in the earth, might take this to mean a man's turning point in finding his courage. But to those of us within the Night's realm, it suggests . . .' "

"The power he took from the Night City," breathed Emma. "He never stopped using it."

"Exactly. But what does that mean about today's Turnbulls?"

Saskia plunged into her stack of books. She looked almost as happy as Nancy did with her feather duster. "If we could just find — ah. The Librarian also pulled this for me. Not the most promising. It's handwritten. Some kind of journal, maybe?"

Emma caught sight of the name scrawled on the flyleaf and snatched at the book.

"Henry. It's his. The Librarian's. Let me — "

"His own notes?" Saskia groaned. "There'll be nothing useful — "

Emma pinned a finger to the page Saskia was trying to flip.

" 'With each ritual, the Turnbull Society confirm their bargain, this unholy hold on the Night City. And with every generation, their stature has grown, as the City delivers to them their wealth, their sovereignty. This they have passed on through their sons, and their sons' sons. Power building on power, down a chain of succession.

" 'But everything has a price. They might command this power, but it does not do their bidding for free. Every year, they must give it something in return. Power for power.' "

Saskia's voice faltered. "A sacrifice."

The world was moving in nauseous shifts. So there was the truth behind Jasper's smiles. The reason he had drawn her close. Hadn't it always felt like a mystery? Why Jasper would want her, above all those girls waiting for his notice; those beautiful others who had been of his world. Who had come from the right families and schools. Now, of course, it made perfect sense. Because those girls had come from power. If they had gone missing, it would matter. Important people would care.

She had been stupid. Fatally stupid, thinking he had wanted her, alone and unimportant, because — because she loved photography, like him. Because she had traveled. Because she was special. It sounded so hollow now. The kind of thing only someone desperate would swallow. Bile crept up her throat.

How his eyes had glittered, when they fixed on her. How hungry he had looked.

"He — they *sacrificed* me. For money. For power." She tried to laugh. It came out a bark. "But they can't get away with it. Even in the mortal world. The police must have asked questions. Like who I was with that night. I *disappeared;* they'll have to have arrested someone. One of them, at least."

"I wasn't sure whether to show you," Saskia said. "I looked at mortal newspapers too. They have them on file here. There were a few about you. This one — "

It was an edition of the student newspaper, dated nearly a year earlier. Emma smoothed the front page.

"SECRET SOCIETY" EMBROILED IN
MISSING STUDENT CASE

As Emma read, she began to shake. So the Turnbulls had been able to deny it all. To lie about where she had been and what they had done. "Little to no relationship with Emma Curran." That was how Jasper had put it.

Emma's claws were scoring gouges into the Librarian's armchair. She felt a vicious delight as it yielded under her. The snap of threads, like tiny sinews. The muscular padding, ripping under her claws. She barely saw the study or Saskia's worried face. Red coats whirled before her eyes. The fox sang through her blood, reminding her that she was a hunter, that this is what she was built for —

to tear and kill
blood on claw and jaw

She laughed aloud.

"I am going to *rip* them apart."

It was marvelously simple. She would start with the first, and move along them in a line. Shredding through dinner jackets and bow ties as though they had been the velvet skins of voles. Then to the rich flesh beneath, their blood a wash of color over her claws. She would leap last for Jasper's heart, feel it burst like overripe fruit between her jaws. She was death and darkness and the night. He would cry before she was done.

Saskia's voice stopped her at the door, pained and urgent. "You can't. None of us can. Emma, no one in the City is allowed to harm them. They're marked. Special, somehow. They're the only mortals we can't touch."

Saskia's words made their way into Emma's brain, slow as molasses. She had to struggle back from her dark visions. To coax a mouth open to snarl to form words instead. "Marked?"

"I've only seen one once. It's really obvious. Like a glowing sign on their backs."

"But how do you know we can't hurt them? Have you ever seen someone try?"

"No, but — "

"The Judge said I was marked too. Can you see that?"

"No, Emma. I can't see anything. I would have told you, you know that."

"They let him go." Jasper's face leered from the newspaper. Laughing at her. "They let all of them go. Like he — like they didn't take everything from me," Emma spat. "I'm here, but they get to go on with their lives? And no one does anything to stop them? No. *No.*"

"Wait!"

The door splintered against the wall.

The corridors of the Library rumbled with Emma's growl.

CHAPTER 30

SHE WAITED, CLOAKED IN THE SHADOWS OUTSIDE THE TURN-bull Clubhouse. The town house stood aloof in its cobbled crescent, cold under the night sky. It seemed to sneer down at her: crouching by its bins, surrounded by the stink of the Turnbulls' discarded bottles and the decomposing scraps of meat from their plates. It only spurred her rage. A panicked part of her fluttered at her rib cage, trying to remind her that consequences existed. But something in Emma was ready to bare its teeth. She was tired of being afraid.

The clubhouse door swung open, and someone in a dinner jacket and a wine-stained cravat stumbled out. On his back was a glowing green mark, like a complex hieroglyphic. So it was true. The Turnbulls were special, protected by their bargain with the Night City. The mark a warning that they could not be harmed.

A growl rumbled in Emma's throat. Her first draining was going to be a Turnbull. And the second. And on and on until the debt was paid.

She had come to hunt.

Piers Popwell did not have a great deal in the way of compassion or humility, but he did have a very keenly developed instinct for survival. Which is why, when most people would not have seen anything to be wary of in the cheery, halogen-lit street outside the Turnbull Clubhouse, he stopped and sniffed the air. All quiet and dark. There was nothing to hear beyond the muffled cheering inside the clubhouse. Two of the slags from the women's hockey team had been throwing up in the soup tureen when he left. Classic banter, that. Chuckling, he wove briskly down the steps.

Alert as he might be, he did not see one of the shadows separate from the others and follow him. It crept closer and closer, close enough to stretch out a hand. Close enough for a chill to blow on his neck, as of a cold breath. Close enough that fingers tipped with claws might reach around his neck to trace his throat . . .

There was a scream, high and unearthly. Piers spun round, taut with fear. No one there. He tucked his chin — which wasn't really weak at all, Mother said, it was all a matter of angles — into his cravat, and continued marching up the street. Perhaps more quickly than usual.

A fox stared at him with baleful eyes from the shadow of a bin.

Emma had crept after Piers, sensing her quarry's breath. But just at the moment of triumph, when her claws were poised to score the soft white flesh of his throat — a terrible pain came, chiming through her teeth. She must have screamed, because it burned as though she'd touched a frayed wire. She lost her command on the shadows that hid her. And then Piers was turning. In another moment, he'd see. That could not happen. She had reached for fox form, frantic as it slid from her grasp like a slippery fur coat. There was no more room for error. She stopped, breathed, found the edges of her fox form. Willing herself to be firm, she pulled it around her.

And it worked. She had not been sure it would, not until the new skin closed around her and cobbles pressed into her four paws. She had actually managed a full transformation, and to stay in it. But her satisfaction had been short-lived.

Piers turned a corner and disappeared. Unscathed. A snarling wind of hatred and disgust swept through her. And as she tasted its grit on her tongue, she realized it was not for Piers. It was for herself. She had chased after the Turnbulls, all that time ago. Had let them dress her in ears and a tail. She had abased herself for their stupid cheers. And now she skulked by their refuse, not even able to land a scratch on them. Emma's fox form shivered in her grasp like a coat in a gale, threatening to fly open.

They had nothing to fear. *She* was nothing to fear. She could not even use the claws and fangs she had made for herself —

A passing car roared by, and Emma lost her grip. She shot back up into human form. She patted herself wearily. Her clothes were still there, at least. Nancy had drilled it into her to treat fox form as a skin she pulled over her own. Transforming that way seemed to keep clothes trapped under the layer of fur. Otherwise, she risked leaving behind every stitch she wore.

She'd done that once, when she'd been so tired she'd tried shoving herself straight into fox form, like someone slamming a door. The fox shape had not stuck, and she'd found herself crouched naked on the floor of the pantry, her clothes in a heap beside her.

"Never mind, love." Nancy's cheeks had been pink from the effort not to laugh. "That was almost a full transformation. It'll be easier soon."

"But when?" Emma knew she was whining. "Please tell me you had this much trouble with shape-shifting."

"I can't say that, exactly. But don't worry, love, it was different for me."

"Different how?" Emma struggled with her gown. The sleeves were laced to the bodice, which was hooked to the skirt, and every cursed fastening needed tightening.

"I chose this." Nancy's soft fingers made quick work of the fastenings at Emma's neck. "Being a fox maiden. I wasn't trapped or tricked, or surprised to get here, like the rest of you. I couldn't wait to transform."

"You *wanted* it?"

"Oh, yes. Arm up, now." Emma raised her arm obediently, and Nancy bent over the lacing. "I wanted the adventure, like. Always dreaming of it, I was. A world bigger'n I had. And I got it, too. Other side now."

Emma switched arms automatically, deep in thought. "Wanting it — helped?"

"Your mind's a powerful part of magic, Emma. You force your body to do what it's scared of, it fights you. But you find something in it that brings you joy? Then you'll get along, right enough. You just have to listen." She had patted Emma's shoulder and stood.

Cursing Piers, Emma drew back to the wall behind the bins. The clubhouse door burst open again, spilling a tide of girls in hockey uniforms and murderously high heels. As they staggered down the steps, something sparked in Emma's brain. She pulled the shadows around herself and ran straight up the stairs, weaving among the group.

"Oy, did you — "

"Stop pushing me!"

Drink-blurred eyes might just have caught the billow of a shadow at the top of the steps, as of a cloak fluttering. The person beneath it, leaping. But the University Women's Hockey 1st had enjoyed too loud and punch-soaked a night to be interested in shadows. The last of them traipsed down the staircase. The front door swung shut.

Pressed into the shadows beyond, Emma's breaths echoed in the dark. The cold marble grandeur of the Turnbulls' entry hall lay dozing before her. A vixen's smile spread over her face. There were more ways than one to hurt a Turnbull. And she was in exactly the right place to start.

CHAPTER 31

MEMORIES HAUNTED THE GRAND STAIRCASE. HUGO, FLORID FACE beaming in the tailcoat and tie of the Turnbull annual dinner. Julia beside him, pale as a phantom in her mermaid lace gown. Emma herself running up the steps, red gown streaming behind. Alive as a flame.

At the top of the stairs, the ghosts left her. Fox instinct ran through her, a live current. *Beware.* She flattened herself against the wall. Voices murmured ahead, from a door thrown open to the passage. A door burned into Emma's memory. The dining room, where they had served her plates of bleeding flesh. Where she had broken their bowl. Where she had seen Jasper's expression change to cold, implacable anger.

She had to force her feet forward, every step silent and sinking in the thick carpet. Firelight flickered from the doorway, casting silhouettes on the wall. She caught the outline of a bow tie, the edge of a tailcoat. Emma pressed herself to the doorframe and peered in. Turnbulls sprawled in chairs dragged around the fireplace. Glasses of port dangled from their hands, tawny as the flames behind.

Francis Carr, once her partner for dinner in this very room. Eddie Spencer, Guy Cavendish, Philip Cranbottom, Atticus Tremaine, and Rory Clarke. Their names were growls in her throat.

"They were back again," one of them was saying. "Asking questions."

"They're journalists." Atticus Tremaine yawned. "That's what they do."

"They're not meant to." Guy Cavendish was petulant. "That was supposed to be all sorted — with the newspaper group and all. I thought we had a deal."

Francis plucked at his bow tie. "It's worse at home. The questions, I mean. My sister won't leave it alone. Asking about the girl. Even my father — "

"Questions are to be expected. Even now. We just need to be prepared, that's all." The deep, cool voice was Rory Clarke's. "They've not reopened the investigation, remember that. The thing that has them so excited at the moment? It's just an appeal. That friend of the girl's. Nate Oluwoggy, or whatever his name is."

Emma's fingers curled to claws around the doorframe. Calling her "the girl." Like she had no name. Like she wasn't a full person to them. Only the fading sting of her encounter with Piers kept her from lunging, teeth bared.

"Can't he leave it alone?" Guy flung himself back in his chair.

"No one can touch us if we keep our stories the same." Rory's gaze was calm. "We were all together, and Jasper was with us. All night. Didn't leave us for a moment."

"And why are we still covering for Jasper? Come on, we're all thinking it." Eddie Spencer looked around for support. "He's been the weakest link here. No alibi. Stupid mistakes in the interviews. *We* all stick to the PR lines we're given. But no, he just — "

"This is what we do," Rory cut in. "This is how the Society works. If one of us goes down, we all could."

Someone snorted. "And if *you* want to piss off the Balfours, Spence, go for it."

Philip Cranbottom smiled thinly. "Think, Eddie. Jasper's not the only one that's been covered for, is he? Remember when you got into that spot of trouble last year? That party. The Baldock girl, Imogen — "

And like a fist to the stomach, Emma remembered. Imogen at the party in Jasper's rooms, dancing barefoot. Staggering between two boys. Being led to one of the bedrooms. Imogen, who disappeared from the University not long after. Emma had been there while something happened to Imogen. While these boys *did* something to her. Guilt burned her throat, sour and sick.

Eddie turned on Philip. "Too much to drink, had some fun, regretted it the next day? That's not the same."

"Her aunt was threatening to raise quite the dust, though. You're lucky you had Balfour senior to back you up. Made it go away, didn't he? Him and my father. Stupid story like that, could have wrecked your career."

"Now it's our turn. We stick up for Jasper," said Rory. "Ride it out."

Francis Carr nodded. "Look, wherever the girl is — "

Philip Cranbottom's voice was a whip. "Do not talk about where the girl might be. Never. We do not know. We do not even *suspect*. Remember that."

Emma's lip curled. Such liars, all of them. But it amused her to think that in one sense, Philip had spoken the truth. Because the boys in front of her did not know *exactly* where she was. That she was a mere fox's leap away, fingers tipped with claws. And that while they drank and gossiped, and wasted the power they'd been given, she was making her way farther into their stronghold. Unstopped. Unstoppable. And somewhere in the shadows of the clubhouse, she would find the key to their destruction.

The key to their destruction looked rather like a broom cupboard, at first glance. But something about it made Emma stop. The metal around the lock was bright with new scratches, as though it were in frequent and recent use. Strange for a cleaning cupboard to be important enough to lock. Or to be in a passage velvety with dust, come to that.

So Emma tried the handle. Locked, as expected. She turned her attention to the floor. Dust lay thick as frosting on a cake; footprints stood out like deer tracks. A fat, layered trail ran down the center of the corridor and turned off at this door. But there was also a second path, narrow and lightly trodden. The prints ended beneath a gilt-framed portrait of a cavalier. Emma approached the painting, triumph tingling in her fingertips. Sure enough, she found a ledge carved into the back of the frame. And nestled inside, a key.

It turned smoothly in the lock. The door swung open. A window lit the outline of a tiny room stuffed with shelves and filing cabinets. In the corner was a door, half hidden by a curtain. Emma pulled back the drapes and hissed. A Turnbull mark glowed green from the wood. And no matter how she tugged at the door, it would not open. Defeated, she turned back to the room. Every surface held piles of paper, folders, box files. A records room. Emma slid the outer door shut and sloughed off her cloak. Time for a different kind of hunt. If — *when* — she went back to the mortal world, she could not rely on the City to bring down the Turnbulls. To destroy them, she needed their secrets.

And after several hours of sifting, Emma knew she had them. Her hands shook. It was too much, too big for one person to comprehend. She had thought she had known the Turnbulls. She had known nothing.

Some records were clearly for the boys. Catering invoices for dinners in the clubhouse, a quarterly bill for the cleaning of silver. And transactions with other services. Like the proprietor of a nearby escort agency, who had apparently complained of her girls coming back with "injuries" and consequently received a sum that made Emma open her eyes very wide.

But the majority of the recent records belonged to the older Turnbulls, the alumni. Records of business deals, legal documents, party donations. Cozy letters between senior Turnbulls and the heads of media conglomerates, outlining a "mutual friendship." To her surprise, the Baldock Group was among them. Whatever had happened to Imogen, it seemed her father had not let it affect his business dealings. The Turnbulls downstairs had expected the media to leave them alone, as though there had been a deal agreed: Reading between these delicately written lines, she now understood their confidence.

Emma read on in disbelief. Corruption, tax dodging, political expense scandals: It seemed impossible for every one of the

313

crimes to have gone unpunished. But they had been. She saw the letters from the business managers and lawyers, on thick, expensive paper, outlining the success of one "campaign" or "initiative" after another. The words "covered up" were not used, but that was the gist of the messages. With enough money, it seemed, you could buy your innocence.

And perhaps the Turnbulls had other helpful tools. In a file marked LEVERAGE, Emma found dirty little sentences on what seemed to be every important person in the country. Jotted notes in jerky, contracted language, as though only intended to jog the memory. Emma could make out some of them. Infidelity, addictions, embezzlement. Some mentioned children in ways that made her swallow and shove the file from her, shaking. The Turnbulls had enough ammunition to blackmail their world into submission.

She turned to the shelves, where gilt-edged books listed members by year. She flicked through a few. With every page, every name she recognized, the tension within her cranked another turn. Politicians, as expected. But also royals, film stars, authors. Surnames that headed the banks and consultancy firms that left recruitment flyers for the students in the mail rooms. The Turnbulls were everywhere.

No, she corrected herself, they were not. They were in one place. At the top.

Emma felt as though she had been looking at a painting upside down. All this time, she'd thought of the Turnbulls as a University club. But these years, this clubhouse, were just a training program. The real center of the Turnbull Society was its alumni. The point of the Turnbulls wasn't to be the most powerful boys at the University; it was to become the most powerful boys in the country.

Emma leaned back in her chair, overwhelmed. These had just been the most recent records. And the Turnbulls were so sure of their power, they were happy to leave this evidence here in plain black-and-white writing, behind one simple lock. Perhaps they were right to feel safe. Whatever they did, succeeded. Whatever they hid, disappeared. They had connections in the media, the courts, the government. She had wondered once what men like this would even bargain for from the Night City. Men who had everything. Now she realized. *Everything* was the bargain. How else could such a small group of mortals have held so much power over so many generations?

The scale was staggering. Of course the Night City hated their bargain. It must be crippled by this flow of power to the Turnbulls. What reward would it give the person who helped it break free?

That recalled Emma to reality. The information she'd found might have swayed a mortal's opinion. It had certainly made her burn with fury. But the Night City would not care about any of it. The only Turnbull dealings it cared for would be magical. She looked again at the door in the corner, and the Turnbull mark glowing from it. The only magical thing in the room. Whatever was behind that door, it was treated as more in need of protection than the secrets here. It was where she needed to be.

But try as she might, the door would not open. Emma tried force, then cunning. Nothing shifted it. She searched every inch of wall, but there were no keys hidden behind paintings here. Jamming her claws into the lock only resulted in a nasty jolt and a strong smell of singed fox.

Defeated, Emma slumped against a filing cabinet and waited until the Turnbulls stumbled out of the house. She heard a dim bloom of voices and a muffled door slam. Then she slunk through the darkened house with every muscle tensed. The Turnbulls' mortal crimes weighed on her as though she were part of them. Because now she knew. And it was her responsibility to make sure the world did too.

But she forced herself to leave the records room without taking anything. Not tonight. Missing papers could put the Turnbulls on alert. Given warning, they might destroy the evidence in the records room and the secret space beyond. Emma had to get through that locked door first, before giving them any reason to suspect that they were under attack. Her reward from the City depended on it.

So she padded through the warren of disused passages at the base of the clubhouse, until she found a disused storage room at the back of the building. A perfect entry point for someone who wanted to remain inconspicuous. She broke the lock on the window and climbed through. From the alley beyond, she turned to glare at the Turnbull Clubhouse. She was not done with that secret door. And now she had a way back inside.

CHAPTER 32

THE LOCKED DOOR WITHSTOOD ALL HER EFFORTS TO OPEN IT. Emma had returned, more than once. Each time, with a new idea. Each time, disappointed. The opening charms she bought at the night market had no effect. Trying to pry off the hinges only stung her claw-tipped fingers numb.

As the moon waned and fattened once more, Emma felt numbing despair creep in. For the first time, she truly considered that she might fail. That she might never escape the Night City. Even as the spring bloomed lovely around her, Emma felt only the cold of the rainy nights. Her sisters could not tempt her to their jaunts in the Night City. Not the fairy horse auction at the night market; not the brandy raid in the Master's Sitting Room at Granville College; not even the ballet of the bats in the starry groves of the University Arboretum. Hunting was the only thing that settled her. At least she was earning something toward her escape. Even if it was a droplet against the sea of her thousand-year debt. And so Emma stalked her prey.

One evening, Emma perched in an alder tree by the river,

waiting. The University track team ran the path below, and they would be rich pickings. But the runners were late. Emma peered down, looking for them.

Something else caught her eye instead. In the thicket that stretched beneath the alder to the river, she saw thatching. Emma slid down the tree and waded forward. There was a hut hidden in the bracken, low to the ground and roofed with dripping reeds. It would be invisible from the path and the water. The air was quiet there. Almost too quiet. There was no birdsong, no friendly rustle of squirrels. The opening of the hut gaped at her like a dark mouth.

A voice hissed from its depths. *"What do you wish?"*

Emma backed away.

"Do not leave, little one. Enter."

"No, thank you," Emma said, as politely as she could. "I must go."

"And leave behind the thing you want most?" the voice caressed.

"How would you know what that is?" Emma crossed her arms, skeptical to the core.

"No corner of the heart is secret to the water hag."

"The water hag?" With a jolt in her pulse, Emma remembered the fox maidens' tale. "You take memories."

"I show memories," the hag said. *"We all have things we wish for. Things lost in the past. A lover, left in the mortal realms? A babe, perhaps, or a long-gone home? Do you not have something you wish for?"*

Her mother's hands, warm on her shoulders. The rosemary smell of her. Something yawned inside Emma: a hole that screamed like a tiny lost child. If she could just feel her mother holding her one more time.

Emma hushed the voice warning of danger. She was a fox

318

maiden now, armed with claws and teeth. The hag should be wary of *her*. She ducked into the hut's entrance.

"And if I do have something? A memory?"

"Then I can help. I need only an item — and coin."

Emma crawled in. The inside of the hut smelled as damp as the outside. A fire glowed at the center of the gloom. Beyond, a dark figure waited.

The water hag. She did not wear a wig of weeds, as Nancy had predicted. Her hair was a pale cascade, knotted with talismans of bird bone. Within the tangled mass, her face was unlined. But her eyes were ancient pits, and the fingers that reached for Emma were glassy, as though the fingerprints had worn smooth from use.

"Come." The water hag's voice was sand over river stones, the grit in it ground fine over centuries. *"Closer."*

Her young-ancient face stilled, as though she listened to a sound Emma could not hear. *"There is a strangeness to you. You carry memories that are not your own. I hear them, whispering. I see a shape of cruel lines, fixed upon you."*

"There's something *on* me?" Emma twisted to look at her back. Her skin crawled, as if with wriggling insects.

"Not on, but inside. It glows from your soul, this rune. A key that locks within the memories of many others…"

"A rune fixed to me. To my soul," Emma said, with a sick realization. The Judge's ruby eyes loomed before her. *Marked by the bargain with the Turnbulls,* he had called her. Branded as a sacrifice by a thing *affixed to your soul*. But then Saskia had told her that whatever marked her, it wasn't visible. So Emma had stopped wondering whether the thing on her was a literal mark, like the rune the Turnbulls wore on their backs. Or whether there might be someone who could see it for her. If she knew what this sacrifice mark was, and what it held, could she find a way to destroy it? To free herself?

The water hag regarded her curiously. *"I could read the memories that cling to this rune, should you wish."*

What memories would be trapped within such a mark? Those of the Turnbull who had placed it, perhaps? Or someone else? Emma's nails bit into her palms. The Judge had said that the bargain was *of long standing* and *paid before now at the appointed time.* So she could not have been the first sacrifice. Others had worn this mark before her. She imagined it clawing into them, drinking away their souls, those unlucky ones who had not been protected as Emma was by her fox's skin. She thought of small pieces of those souls catching on the mark, staying trapped like food stuck between teeth.

Emma scrabbled backward. She had to get away. She could not witness those kinds of memories. But she did not even make it to the door. Those memories might hold the Turnbulls' secrets. She needed those secrets to trade with the Night City for her reward. So she could go home, destroy the Turnbulls, and not even need the locked room to do it.

"And you can show me these memories, even if they aren't mine?"

"Oh yes. I read memories held in objects, not just people. Will you hear my terms?"

Emma would taste the memories within the mark, the hag said. But once tasted, payment would be due. The memories would become the property of the water hag and be wiped from Emma's mind. The memories of nightdwellers did not have the blazing vitality of the mortal kind, but they still held some value. Added up, they paid the water hag's dues to the Night City. Emma would understand.

Emma edged back. It would be no use discovering the Turnbulls' secrets if she could not remember afterward. There had to be another way.

"What if I offered a trade?" she faltered. "A memory for a memory, yes. But you take other memories from me instead, and I keep these."

The water hag's gaze bored into her. *"The memories here are strong. I can feel them. Their intensity gives them value. What could you give as equal?"*

Emma thought fast. It was a gamble, and she would need Nat's performance skills to pull it off. "Take the thing I valued most in my mortal life." She paused for dramatic effect. It was what Nat would have done. "Take my law studies."

The water hag leaned in.

"My learning at the University meant everything to me. Everything." Emma tried to look wistful and noble. "Take those memories." She hoped she had been convincing.

Firelight glittered on dark eyes. *"Very well."*

The water hag stoked the fire and bade Emma close her eyes. There were rattlings and chants. Smoke puffed up Emma's nose, acrid and scented with herbs. It made her cough until her throat tore. She wiped bleary eyes.

And found herself within the first memory. She was in the Turnbull Clubhouse. It was her own memory, exactly as she recalled it. Jasper held a jar aloft, poured four red drops into the Turnbull bowl. Emma felt the press of the next memories, calling her away. But she lingered another moment. Because here, Julia was beside her. Memory-Julia turned to Emma with light in her eyes. Emma wanted to lean into her warmth, but the memory-body would not move. And so she watched Julia fade and the next memory take hold.

She was in the same room; a table stood at the center with the same ritual objects. But the boy above the bowl was not Jasper. And the memory-body was not hers. This girl—*Lucy, her name was, Emma heard it in her mind*—had almost sweated through the shirt the agency had made her wear, and she was worried. Her arms ached after hours of carrying trays. The money for the gig was good, she was reminding herself. And though her friend had said they'd be the worst kind of posh boys, they'd been fine so far. Even asked her to stay after dinner for drinks. Which made it hard to go home, not without being rude. But things were getting strange. They did some weird shit, rich people. Emma lost track of the girl's thoughts then. Because she had looked at the crowd of Turnbulls behind the table. And she had seen Jasper and Richard. For them to have been at the University in this memory, this girl had to have been sacrificed the year before Emma. But they could not have sacrificed two girls in as many years. Once a generation, she'd imagined. To claim a soul every decade or two was monstrous; unthinkable, even. But one a year? She lost her grip on the girl, and the current of memories took her.

The next sacrifice was sobbing. Clutching the wall of Wessex College, falling. Something was happening to her. Her thoughts were draining away and her name and herself —

Gray flooded the world. Faces loomed close, asking *What's wrong?* and *Can you hear me?* and none of it mattered. It was too much trouble to move. There was nothing left inside. No feelings, no memories. Just numbness.

Emma reeled back. The first memory had shown her the ritual and the boys; this girl had given the story of her draining. Left alive, but empty. Her soul, her self, taken. She must have been on her way home when it happened. Emma tried to stay, to see if she was safe, but the next memory was upon her. And they began to flick faster now. Over and over, she saw the Turnbull Clubhouse, the bowl and the runes, the boys in tailcoats. She felt one memory-body after another wrack with screams, with sobs, as thought and soul and self spilled out like warm blood. She wore a miniskirt, an A-line dress, finger-waved hair, a corset. Often now, there was a servant's apron over her dress. And still the memories roared through her. Men bent over her: in breeches, in powdered wigs, in lace cuffs. Then ruffs, cloaks, doublets. The Turnbull Clubhouse she knew gave way to smoke-blackened beams and a floor strewn with rushes.

There were so many girls. Too many. Dimly, Emma felt tears track down the face of her living body, far away in the water hag's hut. But she was down in the screaming. Now the Turnbulls had her by the river, and the damp was soaking through her shift. Only her shift; they had taken her clothes. They put a bowl before her on the ground, forced her over it, hands and knees, like a beast. They pulled her hair back. A man crouched next to the bowl. He had a knife. She was trembling now, and her bowels went, but he did not flinch. He patted her forehead, as you might a cow. His eyes were cold as snow, she thought. Then his knife moved. And she was gone.

Emma came to gasping, clutching her throat. She felt the sear of the knife's slit, hot on her skin. That memory had been different. They had not just drained the girl of her soul. They had killed her.

"Well? That was the last, and oldest, memory." The water hag emerged from the dark.

But Emma's voice was locked within her. There had been so many. She had held a thousand women's breaths in her mouth, felt their fear, lived their pain. The sacrifices had been happening for centuries. And the Turnbulls would do it again. They would keep doing it unless someone stopped them. Unless she stopped them.

"It is time for your payment." The shadows within the hut thickened.

"Yes, my studying memories," Emma said brightly, edging her foot from the dark tendrils. "You can take them now."

"You thought to trick me?" hissed the water hag, lunging from the dark. Her hands were shards of ice on Emma's shoulders. *"With memories so weak and thin, you discard them without care? No, what I take must be warm and alive, as close to you as the beating of your heart."*

Cold dripped through Emma, like fingers probing at her mind.

"And what will be worth a thousand years of memories, I wonder? Your name? Or the ones you love, perhaps? I see a mother. And friends. The boy, all jokes and aliveness. And the girl. Their memories glow within you, so rich…"

The very reeds of the hut were wailing, the air a whirling shriek of smoke and shadow. She had to have something of value to trade, if she could only think of it. She could not lose Nat, or her mother, or Julia. She could not lose her name.

And an idea flashed before her. "I know how to pay you."

The air in the hut calmed.

"I need to keep the first of these memories," Emma said. "I must. I have to remember that there were others like me, once that had this mark, and what happened to them. The mortals who did this — I can't stop them unless I'm armed with something."

The water hag's eyes narrowed.

"But you may have the rest," Emma hurried on. "All the rest — nearly a thousand years of memory, which must mean something. And to make up the difference, take something of mine. Something of true value, this time."

She held out her hand to the water hag and brought a memory to the surface. She was five or six, and it was the first time she had seen a horse. She had been gripping her mother's hand, and seen the great tapered head turn, and the horse's eye come to rest on her. And in the moment she saw the intelligence in those velvety depths, she knew that she wished to understand animals more than anything.

The water hag drew in a satisfied breath. *"Ahhhh. That will do."*

Fighting the impulse to claw her memory back, Emma let the water hag take her hand. The hag fanned the fire, and Emma coughed till her sinuses ached. Smoke curled through the caverns of her skull.

A pleasant numbness swept through her. She knew that she had seen centuries of memories clinging to the mark set within her. She had just seen them, after all. But their contents were a watery blur. Only Lucy's memory remained.

"I have known powerful men," the water hag said, watching Emma cough out the last of the smoke. *"That is what cast me into the Night City. Mine did not have such clever, sorcerous tools as*

yours, only the ordinary brutality of fist and muscle. But their effect was the same."

She gripped Emma's hand, and her touch was no longer ice.

"Take this one back."

It was the girl kneeling by the river. The first sacrifice, her fear as fresh as if her blood had spilled yesterday, not a thousand years before.

"It is wise to know the beginnings of things. Therein can you find their end."

"I don't understand."

The ancient eyes kindled. *"I wish you victory. We do not all get our revenge. May you bring your enemies to their knees."*

Emma felt the kinship blaze between them. "I can take them lower than that, I think."

The water hag cackled, high and eerie. *"Oh, I like you. May we meet again."*

Crawling from the hut, Emma thought she might forgo that pleasure. She would rather be in the mortal world. And she was going to make it happen, if she had to force the whole Night City to bend before her to do it. The encounter had given her new fire. Yes, the memories had shown her no magical secret to destroy the Turnbulls. But they had given her a thousand more reasons for revenge. Her skin still sang with the feel of Lucy's heart beating, and the edge of her nerves. The Turnbulls had to pay.

Emma pushed through the bracken, breathing in the scent of the river. And it came to her that memories were not all her time in the hut had given her. There was something the water hag said. It stuck in her mind, a barb. The hag had described Emma's sacrifice mark as a key to those memories. A chance phrase. But Emma's mind threw up a thought to follow: What if other marks could be thought of as keys? There was a magical lock she had been beating her brains out to open. Which, logically, would require a magical key. The secret room at the Turnbull Clubhouse had borne the Turnbull mark. What if the mark itself was also the key?

Emma ran, shoving through the rest of the thicket to get to the river path. It made perfect sense. Only those who bore a Turnbull mark would be able to pass through that door. Which posed a problem. Her first rash impulse was to seize one of the boys straight from the street. But she'd not even been able to scratch Piers before the pain blinded her. She could not imagine trying to manhandle one of them to the upper floor of the clubhouse.

At the sound of voices, Emma stepped off the path into a tree's shadow. The University track team thundered past. Emma let them go. She had more than hunting to think of now. She would need help to open that door. And Robin had promised to give it. Well then, she would have to see what he could do for her.

CHAPTER 33

Two nights later, Robin strolled into the alley behind the Turnbull Clubhouse. He hefted a sack on one shoulder. A large, ungainly sack with a distinct odor of damp soil.

"Shall we, lady fox?"

His cheerfulness seemed to dare her to ask about the sack, so she said nothing. Robin had his own reasons for everything. Annoyingly, they usually seemed to be good ones. So she kept her lips pressed tight when the sack proved to be just as difficult as it looked to squeeze through the window, and when it left the Turnbull carpets smeared with soil.

As they entered the mortal records room, Robin only sniffed. But Emma found her steps slowing. There was *so much* here. Enough to bring the Turnbulls down, if she only had a way to spirit it all out before morning. If only —

"Lady?" Robin cocked his head. She joined him by the inner door, where the Turnbull mark glowed baleful and green.

He swiped a finger down the wood. "Basic, but not bad for

mortals. At least one of them must be practiced in runes. That's useful to know."

"Can you open it?"

"Not by myself. It can only be opened by someone with a matching mark." Robin's teeth flashed white in the darkness. "And *that's* why I brought a friend."

He leaned over the sack and rummaged.

Suspicion dawned. "Oh no. You didn't."

Robin straightened, holding what was unmistakably — or had once been — a human torso. Brown and leathered, bone showing through desiccated flesh, clasped to Robin's chest like a dance partner. A Turnbull mark glowed feebly on its moldering back.

"I dug him up for you," Robin said soulfully. "Don't you like him?"

Emma spluttered.

"I used the surnames you gave me, O star among ladies. Took a little trip to the graveyards. Popwell, Wellesley-Jones, Spencer, Tremaine. Plenty of those buried here. Not all Turnbulls, but it only took me a few graves to find this fellow, mark intact. Say hello to Sir Walter Tremaine, sixth Earl of Kelmsloe."

Emma stared at the very old, very dead wristbone offering itself for her to shake. She then looked very deliberately up at Robin. He grinned at her. And though part of her was sure she ought to be appalled, she found herself grinning back. Admiring the cunning. The Night City was rubbing off on her, it seemed. And strangely, that didn't feel like a bad thing.

Robin pressed the fraying torso to the door. He let Sir Walter's wristbone rest on the handle and slipped his own strong brown hand over it to press down. The lock clicked open. There was no light in the room beyond. Emma reshaped her eyes into a fox's, while Robin cursed and dug a candle stub from his belt-pouch. Within lay a dreamscape of curiosities. It was like the storage cupboard of a mad alchemist, Emma thought. Robin ransacked the shelves, discarding artifacts. He flung a jeweled dagger aside with disgust.

"Not even five hundred years old. How are we to find anything on their first bargain if they insist on hoarding an eon's worth of modern junk?"

Emma stepped past. Robin was only interested in the Turnbulls' original bargain. But she was more interested in the one that had involved her. Her memory of the ritual shone in jeweled colors, as though the water hag's attention had polished it rich and clear.

Candles flickered around the bowl. Jasper read the incantation from crumbling parchment. The stone pot spilled a drop of red at each compass point. A typed list drowned in the bowl. A knife stirred it all to bind it, flashing through the wine.

Emma sucked in a breath. She was here with Robin, as safe as might be expected for anyone in the Night City. She was not back in that room. But the hands that fisted in her gown now quivered with claws. That wine. She would remember the scent of it until she died. Emma pulled herself to her feet, already reshaping her nose. With a fox's sense of smell, the room came alive. Threads of scent, spinning in the air. And among them, the wine in her memory. Emma picked a silver cup from a shelf: a roaring blaze of scent. But there were other sources. She turned and caught the gleam of a knife resting on a box. A battered blade, blooming with rust stains. She had seen it before. Flashing in Jasper's hand as he brought it down. And the box beneath was just the right size for the Turnbull bowl, that horrid dome of glass-stone wriggling with veins. It had been the heart of the ritual, she was sure. Emma tugged up the lid of the box, blood rising in her ears. Then she slumped, fighting disappointment. The bowl was not there. But there was a lidded stone jar, softened with age. The one Jasper had held in the ritual. Emma held the jar to her nose. What was it, that distracting smell?

The salt-metal scent hit with enough force to bring tears to her eyes. Blood. Emma pressed a fox claw to her thumb and drew a bead of red. She barely had to inhale to know. The blood was the same. This jar had not just held any blood. It was her own.

A smash as the bowl breaks; the chips of stone slicing her skin; Jasper binding the long cut on her palm; droplets of her blood on the floor, on the bowl, on his hands.

Another thought assaulted her. This jar had not held only her blood. The scent was too strong, the jar too stained. There were layers of human blood here. An endless tapestry; hundreds of scent threads. She was holding in her hands the blood of all the sacrifices. The women whose memories she had lived. A thousand years of them.

"Robin." The shake in her voice must have given her away, because he was by her side in an instant. He listened to her, nodding briskly, and she was grateful for his matter-of-factness. One sign of sympathy, and her control would have dissolved.

He sucked his teeth. "The parchment and the bowl would have been ideal. But still, my copper-furred nymph, this is tremendous." He hugged her round the shoulders. "We always suspected they needed tools to help them carry off a ritual of this scale. As mortals, they'd have to. But we'd never have found what they used. Not among this mess. The City will be delighted."

"It will? This is enough, then?"

"Oh yes. For we discover one more surprise." With a magician's flair, Robin flipped the lid from the blood jar. There was a mark carved into it. A rune. Not the same one that glowed from the Turnbulls' backs, as she first thought. The lines were denser, with slashes radiating from the center like starbursts.

Emma's throat closed up around her words. "The Judge said the Turnbulls had fixed a mark to my soul. One that linked me to their bargain. This shape is — it must be the same."

So this was the rune the water hag had seen within her. The thing that had made her a sacrifice. Stamped somewhere deep inside her, like a tattoo she had not asked for. It was a violation.

"We've always known the Turnbulls marked their victims with something. But none in the Night City have ever been able to see it." Emma could have corrected him, but decided not to. The water hag deserved her freedom from the prying eyes of the City. Robin replaced the lid on the jar, gleaming with glee. "It is the essential clue. Without it, we could not guess what magic the Turnbulls used to force such a strange bargain upon the City. Whether alchemical or runic, in a common language or an ancient tongue. Centuries of scholars have searched for the missing proof of their methods. And now here we are, finding it."

He could not have said anything more calculated to cheer her.

"That sounds . . . valuable," she said slowly.

"Oh yes." His smile was growing. "The reward should be considerable."

"Enough to send me home?"

"I think so."

Emma was not sure whether the gasps fighting to escape her throat were sobs or laughter. Light danced in her chest. The floor under her boots was the slanting deck of a ship. She had done it. She had her path home.

She was going to climb the stairs of Gabriel Tower again. She would sit in the front row at Nat's next play. She would lounge in the sun with her mother, lazily debating the classification of a plant. It was over, this nightmare of darkness and blood and claws. Whatever the Turnbulls had done to her, she had undone with her own work and cleverness. And with a way back to the mortal world, she would make them pay.

Robin was looking at her oddly. "And you're sure that's what you want? You could stay, you know."

"Stay?"

"With that reward, you could be free of your collar. Attain a minor position at Court, even. Think on it. I should hate to pine for you. We might do great things together, lady fox." He flashed her a mischievous smile. "And it could be fun."

"Fun," Emma echoed. She pictured running through the gilded corridors of the Court, gown flying behind her like wings. Silver halls lit with fireflies; trees of jeweled fruit; adventures with Robin. Regretfully, she released them all. "I can't. Not with what I've seen in that records room. In the mortal world, the Turnbulls are untouchable. I'm the only one who knows what they've done. With those secrets, I might be able to bring them down. I have to go back. I have to try."

Robin sighed. "I feared as much. Your streak of the heroic is most inconvenient, my lady. I hope you know that. Well, I shall take these to the Court for our reward."

He lifted the box that held the silver cup, the blood jar, and the knife and swung the sack over his shoulder. He had found time to repack Sir Walter in his earth-stained travel compartment, it seemed. The door to the secret room closed behind them. Robin strode out to the corridor; Emma stopped in the records room.

"Leave me here," she said firmly.

"Lady mine, there is enough paper for twelve to carry. And you cannot take any of it without alerting them to your theft. It's a hopeless case."

"I'll decide that." She gave him a vixen-like grin. "You get Sir Walter back to bed."

His eyes met hers, full of suppressed laughter. "I bow to your wish, my lady."

Emma paced the corridor, hoping her brain would hunt up a clever solution. But Robin had been right. She could not take any of the files, not without the Turnbulls suspecting their secrets had been compromised. But with what remained of the night, she might be able to copy out a few documents. It was not perfect, but it was something.

The glint of a frame caught her eye. The wall here had been given over to photographs. They ranged from modern color to the blurred grays of the earliest age of photography. Young men in tailcoats and waistcoats stared from every picture. There they were. Jasper, Piers, Richard. All of the Turnbulls she knew, posed in proud rows. She strolled back through the years of photographs. There was Francis Carr's lantern jaw on a 1967 Turnbull. *Eustace Carr.* And in the gray tones of 1920, a man so sharply lovely, he might have been Atticus Tremaine's twin. *Lord Archibald Tremaine.* Speeding forward to the eighties, the cold eyes of Jasper's father peered haughtily from a frame. *Lionel Balfour.* But it was not there that Emma stopped. It was not there that the blood fled her cheeks, or her lips peeled back in a snarl. She stood rigid, with fingers clawed, staring at a face in another photograph. She tore it from the wall and let it smash on the floor.

An idea ripped through her like a wildfire blown by a gale. She might not be able to take the records from the clubhouse. Not without the Turnbulls noticing what was gone. Unless all of it was gone. Every paper. Every wall. Every trace of the Turnbull Society.

She worked quickly. There were a few hours before morning. Enough time for a fox to slip through the streets to the House of Foxes. And soon after, for a blur of copper forms to lope back across town. When they got to the clubhouse, the fox maidens asked no questions. They set to work ferrying the boxes and files from the house. Emma waited until they had all gone. Every file, every letter, whisked away. She padded from the empty records room, listening as her sisters' song fluted from the alleys and chimneys outside. The last task would be hers alone. It was hers by right.

The photograph crunched under her boot as she passed. She did not look at the face beneath the cracks. A blond young man, with a nose that might seem challenging on a twenty-year-old girl, but fit perfectly on that square-jawed countenance. Taller than the others around him. Just as she was. *Hugh Pelham,* read the caption. Had he kissed her mother by the time that photograph was taken? Had he already known he would leave her? That he would grow up to be a man with a house in the loftiest enclaves of London, with expensive cars and tailored suits and a family that shone in the reflected glow of his wealth? A man who wore a Turnbull mark on his back.

A man whose fortune had come from somewhere. From a bargain. A ritual. From somebody else's sacrifice.

Emma stalked downstairs and flung open the doors to the dining room. She had one more memory to make here. It only took one shining claw, trailed along the fire grate. Sparks leapt in its wake, spilling onto the hearth rug. Puffs of flame that caught and spread. Emma stooped to light a candelabra from them. She held it aloft and spun for one last look at their room. Their cozy chairs for drinking. Their crystal, their silver. They had so many things, these boys.

Emma touched the candelabra to the base of every heavy velvet curtain. She heard the animal growl of fabric catching light. Flames, red as foxes, licked the ancient timbers of the Turnbull Clubhouse.

But that, of course, was not the last of it. Burning a building was one thing. Burning a society to the ground required more. Emma slipped out into the dark. There was one last domino to fall.

Olivia Farquhar tore her fingers through her hair. She'd run out of coffee sometime between midnight and dawn, and Chaucer was still refusing to cooperate. Her nonexistent essay was expected on Professor Lindman's desk in two hours.

A knock rang out across her room. Startled, she darted to the door. There was no one there.

Then her gaze dropped.

Someone had lined the corridor outside her room with filing boxes. The closest was open, with a sheet of paper on top. She bent and scanned it. A second later, she was dialing the number of Mus Khan, her coeditor at the University student newspaper.

"Mus, you have to get over here. Now."

Mus was still grumbling when he reached her room, tugging a hockey hoodie over *Doctor Who* pajamas. He found Olivia cross-legged on the floor amid a sea of paper.

"Come in," she said, without looking up. "You've got to see this."

He studied the sheaf she handed him and swore softly. "These are real?"

"Real as they come. Someone dropped these off this morning and ran. Look at this one — we wondered why none of the bigger press picked up the Turnbull angle of the Emma Curran case. We argued over it, you and I."

"A total media blackout?" Mus sank to the floor next to her. "We didn't know who we were reckoning with."

"And now we do." Olivia dug through a box, face intent. He knew that look. Once she had a story between her teeth, she never let it go. "Someone's dropped us the scoop of all scoops."

"Should we . . . give it to someone? Like, a proper journalist? We've barely scratched the surface, and it's practically enough to take down an entire Cabinet Office."

"None of the bigger outlets will touch it," Olivia said impatiently. "Look at these letters. They'd be scared stiff. In fact, if we publish any of this, we might as well kiss goodbye to the nice media internships we were looking forward to."

"So what do we do with it, then?" Mus grinned. He already knew the answer.

Olivia smiled, impish as ever. "What we always do. We publish."

CHAPTER 34

THE NEXT MOONRISE FOUND EMMA IN THE NIGHT MARKET, HUM-
ming with satisfaction. The University had imploded. The student paper had never flown from stacks so quickly. Students stood
in doorways, waving copies. Academics gathered in conclaves of
tattered knitwear, dissecting details. Expensive cars with silent
engines flew up from London, spilling dark-suited government
advisers and lawyers who hounded the offices of the University
chancellor. But the paper would not back down. It had published
three special editions and counting. Pickup on social media was
moderate, at first. And then the first national outlet had caved. After
sending its own fact-checkers to the student paper's offices, where
the evidence boxes were closely guarded, it ran an article verifying
the claims. The internet fell upon the stories with slavering fervor.

Emma had run through the streets, picking up every discarded
sheet of newsprint she could find. She burned with triumph at every
page. Two more national papers had joined the first. The Turnbulls'
fall was public. And yes, it might be a small ripple, for now. Only
a few stories had made it to print; and those not the most lurid in

the records room. But Emma could picture the future. The shame-faced paparazzi walks in front of family castles. The cars sold, the helipads shut down. Turnbulls leaving courtrooms, heads bowed, chased by whispers that would not cease. The shame. The pain. The justice.

"Lady fox. A sight to gladden my heart."

Emma looked up. Robin leaned against the sugarsmith's stall, all curly beard and mischief.

"I have news." Robin tossed the stall keeper a coin. A large one, Emma noticed. And his tunic was far finer than any she had seen him wear before. There were pearls embroidered on the velvet. But the tree of the Night City was missing.

"That's not a messenger's tunic." A long-lurking suspicion surfaced. "But you've never really been just a messenger, have you? What messenger would be given secrets the Night City would not even trust to its Court?"

Robin took a twinkling sugar bluebell from the stall keeper, presented it to Emma, and steered her to another stall.

"None can match your cunning, lady fox. It was, perhaps, convenient for me to wear the uniform. Messengers go everywhere: unseen, unremarked. Unremarkable. A useful costume to carry out my work. I am sent to handle matters that require . . . discretion."

"You mean you're a spy," said Emma, savoring her bluebell. It tasted of spring mornings. "And a good one, I suspect."

"I believe the mortal term is 'spymaster.' " He bowed. "And the Night City has given no complaint of my services."

"So what is this 'news'?"

His whisper was warm in her ear. "I have your escape."

The words sent spirals of shock down her spine.

"A lordling recently displeased the Night City and was sent to the mortal realm."

"I heard," said Emma dazedly. "For a week and a day."

She had not wanted hope to break her. So she had told herself that spreading the Turnbulls' secrets could be justice enough for her. That if Robin's promise of escape never came true, she might live a satisfied life with her sisters in the House of Foxes, hunting her enemies from the shadows. But it had always been a lie. Now her escape was before her, she felt her hunger for it. Tasted it, like the sugar on her tongue.

"Of course you heard," said Robin approvingly. "You know how to listen and observe. Do you know how rare that talent is? You are wasted in the mortal realms. If you stayed here, I'd have a job for you. But no matter." He sketched a square in the air. "The lordling was sent through a door like this. A hole in the veil between the mortal realm and ours, if you like. But one with a special attribute. Those who pass through it emerge as mortals. It was built in days gone by, when 'playing mortal' was a favorite amusement of the Upper Houses." He grinned. "A moon's worth of mischief, and then they might return through the door to our world, and be mortal no more. Now it is forbidden. The door is heavily guarded. Any approaching without the Night City's warrant would be torn apart by the gatekeeper."

"I do not think I'd like that," said Emma carefully.

"Nor I. So you will be granted a boon. In exchange for your reward — the entire sum — you will be permitted to pass through this door. Just once, and in one direction. To become mortal. You will be given a token to let you through."

"Like my token of protection?"

"A good deal shinier than that, O diamond on the slipper of dawn."

"So where is it, this door?"

"Beneath that extraordinary-looking mortal bridge. The wooden monstrosity."

"The Mathematical Bridge, you mean?" Emma had always liked that bridge. It had supposedly been built with no nails or bolts at all. The whole structure, impossibly, was held together by mathematical perfection alone.

Robin shuddered. "Mathematics. Another monstrous creation of the mortal mind. An affront to the beauty of mystery."

Though she loved all things quantitative, Emma let that pass. Escape filled her mind. "So when will it happen?"

"It will take some weeks to arrange, O sure-footed sprite. You would not believe the paperwork involved. I will send word when all is ready."

She tried not to sound plaintive. "And will I see you before I go?"

"Afraid not, lady fox. The Night City has commanded me next to a spot of trouble in the far reaches. It may not be in my power to return within the next two moons. But I shall think of you, safe in the mortal lands."

It was hard to get the words out around the pain in her throat, so Emma clasped his hand instead. "Thank you, Robin. I mean it."

"Any thanks are mine." He touched his lips to her hand. "Farewell, my lady."

And he was gone. She caught a flash of a rosy cheek turning away in the crowd. The edge of a curly beard. Then the night market swallowed him up.

Spring trickled into summer. As the air grew warmer, humans began to linger outside long after moonrise. The city's byways filled with bare legs and laughter. With escape so close, Emma found herself trailing her hands along ancient college walls and fluted bridges in a silent goodbye. There was so much she would miss. Like the lights of the City. The warmth and incense of the night market. Even the feel of the fox beneath her skin.

She could not bear to look at her sisters. To think of leaving them. And so, when Robin's letter finally arrived, Emma said no farewells. She looked back only once, fixing the ring of bright faces around the dining table in her memory, before slipping away from the House of Foxes. The moon was full: This was the night. A Night City clerk would meet her by the river, Robin had said. There she would make her final bargain and cross back into the mortal world.

Emma crouched on the bank, trailing her fingers in the water. The silver fox charm bracelet was a manacle on her wrist: a deadweight of guilt. Her eyes had teared as she'd shut the door of the House of Foxes for the last time. Leaving the fox maidens, with no word or clue of her plan, had felt like tearing a tooth out from the root. But there was no other way. Her reward could not save them all. And she was needed at home. The fox maidens would forget her: The Night City would take care of that. But in the mortal world, her absence was an open wound. The friends she had left behind could not carry on.

She had seen Julia, not two weeks ago, on this very bank. Hunched and red-eyed, staring at the water. Just as she had been when Imogen left. There had always been a loneliness about Julia, Emma realized. She had not seen it when they met. Julia had been a towering figure, elegant and in command. But there was more Emma ought to have noticed. How much Julia had always expected of herself. How harshly she judged herself, and how hard she worked to hide what she thought were flaws. All of that sadness, Emma might have helped to carry. Instead, she had disappeared and added to Julia's pain.

But she had a chance to make things right. When she was back in the mortal world, she would be a better friend. She would fix the hurt left by her absence: for Julia, for Nat, and for her mother.

"Fox maiden?"

Emma brushed her hands together and stood.

A green-wigged Night City clerk tottered down the bank. A river reed brushed their robe, and they kicked it away with a shudder. "And they made me leave the Court for this," Emma heard them mutter.

They held a heavy gold disc as wide as Emma's palm. A gemstone gleamed from its center, with runes embossed on the metal.

"That lets me through the door?" Emma breathed. Robin had been right. This was far shinier than her inked token of protection.

"It is the only way. Even should you find the door and beat your fists against it, you could not pass through without such a token." The clerk drew it back from her. "You are sure you wish this bargain? The entirety of the reward granted to you by the Night City, in exchange for this passage to the mortal world, and the resulting release from your debts?"

"I'm sure," Emma said, impatient. She'd told them what she wanted: Why couldn't they just hand it over?

The clerk tipped it into her palm.

"You must carry it when you enter the river. The door is underneath the mortal bridge, and its guardian will rip you apart well before you reach it, should you approach without the correct token." A cloaked figure hurried from the dark, and the clerk looked up with obvious relief. "And here is the guide to show you the door. Thank the Night, I can't spend a moment more in this wretched damp. A nice, dry scroll room, that's the way . . ."

The clerk's grumbles faded into the distance.

Emma took in the guide's Eel collar and rough jerkin. There was something familiar about his face. Not from the Beasts' Ball, she was sure. Then it came to her. He had not worn an Eel's collar when she'd seen him last. He had been a messenger then, the first she had met in the Night City: the one who had banged on the Sister and Librarian's cottage door. He'd been apologetic about doing it, though. She'd thought he seemed decent at the time, scared as she was.

So she fell into step with him along the riverbank. It was nice to have a friendly face for her last moments in the City.

He nodded ahead. "Not far now. Gate's beneath the bridge. You'd not spot it, but I guard this bit of river, so I know."

"New job? Last I saw, you were a messenger."

"House of Eels now. Volunteered for this tonight. Bit of extra coin."

Quite a step down, for a messenger. She'd not known of any nightfolk entering the Lower Houses, only foolish mortals. But the little servant at Court had mentioned a relative going in for a family debt, so perhaps this was similar. She pitied the ex-messenger his fall, whatever the cause. It was doubly good to be leaving. The Night City was precarious.

"There." The guide pointed. His sleeve was stained and torn, quite unlike his immaculate messenger uniform.

At first, Emma saw nothing but the Mathematical Bridge. Then something tickled the back of her mind. Memories, scented with green things and salt water. Afternoons spent in a silent crouch on a riverbank. Eight-year-old Emma's hands, pressed around a pair of binoculars for a glimpse of seals.

She had always been good at observing. She sank into the quiet place in her mind, the part that knew how to still her limbs and thoughts until she became part of a landscape. There was no need to look for anything specific. Only let the patterns of movement wash over her. And then, just as it had in her mortal days, something stood out. A patch under the bridge's arch where the moonlight struck the water differently. The phosphoric glow of the City danced over the rest of the river: Here, there was dead darkness. She moved closer. There was a hole in the world, like a flap cut in a veil. She was looking straight through to the mortal side.

The guide blocked her with a warning arm and threw a stone. It clunked into the river near the door. The water erupted, ripples frothing outward. Dark scales curved above the surface.

"The guardian? But the token will keep me safe, right?"

"You'll be fine. Just kneel here and look into the water. Straight down, that's right. You'll see the path."

The guide's hands were warm on her shoulders. Emma stared hard into the river's depths. She saw ripples, a few strands of floating algae —

Her head plunged into the water. There was a force on her shoulders, holding her under. It was the guide. As Emma thrashed and screamed, bubbles jetting from her mouth, she felt him rip a weight from her hand. The token. He forced her arms behind her back, and she felt something slide around her wrists. It was hard and cold, and no matter how she tugged, she could not free herself from it.

The guide hauled her back as though reeling in a fish and flung her on the riverbank. She coughed, spitting riverweed. A quick twist behind her confirmed that her wrists had been bound with a silver chain, like the one the Sister had used at the Court. No knots, no breaks.

The guide waved the gold disc before her. "Mine now. Not so quick this time, hmm?"

Strands of wet hair had glued themselves to Emma's eyes. She tried to shake them from her face. "This time?"

Now that she could see him clearly, she regretted it. His face was flushed, teeth bared in a feral promise. "I don't suppose you cared, last time we met. That when you ran, I paid for it. Cast out of the messenger service, forced into a Night-poxed Lower House. All as punishment for 'letting' you escape."

"I didn't know."

"I took this job tonight to pay you back, didn't I?" He grinned. "My turn to get away. Out of the Night City, forever. I'll not take a hundred years of this collar."

He had the token. He had her way home. Emma strained against the chain. It only cut deeper into her wrists. But if she ran at him, she could ram him in the stomach. Emma struggled to her feet.

But the guide closed the gap between them in a stride. He swung Emma by her bound wrists and hissed in her ear. "I took pride in being a messenger. And you stole that from me. Now watch me steal from you."

He shoved, and Emma toppled into the water with a splash. Cold closed over her. She waited for the thump of river mud against her shoulder, then turned and shoved for the surface with all her might. She gasped in air, kicking for the shore, as the river behind her exploded like a pot on the boil. The guardian was awake.

The guard was already climbing nimbly over the Mathematical Bridge's supports, token in hand. She saw the moment his head disappeared, then his shoulders, until only his leg remained hanging out of the hole in the world. He pulled it through behind him. He had gone.

Emma snarled, and it was the sound of blood and fury. Then a current surged against her legs. Something powerful was moving through the water. Emma pictured prehistoric jaws stretching for her and flailed harder for shore. She needed her arms. Forcing her panic away, she thought of wrists shrinking, of hands made small. Fox paws, fox forelimbs: so narrow, so easy to slip free. It worked. The chain slid off, and her arms churned in a desperate paddle. But there was a sudden lightness on her wrist, and too late she grabbed for the fox bracelet that sank beneath her. Paws became fingers, but not fast enough. The silver fox charm winked into the murk. It had been her reminder of her bond with her sisters, and she had hoped to keep it with her always in the mortal realm. But now it was gone. Just like all of her hopes and plans.

Just as the ripples behind her licked her toes, she heaved herself onto the riverbank. The guardian's scales grazed the surface and disappeared. She was no more threat to the door. Emma flipped onto her back, cold to the marrow. Stupid, stupid; she had been so stupid. She did not want to be warm. She did not deserve it.

Emma clung to that thought as she stepped dully into the hall of the House of Foxes. She waved away the fox maidens' cries of alarm. They wanted to warm her, to dry her, but she could not let them. She did not deserve them either. If they knew the secret she'd kept from them, they wouldn't want to love and care for her like that. The silver fox bracelets swinging on their wrists were an unbearable reminder. Hers was at the bottom of the river. Because she had tried to leave the fox maidens behind. She'd had an unimaginable reward. Shared, it might have at least helped her sisters. But she had been selfish. And she had lost everything.

Turning out her pockets in her bedroom, she found a sodden mass of paper. But she had used up all of her feelings, so there was no grief left in her when she saw the token of protection, ruined and bleeding ink. The Boars could come for her now, and she would have nothing to stop them.

Then something stirred beneath the numbness. Not sorrow or regret. No, what she felt was fury. For the victims whose memories burned within her, demanding justice. For the bruising around her wrists from the chain, and the weight of the Turnbulls' crimes, and the sheer cruelty of her bargain with the City. While she was trapped here, the Turnbulls got to carry on. A few newspaper attacks could only do so much. There would still be more sacrifices, more wealth, more power for them. And she was more helpless than ever.

Then the thought came to her.

She finally had nothing left to take. No token, no bracelet. Not a single shred of hope. Buried under debts that would keep her enslaved for centuries. She had nothing. She was nothing.

So she was free. Because she had just become the most dangerous weapon of all.

A person with nothing to lose.

CHAPTER 35

OF ALL THE BALLS THAT LIT UP THE UNIVERSITY ON SUMMER nights, St. Dunstan's was the grandest. It was always on Midsummer Eve. Just as the Night City gave itself over to Midsummer revels at the Court, the mortals threw aside exams and work for a dreamscape of champagne and strawberries and dancing. Competition for invites was intense. The favored few milled inside the college grounds, ushered in by burly security teams. Outside, shut-out students attempted ever more outlandish schemes to gain entry. The inexpert disguised themselves as booked performers, only to be checked against a list and thrown out by security. Others scaled the walls of surrounding buildings, in full formal dress, timing their drop into the ball grounds to avoid the guards patrolling the perimeter. On this occasion, the most extreme — suspected in later years to have been the water polo team — stripped down to trunks and swam the river, with tailcoats stashed in waterproof bags strapped to their backs. Emerging dripping on the unguarded riverfront at the rear of the ball, they wriggled into immaculate white tie attire and strolled into the thick of the party.

Taken as a whole, it was perhaps not surprising that so many of the University's graduates were recruited into the nation's secret services.

But a fox maiden needed no such subterfuge. Emma simply gathered the shadows around herself and walked past the guards. Inside the ball, she let the shadows fall. Her gown of mist wreathed her shoulders and floated from her waist in shimmering swathes. A velvet bag hung from one wrist.

She was beautiful. She was magnificent.

She was alone.

Through the ancient courts of St. Dunstan's College, the only one alone. Students streamed by in groups, a whirl of giddy laughter and corks popping. Perhaps she had once been that young. A lifetime ago, when her worries had been of essays and friends, and what to say at parties. Now she had no age, and never would again. She felt ancient to her bones next to these children.

Emma lifted her eyes. Above the chocolate fountains and Ferris wheel, above the hectic flush of fireworks over St. Dunstan's Cathedral. Up at the moon, hanging like a clean, cold eye in the sky.

It was time to hunt.

In the end, it was easy to find them. Their table was the largest on the lawn. The marks on their backs glowed through their tailcoats. Every face the same color, every laugh a needle in Emma's ear.

Beside each crisp white shirt and bow tie sat an elegant girl. None of them were Julia. Emma's breath came easier. Her friend ought to be far away from what she was about to do. She needed no emotional ties. No distractions.

The velvet bag weighed almost nothing on her wrist. And all she had to do was reach inside.

She had been careful not to disturb the order of the bottles in the sickroom. While the House of Foxes slept around her, she had robbed its store of deathsleep. A few grains kept Sara unconscious, so Emma had taken a palm's worth. More than enough for nine strong young men.

The tenth, she had hoped not to see. Hugo was a warm presence in her memory. So kind, so helplessly adoring of Julia. She did not want to believe he was complicit. Of all the Turnbulls, he alone had not been party to hunting her through the streets. He had been back at the clubhouse, passed out on a pile of coats. And she had not seen him join the Turnbulls in a single photograph or newspaper quote since. As though he had split from the club entirely. Rejected them, and all that they stood for. She hoped he had. Then she might have a reason to spare him.

The others were different, though. They would pay for what they'd done. The Turnbull mark protected their bodies from a nightdweller's blow or bite. But there was no such mark on the objects around them. Nothing to stop her from sprinkling powder in an unattended glass. And once it touched their lips, no mark could keep them from sleeping long enough for her to drag them down to the Court and in front of the Judge. And then —

Then what? The Judge was clever enough to ensure they would be trapped in the Night City. Just as she was. Their glowing mortal lives, their families and futures, would all be gone too. And wasn't that fair?

Wasn't it?

Was it?

A golden head ducked from the champagne tent. Emma knew that the crowd could not actually have parted. That the music could not have stopped. But there he was, moving toward her. The face from her dreams. At last.

Jasper dropped into an empty seat on the edge of the group. Tawny, disheveled. Knocking back champagne from a glass in each hand. It was rage that made her heart pound so, she reminded herself. And if her limbs were trembling, that was eagerness born from daydreams of ripping out his throat. Emma's lungs burned with the effort to breathe. Her cloak of shadows flickered and dissolved.

There was a blur of movement, and horror pounded through her. She was standing there, visible to any mortals who cared to look. But it was only Richard and Piers, rising to take their dates to the champagne tent. The rest of the Turnbull group followed in a braying cluster, except Jasper. He stood, wobbling on his feet, and stumbled away from the lights and laughter, fumbling a lighter and a crumpled cigarette from his pocket. His tailcoat fluttered around a yew hedge shaped like a dragon, disappearing into the sunken garden.

Emma's gaze flicked a moment between the bright champagne tent, where Turnbull glasses gaped welcomingly for the touch of deathsleep powder, and the shadow-wreathed garden. She barely noticed the velvet bag dropping from her wrist. Her gauzy skirts flitted across the lawns into the darkness.

And behind her, an impossibly tall, thin figure choked on his drink.

In the darkness of the sunken garden, the wind was rising. Shivers ran through the moon-silvered rosebushes. Emma prowled through the beds, snapping off blowsy heads as she went. Petals dripped in her wake, like a trail of blood. This year's growth still bore the rot-sweet smell of the flood.

Jasper struggled to light a cigarette. She watched him through the thorns. She'd had no idea who he was. Not when she yearned after him. Not when their skin finally met, that day on the roof. Not even in the dark and echoing Senate House, when she'd watched his eyes turn cold. She'd thought he was golden. But he was as rotted through as the rose garden itself.

He was as beautiful as ever. In a way, now they were a perfect match. If he had been vicious and dangerous all along, this new Emma could finally equal him. One hunter to another.

The Turnbull mark glowed eerily from his back. She stepped from the roses, prepared to strike.

"I still dream about you."

Emma wished she could scoop her words out of the air and back into her throat. That was not the speech she thought she was about to make.

Jasper dropped the lighter, blank white horror on every feature. "Emma? No. Please, it can't be . . ."

"I know you didn't feel the same way. Now I see it." She cut across him. "But was any of it real? The things you said we'd do together, the traveling, the sailing? The way you kissed me. Was it all a trick to get me where you needed me?"

Her cheeks were wet. She was supposed to want to tear out his throat, not curl up on the ground and sob. Anger would have felt strong. Clean. Not like this squirming agony in her chest.

"Did you know from the start that you were going to sacrifice me? For your precious Turnbull Club, so your father would think you were a good little president? Go on, Jasper, what was worth my life — "

She stopped, partly because he was running his fingers over her face as though she were a precious vase, and partly because he definitely wasn't listening to her.

"You're alive," he whispered. Then, to her immense surprise, he burst into tears.

It is a slightly cruel observation, but — perhaps because men of Jasper's cast so rarely allow themselves to cry — when the dam does finally burst, their listeners are often treated to the most bizarre sounds known to humanity outside of walrus mating season.

Emma listened to the *hnnurgghs* and *guuuaahhs* with a patience born from extreme guilt at finding them so embarrassing. By some strange balancing alchemy, her own tears seemed to have cleared up. She felt almost cheerful.

"Jasper . . ." she tried.

"Bleeeghhhsnuff."

"Jasper, what's wrong?"

"Hargleweggh . . . uffgh . . . I thought you were dead," he managed, and hacked up some phlegm.

Her heart softened. How had it never occurred to her that her sacrifice might have been an accident? A spell gone wrong. Jasper, wracked with guilt and despair. That perhaps he truly had cared for her, after all.

She pushed the thought from her. He was her enemy, and he had drawn her in deliberately. She'd thought he was a simple, impulsive boy who had made her feel special because he liked her. That had been her mistake. If his tears now were a ruse, she wouldn't be fooled.

"I'm not dead."

An expression of purest joy lit Jasper's face, as though he were looking at Christmas and a divine manifestation and a gleaming IMOCA 60 racing yacht all in one. He was so beautiful when he smiled. Her heart sped horribly, and she reminded herself she hated him, hated him, hated him —

"You're not dead." He beamed. "So I didn't kill you. I didn't kill you, and you're here, so I can't go to jail for it."

"You — er — thought you had killed me?" prompted Emma, feeling that the conversation was not running quite as expected.

Jasper strode around, pounding one hand into the other. "Well, I wasn't sure. I drank so much that night, and I had this total blackout after I saw you — at the Senate House, right? And then you were gone. The others said they'd cover, tell the police I wasn't with you, and they had this look. Like they really thought I'd *done* something. I was so scared. I couldn't remember, and I thought, what if I *had* . . . My dad wouldn't let me say anything. Not to the police. Not even to him. Like I really was a — a murderer, and he didn't want me to confess."

His face darkened. "Why didn't you come forward? You have to go to the police. Tell them I didn't do it . . ."

"Jasper — "

". . . Now I can have my life back. Leave this charade, get on my yacht. Forget the University and my father. I won't need his money and his lawyers anymore."

"Jasper," she tried again, less patiently.

"There'll be no more press to pay off, just me and the waves — "

"Jasper. Let me get something straight. Did you or did you not think I was dead because you sacrificed me in an ancient ritual, performed by the Turnbulls since the founding of the University, to bring them — I don't know, riches or happiness or three wishes — from the elemental power that rules this place?"

He could not have looked more bewildered if she had started juggling owls in front of him while singing the "Marseillaise." The world twisted. "Jasper. Secret society. Ritual sacrifice. Ancient magical power. Are you following me? Your dad might have mentioned something?"

She had been so sure, for so long. That he had brought about her fall into the Night City, step by engineered step. It had made sense. He was the president of the Turnbulls. The Turnbulls had made the deal with the Night City. She had been sacrificed to the Night City.

And yet. The more she looked at him, the harder it was to see him as the mastermind. If the degree of confusion on his face was fake, he was a better actor than she could have imagined. And when had Jasper ever been calculated? He had never made a plan more than a day in advance in his life. She had once found that charming and spontaneous.

The suspicion in her mind was now fully formed. "You don't know anything, do you?"

And he didn't. She could see it now in his blank, handsome face. He was just a nice, lucky, selfish boy. He had never questioned what it meant being part of a club because of how important his parents were. He had never had to consider how to fit himself to the world, because the world fit around him.

But he was not a murderer. Perhaps he'd even cared about her, in his own way. The relief was meaningless. Beneath the screaming urge for revenge, she realized, she'd just wanted to know who had sacrificed her. Why they'd chosen her. Now she had no answers.

Nowhere to go, except back to a life of draining and debt. She snapped one last rose from its stem.

"Look, Jasper. I'm saying this as a favor. Don't tell anyone you've seen me. They won't believe it, and it won't go well for you." She turned for the steps. "I'm not back. I never will be."

He really was beautiful, even when he was staring with the expressive confusion of a goldfish trained in mime. Perhaps his eyes were a little fishlike. She'd never noticed that before. If his gaze was vague, she'd thought it was soulful. When he'd left yet another decision to someone else to bother with, she'd called him a free spirit. She'd pinned her dreams to a boy who coasted through life with more charm than brain. She'd painted in depths where there were none. Perhaps she was more like her mother than she'd thought.

She trudged up the steps from the sunken garden back into the ball.

Nine steps later, an arm swung out from the dragon-carved hedge and clamped around her throat.

CHAPTER 36

EMMA STUMBLED OVER THE UNEVEN GROUND. HER CAPTOR DIDN'T slow. He dragged her onward, his arm around her throat. He stripped off his white dress gloves — awkwardly, given he was also holding Emma — and balled the musty cotton into her mouth.

Emma clawed for fox form. It would not come. Fear crushed her in its grip. She tripped, landing hard, and lifted her head to a chorus of green smells. The river lapped at the bank before her. Her tormentor was kneeling to free a punt. She was being taken somewhere else, then. Emma looked at her hands, pressed into the mud. There, on her left hand. Just one fox claw had appeared, razor-tipped and perfect.

Emma covered her left hand and let herself be shoved into the punt.

"Well," said her captor, some minutes later. "Isn't this cozy?"

Emma's hands were bound with a white bow tie. The rest of her was strapped to the backrest of the punt with what had once been a mooring rope.

The figure poling the punt took no notice of her discomfort.

Poor, dull, dependable Richard, always in Jasper's shadow. She had liked him, pitied him, even. She had underestimated him. Overlooked his passion for history and tradition. Forgotten who had handed Jasper every object on the night of the ritual. She barely recognized the face above her. The cold eyes. The frustration and fury.

"You know what? This is boring," he said at last. The punt rocked as he lunged. Two plump pink fingers forced their way into Emma's mouth. Before she could recoil or scream or —

bite tear rip him

— a ball of damp white cloth had fallen into her lap, and Richard was back up on the till, looking down on her. She took a deep breath.

"Scream if you want," he said politely. "We're past any of the river colleges. I don't think anyone will hear you. But if it makes you feel better, please do."

Emma screamed until her throat burned, until every breath tore ragged strips from her lungs. They both listened as the noise died away.

Richard was breathing heavily from poling the punt along, haystack hair pasting to his forehead. And Emma saw, for the first time, the cold glint of the combat knife strapped to his waistband. So when he began to talk, she didn't interrupt. Instead, she worked her claw at the cloth binding her hands. Barely moving, tearing thread by silent thread.

"I wonder." He stabbed the pole into the riverbed. "Can you even imagine the trouble you've caused?"

Apparently, she didn't know how difficult it was for him. She couldn't appreciate the stress he'd been under from the Turnbull alumni. She hadn't been there, facing the old boys in their boardrooms in London. For the first time in centuries, the ritual had not produced its reward. The Turnbull list of demands had not been met.

She wouldn't be able to appreciate the scope, of course. Deals fallen through. Investments failed. Could she imagine the litany of collapsed election bids, the corporate fraud scandals that had surfaced? No, of course she couldn't. It had been a blow to the senior Turnbulls. One they wouldn't forgive.

Half the graduating Turnbulls had failed their exams, and who did the old boys blame? Him. Not their sons. No, indeed. Their precious sons didn't even have the burden of knowing the Turnbulls' history. Perhaps the brighter ones guessed some of it. But the full knowledge was Richard's responsibility alone. That was their decision, the old boys, to keep their secret safe. Only one Turnbull in each batch at the University was allowed to hold the knowledge of their ritual. For three years, he'd served the old boys faithfully. They hadn't even deigned to keep Richard as the president of the Society — though who could deserve it as he did? — yet he'd been expected to do all the work, messing about with bowls and incantations to smooth the way for their heirs. And who do you think they blamed when it had all gone wrong?

They'd left him on his own. They'd taken the ritual bowl back to London, to do their own trials. None of which would work, of course. The senior Turnbulls weren't capable of understanding such elemental power. But he, Richard, had done his own research. His own experiments. The first man since John de Turnbull who had even come close to harnessing the mysteries of the Power. Not that the members gave him the respect he was due. He alone . . .

Emma was astonished to find that she was feeling – bored? She should have been fascinated. Here was the explanation she'd longed for. But the sheer self-pity of the man. He was actually looking to her for sympathy, eyes glistening.

The smallest snap. The last thread on the bow tie had given way. She tensed, sure Richard had noticed, but he droned on. Her hands could be free with a shake of her wrists. Her body was still tied to the punt, but that might change once they made land.

Richard climbed down the punt and loomed over her. He had drawn out the knife. Long as her forearm, it swam toward her through the gloom. She heard the water lapping at the banks, the rasp of her breath, her heart beating once more, once more.

The point of the knife came to rest on her neck.

And in a book-filled cottage across town, the Sister jumped out of her chair with a curse.

Julia Colefax-Lee had spent the last year keeping her head down. Literally. She barely remembered the last time she'd raised her eyes from her shoes. People's faces were horrid. Their voices were too loud. She'd heard them all whispering. Wondering why Hugo still put up with her.

She tugged a strand of hair. She wasn't going to panic. He would be back soon. The queue for the champagne tent was long. Maybe he'd had to stop to say hello to — Well, he said he didn't speak to those boys anymore. The Turnbulls. She tugged her hair a bit harder. She realized she'd forgotten to wash it again. Then a hissing nearby caught her attention.

Julia recognized Nat Oluwole's tall, agitated form, pouring a static-burst of whispers into the ear of a blond in a glittering mirrored gown. Venetia Kent, as lovely and vicious as ever. An odd alliance had blossomed there. They'd worked together on the committee for Emma's memorial service, and found common ground. Venetia had wanted to see the Turnbulls brought down as much as Nat did. She'd always hated that aura around the boys, the feeling that they could get away with whatever they wanted. Nobody loathed being the second-most powerful in a room more than Venetia. And Nat had been in a frenzy to go after the Turnbulls when the police wouldn't. To keep looking until he found what they did to Emma, and some way to prove it. He had promised Emma's mother, when Dr. Curran had eventually left England. She had flown in after Emma disappeared, blazing with cold fury, and spent months hassling every police officer within reach. But door after door closed in her face. Emma had been taken by an unknown assailant, they said. Her daughter had likely been dead for some time. It was best for her to accept that. But Diana Curran had refused to accept it, and so had Nat. When Dr. Curran finally boarded a plane out, determined on following up leads with her international colleagues — with the slim hope that Emma had fled to a former home, perhaps in Tasmania or the Philippines — Nat had picked up her campaign. He seemed to have found Venetia a willing coconspirator. But Julia had only wanted to keep her head down. On her pillow, preferably. She was just so tired. They'd messaged her a few times. Did she want to interview a potential witness with them? Did she want to help them coax shopkeepers into showing their CCTV tapes? Julia had ignored all of the messages, numb to the core. Everything had been too tiring, for a long time now.

Venetia didn't lower her voice at all. "No, she'll be useless. She's crazy." A frenzied burst of hissing. "I don't care if I 'shouldn't say that,' Nathaniel, she literally had a breakdown and now she's some kind of freak shut-in." More whispering. "Fine. *Fine*."

Julia's breath faltered. She edged away, but Venetia had blocked her escape. A pale hand closed around her arm like a python's coils. "We need your help."

Nat's kind face loomed over Venetia's shoulder. "Venetia, let go of her! Julia, this will come as a shock — "

"What will be a shock?" said a hearty voice, with a hint of warning. Julia felt her breath come more easily. It always did when he was near.

"Oluwole, good man, how are you?" Hugo pumped Nat's arm with enough vigor to set him shaking like a scarecrow in a gale-force wind.

"Sorry to be so long, Jules, I got caught up with Jasper. Said he was seeing things, like — Well, doesn't matter, couldn't have happened. Poor old guy, he's really come off the rails."

Hugo's broad shoulders sank. Julia heard the defeat in his voice and rubbed his arm. He could never bear to know someone was in trouble and not help. It was why he had been so easy to fall in love with, once she'd had the idea.

Nat's voice was strangely intense. "I don't know what Jasper said, Hugo, but I'll tell you what I just saw. Tonight. *Emma*."

Hugo's broad brow creased.

"We both did," Venetia cut in.

Julia felt a noise escape her. Because Emma was gone. Julia had run ahead that night, and Emma had disappeared. She could still see Emma's face, fading into the darkness. Her brain tortured her with fantasies of going back, of taking Emma's hand and refusing to let go. But she had not done any of those things. And so Emma could not be here, alive. Because Julia had failed her.

Nat took one of her hands. "Julia, I don't know how, but Emma is *here*. We saw her. She ran off, but I need" — his voice cracked — "we need to find her."

It was too awful. They'd both gone mad. Julia turned to Hugo, longing to hide her face in his lapel. But he was looking past her.

"Oh my God," he rasped. "I know where she went."

Julia reeled back from him.

"Jasper kept saying he saw it. Emma being taken toward the river, too far away to catch up. I thought he was raving, but — Richard. He said it was Richard."

Julia felt their eyes on her. They seemed shocked. But all she felt was numb certainty, an echo of something known already. She'd never been able to explain why she stopped answering Richard's messages after Emma was gone. Her mind never let her examine why she felt she had to walk a different route home from lectures. Why she'd struggled to breathe in bed every night until Gabriel College let her switch rooms to one in the modern block, the one with keypad entry and security cameras. Why she jumped at shadows.

Now she was sure. Richard had always understood her. He had known the stinging pressure she'd worn like a noose all her life. Her family's demands for her to succeed. To exceed. To prove worthy of her position. He'd said he felt it too. Felt the way it warped the inside of you until living felt like a soundless scream. But there had been a difference between them, she realized now. She had directed all of that pressure and rage in on herself. But Richard's fury was for the world around him. A cold, steely undercurrent. So if Richard was involved, she knew one thing. The others weren't afraid enough yet.

She strode from the group. Above her, the undersides of the leaves showed white in the wind. Lanterns strung between trees creaked. The weather was rising. The others scampered behind her. Or, at least, she thought they did. She didn't turn to check. The ground near the riverbank was churned up. There were no punts tied to the mooring posts. And there was a handprint in the mud.

"Julia, wait — " Hugo was panting to keep up.

"The towpath. There's nowhere else to take her."

"But which way?" Nat's tailcoat was whipping in the wind. "South, toward Regent's College? Or North to Gabriel — to the Meadows?"

"Lots of nice lonely murderous spots there," Venetia drawled.

"*Not helpful,*" Nat hissed, a wary eye on Julia.

And then they heard the scream.

South, then. And Julia found herself, with a suddenness that dizzied her, panting through the dark. The river gleaming in sly little ripples beside the towpath. Her gown catching on brambles. The others ran behind her. College after college passed, and there was no sign of Emma.

"Maybe we should stop. Regroup. Call the police."

"There's no signal."

"Richard could have taken her anywhere. Back into town. Or had a car waiting."

A year without slipping on her running shoes — and without eating or getting out of bed much either, if she were honest — was making itself known. Julia's breath was coming in gasps. But her body felt as though it was waking up. Moving through a memory of someone she had forgotten how to be.

"No," she said. "If it's Richard, he's taking her to the Library. He's always had a key. We're going there."

CHAPTER 37

RICHARD WELLESLEY-JONES FELT ENTITLED TO A LITTLE grievance.

A sacrifice had never escaped. A sacrifice had never been linked to the Turnbulls. Yet there she sat in the punt, staring and insolent. And in the past year, the Turnbulls had been hauled before the lowering stare of cameras and columnists. Centuries of secrecy shattered. Because of this nothing. A girl so unremarkable, her own father hadn't bothered with her.

Although. Was there something about her? Something that hadn't been there before. Weak, malleable Emma Curran had not had eyes that sparked with the light of burning stars. The creature that faced him was no girl. The lines of her were too perfect, as removed from humanity as a drawing or a statue. She sat with the eerie stillness of a predator in wait. Richard crushed the instincts that were insisting, quite firmly, that he should turn and flee.

He pressed the blade to her throat. An uncanny chill radiated from her skin.

"What happened? You don't seem — human anymore."

"I'm not," Emma agreed, one eye on the knife. "I made a bargain. It changed me."

Richard's tongue flicked around his lips.

"A bargain?"

"I pledged my service to — a power."

Strange how he almost believed her. It was impossible, of course. Centuries of Turnbulls had tried to unlock the secret and failed. Only John de Turnbull's first bargain had held: Each year a sacrifice was made, and the Power granted the Turnbulls their list of demands. A list carefully drawn up by the alumni, each jockeying to have their interests represented. Generations of wealth, political power, and fame stemmed from that bargain. But no Turnbull had ever succeeded in making a new bargain with the Power. To force it to answer their will whenever they pleased, and not just once a year.

Richard found his hands were taut, knuckles showing white through the skin. He had always known that he would be the one to do it, the one destined to forge a new path for the Society. Midnight hours spent in study of the rituals. The cuts on his hands he had explained away with clumsiness, the shapes drawn in blood and then wiped away, night after night. The gray dawns rising on endless failure.

And then there had been one night, the September the University was buzzing over Jasper's return. The hunter's moon high over St. Dunstan's College, silvering the sill of Richard's bedroom. He had been so close. Each time he tweaked the words of the bargain, changed the shape of a rune, the force that coursed from the Turnbull bowl grew more electric. Ritual by ritual, he had felt his work shaking the veil between the human and the magical. And that night, he felt the magic catch. Felt the bargain start to take hold. The bowl glowing in his hands, the roiling of the great Power bucking beneath his grip. He had been so close to mastering it. And then the force had surged, become a flood. The current singed his skin from the inside. He could not keep his hold. The capillaries in his nose had burst, warm blood streaming over his mouth. He fell backward.

And the bowl was cold. The Power was gone.

He had staggered to the window. Below, dark eddies of water were lapping at the foundations of St. Dunstan's. They reeked of magic. The Power had called them up, he knew it. He had come too close to breaking through its barriers, to forcing it to his will. He had threatened it. And like a wild beast, it had lashed out. He had watched well into the dawn, as the Power drowned the whole city. Oh, they had wailed about the flood, those petty people with no sense of what had been at stake. The bursars yammering to the press about historic carvings. The shops moaning about a bit of water damage. As though that compared to the loss of the power that had so nearly been his.

Even after the flood receded, it left the city drenched in a film of magic. Like a shield. Every bargain he attempted after that fizzled and died before the first rune was complete. And so he had been denied even one bargain of his own. Yet this creature sat there, claiming to have made one by herself. He could have laughed at the lie.

The funny thing was, the sacrifice wasn't meant to have been her. He had chosen carefully, all that time ago: one of the hired help taking coats at the Turnbull annual dinner. Just as the old boys instructed, he tried not to use University students. He tried to be fair. Students worked hard. They earned their place. Well, apart from the diversity schemes flooding the University now. Anyone who could scrape together a few Cs and a woke-enough sob story. He wouldn't have minded using them. But there was far too much scrutiny there. It would bring too much trouble.

Caution was the key. The ritual was discreet. Not a whisper of scandal, in all the generations of the University. They never disappeared, the ones marked for sacrifice. Nothing so flashy. The serving girl he'd chosen should have gone home to her bed that night, woken up. It would have taken a day or so for the magic to fully drain her. After that, it would have just looked like a breakdown. There but not really there. Sometimes you got ones that walked into traffic or fell down stairs, too drained to care. It was very neat.

Or it should have been. He sometimes thought of that coat attendant, living life with no notion of the part she could have played in securing the future of the nation. But Emma had squeezed her way into the Turnbull annual dinner. Before then, he'd been mildly amused by her. Liked her, even. She wasn't bad, for one of Jasper's attempts at rebellion. But then she, a grasping nobody, had broken their ritual bowl. Handed down, ceremony to ceremony, since the founding of the University. It had survived the Reformation of the monasteries and German bombs. But not Emma Curran.

It was funny to remember. He had actually thought it was fated. Because in breaking the bowl, she had left her blood all over it. All of those lovely little slashes on her fingers, the pulsing slit on her palm. She made it so easy. Marking a sacrifice — oh, it took ingenuity. You needed something of them for the ritual, you see. Hair was the easiest to get. Mixed into animal blood, it could do the trick. But pure human blood was the best, the strongest. The oldest way.

Richard let the knife probe the soft skin of her neck. He watched her face, imagining the pain.

She was smiling in a way he didn't like.

"Thank you," she said.

He found himself peering closer, trying to see behind the mask. The tears she must be holding back. The fear and sweat of the cornered beast.

But she was still smiling.

"You've made me see it clearly. I thought it was my fault. Who I trusted, or what I drank or what I'd said. That I'd brought it on myself, somehow. But none of that mattered. Because it was always about you, and what you chose to do. It wouldn't have mattered if I'd been wise, or perfect, or hadn't been there at all. You would have found someone else and done it to them."

At last, the tear gleaming down her cheek. Somehow, it didn't give him the satisfaction he had hoped. No matter. He caressed her cheek with the flat of the blade.

"Oh, I agree. Really. You don't matter."

And then the punt nosed against the bank. It was the moment Emma had been waiting for. Richard sawed through the rope that tied her, and heaved her onto the riverbank. Her fox instincts coaxed her to stay cunning and limp until the sweet, solid ground met her limbs.

run run run
this way and only this

She spun to her feet. But Richard stepped into her path, and she ran into him at full tilt. Pain ripped through her as the mark on his back flared. Worse than her brief brush with Piers, worse than she could have imagined. No creature of the Night City could attack a Turnbull. She fell, and darkness rushed the edges of her vision. But there at its center, she watched Richard's face change, from confusion to understanding to a vile, hardening glee.

He bent over her, and the ghostly glow of the Turnbull mark on his back cast a halo around his face. He pinned her body to the ground with one hand. But he left her arms free.

"Go on," he said softly. "Hit me."

Emma glared up at him.

"Hit me, Emma." His smile widened as he took in her prone body. "You can't. Can you?"

His finger drew a line down her collarbone to her rib cage. "You. Can't. Touch. Me."

He flicked her skin at every word. Emma flinched, and the light in his eyes grew.

"Well, this is going to make things easier. You're coming with me, Emma. And together, we're going to finish the ritual you spoiled."

He pulled Emma to her feet and wrenched her arms behind her. The Library loomed above them.

"You see, I've been wondering. Do we really need all the trappings of the ritual? The people, the props. Sometimes, the old ways are best."

He forced her toward the building.

"I've read the histories. The Power has always liked a blood sacrifice. And I'm sure yours will be acceptable."

CHAPTER 38

FIREWORK FLASHES FILTERED THROUGH THE LIBRARY WINDOWS, staining the stacks pink and green.

"You probably don't know this. We're actually on top of the very source of the Power."

Richard, Emma reflected grimly, never seemed happier than when *explaining* something. She was thankful, at least, that this had distracted him from knife fondling and outlining her death in detail. But if he was going to murder her, he might at least have had the decency not to lecture her on the way.

Richard seemed to take her silence for dumbstruck awe. As he tugged her through the stacks, his voice rose with a true historian's fervor. "Yes, this very library. The texts say that it was originally the site of a holy spring. A pagan temple to the Power. The founders of the University recognized what it was and built over it. This is where those early members of the Turnbull Society brought their sacrifices. Just imagine."

The quiet was shattered by a smash. It could not have come from one of the windows around them, which were all intact. Sound traveled strangely in the Library.

Richard dragged Emma on more quickly, pulling her into a windowless corridor. He used the knife hilt to flick the light switch. Emma saw chipped tiles and noticeboards crowded with flyers for typing services and language exchange partners. It was a distinctly unmagical place to die.

Then the tiniest *plishing* sound drew her attention to the wall beside them. Set into an alcove was a stone drinking fountain, the kind Emma associated dimly with pictures of Rome. There was a face carved into it, one whose beard and hair fanned out as though drifting in a current. A stream of water poured from his lips into the basin below. The stone itself was curiously smooth and glass-like.

Emma had the opportunity to notice this detail, since Richard had forced her down until she was bent over the basin.

"Yes," Richard crooned, breath hot on her ear. "When your blood drains into this fountain, it will wash straight back to the Power. That's how it used to be done, in the ancient times. Through your sacrifice, your pain, the bargain will be fulfilled. And everything will be back to how it should be."

He twisted a hand into Emma's hair and pulled, exposing her throat to the knife.

Even resisting the pressure he exerted was enough to send pain singing through her skull. But Emma readied for one last desperate attack, pain be damned —

" — AND I CARED, YOU BASTARD."

The sound came all at once, as though someone had turned the dial on a muted radio. Jasper stood in the doorway, purple-faced, mid-roar. Sound did, indeed, seem to travel strangely in the Library.

Richard pulled Emma in front of him and pressed the knife to her throat.

The purple drained from Jasper's face. He looked like a lost little boy. "Come on, Rich. Let her go. Please."

"This isn't what you think. I found her here. She must have been hiding, all this time. I was stopping her for you — "

"Liar. I could hear you all the way here, as soon as I got in. Saying weird things about powers, threatening her — "

Richard changed tack. "I had to, Jasper. She was a danger to the Society. She was going to ruin us all, our fathers — "

"Danger to . . . ? The Society's only a bit of fun, Rich. Come on, it doesn't really matter."

"The Turnbull Society is the single most important reason this nation still exists," Richard screamed, in a high voice Emma had never heard him use. Behind her, he was shuddering with emotion. The blade at her throat trembled viciously.

Jasper took an unconscious step back.

"Rich, mate. You've been part of my family since we were ten. I love you like a brother, you know that. But I can't let you hurt her. My father wouldn't want you to — "

"Your father? What do you know about *your father?*" Richard hissed. "*I am more his son than you could ever be.*"

His face was transformed, rigid and white.

"He trusts me with things. Things he's never told you. I used to wonder why. After all, you're his 'real' son. And then I saw. It's wasted on you. All you want to do is run away on your little boat. Play with your camera. Maybe that's why he never told you."

"Told me what?"

"He told me when I was ten. After my dad's funeral, when he was driving me back to school. About our ritual, and what we owe to the Society. He said my father wanted me to know. But it had to be a secret, because you weren't ready yet."

"I would have told you. I waited years. Every term at school. Every holiday I spent at your house. For you to ask a single question. But you never did. You just take everything your father's built for you, and never once asked where it all came from."

"Where what came from? Why are you saying this?"

Richard laughed, a bitter, mirthless thing. And as he told Jasper the truth of what the Turnbulls were and what they did, it struck Emma then that there were two types of evil, among these boys raised to have everything. It was easy to hate Richard's type. Wielding the knife, plotting the Society's rise to power, sacrifice by sacrifice. But what of Jasper, and the others like him? Coasting through life on golden waves of luck. Enjoying privileges without the pain of interrogating them. Because it was fun, being rich. Being sought after. It was convenient to think that this was the natural order of things: a little unfair, perhaps, but out of one's control. And that, in itself, was an evil. To be able to look away, to avoid seeing where your joy had been sucked from someone else's marrow. Emma felt a prickling of guilt: She wasn't sure she'd been all that innocent of that herself, in her mortal life.

Jasper shrank from Richard, shielding his face as if to ward off the words. "No. I don't want any of this."

"It's not about what you want," Richard said, implacable. "It's about the country, and what's best for it. We've spent generations, centuries, keeping it stable. We have to do what it takes to protect it. You and me. We're meant for it."

"But killing people — " Jasper looked sick.

"Look, that's an extreme — oh, you should hear your father explain it. Like he says, you have to make tough decisions when you're the ruling class — " Emma twitched, and Richard smiled.

" 'Ruling class.' It's become such a dirty term, hasn't it? We pretend it doesn't exist anymore. But who's in charge, Emma? Who is it, in your Parliament and your news reports and your boardrooms, hmm? What do they have in common?"

He tapped Emma on the nose with the knife, and she flinched. He turned back to Jasper. "We're still there for a reason. We rule because we know how to. We're brought up for it. We give up so much, to run the country for people who'd rather spend their time watching reality TV than make a single difficult choice to keep the economy going. We're the only ones willing to do what it takes. To make the necessary sacrifices."

Emma held still. She only needed Richard's attention to slip, just a little. If she got out of his hold, she was quick enough to outrun him.

"I don't know, Rich. It doesn't sound quite, like — fair."

"Fair? What's fair? Maybe it's unfair we get the best schooling because our parents can pay for it. But that has still made us the best. The most qualified. What are we meant to do at the top, hand things off to people who aren't as prepared, aren't as good, just because it would be nicer? History isn't nice."

But history had always been written from their perspective. The Turnbulls, and people like them. So whose fault was that? Emma never got to finish the thought. Because Richard dropped the knife. Because crashes rippled through the air. Because framed in the doorway were three figures with axes in their hands. And boars' heads.

But the Boars were never allowed in the Library. The Night City would not permit it. Which meant that something, somewhere, had gone terribly wrong.

Richard went slack. Emma ripped herself from his grasp and plunged blindly into a dark reading room. Behind her, someone started to scream.

CHAPTER 39

THE GROUP FOUND THE LIBRARY unlocked. THEY FORGED into the deep-sea silence, the bookcases dark alleyways around them. Nat forced them on the darkest route of all, where the firework-stained light from outside barely reached. Hugo took out his phone, but its anemic glow only lit a few steps ahead.

"I hear her again. That way, through the theology rooms." Nat veered off through an archway.

"Can you tell me why, exactly, we're following a sound that none of the rest of us can hear?" Venetia hissed.

"We can't let him go alone," whispered Julia. "I don't think it's safe here."

Venetia glanced at the darkness around them, then gave a laugh that almost succeeded in sounding careless. "What? There are four of us and one of Richard," she said, at a normal volume. Julia flapped her hands frantically, miming silence.

Venetia ignored her and spun on her toes through the archway, pale hair floating behind her. "Scared of the dark, Julia? It's just a library. What is there to be afraid of?"

Hugo lifted his phone. Its glare glinted off two murderously sharp tusks. More emerged from the darkness. Poleaxes gleamed. Heavily booted feet stepped into the light.

Julia did not wait for her mind to catch up with her eyes. She ran, tugging Hugo and Venetia along the corridor with her.

"Take the mortals. Block the way here. But find the fox." The voice behind them was a guttural rasp. Gold bandoliers stretched across broad shoulders.

The poleaxes lowered. The boots pounded forward in file.

Julia saw Hugo risk a glance over his shoulder, then snap his gaze forward. His face was a study in horror.

Behind them, thudding footsteps broke into the artillery fusillade of an all-out run.

But sound must, indeed, have traveled strangely in the Library. Because only three reading rooms away, Emma was creeping through a dense, moth's-wing silence. She peered around each bank of desks before plunging for the safety of the next, the fox a welcome melody in her mind.

> *we run from the hunt*
> *they shall not catch us*
> *for we are quick we are clever*
> *Together,* thought Emma.
> *together,* the fox agreed.

Somehow, once Richard's hands no longer held her, her panic had started to dissolve. She was still too shaken to manage a full transformation. But she had been able to reshape her eyes, her ears, her nose, until her fox senses came flooding back. The dark Library was no longer a mystery. The fox's song hummed in her blood. She felt a comforting brush against her thoughts, like warm fur.

Then a ribbon of scent hit her nose and held her rigid. *Known smell. Boy smell.* But it was not Richard's acrid sweat or Jasper's cologne. Trusting her fox instincts to keep her from hitting sharp corners, she pelted ahead blindly. Her breath came in pants, in gasps, in great chest-heaving sobs, and then he was there. She flung herself at him, letting the fox parts of her melt away until she was Emma, only Emma.

"Emma!" Nat held her tight. His owlish face was wet with tears.

She pulled back, shaking. "You can see me."

She had once spent hours talking to a boy who could not hear her, because missing her friend had pierced a hole in her soul. She had gritted her teeth against the pain when he walked away, because pretending had been the best part of her day. And now here he was, looking at her. Actually seeing her. It felt like sunlight. It felt, just for a moment, like she was warm again. Mortal again.

"Of course I can see you. And I'm never letting you out of my sight again." Nat seized her in a crushing hug.

"Me either."

"There you are, Oluwole. Look what we've found!" A jubilant Hugo burst into the room, dragging Richard by the collar. Richard was smudged with dust and bruises. He slumped in Hugo's grip, looking utterly defeated. Julia and Venetia followed, panting.

"My God." Hugo stopped short. "Emma! It really is you. Alive and . . . well?"

He looked uncertainly at Emma's strange, sharp beauty: clear and cold and terribly inhuman. "Er, alive and here, at least. Now, not to worry, we gave those piggy fellas the slip a ways back. I'll be damned, they're fast buggers. Still, not up to our tricks. They ran right by our hiding place and never a twitch."

"More likely they lost interest in us. I would have, if it meant traipsing into that bug-infested cupboard you shoved us in," said Venetia. "They found some nice glass cases of priceless manuscripts to smash up instead."

"This one" — Hugo gave Richard a shake — "we found pelting out of the printing room as if the hounds of hell were on his tail. Thought he might have something to say about where you were, Emma. Didn't we, Jules?"

Julia stepped around Hugo as though she had not heard him. Her eyes were huge. Tears trembled on her lashes. She slid her arms straight around Emma, and her voice cracked. "You're alive."

She straightened up, leaving behind the hunch she had worn every day of the past year and a half. "It's time we leave. We need to get Emma somewhere safe, and those monsters are still between us and the door. And we have to deal with — "

Her glance rested uneasily on her ex-boyfriend. Richard drooped from Hugo's hold on his collar. His encounter with the Boars seemed to have shaken him beyond words.

But before anyone could move, a marble bust fell from above. It shattered a breath away from Nat's head. They craned their necks up to the gallery of the reading room.

It was filling with boar-men. They ran.

382

"They're behind us," Nat panted in the corridor. "We can't get out through the south wing now."

"Try the other way, then." Hugo tugged Richard along grimly.

Emma's fox instincts screamed a warning. She managed to pull Nat and Julia back from the door in time. "No, can I hear them there," she gasped. "They're in the north corridor too."

"At both of the ways out. So we're trapped," Venetia said acidly.

Richard croaked something.

"What?" Emma waved at Hugo to loosen his grip on Richard's collar.

Richard rubbed his throat and coughed. "The military history room. I have — the key. Round my neck."

"A room that locks . . ." Emma hated to consider anything he said. But he had dropped his knife by the fountain, whereas the Boars were closing in with pikes and swords intact. "We'd be safe there from the Boars, at least."

"Stellar thinking," said Venetia. "Let's trust the deranged kidnapper."

"This can't be a good idea," Nat muttered.

Emma looked round at them all. "Our best plan is to hide until the Boars pass, then make a run for the exit. I hate to say it, but the military history room is the only place we'd have a chance of barricading ourselves in that long. Nowhere else locks."

"How would we get there?"

"We'd have to cut through the Greater Reading Room." Emma had spent enough time in the Library to know its layout. So she crept ahead with Venetia to scout out the way.

Close to the door of the Greater Reading Room, Emma tripped over something curly and shivering. It whimpered and tried to shrink back under the book trolley it had chosen for a hiding place, golden curls askew.

"Don't hurt me, please. My family — they're important, rich — my father can pay you, anything you want."

"Dear God, how pathetic." Venetia's voice dripped disdain. "Come out, Balfour. It's us."

"Venetia? Emma?" he scrambled out. "Are the monsters gone?"

A year and a half of hatred was hard to shake. Emma found she had to force the words through her teeth. "No, but we've found somewhere to hide. Through the Greater Reading Room."

Jasper paled. "But they're there too, the monsters."

Hugo, Julia, and Nat arrived in a clatter of footsteps, Richard in tow.

"We have to move," Nat said. "Now. They're right behind us."

Emma calculated quickly. They were out in the open here. But in the Greater Reading Room, they could use bookcases as cover. There, they had at least a chance of creeping past the Boars.

Emma steeled herself to be brave, to shake off the last of her shock and fear from Richard's attack. He, at least, was no longer a threat. He slumped behind Hugo, a broken man. But she still had to be strong. To keep her mortals alive. Even if the darkness of the Library pressed around her, feeling thicker than ever.

"Stay off the central walkway," she warned the group. "Stick to the shadows between bookcases."

"We're with you." Nat took Jasper in a firm but kind grip, like the owner of a cowardly puppy, and tugged him from under the trolley.

"N-no," panted Jasper. "Stop pulling me — the monsters — "

They slid through the doors.

The Greater Reading Room was a cathedral to books. The one room could have fitted whole libraries. Emma squinted in the dim light. She just made out a cluster of shadows moving at the far end, gathered around something. Smoke spiraled up to the magnificent vaulted ceiling.

But their end of the room was deserted. There was only one guard ahead, ambling along the central aisle. Emma signaled to the mortals to creep forward. They slipped around the bookcases in ones and twos. The darkness seemed thicker than ever. Emma began to hold out hope they would make it through unseen. They had already covered a quarter of the reading room without drawing the Boars' attention.

And now Emma made out the origin of the smoke. The Boars had built a bonfire of broken desks and bookcases. Now they were piling ancient tomes in stacks by the fireside. So close to the flames. An invisible hand closed around Emma's throat. The Boars had to have gone mad, or rabid. They were going to destroy the Night City's own hoard of books: its most precious treasure, the knowledge it had taken centuries to build. Beloved, irreplaceable. That they dared such a thing filled her with dread.

And anger. It surprised Emma to find how much it mattered. They weren't her books. But the Library stood for everything the University was. Or what it ought to have been. Because the place she studied shouldn't have been about the Turnbulls, or money, or tradition. Or inner circle after inner circle that only a few people got invited into. This building, and these books, were what it ought to have meant. Knowledge, free for anyone who came in.

But it would all burn so easily. All that polished wood; the paper kept carefully bone-dry. The whole Library could go up in an instant. There would be nothing left to save. Someone ought to stop them.

But there was no one. The Library was deserted. The nightfolk were at their Midsummer revels. The mortals were sipping champagne in punts, gazing at the fireworks over the St. Dunstan's ball. There was only her.

Emma saw Nat across the aisle, hiding behind a bookcase. She heard Julia's breathing beside her. Her first duty was to her friends. She was the only one with the cunning and claws to get them all out. There was barely half a room to cross. The Boar on patrol was not even looking. They might just be able to get away safely. All they had to do was keep quiet.

There was a shattering crash. With the urgency of a shivering Labrador, Jasper had squeezed his way into Nat's hiding spot, tipping the whole bookcase over in the process. The guard turned, yelled, raised his hands. The bookcase landed on top of him. There was the crack of a severed neck. His poleax clattered to the ground.

Emma heard the first shout of alarm. Boars spilled into the central aisle, a tide of them, more than Emma had yet seen. Boots crunching in formation, file upon file of sharpened tusks and weapons scarred with use.

Eyes telegraphing murder at Jasper, Nat worked quickly to topple the next bookcases onto the coming soldiers.

Emma shoved Julia behind her. "Help Hugo and run for it — I'll get the others out."

"Of course you will." With a fond smile, Julia tucked Emma's hair back into place, out of her eyes. "You've become quite the hero while you were away, haven't you?"

Emma watched her go, thinking hard. She needed to get the Boars to fall back enough that she could get the remaining mortals past them. She had to act as a distraction.

Emma leapt, a whirlwind of shadow and claws. The Boars were far more powerful, and she was afraid of them. But she was faster. She landed quick shallow scratches, which bled nastily. The world became a maelstrom of screams and bodies. Emma saw Hugo sling Richard over one shoulder like a grain sack. He and Julia reached the far door and ran through. They'd be able to lock themselves into the military room.

The Boar in front of her backed away in horror. She followed his gaze over her shoulder.

"Night above," she said blankly.

In the center of the reading room, one Boar after another swayed and gently toppled over, like windblown meadow flowers. They were doing so because their heads had been sliced clean by the cobra-like progress of a poleax. At the other end of the weapon, Venetia's teeth were bared in a grim smile. Her pale hair was spattered with red, and shreds hung from her ball gown.

As Venetia beheaded another Boar, Emma saw Jasper scrabble through the door. With a final vicious thrust, Venetia flung the poleax down and sprinted out after him. Emma hoped Nat had already gone. She looked around for him, but saw no sign of long legs or skinny shoulders.

Something caught her feet, and she tripped. When her eyes came back into focus, a Boar was already standing over her. She wheezed up at him. He raised his sword high with both hands, ready to bring it down into her heart.

A metal spike went straight through his throat.

The Boar's sword clanged to the floor. Scrambling to avoid the spray of blood, Emma pushed herself backward, rasping and coughing. She collided with something and looked up to find Nat's upside-down face peering at her. He looked rather green.

"Thank you," wheezed Emma, resting her head against his knees for a moment.

Nat lowered the blood-tipped spear and helped her stand.

A Boar reared up in their path, a battle-ax in each hand. Emma ducked under one raised ax arm, whipping Nat after her. Long arms flailing, he managed to score the spear along the Boar's thighs to the back of its knees.

"Oh God — sorry — well, not sorry, but — "

It dropped forward with a howl of agony, its hamstrings severed and dripping. It was enough to get them to the door. Emma pushed Nat through.

Then a cry rolled through the reading room. She turned, horror-struck. The Librarian stood over a pile of ancient books, screaming at the Boars. All alone, and they were closing in around him, but he kept roaring in their faces. She shoved the door shut on Nat and ran for the old man. She could drag him out.

But something hit her across the middle. A wall of muscle. The stink of old leather and blood. She looked up, and a Boar grabbed her by the throat.

A patch of darkness was moving outside the Library. The keen-eyed might have spied a skulk of hooded figures within.

"Were those the — " said a shadow.

A second shadow pulled it back from sight of the doors. "The Boars, yes. Quiet, foolish girl, or you'll have them on us."

"But what'd Emma be doing *here*? I thought she'd go — "

"I am trying," gritted a third voice, "to maintain a tracking spell. Could you stop talking?"

"Sorry, love. But if the tracker's leading us here, are we sure the thief we're following is Emma?"

"The ward spells on my deathsleep jar don't make mistakes, fox girl," the second shadow growled. "Emma's traces were all over them. We may have found her bag in the gardens — though the Night only knows why she'd drop it there — but the trail carries on here."

A crash echoed from the Library, followed by guttural roars. The shadows flinched as one. "Boars in the Library," the second shadow continued, sounding shaken. "They were forbidden to enter centuries ago. And the City would never allow them to destroy its books. I fear — "

There came a splintering crack from deep within the Library, and a howling scream.

Saskia ripped away her cloaking shadows. "Emma's in there. We have to help her."

But Nancy pulled her back, pointing a silent finger. Boars stood at attention before the doors, pikes sharp against the sky. The outlines of tusks and weapons glinted behind every window.

The Sister gathered the fox maidens around her. "We must tell the Night City. The Boars chose a clever time for whatever devilment this is. With the Court so wrapped up in the Midsummer revels, it's the Night's own chance that no one's heard what's going on."

"We can't interrupt the revels. They'll string us all up."

"We have to try. Hurry, to the Court."

Saskia's mouth was set in a mulish line. "And leave Emma alone here?"

"We must. If Emma is inside, the best way to help her is to bring assistance. We must trust that she is clever and strong enough to hold out until it comes."

The Boar flung her like a rag doll. Emma barely had time to register that she was flying through the air. To throw her hands around her head —

Her body skidded across the stone floor. The air exploded from her lungs. All she could make were little squeaky gasps.

When her eyes came back into focus, the Boar was already standing over her.

"Look, a little fox."

Above her was a cliff face of chest crossed by gold bandoliers. Small, cold eyes stared down. Eyes she had seen before, on a dais. In a ballroom.

"Come to join our game?"

Emma's eyes flicked round at the surrounding soldiers, then back to the Boar commander. "I am a citizen. The Night City wouldn't want you to hurt me."

Squealing laughter ran around the room.

"You think we answer to the Night City now, little fox? No, we think it is time for stronger leadership. The City has forgotten how to respect power. Look at this Library. One of its great centers of magic, left empty and open for any to seize? Careless. Yet the City and its Court are too wrapped up in their Midsummer revels this night to notice. They choose to debauch themselves blind: We choose to take our chance. For once this Library burns, the City will be weak. And then there will be a new rule. Our rule."

She heard satisfaction warm the grating voice. "We will make things right. We will bring order. True discipline."

Emma imagined a world ruled by Boars, and shuddered.

Two soldiers dragged the Librarian across the floor and cast him down next to Emma. She felt for his hand. The old man was shaking.

"You cannot do this." His pale eyes blazed up at the Boar. "You cannot destroy these books."

The Boar commander picked one book off a stack and squeezed. Taloned nails punctured the leather binding.

"Oh yes," he said, "I believe we can."

He tossed the book backward. It hit the bonfire with a sizzle.

And the air exploded. The shiver knocked Emma flat on her back. She gathered the Librarian to her, trying to shield him. A snarl shook the timbers of the bookcases. Whispers cascaded out: a hissing torrent of rage.

It was not something behind the shelves: It *was* the shelves. At the first contact of book to flame, the Library had come to life. And it was *furious*.

The Boar commander, leering overhead, was yanked back. He fell on his stomach, scrabbling at the floor.

Emma pushed herself up. Snakes of darkness had him by the

ankles, dragging him into the shadows between the stacks. Emma saw blood well around the shadows' grip, as though they bit into the flesh. The Boar screamed, high and horrible.

Emma had been right, earlier. The Library darkness was thicker than usual. Now she saw it leaking from the space between books: a living tide of hungry fingers sliding across the floor. Emma pulled the Librarian closer, but the darkness did not touch them. It only nosed at their feet and streamed on.

Around the ankles of the Boars it went, like living shackles. The reading room echoed with their howls. The dark closed over the bonfire, snuffing it with the snap of a fist bursting a bird's heart. And then the floor shuddered.

The Boars began to sink. Stone sucked greedily at their legs, their shoulders, as the Library pulled them down. The flagstones closed up as the last tusk disappeared. Emma rolled to her side and pressed her ear to the floor. Far below, as if encased in several tons of stone, she heard their screams.

In the silence that remained, Emma lay stunned. She wanted to laugh, or cry, and she couldn't tell which.

"Are they — "

"Trapped. Most horribly." The Librarian smiled with dreamy malevolence. "The Library will hold the Boars until the City comes to take them for punishment. And the punishment will be grave indeed, for those who have violated the Night City's most holy place, destroyed its books, and broken the bonds of their agreement."

"That was — Did you know the Library could do that?"

"This Library is capable of many things. I am not sure if even the City knows how well it is able to defend itself, if ever it needs to." The Librarian patted the side of a bookcase as lovingly as if it were the flank of a favorite horse. "It is all done now. All is well."

Emma choked, burying her face in his brocaded front.

"There, child, there," the Librarian soothed.

Emma found herself sobbing an incoherent string of words into the Librarian's shoulder: about Richard, and rose gardens, and knives held at her throat. All the while, a knotted hand stroked her hair. Eventually, the sobs slowed. The Librarian's words began to sink in. All was well.

Something struck her, and she looked up. "My friends, the mortals. They don't know. I must go tell them."

"Go, then, child." She helped the Librarian to his feet. He looked at the mess ruefully. "I must take what care I can of the books before my sister arrives. She will wish my full attention to scold me for running into danger."

So Emma left him and slipped past the remains of the bonfire. Past the splintered bookcases and the charred books scattered across the flagstones, and into the silence of the Library. It was over. They were all safe. The mortals were safe.

A bitter note crept into the sweet. There was no more fighting to do, which meant it was time for the worlds to separate again. It was time to say goodbye.

CHAPTER 40

THE MILITARY HISTORY ROOM WAS CLUTTERED WITH GLASS CASES holding muskets and ceremonial daggers. Rifles and sabers hung from the walls. Richard slumped on the floor against a display case. Hugo stood guard in front of him. In the other corner, Nat and Julia were binding a scratch on Jasper's arm. With the unerring instincts of a cat, Venetia had perched herself on the windowsill. There, she was dividing equal attention between looking down on them, and grooming the gore out of her moonlight hair.

They all looked up when Emma came in.

"It's over. We're safe. The Boars are gone."

Nat and Julia clutched each other. Jasper buried his head in his hands. And across the room, Hugo gave a sudden intake of breath.

They turned. Hugo was standing very still, his chin raised. A gold-hilted knife rested at his throat.

"And to think, I hadn't been sure about putting this on display." Richard smiled and tilted the dagger. His air of defeat had fallen away, as if it were a disguise he had shed. He had been waiting, Emma realized. For the group to be distracted. "Officer-class ceremonial knife. My great-grandfather's, actually. From the time of the Raj."

Behind him, Emma could see the display case hanging open.

"Family heirloom."

Julia stumbled toward Hugo. Richard tutted, and a line of red welled along Hugo's throat. Julia stopped abruptly, her hand reaching for nothing.

"No closer, Jules, babe. Hugo's a friend. I don't want to hurt him. It's her I want." He jerked the blade at Emma.

"You're going to come with me, Emma. And you are going to get on your knees and let me finish the sacrifice. Otherwise — " Hugo gave a muffled grunt of pain. Richard had pressed the flat of the blade to the open wound. "I will be forced to kill him. And I will."

Emma took a single step before Jasper and Nat seized her arms. Nat hauled her back. "Don't listen to him, Emma. He won't do it."

"Let go. I have to — "

"He's bluffing," offered Jasper, from her other side. "We've known Hugo since nursery."

The knife lowered. A pleasant smile curved Richard's cheeks. "Oh, since nursery, is it?" he said. He plunged the knife backward into Hugo's gut, his face curiously detached. "I'd forgotten that."

Richard grunted as he dragged the blade up through Hugo's middle. The knife moved slowly, jerk by jerk, as what was inside Hugo made one last struggle to stay in. The sliced edges of his dress shirt gaped white, then red. A rounded edge of liver slipped out, then the darker gleam of intestine. Blood spattered. Richard twisted the knife up. Hugo gave a strange, wet gasp and fell, blank-eyed.

"I don't do these things because I want to," Richard said, panting. "I do them because you're making me."

Blood flecked his lips. The knife in his hand was red and syrupy. Emma's legs weren't working properly. She couldn't feel them, at least.

Julia threw herself on him with a scream. Richard recovered his footing, and held Julia's face between tender hands. As much as they could be, with one holding a knife.

"Pretty Jules," he murmured. "We would have lasted. Even after you ran to the gutter press. I would have forgiven you." Runnels of blood trickled down the blade and over his hand, onto Julia's face. Richard smeared one away with his thumb.

His voice changed. "So. Emma?"

"Don't — " she croaked, but Richard had taken the knife and passed it across Julia's throat. Her beautiful, delicate throat. Surprise painted Julia's features. She sagged slowly, her ball gown crumpling beneath her.

"Too slow. When I say come to me, I mean now." He gazed down at Julia, lying at his feet. Her bubbling gasps filled the room. "So much blood. And no use for it at all." He looked sad. "There, she's quiet now."

A keening filled Emma's mind. She had time to notice Venetia, up on her windowsill, a hand clamped to her mouth. Jasper and Nat, unmoving as statues. Julia's awful gape.

In fact, Emma had the feeling that the rest of the world had slowed down. Only she and Richard looked across at each other in true time. For once, she knew exactly what she was going to do.

She felt the warm, grateful pull of her muscles, the thriving pulse that sung its willful song: alive, alive, alive. And, as each step carried her closer to Richard, she felt for what lay beneath it all.

The fox.

From far away, she heard Nat's gasp; felt the currents of air as Jasper stumbled back from her; saw the shock in Richard's florid face.

She was a fox now, and running. The hunter chased her. Once he had her scent, he would not stop. She would flee, he would follow, and she would lead him far from her mortals.

run run run
this is the hunt

Her breath rasped, and the reading rooms blurred into one. His footsteps were close behind. She forced a faster pace. A solid door was just ahead. She spat herself back into girl shape and wrenched the handle with human hands.

"Come on," she muttered. "Please."

It opened under her desperate fingers. She sped through into the shadows beyond, slamming the door shut behind her. Panting, Emma looked around at a reading room dotted with four doors, one at each compass point. A staircase spiraled to an upper gallery. Beneath, a tapestry hung in an alcove: a tree laden with fruit, a river winding round.

She recognized it. She had spent hours searching through the books here, all magical texts about mortals. She'd spent almost as much time trying to find the room itself. The Library had often sent her spinning in circles around it, through the same few useless galleries, before it finally relented and let her in. It had felt like the Library's little joke. She had always suspected it had a sense of humor.

Perhaps it had a sense of friendship too. Emma waded through the darkness and placed her hands on the nearest bookcase. Feeling utterly ridiculous, she whispered to the Library. She asked for help. She pushed its attention toward the bloodstained man with her death in his eyes, whose footsteps drummed closer and closer to the door. She spoke of hiding this room from him. Of sending him through an endless loop of darkened rooms, a closed circle that would not let him in or out. She promised hours of faithful service, reshelving the most jumbled collections and dusting precious books.

Richard's footsteps were at the door. And then she heard him pass by. His rage-filled grunts circled the room, but did not find a way in. Emma's spine began to uncurl from its hunch. She heard his first cry of frustration. Richard's footsteps turned, pounded the other way, his breaths rasping thick with fear. This time, his cry was of horror. The Library had trapped him. Outside Emma's hiding place, he ran in his own dark and doorless corridors, looping eternally around the room.

"Let me out — someone — "

Emma smiled with satisfaction. She stroked the bookcase in silent thanks. But it struck her that she could not stay there waiting, like a fox trapped in her den, listening to the footsteps outside. She, with the weight of a thousand ghosts at her back. With her friends' blood freckling her skin. She was meant to make him pay.

The plan came to her then. Simple, clean. Obvious.

She called to him.

"Richard." It was a song, a taunt.

Outside, she heard his footsteps falter. She flitted closer, to the very wall that divided them. She called again.

"Richard."

She heard him curse. She danced along the edges of the room, calling as he ran, always just ahead of him.

"Can you really not get me?"

Heavy feet stumbled on the other side of the wall. "What are you doing, witch?"

Emma let her laugh echo, high and eerie.

She heard a ragged intake of breath. He was afraid now. Good.

"Do you like the dark, Richard? The running? I hope you do. Because you'll never leave it." She had become good at lying, she realized, with all her time in the Night City. "You will die here. Imagine that, Richard."

A sound from the nearest wall suggested he had slumped against it, and slid to the floor.

"I will get you. I will kill you." She heard his fists thump the wall. But he was panting as he said it.

Emma slid to the floor on her side of the wall. She could hear the wet rattle of his breath, only inches away. It was almost intimate.

"You know, this is the second time you've run after me and not caught me," she mused, as if at random. "How frustrated you must have been, the night of your ritual. Chasing me through the streets. So close, until I . . ."

She held her breath. He might not pick up the lure she had left dangling.

". . . until you made a bargain."

Emma closed her eyes in silent gratitude. He had taken the bait.

"I did." And she let her voice puff with pride, smug and unbearable. She was quite pleased with her next crow of laughter. "And to think of you, all learned and expert, with your bowls and your runes, failing and failing. Always a failure. When I did it the first time, all by myself, running from you, and all I needed was desperation and a plea, and a bit of blood to open the way — " She let her voice squeak, as though she'd stopped herself.

"So that's it." There was glee in Richard's voice. "Of course. Our bargain was complex. So many elements to fail. But yours was simple. One request, one person: your promise sent straight from you to the Power — "

"The Night City," Emma corrected, as officiously as Richard might have, then let her voice spill over with horror. "No — I shouldn't have said — the proper name, we use it only — "

She hoped Nat would be proud of her acting.

" — only for bargains. I see." He was wrong, but it didn't matter. She had just wanted him to hear the right name. Richard chuckled. "*The Night City.* You won't understand, you idiot, but you've given me exactly what I need to end this."

"End this? End this how?" She added a touch of terror. Tried to sound weak, an idiot. A thing she never had been. Richard was the one who didn't understand.

From the other side of the wall came a muffled sound of pain.

"I give my blood, to open the way."

The wall scraped as he pushed himself up it.

"The desperation of the trapped." His footsteps began to thud again, moving around the outside of the room. "Pounding heart, painful breath. And oh, would you look? I have that." He was wheezing now. "And what was the last you said? Oh, yes. The plea."

She heard him raise his voice, sonorous. "Great Night City. I pledge you this bargain. I will offer you just payment — "

Emma steeled herself to jump in. The interruption would infuriate him. But she had to say it perfectly. Every word mattered. "No! The Night City won't let you break in here to hurt me, it can't — "

"It can and it will." Oh, there was real venom in his voice now. "You think you can do what I can't? I command these powers. You are nothing."

The repetition of the idea was important. She needed him to pick it up.

"Oh please, don't let him in," Emma declaimed to the heavens, borrowing Nat's favorite dramatic tone. "Don't let him break in here so he can finish his ritual, please — "

"Great Night City," he roared over her interruptions. She had stoked his fury well, she noted with satisfaction. His voice was shaking, the words tumbling over one another. The sound of a man primed to make a mistake. "Let me in, damn you. Take my bargain. Come on." The walls rattled with his pounding. She heard the grit of exhaustion in his snarl. "Please. The old boys won't take me back without it. The Balfours don't have a home for me, not if I can't fix things. I need this. Wherever she's hiding, just let me through so I can finish our ritual. I'll pay whatever you want, if you give me that."

Emma squeezed her eyes shut and her hands over her mouth, smothering laughter. He had done it. He had thrown himself, tongue-first, into her trap. For the Night City loved its tricks with words. And there was a vast difference between a bargain to kill someone and a bargain to break into a room *so that one might* kill them. She had only to wait for what came next.

The nearest door swung open. Richard stumbled in, disheveled and sweating. Emma perched on a desk, waiting.

He stalked toward her, blood soaked and awful. One thick pink hand yanked a reading lamp from a desk. He hefted the heavy bronze in his arms. His eyes traced a path through the air to Emma's skull, as though rehearsing the blow that would crush it. Emma felt sweat dampen her back. Something ought to have been happening by now. She had bet her life on it. He had made a bargain; the Night City would come to collect. But he was nearly on her. She readied to spring, every muscle taut.

His gaze tracked over her head and stopped. Emma looked back. The corner of the tapestry was fluttering. Then it blew back, as if in an invisible gale. Behind was an earthen passageway, tree roots tangling into the distance. Richard stepped closer, mouth soft with amazement. At the end of the tunnel, Emma could just make out a carved door with a crystal knob. A door she had seen before, although she had come to it by a different entrance.

Emma stilled the joy leaping in her chest, and cued herself for a performance. She huddled her face into her hands, sobbing as best she could. With the adrenaline and the horror of the night, it was easier than she thought to call up some real tears.

"What is that? Answer me."

She lifted her face, shining with tears. "It is the Night City's place." Then, with an obvious shudder: "It is bad, wrong, don't take me there — "

He dropped the lamp. "The Power, guiding my hand at last." He took her by the arm, pulling her into the passage. "It wishes me to deliver you. It shows me the way."

The earthy scent of the Court tunnels wrapped around them. Mineral streaks glowed from the walls, bright enough that Emma could make out the door of the Room of Choosing, growing closer. A room that appeared when mortals had a bargain with the Night City, left unpaid. The sign of a debt, soon to be collected. She smiled to herself.

Richard wrenched the crystal knob of the door and tugged Emma through behind him. There were the five pillars with their glittering objects; there, the skeleton monk in his corner; and there, with its bright black eyes and mushroom skin, was the wizened creature who had guided her. She bowed to it. Respect was always worth showing. Emma knew the moment the creature recognized her. It visibly brightened, its thistle-flax beard twitching. She had always thought of it as a friend. She was glad to see it remembered her, and kindly.

For more reasons than one. Emma melted a step behind Richard and placed a finger on her lips, jerking her head at the Turnbull. She traced her bruises and the blood on her gown and again pointed at Richard. The creature gave a sly, sharp nod. She knew it understood her.

Richard strode to the pillars. The feather, the droplet, the ball of light, the rat teeth, and the claw floated gently above them.

"Treasures of the Power," he breathed. He beckoned the creature. "You there. Servant of the Power. What do these do? Are they how I must fulfill the ritual?"

His tone made the creature stiffen. Before it answered, Emma slid in. "They will complete your bargain," she said, choosing her words carefully.

Richard snarled over his shoulder. "As if I would trust you."

"Oh no, the little once-a-mortal does not lie." Overlarge black eyes glinted at Emma, and then back to Richard. Emma saw the mischief in their depths. "No, indeed. These will complete your bargain. Although—"

Richard turned away without thanks. The creature's eyes narrowed.

"A trial of my worthiness," Richard murmured, staring at the objects. "Of course. To fulfill my bargain, to repair the Turnbull ritual, I must choose."

"Choose, yes." The creature puffed its chest and drew itself up, delighted to perform. "Debtor, for the City's payment / You must choose—" it began proudly.

"Leave off all that," Richard snapped. "I'm trying to think."

Needle-sharp nails quivered, as though thirsting for the touch of blood. Richard remained oblivious, musing before the objects. "I see it now. Each of these must grant a gift, a power . . . but I must choose correctly. Only one will prove me worthy to command the Night City: to fulfill the Turnbull ritual that was broken."

Emma and the imp eyed each other, bemused. There was very little need for subterfuge when a victim was quite so determined on deluding themselves.

"A feather for obedience, as in the blazons of heraldry."

He went on down the line. Emma could only watch in awe as he confidently misinterpreted every object.

"A teardrop to grant purity. The sun, for glory." He passed from the glowing ball to the rat teeth and broke off, clearly puzzled. "An odd shape. Alchemical symbol, perhaps? Made of gold, for wealth. That's it. And this claw — "

The amber claw on the final pillar was not glowing, as it had for Emma. But Emma could not bear for him to approach it. It was time to lure him into the final trap.

"Don't tell him about the ball of light." Emma shrieked, flinging an elbow over her head. "Oh, creature, I beg you. Let him not have that power — "

"Power?" Richard turned.

From under her arm, Emma winked at the creature, who was looking rather startled.

"The ball," she said, through clenched teeth, "which he called a sun."

The ball of light swirled upon its pillar, an angry star. Richard eyed it hungrily.

"Ah," said the creature, eyes glittering. "Yes. Shame on the little once-a-mortal, seeking to hide this power from the so-noble gentleman." Its voice dripped with glee. "I can tell him all about it."

"Those who walk the path of power
Wear the gift of mortal skin:
They shall owe no gift of service,
But only that which lies within."

Richard looked at the creature with dislike. "Can't you do anything but talk in riddles? Still, doesn't matter. A child could solve it.

This light bestows a power that only a mortal may wield. They 'owe no service,' because it gives them command over all. The Night City, bargains, that kind of thing. But this is only for a certain, worthy mortal: judged by 'that which lies within.' Do I have it?'"

"Not allowed to give clues." The creature stared up with barely concealed venom.

He had missed every warning in the words. Every hint of danger. Just as Emma hoped, Richard stretched out his hand for the blazing ball. His fingers closed around it.

And the Night City seized him. She saw it happen. Power streamed down his arms, the fire of life and thought and soul. His face grayed.

What's within a mortal, then? Emma heard her voice echo, from long ago. *Oh. Mortality. You give what you contain. Everything that you are. And you're gone.*

The ball of light drank deeply, growing brighter and fiercer. It was just what he had planned to do to her. What Turnbulls had done to victims for centuries. A full draining.

The ball burned unbearably bright. Richard crumpled to his knees. And a vision flared behind Emma's eyes. A rune blazed green against the darkness of her eyelids. A knot of cruel lines, a sunburst of shards. The rune of the Turnbulls' blood jar and its victims: the rune affixed to her soul. With a blinding pulse of green light, she saw it shatter. The rune's debt had been paid: the essence of one mortal soul drained into the Night City. But not hers. Because she had tricked Richard into giving his own soul to the Night City instead. For the first time, one of the Turnbulls had been the sacrifice for their own Society's bargain. And so Emma was free of them. Of their rune, of their debt, of their greed. Free. The light behind her eyes cleared. She blinked them open.

Richard looked up at her, a perfectly animate man. But his face was empty. Even his body looked diminished, like dough collapsing on itself. He gazed without interest, without fear. Without anything. The ball of light dropped from his hand, rolling into a corner.

"All drained." The creature kicked him and chuckled, a rasp like a cricket rubbing over a rusty chain. "I have not seen one take the ball in some decades. I do enjoy it."

"Can I have him?" It would cause fewer questions in the outside world.

"As you please. The Night City has no use for the shell." The creature rustled its knife-nails over her hand in the softest of touches. "But you, I may miss. Farewell, little once-a-mortal."

The room began the queasy process of folding in on itself. Teeth clenched against the nausea, Emma pulled Richard to the passage. He quivered in her hold like a soft animal. She pushed him through the tapestry, into the dark of the reading room. As the tapestry fluttered to stillness, the passage behind became a plain stone wall.

It was done. She let Richard slump against a desk. He would make no more rituals. He would wield no more knives. By her own hand, she was free of the Turnbulls and their debt. Their mark on her was gone. In comparison, her hundred years of promised service were a speck in the balance. She would find a way around them. She had done this. She could do more.

"Hullo, lady fox."

A figure in green velvet lounged against a pillar.

Robin looked at Emma. He twinkled, the infuriating creature. "You've been busy, I see. I thought I heard you here earlier, but would you know, I had the Night's own time getting in."

"What are you doing here?" she scolded, to hide how happy she was to see him.

Robin raised a brow. "I was at the Midsummer revels at Court, freshly returned from my posting, and heard the trouble my own dear lady fox was in. I came, of course, on the instant."

"You heard about me — about this" — Emma indicated the splintered mess of the Library beyond the reading room — "at Court?"

"Well, my dewdrop, your fox maidens stormed the Court celebrations for your sake. Quite trod over the musicians. They were almost dragged away to the cells for interrupting the revels, but they stood their ground. I have never seen the jaws of the Upper House lords so slack. It was delicious." He grinned. "They told of the Boars attacking the Library. You cannot imagine the chaos. The Judge stepped in to create order, and gave his commands. The Boars will be held for judgment in a very unpleasant part of the Court, charged with high treason. He comes here himself, to see the damage. But I, along with your fox maidens, was most anxious to see you safe, and so we sped together to the Library. I left them tending to the Librarian."

"They're here?" Emma said, her eyes flooding. "And they did all that, braving the Court, for me?"

A handkerchief unfurled under her nose with a flourish. "You inspire loyalty, my lady."

"Oh, you." Emma flicked it at Robin with a watery grin. "Thanks."

"Do not thank me yet," Robin replied. "I may well need it back.

The Judge will soon be here, and in no kind mood. Somehow, this humble creature always ends up at the lash end of his tongue. It quite oversets my tender feelings."

Before Emma could spare a thought for Robin's tender feelings, a shiver ran through the air of the Library.

Robin looked grim. "That would be him. Come, lady. We should find the mortals and bring them. The Judge will command our presence."

CHAPTER 41

EMMA PACED OUTSIDE THE GREATER READING ROOM. HER BALL gown trailed through fire-charred debris, blackening the hem. She didn't mind as much as she might have. The dress was already a patchwork of blood and river mud. Her feet crunched over the skeletons of shattered bookcases. She didn't mind that either.

On this side of the door, she knew what she was. Free of the Turnbulls' cruel bargain but still bound to the Night City by her collar, her Oath. Reunited with her friends but lost to them the moment they left the Library.

On the other side, the Judge was waiting. And she would find no softness in his ruby eyes. She had broken the Night City's law by speaking to mortals in the Library. And the City was not kind to lawbreakers. It had not cared that Sara had crossed its boundaries from desperation. Or that Emma had been made a sacrifice against her will. The City had always demanded punishment. And the Judge had pronounced it.

Emma wrapped her arms around herself as far as they would go, to hold back the cold, sticky feeling behind her ribs. It didn't help. Nat, Jasper, and Venetia huddled in the corridor beside her. Nat was still shaking, the marks of tears on his cheeks. Emma had found him outside the room where Hugo and Julia lay, his knees curled to his chest. He hadn't been able to go back in. But he had pulled off his tailcoat, still scented with champagne from the ball, and thrust it at Emma without a word.

Emma and Venetia had used it to cover Julia. Venetia had turned away afterward, fists clenched. But Emma had taken a moment longer to smooth the coat around Julia's neck, as though she'd been tucking her into bed. She remembered Julia doing the same for her, once. Julia's hands had been so warm. It seemed wrong for her to be so cold now. Before she left the room, Emma had stooped to take Hugo's pocket square from his tailcoat, and spread it gently on his face.

The door to the Greater Reading Room swung open. Robin was beckoning.

"Just to warn you, lady," he murmured. "Himself is in no happy mood."

He ushered Emma inside, the mortals behind her. The Judge stalked among the remains of the Boars' attack, his robes sweeping torn books and singed manuscripts. Robin had been right. The Judge's eyes, which usually glowed like coals, now had the blaze of the more unpleasant kind of hellfire. Two spots of actual color had mounted in his cheeks.

"Never seen him so worked up," Robin muttered almost inaudibly, to be answered by a murderous stare from the Judge.

"This night has seen crime upon crime, in measure beyond comprehending."

The Judge's hiss shook the room. Emma blinked, persuading

herself that she absolutely had not seen a flickering forked tongue snap from between his lips like a party streamer.

"An invasion of this Library. This holy place, for all nightdwellers. Books destroyed, in full awareness that knowledge is precious to the Night City, and these books especially treasured. The wanton insurrection — but this shall be examined at trial, not here."

Emma bent her head. Yet again, she was waiting for the Judge to pronounce a sentence. One that might be cruel, and pointless, and unfair. It had not mattered before, that she had done nothing wrong. That others were to blame. So perhaps he would rip her from her sisters and the safety of the House of Foxes. Or — she thought of the Librarian and the Sister — perhaps there were worse things to lose. Like her hands. Her eyes. Emma's stomach churned.

The Judge looked over the bloodstained mortals. As Emma watched, the blaze in his ruby eyes seemed to cool. And when he spoke, his voice no longer made Emma want to hide under the nearest desk.

"The Boars bear the full responsibility for this desecration, this unholy damage, and so they shall bear the full punishment for it. Yet there is another factor to consider. You. Had it not been for your actions, the damage would have been far greater."

Emma lifted her head. She hardly trusted the first flutterings of hope in her chest.

"No bargain held you to this defense of the Library, nor the injuries you have sustained. Yet you sacrificed your safety to fight for it. It was an act of bravery and loyalty, most valued by the Night City. You have protected what it holds dear. You have earned its thanks. And the City cannot leave such a debt unpaid. Everything has a price."

Emma's ears were roaring.

"So, by the Night City's order, just return shall be made for your actions. I am empowered to grant each of you a reward. A mark of the City's favor."

Emma fought the laugh threatening to close her throat, the hysteria bubbling at the base of her stomach. No, the Judge was not taking her hands, or her eyes. He was bestowing a reward instead. She tried to tell herself not to hope for too much. Not to dream of bargaining her way out of her collar; escaping the Night City; running from this room as a mortal once more. But her thoughts were wild creatures, and she could not command them.

"What's the reward?" Jasper shrank back as the Judge turned ruby eyes on him.

"Whatever you wish, mortal. Within reason, and commensurate with your deed."

Whatever she wished. The words rang through Emma like a bell.

Nat was the first to kneel before the Judge. Emma couldn't hear a word from the back of the queue, but she couldn't mistake the smile lighting her friend's face. He wouldn't meet her eye as he hurried away.

Then Jasper thumped to his knees in front of the Judge.

"I want to forget," he said. "The monsters, the magic people. Watching Rich kill Hugo and Julia. All of you. All of it."

The Judge nodded.

But Jasper stayed down. A frown furrowed his beautiful face. "While we're here, I also want to win the America's Cup. It's a sailing race. Can I ask for that as well? I'd probably need to do well in the Olympics to get on the team, so maybe it'd be better to set a solo world record — like at the Vendée Globe? That's another race . . ."

Jasper began to explain the finer points of yacht sponsorship, qualifiers, and weather conditions.

"Yes. Yes. Very well," the Judge snapped. "You cannot have everything. But you will have what you need. Just — leave me. I beg."

Venetia was next to kneel. Emma could not hear her whispered request, but she saw the Judge draw back. A line appeared between his brows, like a crease in paper. But Venetia leaned forward, hissing urgently, and the Judge eventually sighed. He nodded.

Venetia rose with a smile, her eyes two pools of venom. The fox stirred uneasily within Emma: a shivering, fur-prickled feeling of trouble to come. But she pushed away the foreboding, distracted. The Judge's eyes had come to rest on her.

"Emma Curran, we meet again. I seem unable to avoid it. But you, it seems, no longer bear the Turnbull mark."

"I have repaid the Turnbull contract." Emma lifted her chin. "The essence of one mortal life has been drained. My debt there is settled."

"It was cleverly done. And I am empowered to grant you a further reward, as I have these others, for your defense of the Library. But yours shall be greater than theirs. For you have served the Night City with more than your courage in battle: Your cunning brought low one of the Turnbulls. And this, despite the power of the mark they bear to protect them. Never before, in all the centuries of this cursed contract, has the Night City found a way to touch them. But you have shown the path. And for that, I am ordered to give a great reward indeed."

"I could go back to the mortal world?"

"More than that. To match your deed, the Night City has ordained that you may live equal to any Turnbull for all your days: with riches, fame, and power beyond other mortals. Perhaps you should like to reign as a queen, or hear your name spoken across all lands?"

And Emma saw herself as he had said. Heads bowing as she walked into a room, wealth and power in her train. Prizes, admiration, love: all falling into her lap. For a moment, it was all she wanted.

But a memory insisted on interrupting. A silver fox bracelet, sinking into the river's depths. A token of loyalty between sisters, lost because she had been fixed only on her own escape. Back then, she had been ready to abandon them to their fates. Now she had a chance to choose differently.

Emma squared up to the Judge. "No. I don't want any of that. If I want power, I'll get it myself. I know I can do it. But this reward — it's big enough for more than just me. So I want to share it."

"Share?" The Judge sounded incredulous.

"I would not have survived the Night City without the fox maidens. Or the Librarian and his Sister. Or Robin . . ."

Robin shook his head. "Not me, lady fox. I have already been well rewarded for our work together."

"Then just those others," Emma told the Judge. "Divide the reward between us."

Robin cleared his throat. "I believe they are close by, tending to the Librarian."

"Very well," the Judge said irritably. "Send them in."

The Sister, the Librarian, and the fox maidens entered the Greater Reading Room. When they saw Emma, the instant relief on their faces melted her heart. The Judge called them forward.

"This fox maiden has elected to share with you a reward, given for her part in this night's doings. Do you accept?"

Their expressions went from relief to shock. The Judge had to repeat himself twice more before it seemed to sink in. The Librarian beamed Emma's way. The Sister had gone pale.

The fox maidens rushed for her. Saskia and Nancy; Frances and Selina and Gertie; the twins. Their scent washed over her: den smell, sister smell. It was warmth and it was safety.

"You took on the Court for me," Emma whispered, hugging them all back fiercely. "I can't believe it."

"After going to the trouble of making you a half-decent fox maiden, you think I'm going to let you stroll around a Library full of Boars and get yourself killed? What a bloody waste of my time that would have been," Saskia said.

Emma felt her heart swell.

"You're one of us, love," said Nancy.

"I am one of you," said Emma. "And when we get out, we get out together."

She raised her voice to the Judge. "They accept."

"Then let them come forward."

The Sister and the Librarian stepped closer, hand in hand. There was so much hope in the Sister's face, it hurt to see.

"I have my own suggestion for your reward," the Judge said. "The Night City has not seen another artist to compare to your brother. I know it was demanded, as price for your return to our world, the sight of your eye and the grace of your brother's hands. Perhaps that last bargain might now be . . . softened. If you will permit me?"

The Sister had begun to shake. She clutched the Librarian as though he were the only thing keeping her upright. He had to nod for both of them.

A ripple of power passed over them. For a moment, all was silent. Then the Sister gave a choked cry and drew off her eye patch. The empty socket below was gone. Two dark, dancing eyes gleamed in her face.

Beside her, the Librarian was staring at his hands. No more were they twisted knots of meat. Each one was fine boned and strong, graceful as a bird's wing. He turned them this way and that, as though the tapering fingers held an invisible brush. Tears traced his cheeks.

The Judge said, slightly stiffly, "I am glad you accepted. I will find great pleasure in your brother's return to painting. I was, in times gone by, a collector of his work."

The siblings stepped back. Emma was sure they had not moved with such ease before.

"I don't pretend to speak for all of the fox maidens here." Saskia's voice rang out. "But this is what I want. For my debt to the Night City to be forgiven, so my service in the House of Foxes is paid off. Not to be made to do drainings, or have my salary taken as dues by some Lower House before I've even seen it. I want to be a free citizen. To choose my profession."

The Judge steepled his fingers. "That would be acceptable," he said at last.

"Then that's what I want too," another fox maiden burst out. A clamor rose, all of the fox maidens calling their agreement in shrieks and barks. Jasper had covered his ears again.

"Then the House of Foxes will fall, and be no more."

"Oh, but no," came Nancy's soft voice. "No, your lordship, that won't do at all."

"Indeed?"

Nancy shook her head. "It's been my home. Why destroy it? We could make it better. This isn't me asking as my reward. I still want my debt forgiven, and that's that. But you need the House of Foxes. If the Boars've gone bad — well, worse — then there's a right old gap, isn't there? No soldiers. No guards.

"Let me lead the House of Foxes and change what it's for. No more hunting mortal folk to collect what the City's owed. The fox maidens could be guardians of the Night City, in the outer world. We know the streets up here better than them in the Court. We can pass among mortals without them noticing — or running away screaming if they did, which is better'n you could say for the Boars."

Emma saw the slight quirk to the Judge's lips that, she was almost sure now, passed for a smile.

"Your friend is idealistic," the Judge said, looking at Emma. "What do you think?"

"Me?" Emma shifted uncomfortably under the scrutiny of the room. "I — Well, Nancy would be the best choice for a head of house. She's practical, too, it's not just ideals. I think you — the Night City — could work with her. You should."

The Judge sank into thought. "Fox maiden, I can grant only the stated rewards at this time. But I will take your proposal to the

Night City. If it is found acceptable, you will receive terms for a bargain." He looked closer at Nancy. "You are the one with the unusual path, are you not? You seem to be using your opportunity well."

"What does he mean?" One of the twins tugged Nancy's sleeve.

"Oh, well. That. The rest of you were human mortals, before you were turned to fox maidens. I — " Nancy paused, with a mischievous smile. "Well, I was a fox."

"You were *what?*" Saskia, for once, looked anything but self-possessed.

Nancy's sharp little nose wrinkled in amusement. "We'll get you there, love. Later. His lordship hasn't finished up yet."

"Indeed. Now the last. So, Emma Curran, with what remains of your reward, do you want to live as your sisters shall? Or will you return to your mortal life instead? The Night City is generous. You have but to ask."

Emma heard Saskia's gasp. She felt, rather than saw, Nat's smile warm her face. But she couldn't raise her eyes from her feet.

"To choose one or the other would be a path you could not alter," the Judge intoned.

It should have been simple. It was all she had wanted. To return to her mortal life. To hug her mother. To study science, and see what she was meant to become. A life where she got to make the choices. How could she give that up?

But how, now that she had seen another world, could she give that up either? The Night City was bound into her bones. She had changed her skin for the fur of a fox. She had walked in shadows and felt the heat of magic in her veins. Could a gray mortal existence ever compare with a world of blood sisters and adventure?

"You could," the Judge interposed delicately, "be granted the right to walk in both worlds."

Emma lifted her head, hope beating a pulse in her ears. "How?"

"You are the first in the records of the Night City to break a mark laid by the Turnbulls. Considering your unique position, if you were willing to pursue the matter further . . ."

"Pursue it further?" Emma repeated stupidly.

"The Night City wishes to be free of the Turnbulls. To no longer serve their ends, even in return for their sacrifices. It wishes to find a way to break the Turnbulls' bargain. Promise now to assist with this goal, and you will be given the power to walk in both the mortal world and the Night City. Do you accept the bargain?"

"Er — any more terms?" Emma said. It seemed suspiciously simple.

"A trifling matter," he replied. "You must spend exactly half of your time in one world, and half in the other. From year's dawn to year's end. Should you favor one more than the other, even by a day, you will be made permanently a member of it."

There it was. Emma looked at Nat, and at Saskia. It was a small enough price to pay to have both.

"I accept," she said. And it echoed through her, sure in every last bone and breath and muscle. The right choice. The only choice, for her. She did not belong in one world or the other. She was made for both.

"Very good," the Judge replied crisply. "Be ready to receive word of your presentation to the High Court."

"My presentation?"

The Judge popped out of existence.

"He likes to do that," said Robin, at her elbow. "Stay well, lady fox."

With a last wink, he was gone.

Then Emma felt a rush of air on her neck. Heard a clatter. There, on the floor, was her silver collar. It had fallen away. And with it, her servitude to the Night City. More collars struck the ground. She saw her sisters touch newly bare necks, eyes soft with wonder.

A siren pierced the air. Somewhere outside the Greater Reading Room, gravel crunched. The vaulted room filled with flashing blue lights.

The fox maidens gathered her in a bone-crushing, icy hug. *They feel so cold*, Emma thought, *have they always been this cold? I must be going into shock.*

Nancy held her tightest of all. "Oh, love, thank you. There's no time — the mortals are coming — but we'll find you, don't you worry."

She released Emma. One by one, the fox maidens melted away. Dark shadows with pointed ears and brush tails scattered across the reading room floor. Only Saskia remained.

She gripped Emma's shoulders, eyes burning with cold fire. Then a pair of chilly lips brushed Emma's, like a touch of honey and ice. Absolute shock held Emma still. But within, her heart was thundering: a dark symphony that fogged her mind and blurred panic with joy. Too late, she reached out. Her hands closed on darkness. Saskia was gone.

"You've done well, girl," the Sister whispered gruffly, pulling Emma into a hug of her own. "And I'll see you soon. You won't be alone, that I promise. Henry? Oh, have your moment, but be quick about it. They can't find us here, those mortal police."

There was a new stillness about the Librarian. The wheezing was gone, Emma realized. "You look different," she said. He did, now she was this close. Younger, and taller, as though the weight had rolled off his spine.

"So do you, child. You look . . . mortal." He traced Emma's face with a gentle finger, then shuffled into the shadowed labyrinth of the stacks. The darkness closed behind him.

The reading room doors burst open, and a squad of blue vests charged in. Emma was left staring at Nat, Venetia, and Jasper.

"What are we doing here?" Jasper blinked. "Why are there police? Oh, hullo, Emma. Have you been away? Feels like I haven't seen you in ages."

Venetia flicked her blood-streaked hair over one shoulder. "I am, as ever," she said, "surrounded by idiots."

CHAPTER 42

EMMA ADJUSTED THE ANGLE OF THE PHOTO FRAME. SATISFIED, she dropped onto her bed. The college had offered her a bigger room. But this one, an attic overlooking the Gabriel College bell tower on one side and the Meadows on the other, had won her heart on sight. It was full of nooks and odd angles. And best of all, its battered door opened onto a living room, opposite a matching door that led to Nat's bedroom. It had been the last set of connecting rooms available at such short notice, the bursar had said.

"But of course," he had stammered, "exceptional circumstances, we all know your, ahem — situation."

She was still getting used to being front-page news. The stares and whispers were unsettling. But there had been one major benefit to being a nationally famous kidnap victim. Whatever she asked for, the University seemed happy to provide. Very happy. Almost anxious to please.

This, of course, had nothing to do with any statements the chancellor had issued during her supposed eighteen-month hostage ordeal. It did not denote any *embarrassment* on the part of the establishment.

In fact, the University's press officers had become decidedly vague in the face of inquiries as to why the chancellor had arranged press calls for Richard and his friends on University property. Or the possibility that he had described the country's newest criminal celebrity as an "exemplary young man," undeserving of "the cruel disruption" to his studies from "baseless, discriminatory rumors." Meanwhile, with much muttering and chain-smoking, the press office were spending their weekends scrubbing every photo of the chancellor with his arm around Richard from the internet.

Emma sat up as Nat appeared in the doorway.

"Hee — hiiii — phhh — " He clung to the doorframe, panting. "Six flights of stairs, Emma," he mourned. "Six. It isn't right."

"That was the deal," she reminded him. "Remember, these are — "

"The Last Rooms Left," they chorused.

It was what they'd said when they discovered that the radiators were purely decorative. Or that the only bathroom was two floors below. Or that the eerie whistling noise in the living room came from a Victorian speaking tube that nobody had bothered removing. They already loved their set of rooms with a passion bordering on obsession.

"And at least this high up," Nat sighed, dropping into an armchair on top of her carefully folded shirts, "nobody can hear us if we scream. Hm. Is that a good thing, in our situation?"

"Nothing has tried to kill me for a week and a half." Emma rescued her stack of new textbooks from their current role as Nat's footstool. "I'll count that as a win."

Nat held one up. "Ah! So it's all sorted?"

"Yep." Emma grinned. "Confirmed today. I start on the natural sciences course in September. I've already picked all the zoology modules. I did the required sciences at school, so they didn't have much more to say about it."

"Welcome back to the University." Nat adopted a lordly air. "Now, as the resident senior academic in these rooms — studying, as I shall be, for a master's in English — Ow, Emma. I'll stop. I was only about to say" — this in an injured tone, evading Emma's hands — "that this calls for a cooking night to celebrate. My auntie's just sent me a new recipe. All in Yoruba this time, so let's see how good I've gotten."

"Spicy?" Emma asked, hopefully.

"The bishop has strenuously warned against making it, which bodes well. My adored father finds bread sauce too peppery. I can't imagine how he coped before he moved to England. But that reminds me — wasn't your father meant to be here?"

"He called. He wanted to stop by for lunch. Between business trips, of course," said Emma. A wry note had entered her voice. "He said he was worried when I went missing. That he felt badly, not being there when I was growing up. But — "

"Go on."

"I'm very proud of myself about this part."

"I'll make a big fuss of you," Nat promised.

"I told him not to bother. I've done without him all this time. I don't need him. I realized" — Emma took a deep breath — "it was my mum I really needed to talk to."

She turned a textbook over in her hands.

"I'd never told her, not properly. How I feel about all the

425

moving. How I've always felt. Leaving my home and my friends, even when I begged her to stay. It felt like I didn't matter. Or just not as much as her work."

"And did you?" Nat leaned forward. "Tell her?"

"I called her this morning."

It had been a strange conversation. Emma's heartbeats had seared her chest. Her breath had felt just as frantic, as hunted, as when she'd run from Richard or fled the Boar. But she hadn't known how much better it would feel, once the words were out there, spoken. She'd said all of the selfish things she'd hidden for so long. And her mother had listened, as though they weren't awful or shameful at all. As though she saw all of Emma, even the hard, vicious, angry parts, and loved her anyway.

"She said that she was the selfish one. That she'd persuaded herself I was coping fine, because she needed to believe it. Because she wanted those jobs; the moves to exciting new places. And it does sound hard, Nat. Being a mother and your own person at the same time."

Emma's mother had told her other things, too. That deep down, she'd been trying to give her daughter the life she'd always dreamed of. Travel, independence: all the things she herself hadn't grown up with. More than that, she'd wanted to be the best in her field *because* of Emma. To be the kind of parent Emma would look up to. Because she worried she wouldn't be enough of a parent, by herself. Without Emma's father. That she couldn't fill in the gaps.

Emma shook her head. "I never knew."

Nat raised an eyebrow. "And how did you feel about it all?"

"Fine," she said. "I told her I was already proud of her. That I never needed another parent. And that what I wanted right now, more than anything, was to have her with me. Not in a research station across the world."

Nat applauded.

"It felt so selfish to say. But it was kind of freeing, being selfish out loud." Emma felt the grin lighting up her face. "She phoned back a few hours later. She said that I always came first, no matter what. And Nat, she's moving here. As in, right here, near the University. She'll live in town until I graduate. She called the University about it at lunch. Apparently, they offered her a job on the spot."

"On the spot?" Nat repeated, stupefied.

"She's that good. The University Plant Sciences Department's been after her for years." Emma couldn't keep the pride from her voice. "It might take her a while to sort out a house in town, so it'll be just you and me staying at the University this summer, just like we planned."

"Just as it should be."

"Although," Emma amended, "that's partly because I'm not sure I *can* go anywhere else right now. There were lots of terms of that bargain I'm not clear about. And we may have to be here for our presentation to the Court, whatever that is."

They traded grimaces.

"Your parents really don't mind you staying here over the summer?" Emma asked.

"Oh, they weren't happy at first. But they want to let me 'do what feels right for me' at the moment, which is delightful. I cannot believe I spent years working myself up to telling my extremely traditional Nigerian father that I planned to give up my bright future to become a penniless actor, and all I got were hugs and great long speeches of unconditional love. Not a single thunderous passage. Not even a tiny bit of disinheriting. I could have done this years ago."

"You know," Emma said, "your smile is a good three inches wider since you came out of that room with them."

"So obnoxious, isn't it?"

A throat cleared. "Um — hello? Anyone here?"

A pained expression crossed Nat's face.

"I'm going to have to try not to laugh at him, aren't I?" he said. "You're going to make me."

"I am."

Jasper edged into the room, in pink chino shorts and boat shoes. He bounced on his heels. He appeared to be looking for something to say. "It's very small in here."

"I like it that way," Emma said.

"Oh, me too. I was just thinking, it's about the same size as the cabin on the *Phoebus Laurel*. We're getting her fitted up at the moment — cupboard for my darkroom, everything. You might've read about the crew we put together, we'll probably race at — "

Nat made a strange, hiccoughing sound.

"Anyway, that's not what I wanted to talk to you about."

Jasper scraped back his golden curls. "I've heard the rumors. My head's not exactly straight about it all, I still can't believe Richard would" — he caught himself — "not that I'm saying you're lying. But people are saying he kidnapped you, the night you went missing. And held you prisoner for a year and a half?"

Emma nodded, keeping her face carefully smooth. It was the story she'd decided to stick to. Richard was in no state to contradict it. He had been blank as a sleepwalker when the police cuffed him in the Library. Later, he agreed placidly to every charge put to him, though in a flat vacant voice that gave even his defense counsel the shivers. Now he sat in a cell awaiting trial, with no apparent interest in life beyond staring at a wall.

"And the things they're saying — he really kept you in a storeroom in the Library?"

"I don't know," Emma said. She was getting practiced at evasion. "He kept me pretty drugged up."

"Yes," Jasper said sagely. "My father's investigators said your blood tests came back very strange."

Emma pictured Jasper's father, cold eyes scanning a report. There was her true opponent. Richard had only been his puppet, groomed to violence by a man who had wanted to spare his own heir the dirty work. He had known how to dole out affection and withdrawal in crumbs, playing Richard against Jasper, until he had molded himself an eager little servant. Of all the old boys, he was the one she feared most. She would have to be ready for his attack, when it came.

Unaware that he'd dropped a potentially explosive piece of information, Jasper slumped against the wall.

"Then it's really true? My God, he was my best friend. Kidnapping a girl he knew was my — well, er — my friend, anyway. He saw what hell I was in, with the press coming after me. I can't believe he would do this to me."

Nat's eyes rolled back in his skull. Emma kicked him. Gently.

"And then to kill Hugo? And Julia? It's fucking strange. But for some reason, that feels more real to me. Which doesn't make sense."

"Yes," Emma said dully. Beside her, Nat's expression had sunk into leaden lines. She knew her face held the same misery. Thinking of Julia and Hugo was a grief that would not lighten. "They figured out that Richard was holding me in the Library. They confronted him. With Nat and Venetia. They rescued me. He stabbed Hugo, then Julia."

"And those hooligans broke into the Library at the same time?" Jasper shook his head in amazement.

"Just imagine," Nat said drily.

"God, the damage they did. What kind of scum smash up all that history? But if they hadn't interrupted Richard when they did, he might have killed us all too. To think I was blackout drunk under a desk, all that time. You know, if I'd been on my feet, I'd have stopped them."

"Indeed?" Nat was straight-faced.

"Yeah. This has been a wake-up call. I mean, I can't even figure out why I was in the Library in the first place. It all goes to show, I need to stop drinking so much. Focus on my health."

"Oh, that's what all of this goes to show?"

"Totally." Jasper nodded vigorously, missing the edge in Nat's tone. "Our trainer for the crew says the same. Actually" — he turned to Emma — "that's something I wanted to talk to you about."

He settled on the bed next to her. "It's just, there's such a lot going on. Dad's devastated about Richard, and there's so much to get ready for the race, and I'm way out of shape, and this last year was so hard for me. I thought I'd come chat to you about it. You always make me feel better."

"Jasper, you should talk to someone about all this. But a professional, maybe? I can't be that person for you," said Emma. Firmly.

Nat had been right. It suited her.

"Oh." Jasper sounded disappointed. "I thought you'd enjoy it. It's just, you're such a good listener."

"I am good at a lot of things, Jasper," she said, levering him from the bed by the simple expedient of pulling the duvet from under him. He startled to his feet like an offended pelican. "Many, many things. And I'm going to ask you to go now."

Nat steered him from the room under the guise of clapping him cheerfully on the shoulder.

"Emma, you are a wonderful person," Nat said afterward. "You also have terrible — *terrible* — taste in men."

Emma spent the afternoon arranging her treasures. Her corals and pressed leaves, a carved dolphin her mother had given her. After some thought, she'd added the photograph she'd taken of a lapwing, that early sun-striped day at the river with Jasper. It was the best thing she'd ever done with a camera. A breath of that long-ago Emma hung about it. Her softness. Her wonder.

As evening fell, the new Emma felt a stillness settle over her. A breeze was blowing from the Meadows. It meandered in through her little attic window, propped open to let in the night air. She'd moved the desk there so she could look across the waving grass, out to the river and the ancient woods beyond.

The turrets of Gabriel College were darkening in the fading light. Beyond, the Night City waited. There was still much she did not know. How to return to the City, if she did not want to be trapped in the mortal world forever. How to break a contract that had been made centuries ago. Where her friends were, and how they were. When she would see them again.

And the Turnbulls were still at large. Even now, from their

boardrooms and town houses in London, they might be planning a new ceremony. But there would be no more sacrifices. Whatever it took, whatever the next year brought, she would stop them. Emma felt the song in her blood quicken. Her hunt was just beginning.

But for now, what she had was this. A circle of lamplight. An empty page. And a book. This was the reason she had come here. To learn. Emma turned the first page of *Animal Physiology*, 5th ed. Some of the knowledge she sought, at least, was right in front of her. She took a breath, and dove in.

ACKNOWLEDGMENTS

A book does not leap into the world by itself. So many people have given their talents and time to bring *The Fox Hunt* to shelves. I'd like to thank them now.

First and forever, thanks to Nicole Cunningham, the most excellent agent to have ever turned a page. Your insight and brilliance have made the book what it is. Thank you for your time, your passion, and your love for Emma's world. They have been the best supports any writer could hope for.

Equally fierce thanks to my editor Liv Ryan, whose talent has transformed *The Fox Hunt*. On every page, I see the ways you have made its claws sharper and its pelt burn more brightly. Emma's story owes so much to your guidance, and I owe just as much to the joy you've brought to every stage of working together.

The same goes for the extraordinary team at Little, Brown. Thanks to Sally Kim, champion of fox maidens; to Emma Littel-Jensen, established early on as destined to work on this book and a creative force to be reckoned with; to Marieska Luzada, whose letter-writing is as exquisite as her outreach; to Eileen Chetti, for your rare eye for detail; to Naomi Glascock, Jennifer Trzaska, and Nicky Devaney for getting the book into readers' hands; to Linda Arends, whose work is the reason *The Fox Hunt* has become a real, finished book; to Taylor Navis, who designed the book's interior and has an almost supernatural affinity for finding the perfect manuscript-inspired typeface; and to Kirin Diemont, who designed the cover and performed an act of magic in doing so. Your skill and imagination have created something truly beautiful for *The Fox Hunt*.

Thank you to Jenny Meyer for working her magic on the foreign rights for *The Fox Hunt*, and to Heidi Gall for the same. Thanks also to Berni Vann on film and TV rights: your instant understanding of *The Fox Hunt* and your vision for it have been a wonder.

Across the ocean, thanks to the fabulous UK team at Electric Monkey: Lucy Courtenay, Lindsey Heaven, Lila Nicholson, Amy Readyhough, and Olivia Carson.

I've been so grateful for the kindness and encouragement of other writers: Victoria Lee, Erin Crosby Eckstine, Emma Törzs, and H.G. Parry. Thank you especially to Lucy Waverley for welcoming me into a warm and brilliant community of writers.

And finally: thank you to the students and staff at Emmanuel College, Cambridge for making my time at university very different from *The Fox Hunt*! I found belonging, encouragement, and a lifelong love of learning at Emma. The people I met there have shaped the course of my life. And so I have borrowed its name for my heroine, and hope this stands as a little nod of thanks for all of the knowledge and friendship I found in its halls.

ABOUT THE AUTHOR

Caitlin Breeze has a degree in Classics and Modern & Medieval Languages from Emmanuel College, Cambridge. She went to Falmouth University for a creative MA, and then on to a career in creative direction, design, and communications. She lives in London, in a tiny house full of books. *The Fox Hunt* is her first novel.

RAISING READERS
Books Build Bright Futures

Thank you for reading this book and for being a reader of books in general. We are so grateful to share being part of a community of readers with you, and we hope you will join us in passing our love of books on to the next generation of readers.

Did you know that reading for enjoyment is the single biggest predictor of a child's future happiness and success?

More than family circumstances, parents' educational background, or income, reading impacts a child's future academic performance, emotional well-being, communication skills, economic security, ambition, and happiness.

Studies show that kids reading for enjoyment in the US is in rapid decline:

- In 2012, 53% of 9-year-olds read almost every day. Just 10 years later, in 2022, the number had fallen to 39%.
- In 2012, 27% of 13-year-olds read for fun daily. By 2023, that number was just 14%.

Together, we can commit to **Raising Readers** and change this trend. How?

- Read to children in your life daily.
- Model reading as a fun activity.
- Reduce screen time.
- Start a family, school, or community book club.
- Visit bookstores and libraries regularly.
- Listen to audiobooks.
- Read the book before you see the movie.
- Encourage your child to read aloud to a pet or stuffed animal.
- Give books as gifts.
- Donate books to families and communities in need.

BOB1217

Books build bright futures, and **Raising Readers** is our shared responsibility.

For more information, visit **JoinRaisingReaders.com**

Sources: National Endowment for the Arts, National Assessment of Educational Progress, WorldBookDay.com, Nielsen BookData's 2023 "Understanding the Children's Book Consumer"